Praise for Shaylin Gandhi's *When We Had Forever*

"A lyrical debut, full of heartbreak, su[...] [...]erous
shot of hurt. Original and fast-pace[...] [...]t kind
of wallop!" —KRISTA [...] [...]g author

"Beautifully written with a twist you w[...] [...] couldn't put it down!"
—HELEN HARDT, #1 *New York Times* bestselling author

"Captivating and emotionally charged with a storyline you won't see coming.
Shaylin Gandhi writes with the depth and finesse of a seasoned author. All the stars
in the sky." —MIA SHERIDAN, *New York Times* bestselling author

"Shaylin Gandhi is a writer to watch (and read!). *When We Had Forever* is lovely,
smart, and layered with emotion and heart. I can't recommend it enough."
—EMMA SCOTT, *USA TODAY* bestselling author of *Full Tilt*

"I was obsessed with *When We Had Forever* from the very first page. The tension.
The angst and the plot twist that literally made me gasp out loud and still lives
rent-free in my head. Shaylin's writing is pure magic."
—NISHA J. TULI, bestselling author of *Trial of the Sun Queen*

"This book is an addictive page-turner, laced with undeniable yearning, visceral
tension, and narrative propulsion that kept me up into the wee hours of the night.
Haunting, erotic, *When We Had Forever* is a must-read love story that isn't afraid to
walk on the dark side and emerge, victorious, in the light."
—EMILY COLIN, *New York Times* bestselling author of *The Memory Thief*

"I've got a new favorite writer! Shaylin Gandhi's ability to weave beautiful prose
with relatable characters and an unexpected plot twist has resulted in a book
that's impossible to put down. I loved every minute of it."
—LACIE WALDON, author of *The Layover*

"Addicting and deeply romantic, *When We Had Forever* is a powerful story of
unwavering love." —ALEXANDRA KILEY, author of *Kilt Trip*

Also by Shaylin Gandhi

When We Had Forever

To learn more about Shaylin Gandhi,
visit her website, shaylingandhi.com.

WHEN WE HAD FOREVER

SHAYLIN GANDHI

CANARY STREET PRESS

**CANARY
STREET
PRESS™**

Recycling programs
for this product may
not exist in your area.

ISBN-13: 978-1-335-23087-4

When We Had Forever

For questions and comments about the quality of this book, please contact us
at CustomerService@Harlequin.com.

TM is a trademark of Harlequin Enterprises ULC.

Canary Street Press
22 Adelaide St. West, 41st Floor
Toronto, Ontario M5H 4E3, Canada
CanaryStPress.com

Printed in U.S.A.

To every woman who's ever been deceived:
the good ones are out there, I promise.

THE END

When my marriage ended, I was in the bathtub.

Not that I realized it at the time. I only found out later, and for weeks afterward, I wondered. At what moment did I stop being a wife?

Months have passed, but the question still gnaws at me on rain-drenched nights as I lie awake, watching bleary red numbers mark time from the nightstand flanking the empty side of the bed. Or it blares through my brain without warning, like on the morning I dig through the kitchen cabinet and find my husband's favorite mug in my hands.

I squeeze the cup until my palms ache. In my imagination, long fingers wrap around the mug's familiar slogan—"The Difference between Your Opinion and Coffee Is That I Asked for Coffee." Those same fingers once skimmed down my shoulder while I showered, or trailed against my neck as I wrote. Now they'll never touch me again.

At what moment did I stop being a wife?

The floor tilts. My stomach shrinks as I stumble from the

gleaming kitchen to the hallway, where I wrench open the storage closet door.

I should be careful and nestle the mug in among the other orphaned things that carve an endless hole through me. But with no one here to witness my lack of restraint, I just bang the cup down on a stack of architectural magazines and sag against the wall. Yet the closet's relics seem to whisper, and the question only grows.

What the hell was I doing when my marriage ended? Running my razor up my legs? Letting the gathered gobs of shaving cream float away like little foamy icebergs? Leafing through the book that lives on the teak bench beside the tub?

At what *exact* moment did I become a widow?

I feel like I should know. I should've felt a pang in my chest, maybe, or a sympathetic gasp for air when my husband took his last breath in this world.

Instead, I felt nothing. Only later, during that nightmarish phone call I now recall in snatches—*car accident...your husband... died on impact*—did I understand the world had changed.

Afterward, when the police report followed, I pieced *some* details together. I now know I became a widow on a Sunday afternoon, while in the bath. Maybe while shaving my legs. Or maybe...

There's another possibility for what I might have been doing at 3:32 p.m. on February 18. I could've been thinking about *him*. My brother-in-law. The man who knocked my life off course without ever having met me, without even knowing my name.

Not that I think of him often. But I did that day.

Now I double over in the hallway, propping my hands on my knees. My husband's gravelly concern seems to echo off the polished tile as though he's standing right next to me.

You'd feel better if you went for a run, Mina.

My coffee is still steeping in the chrome-and-glass French press in the kitchen, but I leave it be and obey the ghostly suggestion. Funny how, when my husband was alive, those words used to lodge between my ribs and stick there. I even suspected him of deriving more relief from my runs than I did, because he always sent me off in those neon moments at the start of a fight, when everything in me began to glow white-hot.

Except he wasn't wrong. Running *did* help. I can admit that—now that he's dead. Now that him being right doesn't feel like it robs me of anything.

By the front door, I yank my beat-up purple running shoes— two lonely daubs of color in this ocean of black and gray—from their designated cubbyhole and shove them onto my sockless feet. I don't care that I'm only wearing rumpled pajama shorts and an oversize T-shirt I once got from volunteering at the animal shelter down the road. Any runner worth her salt always dresses for the second mile, anyway.

Outside, the forest blurs in the silver wetness. It's a typical March morning in coastal Washington; the evergreen spires soar skyward while the tang of ocean piggybacks on the drifting mist. I inhale, hoping the gauzy air will file down my broken edges to the harmless contours of sea glass.

If only it were that easy. If only I could fill the hollow ache where so much has been torn out.

Not that it's my husband's quiet urgings to run that I miss. No, I yearn for the breathless, early moments we spent admiring star-strewn skies. And the years afterward, when the metronome of his heartbeat lulled me to sleep. I miss the hopeful way he searched my face whenever he came home with a just-because gift, as if never quite trusting that *he* was the gift. That for me, material comforts paled in comparison to the way his hand felt in mine, or how, on the rare occasions we traveled together, the world came alive for us.

Those things are gone now, taken from me in a single moment I didn't even notice passing me by.

I take off sprinting. Once upon a time, I ran light-footed, free, but now I let my whole body absorb the impact. It's the only way to silence this horrible question.

What were you doing when the love of your life died? Thinking about his awful brother? A man you hate?

Inside of a mile, blisters bubble on my sockless feet, but I pause only long enough to scrape my chin-length hair into a messy top-knot, then continue running. Five mindless miles whirl by. Six.

When the road ends, I stop in the empty cul-de-sac. The trees stare down, each piney knothole like a glowering eye, and I nose my shoes over the edge of the pavement. Maybe I should just keep going. Find a way to outrun this sucking grief.

But behind me, the road awaits. I hate the idea of turning around—of coming this far only to go backward again—but sometimes that's the only choice.

Sometimes the past is all we have.

BEFORE

The day I met Michael, I hit him in the face with a pie.

It's a breezy Sunday in June, and downtown Seagrove bustles in a way I rarely see. In the summer, our quaint seaside enclave attracts its fair share of visitors, but a typical weekend sees tourists strolling past the muted green-and-red shopfronts at leisure, coming from or going to the beach in no particular hurry.

Today, though, Seagrove hums with life. The animal shelter I've volunteered at for the past three summers has organized a fundraising carnival, complete with vendors hawking sweet-smelling funnel cakes and booths offering massive stuffed animals to anyone who can land a wooden ring around the neck of a bottle. Laughter mingles with the bright cries of gulls. Peaked canvas tents rub shoulders, each one crowned with a jaunty yellow flag that flutters in the breeze.

The liveliness of the day takes the edge off my guilt. It's almost like Seagrove has arranged this send-off for me. Like in its mind, I'm not making a gigantic mistake, even if everyone else seems to think so.

And by *everyone else*, I mean my best friend, Kate. She strolls along beside me, turning heads in a fluttering floral sundress that showcases the stunning length of her legs. Buttery hair cascades down her back, and with her oversize sunglasses and sun-kissed skin, she looks like an incognito celebrity summering at the seaside while hoping no one will notice.

Everyone notices.

Not that Kate notices them back. She just measures out bites of funnel cake, as if tearing her guilty indulgence into tiny pieces will somehow vaporize half its calories.

"So." She pops a tidbit into her mouth. "Am I ever going to see you again? I mean, I know we always said we'd move away after college, but I thought that meant to Seattle. I didn't think you'd get on an airplane and ditch me completely."

I swipe her next morsel of cake for myself. Something that's thickening my arteries with a single bite has no right to taste so delicious, but the sugary greasiness makes me groan.

"Rude," Kate says.

"I'm not ditching you." I suck my fingertips clean. "And I'm not getting on an airplane for another month. You know you're welcome to come hang out with me in Seattle 'til then. The house I'm staying in has two bedrooms."

"That old lady's house, you mean? The one who just died?"

I give her a significant look. "If by *old lady*, you mean my great-aunt Rosalie, then yes."

Kate sniffs. "Oh, come on. She was ninety-three. That definitely counts as an old lady."

I sigh, but know better than to expect delicacy. Kate's about as delicate as a herd of stampeding buffalo. And to be fair, I only met my great-aunt Rosalie once. I don't remember much more than her shouting orders at me to make fried-bologna sandwiches so she wouldn't miss the faith healers on TV.

"It's a house," I say with a shrug. "And it wouldn't cost you anything."

Kate's nose crinkles. "Didn't she have like, eighty cats?"

"I'm pretty sure it was three."

"Whatever. It probably stinks in there. Besides, what would I do while you're busy listing her stuff on eBay all day?"

"Um...the usual Kate things? Make salads? Do absurd amounts of cardio?"

"Okay, that is halfway tempting." She drums her fingers against her chin. "But what about when you jet off to Greece next month?"

That oh-so-casual question ripples through me, building toward either excitement or terror—I can't tell which. "Then you could wave goodbye to me at the airport?"

"Gee." Kate's tone goes flat. "Wave to my best friend while she leaves me behind. Sounds awesome."

I wince. "I told you, I won't be in Athens forever. Just long enough to break a few hearts and get a really great tan. Then it's back home to do real life."

I don't add that if I had my way, I'd hopscotch around the world for a year or three or ten. There's no point in saying so, because there's no way in hell my mother won't force me to come home. It doesn't even matter that I'm twenty-two. Protective is essentially her middle name. Or maybe Petrified.

Corrine Petrified Sutton. It does have a certain ring.

And honestly, I'm no less terrified myself. I'm still working up the courage to tell her I'm going abroad. I figure once I do, I'll have three months of freedom, maybe four, if my courage and my bank account hold out that long.

"Why Athens, anyway?" Kate says. "It's not like you speak Greek."

"Why *not* Athens? Give me one good reason. Besides the fact that I'm a stupid American who only speaks English."

"I don't know, maybe because it's five thousand miles away?"

"Six thousand, actually. If you count from here."

My best friend gives me *the look*. The Katelyn Archer special.

Those ridiculous sunglasses hide half her face, but I can visualize her enormous brown eyes crinkling, the upward hitch of each brow, and feel her ice-cold stink eye.

She thinks I've lost my mind.

I drag my flip-flop over a crack in the sidewalk. Second to my mother's inevitable horror, this is the biggest downside to moving to a country I've only seen in pictures—the fact that my best friend feels betrayed by it. In high school, Kate and I promised we'd get an apartment in a glittering city someday and spend our nights in too-loud clubs, teasing boys and getting drunk enough to take taxis home. We'd stay up until 3:00 a.m. on work nights, eat whatever we wanted, and throw impromptu dance parties with nothing but the two of us and a giant bowl of kettle corn. We wouldn't just live together, we'd *live*. Together.

At least that's how I envisioned it. Maybe Kate planned on persuading me to color-code my wardrobe—*Why wouldn't you? It takes all the guesswork out*—and sedately watching the nightly news while enjoying a single Ferrero Rocher chocolate for dessert.

But we would've worked it out. We still can. It's not like I'm leaving forever.

"At least explain how you picked freaking Greece." Kate adjusts her sunglasses. "And do *not* say you threw a dart at a map."

I mask my chuckle by pretending the funnel cake went down wrong, but in reality, that's *exactly* how I settled on Athens—in the most clichéd and illogical way I could think of.

It felt so wrong that it felt right.

Saying that would only piss Kate off, though, and I'd rather keep her happy, partly because I love her, and partly because I'm a selfish jerk who still needs to beg for a ride to Seattle tomorrow—a six-hour round trip I'm sure she has no interest in making.

I don't exactly have a choice, though. My car conveniently

picked today to die in a gush of black smoke and metallic screeching, and in less than twenty-four hours, I have to meet with Rosalie's grandson. The month-long job of selling off my great-aunt's estate will earn me the last twenty-five hundred dollars I need for my plane ticket.

I can't, under any circumstances, screw that up.

Kate eyes my theatrical coughing with skepticism. "You know I'm only grumpy 'cause I'm gonna miss you, right?"

"I'll miss you, too," I say honestly. "And please don't hate me, but is there any way you could take me to Seattle tomorrow? I have to meet my cousin Patrick at eleven, but my car died."

Kate sighs and tosses her remaining cake into a nearby trash barrel, then dusts her hands as if offended by the residual calories clinging to her skin. "Can't one of your parents take you?"

"It's Monday. They're working."

"Okay. So not only are you ditching me, you want me to aid and abide you, too?"

I pause. "Aid and abet?"

"Whatever. I'm not the writer. You know what I mean."

"I can pay you." I don't hide my pleading tone. I'll have to recalibrate my budget, but only a catastrophe of the highest magnitude could stop me from showing up for that job tomorrow. "Gas money, plus enough for your time. And some extra, just because I feel like crap for having to ask. Really, really desperate crap."

Kate props her hands on her hips. "Mina. Come on. I don't want your money. I know how hard you worked to save it. Can't you just...I don't know. Cheer me up. Make me laugh. Hit that guy in the face, actually, and I'll do it."

My brow knits. I have no idea what she's talking about until she points to a guy in a nearby booth. Pie crust and creamy goo slather his face and sage-green button-up.

Like everyone else, he's staring. Unlike everyone else, it's not at Kate. He's looking at me.

Something sparks inside my chest. Which is ridiculous, because I can't even tell what this person looks like. I can only say that his saturated hair resembles dark straw, and his eyes are a color I've never seen before. I don't know what to call them, but they remind me of the ocean. Not here, where the water is broody and sullen, but somewhere tropical. Someplace where coconuts thud into welcoming white sand.

And he has a body to die for. Even the layers of whipped cream can't disguise the fact that he probably spends a lot of time picking up weights and putting them back down again.

"I'll definitely hit that guy in the face," I murmur. "I think I'd hit him in all kinds of places."

"Ew." Kate doesn't bother to lower her voice. "He's probably a troll, underneath all that."

The guy grins, and I think, *I didn't know trolls came equipped with such perfect smiles.*

Someone says my name. I glance around to find Darlene, my former supervisor from the shelter, standing behind a table that offers an array of whipped-cream pies.

I return her grandmotherly smile. White-haired but spry, Darlene wears glasses as thick as old-timey Coke bottles, bakes apple pies from scratch, and develops an uncanny ability to swear like a sailor after a single drink.

Briefly, I mourn the fact that I don't have any alcohol to offer her. At least that would lift Kate's mood. There's nothing quite like hearing a seventy-five-year-old woman dispatch the f-word with gusto.

"Mina, dear," Darlene says. "It's good to see you. And congratulations on your graduation."

"Thanks." My gaze wanders back to Mr. Pie Slop and his tropical eyes. He's put his flawless teeth away and settled for watching me intently.

I watch him right back. If he's affiliated with the shelter, I should recognize him, but we've definitely never met. "How much to throw a pie? And who's your willing victim here?"

Darlene pushes her Plexiglas lenses up. "Five dollars gets you three pies. And this is Michael...erm...Drake?" She says his name like she's not sure. Like she's only just met him.

"Michael Drake." I roll the name around on my tongue, then slip Darlene a five. "What do I get if I hit him?"

"Nothing. It's just to help the animals," Darlene says.

In the same moment, Michael says, "Pure, sadistic gratification."

Despite the day's balm, I shiver. His voice skims down my spine, making me think of aged bourbon and expensive leather and curling blue cigar smoke. It sounds older than the rest of him, though it's hard to pin down his age with all that glop coating his face.

Regardless, his answer tells me he's smart, maybe even well-read, though the second part seems optimistic, considering he'd have to sandwich any book time in between all those biceps curls.

"Michael Drake." When I repeat his name, something flashes in his eyes. "Where'd you come from? I thought I knew everyone in this town."

"You probably do," he says. "I'm just visiting. For work."

I raise an eyebrow. "Nobody comes to Seagrove to work. Only to get away from it."

He chuckles. "Fair enough. I'm here on a corporate retreat. Most of my company's down from Seattle for the weekend. Maybe you've heard of us. Forsythe & Winter?"

"Oh, yeah." Kate pores over the pies. "Some fancy architecture firm or something, right? Here, Mina. This one looks the messiest."

I accept her offering, which indeed looks capable of inflicting maximum splatter. Whipped cream slops over the pan, leaving sticky white gobs on my red shirt. "If you're just visiting, what're you doing in the pie-throwing booth?"

Michael shrugs. A few dollops slide from his shoulders onto the grass. "One of my coworkers was supposed to come, but he got sick and sent me instead. He's from here originally, actually. Ben Gallagher."

My mind races down the hallways of memory in pursuit of that name. Ben Gallagher, yes. Except I always knew him as Benny. He was two years ahead of me in school, at least until his sophomore year, when his parents got divorced and his mom moved them to Seattle.

I haven't seen Benny in years and had no idea he'd ended up working for a high-end architecture firm. I *do* know his dad still lives here in Seagrove and happens to be Darlene's nephew.

"Huh," I say, as connecting threads stitch together in my mind. "Small world."

"Not really." Michael's attention remains on me. "It was Ben's idea to do the retreat here. He talks about this place all the time. Still swears he's going to move back someday."

I ponder that. I can't imagine escaping this Podunk town and then returning *willingly*, but to each their own, I guess. "Well, Benny must've made you a pretty amazing offer to convince you to have pies thrown at you all day."

"Nah. He asked, and it sounded like fun. So here I am."

"You thought getting doused in whipped cream sounded like fun?"

"Does it not?"

Predictably, Kate grimaces and smooths her perfectly ironed sundress. Meanwhile, I fight a smile. Getting coated in pie doesn't seem like *fun*, exactly, but it does seem like the kind of thing someone who's already living life out loud—instead of just planning to start next month—would do.

I don't want to give this stranger too much unearned credit, though, so I aim my pie while lobbing another question. "So you're...what, some kind of architecture nerd?" At the very least, I want to see if poking fun will make him stop staring.

It doesn't. He grins. "Yeah, I probably qualify as 'some kind of nerd.' But you don't get to say that like you aren't one, too. Takes one to know one, writer girl."

His comment lands just as I throw, and my pie goes splattering off into the grass. "Wait. How'd you know I was a writer?"

"Your friend said so." His glance flickers toward Kate. Barely. Then back to me.

I flush, realizing he must have been listening to our earlier conversation. Attentively.

"And it's a good thing you've got brains," he continues, "because judging by that throw, a career in baseball's off the table."

He softens the jab with another non-troll-like smile. I slit my eyes in response, warming to Kate's challenge as she places a second pie in my hand.

I've insulted Michael Drake, and now he's insulted me back, and not only do I desperately want to win a ride tomorrow, but I'd really love to nail this guy in the face. Just for the pure, sadistic gratification.

"Keep talking." I heft the pan. "You'll regret it once I've gotten whipped cream up your nose. And if you actually knew anything about nerds, you'd know better than to taunt one. We're secretly dangerous."

"Oh, god. That's right. Never mock a nerd." His eyes widen. "Is it too late to beg for mercy?"

"Beg all you want. My heart is a cold one." I toss.

"Guess I'll just have to move, then." He steps neatly from my missile's path, leaving another forlorn tin glinting on the ground.

"Hey! You cheated!"

"I absolutely did," he says, without a trace of shame. "How else can I make sure you lose your bet?"

Off to the side, Darlene frowns.

I grab my final pie. "Why on earth would you want me to lose my bet?"

Michael considers me with eyes that words like *turquoise* and *aquamarine* don't do justice to. A rabid urge to know what he's seeing rises up. Why fixate on a black-haired, blue-eyed pixie who so often goes unnoticed?

"I want you to lose," he says, "so I can take you to Seattle myself. I'm headed home tomorrow. It wouldn't be any trouble."

My breath hitches. I can't believe he would just come out with that, like he invites strangers on road trips every day.

Darlene's frown deepens. "Now, young man, I know you're Benny's friend, but—"

Kate steamrolls right over that, her tone shrill. "Excuse you, you weirdo! Mina's not going anywhere with you. She doesn't even know you."

No, I don't. But strangely, there's something about this guy's confidence and sea-bright eyes that makes me want to.

"I'd consider it," I say, trying to stifle my rising flush, "except that this next pie's going to hit you in the face. Which means Kate's taking me."

"Damn right I am." She sounds horrified that I'm even having this conversation. "No way are you getting in a car with this guy, Mina. He could be a serial killer. He's probably trying to get you alone so he can make you his next victim."

A dry note sneaks into Michael's smoke-and-bourbon voice. "That's actually not what I'm going for. At all."

I combat the heat blossoming in my cheeks by spinning my pie. Amazingly, I end up looking like an expert, even if I do splatter whipped cream against my neck. "Maybe so," I tell Kate. "But how can he be sure I'm not a serial killer, too? A better one?"

"What? What're you even talking about?" Kate gibes. "You're a girl."

"Are you saying women can't be serial killers?" Michael says. "Because I find that very sexist."

I smother a giggle. "Yeah, Kate. How sexist."

She pushes her sunglasses onto her head and gives me an unimpeded version of *the look*, one that tells me she's not at all pleased that this tourist and I have somehow ganged up on her. "Don't be stupid. Just pie this guy hard enough to shut him up and let's go. I'm taking you to Seattle tomorrow. I'll take you to freaking Canada if you want. Just don't go anywhere with this creep."

I flash a smile of surrender. "Okay, okay. You're the bestest friend ever."

"Obviously," she says, peevish. But her frown eases.

I turn back to Michael. "And you. Don't you dare dodge this time."

"No, ma'am. I'd never disobey a direct order from a nerd." He mock salutes me. "But just so you know, I'm leaving at eight tomorrow. From Seaside House. Just...don't come if you have nefarious intentions. A guy can never be too careful, these days."

Darlene makes a sound of protest. "I don't think your mother would like you getting in a car with someone you just met, Mina."

"Definitely not," I murmur, in what amounts to the under-statement of the century. My mother would handcuff me to the bed if she thought I was even *contemplating* catching a ride with some muscle-bound Seattle architect I've known for five minutes.

Lucky for her, I'm not the sort of person who'd do that.

Then again, I'm not the sort of person who'd move to another country on a whim, either.

My brow furrows as I weigh my options. Briefly, I consider telling Kate she's off the hook for the ride, but I have no desire to deal with the nuclear fallout *that* would prompt.

"Mina?" she ventures. "I don't even care if you hit him anymore. He obviously just wants attention."

Michael Drake doesn't refute that. He just holds my gaze, waiting to see what I'll do.

With a rueful smile at my own cowardice, I say, "I think you're right," and throw the pie.

This time, it's a bull's-eye.

BEFORE

In the morning, an incoming call pierces my awareness, yanking me from a vivid half dream. I bolt upright and fumble my cell off the nightstand, then croak a greeting.

"Oh god, Mina," Kate jabbers breathlessly in my ear. "Please don't hate me, but I can't take you to Seattle today. I'm so sorry."

"What?" I rub grit from my eyes. "What're you talking about? Why not?"

"This is so stupid, but I left my dome light on last night, and now my battery's dead, and… Well, I was just leaving to come get you, but I'm stuck. And I know you have to leave like, *now*, and—"

"Wait, what do you mean, now? *Now* now? What time is it?" Not waiting for an answer, I pull the phone away. The numbers on the screen slap me across the face. "What? Seven thirty? How's that possible? I set my alarm for six."

Or maybe I didn't. I don't actually recall. I just remember climbing into bed, filled with enough excitement that I couldn't sleep for hours, and now…

"Shit," I say. "Shitshitshit."

I jump from bed and race to the bathroom, where I toss the phone onto the counter. I scrub my teeth and yank a brush through my waist-length hair.

"I'm so sorry," Kate wails, on speaker. "I don't want you to leave, but I never would've done this on purpose."

"I know."

"Are you mad?"

"How could I be mad?" I spend all of four seconds wanding mascara onto my lashes, then another three dusting blush onto my cheeks. There. Done. "I should've been up already, and I should've had a backup plan."

"What're you gonna do?" She sounds miserable. "Can you call Patrick and explain?"

I zip back to my room and pull on the clothes I laid out last night—a collared shirt and dressy slacks intended to show that I take the responsibility of rehoming Rosalie's possessions seriously. My cousin is family by marriage, not blood, and he has no obligation to keep this job open if I don't show up as agreed. Especially since we've never actually met.

"I'll just have to find another ride," I blurt.

"Ugh." Kate swears under her breath. "You're not thinking what I think you're thinking, are you?"

My heartbeat churns as I scan the screen again: 7:34. That gives me twenty-six minutes to cover the three miles to Seaside House. Running is my only option—the closest cab company operates out of the next town, and the last Uber I called took forty-five minutes just to show up. "Of course not."

"Oh, thank god." She expels a breath. "Are you gonna ask your mom, then? She can take the day off work, right?"

Only then do I realize Kate's asking whether I intend to catch a ride with Michael Drake.

Oh. Well. In that case, she's going to be pissed.

But we can argue it out later, once it's all said and done. "Look, I'll text you in half an hour, okay?"

"Okay." She tenses up all over again. "But... Don't do anything stupid, all right?"

Just before hanging up, I say, "I won't."

Except...I absolutely will. I've waited my entire life for this. I can't let the opportunity slip through my fingers now.

I pelt from the house with my quilted purple roller-bag in tow. Luckily, I've chosen sensible shoes for my first day, and my shiny black flats slap against the sidewalk as the suitcase clatters behind me.

My thighs burn. Sweat beads my forehead. But my breath comes deep and even, because if there's one thing I excel at—besides daydreaming about places I've never seen—it's running like hell.

Cars honk as I careen through one intersection after another. The boardwalk rimming the beach comes into view. I hurtle onto it and burst through the door of Seaside House, a dusty blue Victorian bed-and-breakfast with a nightly price tag somewhere in the four-hundred-dollar range. Now I *am* breathing hard, but I ignore it and pull my phone out again: 7:58.

Not too shabby.

I glance around. A bank of windows overlooks the beach, where early risers pick through whitewashed driftwood. Round tables topped with lacy cloths dot the room. Two women with flawless salon highlights sit nearby, sipping from steaming coffee cups. I don't recognize them, which gives me hope.

"Hi." I finger-comb my hair, trying to make myself at least halfway presentable. "You wouldn't happen to know a Michael Drake, would you?"

They frown at my heaving chest and sweat-dampened collar.

"Who're you?" one says. "And why're you looking for Michael?"

A breath bubbles out. It sounds like they know him, at least.

"My name's Mina. Do you work with him? I'm trying to catch a ride."

They exchange a surprised look. "Are you a friend of his? Or...?"

"No," I say. "We just met yesterday, but he's heading home this morning, and I desperately need to get to Seattle."

"Oh." The first woman's tone softens. "I think he's still out running. He left about an hour ago, and I haven't seen him since. Unless he sneaked in through the back."

The second woman sips her coffee. "Even if he was here, though, I wouldn't bother. You won't get anywhere with him."

I frown. "What do you mean?"

"Well, Sarah asked if she could carpool with him this morning, and he blew her off."

The first woman—Sarah, apparently—nods. "And not in a nice way. I mean, he's always been kinda standoffish. But something's been seriously off with him lately. I swear he's spent the past month outright avoiding everyone."

"Except Ben," the other interjects.

Sarah nods. "Yeah. Except Ben. Anyway, Michael made it pretty clear he wanted to drive alone today. Sorry. I wish I had better news. But honestly...he's kind of an arrogant asshole, anyway. You're better off going with someone else."

Panic whirls in my stomach. "I don't have anyone else to ask."

Sarah's look turns sympathetic. "I'd say you could come with us, but Brooke"—she gestures at her friend—"drives a Miata. Only two seats. Good luck, though."

"Thanks." I try to gulp down the sudden throb in my throat. Michael offered me a ride himself, but maybe he's changed his mind. Still, I have to try. Asshole or no, he's my only option. "I'll check to see if he's out front. Have a nice breakfast."

I leave as they dig into their waffles. Outside, my phone shows 8:02.

The numbers jab at my gut. Michael's toned physique makes

me suspect he's no stranger to self-discipline, and the fact that he went running at 7:00 a.m. while on a retreat only strengthens that theory. Which means if he said he's leaving at eight, he was probably serious.

I scan the parking lot. Sunlight glints off metal car hoods, and in the far corner...

My pulse jolts. Beneath a stand of lodgepole pines, a blond head ducks into something low and blue. An engine roars.

Shit. If that's him, this is my last chance.

I take off running. The car powers through the lot, gravel fountaining from its tires, making me think there's definitely a man behind the wheel.

I reach the lot's exit. The Audi TT jerks to a stop mere inches from my knees, all throaty rumble and sparkling jay-blue paint. Reflected sunlight glares off the windshield.

I shade my eyes. A power window whirrs down, barely audible over the hiss-crash of waves against the nearby beach.

"Michael Drake?" I shout. "Is that you?"

A low laugh answers. "Maybe. Depends on whether you have any pies with you this time."

The smoke-and-bourbon voice spills warmth through me. I spring toward the driver's side. He doesn't *sound* like he's going to refuse me. "Oh, thank god. My friend's car died this morning, and I ran all the way here, hoping you could—"

When Michael looks up through his open window, the rest of my sentence flies off into the sunshine.

Jesus.

He's got one of those faces made from bold, sharp lines—angled jaw, squared chin, prominent cheekbones. I gape for a good five seconds before noticing the gentler touches like generous lips and a faintly upturned nose, and then I just keep staring. Between the hard lines and the soft ones, there's something intensely...*beautiful* about this guy, yet with his rough, masculine edges, I would never actually use that word to describe him.

And those eyes—glimpses of a welcoming ocean, fringed by long lashes. They seem to record the depths of my inner reaction, as if he sees straight through to some private core.

"Hoping I could what?" he says.

My breath gets lost trying to find my lungs. "What?"

A smile plays around his mouth. Hair the color of old, age-worn gold curves over his forehead, which he reaches up to brush back. "You were hoping I could what?"

"Um…" I blink my way from my stupor. Guys like this don't stroll through Seagrove every day. Or any town, for that matter. "Take me to Seattle."

He smirks. "What do I look like, some kind of altruist?"

The truth rolls off my tongue before I can stop it. "God, no. You look like you shouldn't even know what that word means."

"Wow." He laughs. "Thanks. First you hit me with a pie, then you tell me I look dumb. I'm starting to think I've offended you somehow."

Heat stains my cheeks. "No, I didn't mean…" Yesterday, I assumed he was hitting on me, but looking at him now, that's so very obviously not the case that I can only laugh at my own arrogance. Out loud.

He raises an eyebrow. "And now you're laughing at me. *Mockingly*, if I'm not mistaken."

"Sorry," I say. "It's not that. I didn't come here to insult you, or beg for charity. I just need some help. I can pay, if that helps."

His tropical eyes glitter. "Now you think I need your money?"

I scan the car, which probably costs more than most people make in a year, then his shiny, gilded hair. I bet his shampoo alone is worth more than my entire makeup collection. "Um…"

"You know what?" He waves a hand. "Don't answer that. Just throw your bag in back. You have to be in Seattle by eleven, right?"

My mind blanks. I can't imagine how he knows that. But

then I remember his above-and-beyond attention to detail yesterday. *Takes one to know one, writer girl.*

Must be an architect thing.

"I really, really do." I forcibly unfreeze myself, then toss my suitcase into the trunk, slip into the car, and snick the door shut. Michael rolls up his window, sealing us into a cocoon of chilled black leather and tinted glass.

He watches me click my seat belt, his expression curious and assessing and…something else I can't pin down. I pointedly ignore it and punch Rosalie's address into the navigation. A blue line appears on the map: "Time to destination: 3:02."

I fixate on the path to my freedom, which will deliver me a mere nine minutes late. I only have to get through three hours and two minutes in close quarters with an absurdly gorgeous architect who may or may not be the world's biggest asshole.

Worth it.

"I'm surprised you came," Michael says, ignoring the navigation screen, his foot still on the brake. "I was ninety-nine percent sure you wouldn't."

I arch an eyebrow. "That's because you one hundred percent don't know me."

It's a bold response, so much so that I can't say where it comes from. If my mother could hear me, she'd faint dead away. So would Kate. Well, no. She'd give me *the look.*

Not this guy, though. His half smile blossoms in full. "What's your name?"

"Mina."

"Mina. Huh. I like that, actually. It suits you. Tiny, but impossible to ignore. *Mi-na.*" He infuses those two syllables with more appreciation than I knew they could hold.

To me, my name has always sounded small and stilted, a reminder of my unimpressive size. But when Michael Drake says it with his oak-paneled-rooms-and-red-leather-armchairs voice, I suddenly change my mind.

Mina. It actually has an edge of elegance. Who knew?

"Thanks," I say. "And...you *are* Michael Drake, right?"

I don't know why I ask; he can't possibly be anyone but the pie-covered guy from yesterday. And yet I can't quite believe *this* was hiding under all that whipped cream.

His focus sharpens. "If I said no, would you get out?"

"I... Uh..." Not what I expected.

He waits, not so much as a blink to lessen the weight of those eyes on mine.

I swallow, remembering a story I once read about two war-time pen pals who fell in love by letter, neither knowing what the other looked like. When they finally agreed to meet, the woman wrote ahead to say she'd pin a red rose to her lapel, but when she boarded the train, she asked a kind, homely woman to wear the flower instead—the problem being that she was beautiful, and she didn't want her soldier to love her because of that.

It was a test. At the station, would the soldier approach her, gorgeous but roseless? Or the plain woman wearing the flower? Would he choose beauty or substance?

This charged silence makes me feel like the soldier. Like Michael's asking whether I got into this car because of our easy repartee yesterday, or because of that striking face of his.

"Sorry, but..." I mirror his intensity. "I'm looking for a Michael Drake. Maybe you've seen him? Nerdy architect guy? Likes to walk around wearing a few layers of baked goods? Maybe I should just wait out on the sidewalk. I'm sure he'll show up eventually."

I fumble for the door handle, not at all certain he'll stop me, immensely grateful when he reaches across to still my hand.

When I turn back, he's leaning close. He breaks into a smile, which has roughly the same effect as the sun emerging from behind a cloud.

My breath dwindles. I forgive the fact that he apparently has no plans to depart my personal space anytime soon, because he smells incredible. Like the mossy forest after a drenching rain, when the world glows fresh and quiet, the woods still waking after the fury of the storm. He smells like the beginning of something. Like the start of a new day.

"I guess I'm Michael, then," he says, soft and smoky. "No need to get out."

"Oh. Good. I *was* kind of looking forward to seeing what this car can do." Amazingly, I sound all kinds of casual. Inside, I can't help but marvel at how his name doesn't suit him.

Michael. It's biblical. Angelic.

Aside from the golden hair, this man possesses exactly zero angelic qualities. In fact, looking at him makes me want to commit a cardinal sin at the earliest opportunity.

No, it doesn't, I tell myself. *Patrick. Great-aunt Rosalie.* All I need is a ride. And not the X-rated kind.

Michael doesn't encourage a return to rationality by moving away, though. His gaze lances into me, and every cell in my body responds, a crowd of a million heads all swiveling to fixate on the same thing.

I gulp. "Do you always look at strangers this way?"

His lips quirk. "What way?"

Like you're examining their soul, I almost say, but there's no way that won't sound ridiculous, so I settle for "Like you know them as well as you know yourself."

"Of course not," he says. "I'm not a creep. Despite what your friend said."

"Okay. But you're looking at *me* this way, which makes you...?"

"Intrigued."

"Right." I'm dimly aware that I'm hyperventilating, but I can't seem to make it stop. "And what about me intrigues you?"

"A few things." His smile softens, turning vulnerable and sweet. "For one, not many girls would've sprinted across town just to get a ride. But you did, which tells me you're passionate about something."

"Everyone's passionate about something."

"No." He chuckles. "God, no. And second, I like your face."

A nervous cackle threatens to erupt at the absurdity of hearing a statement like *that* from a guy like *this*.

"You have this natural look," he continues. "Not a lot of makeup. Like you're not trying to fool anyone. Just being you. It's a sign of confidence."

"Actually, it's a sign of me oversleeping by an hour and a half."

His eyes crinkle with amusement. "And you're honest. Most people aren't. At least not like that."

"Well," I manage. "You might actually be onto something with that one."

He glances down, his lashes kissing his cheeks, then releases my hand and retreats. He shifts into gear. "Now that we've cleared that up, are you ready?"

I nod, completely incapable of forming words. What's English? What are words?

"Good." His foot presses the gas. "This should be…interesting."

I flash a weak smile and glue my attention to the road. When my brain finally decides to start working again, I realize how vastly I've misjudged this situation.

Michael Drake might be willing to drive me to Seattle, but I'd better make damn sure I still want to get out of his car once he does.

AFTER

Six months have stumbled by, and still, I find reminders of my husband everywhere. Yet I feel his loss most keenly in the places he *isn't*. In the ragged, gaping holes he left behind.

No second toothbrush sits beside the sink. No hand steals around my waist to tug me close in the mornings. In the evenings, his drafting table lamp no longer spills light into the yard; when I look up from the couch, only my own wraithlike reflection hovers in the glass. There sits a sad-eyed widow, reading her book by the blue flicker of the television, just so some life will fill these empty rooms.

It's August now. A beautiful month, but the sunshine hasn't kept the days from blurring into one long, empty tableau. Last week, I turned thirty-seven without even noticing. I woke up and went to bed without once remembering my birthday.

Not that I would've done anything differently, if I had. That day always comes with its own set of problems. Best to avoid them completely.

Today, Michael's absence presses in, heavier than usual. I

carry my coffee to the living room and stare out through the glass. Sunlight winks through the evergreen fronds as if mocking the cavernous darkness gathered beneath my ribs. I sip, but even the bright warmth of caffeine fails to lift my spirits.

It's obvious to me why. Once, in the first year of marriage, I'd complained to Michael about how intense his work had gotten. Cofounding his own architectural firm meant he'd barely had time for us anymore, which, to be fair, he'd warned me about in advance. Still, he'd apologized by buying me a subscription to the Coffees of the World club. The company had shipped us a bag of beans from a different country each month. That had lasted a year, until I'd met my soulmate strain in the form of a brew from Kenya and Michael had promptly switched the delivery over to a single variety. It still shows up on my doorstep each month, like clockwork.

God, I miss the way he took care of me. Even if I would've traded every ounce of that pampering for more of his time.

The chime of an incoming call jolts me. On the desk, my phone lights up with Kate's picture. I reach over and hit Cancel. The idea of formulating words right now exhausts me, and my gaze wanders to my laptop. Maybe I could just email…

But no. If I venture onto the internet, I know exactly what I'll see. Who I'll accidentally end up staring in the face. And I'd love nothing more than to never think about Michael's brother again.

A high-pitched keening slices through the quiet.

I jerk toward the windows. The sound comes again, from outside. Frowning, I set my coffee aside and venture through the slider onto the porch, then down into the yard.

Beneath the deck, something stirs. A pitiful whine floats from the shadows. The sound hits me in the heart, or whatever I have left of one, and I ease into the darkness, where a shadowy shape shrinks away.

I blink until my eyes adjust. It's a dog. An old Irish setter mix, with muddy brown eyes and a graying snout.

Longing rises tight in my chest. For a moment, I'm seeing another dog entirely, one with a copper coat and wretched breath. One I buried years ago.

God, I'm so damn tired of burying things.

When I blink again, reality returns. What is wrong with me? This poor creature hardly resembles Penny at all.

I push away the hollow ache of loss and crouch. The dog is curled between a bag of mulch and a stack of empty flower-pots. No collar. No visible wounds, either, but she's panting as if she just sprinted across miles of forest. Another whine comes from deep in her throat.

I reach out. Years ago, someone dumped a husky on the shelter's doorstep who'd keened just like this. Darlene had taken one look and diagnosed him with peritonitis, then made a phone call that had gotten the dog into emergency surgery, where he'd had a broken chicken bone removed from his intestines. It hadn't mattered that Seagrove's only veterinarian had been the best man in a beachside wedding that evening. Darlene had worked her magic, the way she always does.

Now a fire lights in my muscles. I don't know if this dog is in the same predicament, but if so, I need to get her to Darlene. Immediately.

The dog sniffs my outstretched fingers, then licks. It's the only encouragement I need to scoop her up. She's all dead-weight, but I stagger around the house to the garage and settle her into the passenger seat of my Genesis. If her condition is as critical as the husky's, every moment counts.

Within seconds, I'm rocketing from the driveway.

Maybe I shouldn't roar across town at twice the speed limit, but every time the dog whimpers, a hot spark flares in my chest. If Penny had ever wandered off, I would've wanted someone to help her. To do anything.

And, if I'm honest, this is the first time since that horrible phone call that I've felt in control of anything. The first time in six months I've actually had a say.

The speedometer's needle edges higher. "Hold on, girl." I take the turnoff onto Darlene's street thirty miles an hour faster than legally permitted. "Help's coming."

As trees whip past the window, I hope like hell that's not a lie.

BEFORE

Michael accelerates down Main Street with one hand draped over the steering wheel, apparently every bit as comfortable piloting sports cars as he is mocking strange girls and being hit in the face with pies.

I surreptitiously wipe my sweaty palms on my slacks. Oddly, the silence doesn't prickle, like it would with most strangers, but waits with a sort of held, anticipatory breath. The interlude gives me a chance to study him, too. To note the finer details, like the fact that he wears no jewelry, except for a twisted silver necklace that bridges the grooves between his collarbones and muscled chest, which are just visible through the V-neck of his black shirt.

He's dressed more casually today, his sleeves short, his jeans well lived-in, suggesting that yesterday's business attire was for his coworkers' benefit. My attention settles on his hands. Like most men's, they're square palmed, but the fingers skimming the dash are long, almost delicate. As with his face, I find the contrast compelling.

Most noticeably, though, Michael Drake radiates a...steadiness. I can tell by the way he drives. He seems like the kind of person who trusts himself. Who's never confused by anything.

As he steers onto Highway 109, he catches me staring. It's the second time now, but I don't bother to hide it.

His smile reappears, so readily that I wonder if I imagined that moment of seriousness earlier, when I asked about his name. "What?" he says. "Am I not what you expected?"

"You're really not. At all."

"Hmm. Is that a good thing? Or are you about to insult me again?"

"I..." I grope for something that won't give me away. "...Just wasn't prepared for the lack of frosting, that's all."

He chuckles. "Should I have showed up covered in whipped cream?"

"I would've been impressed if you had."

"Well, damn. I considered it. I came about this close." He holds his thumb and forefinger up. "But I figured I might not be able to defend myself if you hadn't had breakfast yet. And we've already established that a guy can't be too careful. Especially around nerds." His voice drops to a stage whisper. "I've heard they're dangerous."

His teasing unwinds something in me, and I snicker at the visual of me clambering over the gearshift to lick pie off his shoulder. "You are *extremely* sure of yourself, aren't you?"

He raises a golden eyebrow. "Should I not be?"

It ought to sound cocky as hell, but it doesn't. He says it like he's genuinely curious as to whether I find him lacking in some way.

I absolutely do not. But it won't hurt him to wonder.

"What *were* you expecting?" he says when the silence grows.

It's hard to say. Mostly, to climb into this car alongside a perfectly normal human, albeit one with a distractingly firm body and nice eyes.

I did not expect to feel like I'd strayed too close to a downed power line, or like Michael Drake makes an entire car's worth of air sizzle just by existing. I didn't expect him to use words like *altruist*, or remember details about me most people never would've noticed in the first place.

"Someone less...arresting, maybe?"

"Arresting?" His eyes spark. "You think I'm arresting?"

Well. To hell with it. "Yep. I'm pretty sure that's the exact word I'm looking for."

He flashes me a look of appreciation. "I don't think anyone's ever called me that before. *Arresting.* I might like that as much as I like your name."

"In that case, you're welcome."

He smiles sidelong, as if confirming something he already suspected. "You know, it's funny, because when we met yesterday, I could've used the same word for you."

I give him a narrow look. "Are you teasing me again?"

"When did I tease you the first time?"

I lower my brows and glare, which earns me a spirited laugh.

"Okay, okay," he says. "But really. When you walked by me yesterday, it was like...I don't know. Something I've never felt before. This tingle started in my head, then went down through my chest. It was almost like I recognized you. Or like I'd been terrified about your safety for a long time, then saw you walking down the street, perfectly fine. It was that sense of relief, almost, the kind that goes so deep it's like your bones sigh. Seeing you was this overwhelming experience that had nothing to do with what I was looking at. It was...disturbingly powerful, actually. *Arresting.*"

My jaw slackens. He delivers all this like he's telling me about something that happened at the grocery store. No hesitation or coquettishness. Just utter, transparent candor. "All that happened just when you looked at me?"

"Yeah. I mean, I was listening to what you were saying, too, which might've had something to do with it. But whatever that feeling was, I knew I had to talk to you. If you hadn't stopped at the booth, I would've left Ben's great-aunt hanging and chased you across the fairgrounds covered in pie."

A stilted laugh erupts. I have no idea what's happening, only that Sarah was wrong about one thing. This guy definitely didn't want to drive alone today.

He doesn't really seem like an asshole, either.

"And then what?" I hear myself say. "What would you have said to me?"

"The same thing. That I wanted to take you to Seattle. Though I probably would've had more explaining to do, in that scenario."

I shake my head. "Are you *sure* you weren't looking at Kate while all this was happening?"

"Kate? Who's Kate?"

"My best friend. The runway model you got into a catfight with."

"Oh." The warmth in his voice fades. "Right. She's pretty, I won't lie. But I wasn't looking at her. I was looking at the dark-haired writer who's willing to move to Greece just for the hell of it. The one who knows exactly what 'aid and abet' means."

"Wow." I stare. "You really were eavesdropping."

"Shamelessly." He steers the Audi through a tight curve with enough speed that my back melds with the leather seat, but he seems so sure of his ability that I end up feeling sure of it, too. When the g-forces loosen their grip, Michael looks over again.

The touch of his eyes burns a path down into some eager, uncharted part of me. Heat flickers and flares in my belly.

I jerk my gaze away. It's entirely physical, I tell myself. The inevitable reaction to sharing a car with someone so striking. So what if that someone also happens to function with a degree of openness I've never encountered *and* appreciates my vocab—

Nope. I steer my thoughts back into their lane. *Patrick. Ro-*

salie. I have a job to do. A foreign country to get to. A life to go live. In three hours, I'll leave this unexpectedly arresting man behind, and after that, in all likelihood, I'll never see Michael Drake again.

Which is fine.

Totally, completely fine.

I fiddle with my purse strap until the sparkle in my blood dissipates, then retreat to the bland, superficial topics strangers usually default to.

Michael's amused expression makes me suspect he knows what I'm doing, but he doesn't protest. He answers all my questions, though his terse responses regarding architecture soon spur me elsewhere. When I ask about his hobbies, he catches me off guard by waxing poetic about books and nature. He hikes. He camps. He *does* read—fifty pages a day, without fail, apparently as a form of mental self-discipline.

"You seem surprised," he says when my writer's heart swells to such a size that words fail me.

"I am."

"Why, because I look like a jackass who doesn't know what an altruist is?" Light dances in his maybe-turquoise eyes. He's teasing again. Or fishing for compliments.

Either way, I'd have to be dead not to engage. "That's not what I meant, and you know it. I just meant..." I sweep a hand up and down to indicate his sheer male exquisiteness. "You know. Don't make me say it out loud."

He flutters his lashes. "But it'd be so much more fun if you did."

My god. He's incorrigible. "Okay, you look like the kind of guy who lives at the gym and breaks a different girl's heart every weekend. Not the kind who *reads*. There. Happy?"

He laughs. "Well, you wouldn't be *entirely* off base with that. But I probably don't do either of those things as often as you think, and I'm more than just a pretty face."

Again, it should sound cocky, but again, it doesn't. Probably because there's no debating whether or not he's attractive. He is. Statement of fact.

"Clearly," I say. "But I can't believe you read actual books, every day. No one does that anymore."

"I know." His voice roughens, mournful. "Focusing on anything more than a scroll through Instagram is like a dying art. But that's exactly why I read. So I can stay capable of actual thinking."

My inner nerd begins to salivate. "Did you read this morning?"

"Yep."

"Which book?"

"It's called *Consumed*. About evolutionary psychology and its impact on consumer behavior. It talks about how, on a subconscious level, our genes govern our buying habits, which essentially means—"

"Yeah," I say. "I get it. Behavior that evolution grafted into us a long time ago still affects our choices today, right? Like, people might do things that seem irrational, buy things they can't afford for no apparent reason. But deep down, there *is* a reason, buried somewhere in our DNA. You just have to go back a few millennia to figure out why it's there."

He looks startled. "You've studied evolutionary psychology?"

"No." I laugh. "I have an English degree."

He zeroes in on my face. "Then how'd you know what I meant?"

"I'm a nerd, remember? I read everything. Similar to someone else, apparently."

Michael's gaze returns to the road, but something in his posture tells me I still have every ounce of attention not dedicated to driving. "Well, there you go. Even if we ignore what you look like, the fact that you said what you just did tells me I was staring at exactly the right girl yesterday."

My face heats. I don't know which part of that to address first. "Ignore what I look like? What do I look like?"

"Like the kind of girl who could break my heart. Forget the other way around."

A beat passes. "Are you making fun of me?" Not that I'm unattractive—I actually like the wide-set blue eyes and dainty doll's mouth I see in the mirror. But I don't usually stun people like Kate does, and palling around with her hasn't exactly led to a flood of choices in the romance department. Guys almost universally gravitate toward her first, and I've never had any interest in her leftovers.

"No." Michael chuffs a ragged laugh, almost to himself. "You're not one of those weekend conquests you just talked about. You're the kind of girl that leaves permanent scars. I can tell." The way he says it strikes me. He sounds, of all things... *pleased* by that.

My blush blossoms in full. I angle away, hauling myself back from the brink of some luscious abyss I don't dare jump into.

On any other day, I'd dive in headfirst. Even now, I want to so badly it hurts not to. But I can't. Won't. *Patrick. Work. Greece. Freedom.*

I need to keep this guy at arm's length.

I have my work cut out for me, though, because no matter how benign the topic, Michael always veers toward something deeper. It's like he doesn't have a setting called *small talk.* He's unabashedly interested in the world and its ways, and has thoughts, theories, about everything. He wants to know mine, too. As the miles melt away, he asks about my innermost dreams, my writing, what I'd do if today was my last day on earth. Then he listens, rapt, as if I might say something ingenious and it's his job to watch for it.

"One day to live?" I echo. I don't even have to think about it. "That's easy. I'd leave the country."

"Really? Why that?"

"Because I've never done it before."

His eyebrows jump. "You've never been to Mexico? Spring break in the Bahamas?"

"I've never even been to Canada." I grip the seat as he guides us through another serpentine curve. "Which is crazy, because I've dreamed about other countries since I was little. But the closest I could ever get was reading. Then writing my own stories, eventually. In high school, I used to make up these travelogues about all the languages I'd heard, the streets I'd wandered, the new foods I'd discovered. I was obsessed with writing it down, and I've always wondered if reality would match up with the dream."

His long fingers drum against the wheel. "So that's why you're moving to Greece? To find out?"

"Yeah. That, and..." I trail off. There's another reason. A fantasy, more like. One I haven't even told Kate about. But the confession will only make me sound starry-eyed and naive, so I pretend to find importance in the greenery rushing past the window.

"What?"

"Nothing. It's...nothing."

"It doesn't *sound* like nothing." Michael's eyes slit. "Let me guess. You want to be a travel writer? Combine your two passions into a way to make a living?"

The question lands low and solid in my belly, and for a moment, I can't speak. I can only stare at him while something inside me rearranges itself.

"Am I off base?"

"No." My voice comes out flimsy, no more than a breath. "But...how'd you do that?"

"Do what?"

"Read my mind."

The smile that never quite leaves his lips flares again. "I

didn't. I just paid attention while you talked. Put the pieces together."

I suck in air so hard my bottom lip folds under my teeth. Whatever's happening right now, I have no idea how to handle it. Kate and my parents listen well enough, but with them, expectation lurks just beneath the surface. I only have to say the wrong thing, *want* the wrong thing, for the skeptical glances to begin.

Meanwhile, Michael's expression holds such obvious acceptance that something suspiciously close to tears tickles at my eyes.

I clear my throat. Twice. It still doesn't chase away the burn.

Thankfully, the road claims his attention again. "My only question is…if leaving the country is important enough that you'd spend your last day doing it, why haven't you already? You said the closest you could get was reading, which makes it sound like something was holding you back."

I gulp. I almost wish he weren't so astute. My eyes drop to my lap as memories march past—all those nights when my mother camped out on the living room couch, poring over old photographs and building mountains of tear-stained tissues.

I think of the times she waited outside under the porchlight if I overshot curfew by a single minute. And my sophomore year of college, when I broached the subject of studying abroad in New Zealand.

Not a chance, she'd said, twisting her wedding ring around her finger, the way she always does when she's anxious. *Don't you remember what happened to your brother? And to Margo? How can you even consider it?*

How, indeed.

I look up. My gaze tangles with Michael's.

Oh, god. I'm going to tell him. About all of it. How my brother, Jasper, died in another country the day I was born, how a fear of foreign places has held our family in a clenched fist ever since. How I spent my childhood burying my long-ings so deeply I fear I'll forget them myself someday. How I once had two best friends, until Margo went off to a foreign-exchange program in high school and never came back, thus solidifying my parents' terror forever.

Long-buried truths tumble up my throat like caged animals starving for freedom, and—

My phone rings.

I seal the words behind my lips, shaking myself. What the hell am I doing? I fish through my purse, then suppress a groan at the name on the screen.

My mother. How fitting.

I flick the button. "Hello?"

"Mina?" She shapes my name into something small and fretful—she always does, at least until I convince her I'm safe. I forgive her in nanoseconds, though, the way any daughter with an ounce of compassion would. "Are you okay? Where are you?"

"Mom, I'm *always* okay." I use my gentlest tone, this ritual ageless by now. "I'm on my way to Rosalie's."

"Oh, good. I just wanted to make sure you got on the road all right. You're with Kate?"

I glance at the specimen beside me. From a certain angle, he *does* kind of look like a male version of my best friend—blond, toned, ferociously good-looking, enough that I feel like I'm staring directly at a light bulb and might incinerate my reti-nas if I don't look away soon. "Yep. With Kate. She's driving."

"Hi, Mom," Michael says in a falsetto so absurd that I make a snapping motion with my hand in an attempt shut him up.

He winks.

I glare.

Thankfully, the road noise proves significant enough that my mother doesn't catch the exchange, because relief colors her voice. "Well, tell her I said hi. And text me when you get in, will you? Just so I know you're safe."

"Of course." As if I need the reminder. "Love you, Mom."

"Love you, honey."

After hanging up, I shake my head in disapproval. "Nice."

Michael chuckles, clearly pleased with himself. "What? I was only playing along."

"No, you were playing with fire, was what you were doing."

His amusement only deepens. "Is she really that protective?"

"You have no idea."

"Oh, come on. Aren't you in your twenties?"

"Yeah, but...she has her reasons."

He must catch the tightness in my voice, because he sobers. "Oh. Well, damn. Do you want to talk about it?"

"No. I really don't. Thanks." I firmly replace the lid on the can of worms I was about to upend in his lap. "Besides, it's your turn. I told you my answer, but you haven't given me yours. What would you do if you were going to die tomorrow?"

"That's easy," he says, and I wonder if his mirror of my answer is intentional. He gestures between us. "I'd do this."

"What, drive me to Seattle?"

"Yep."

I roll my eyes. "No, really."

"Really."

My god. I should've known better than to ask. It seems no question is harmless with this guy. "You're telling me the top item on your bucket list involves three hours in a car with a stranger?"

"Not exactly." He shifts his hand from the top of the steering wheel to the bottom, which makes the muscles in his forearm dance in a way I try my best not to notice. "I'm saying I don't have a bucket list."

"No way. Everyone has a bucket list."

A lock of gilded hair sneaks down over his forehead. He rakes it back, revealing a crease between his brows.

Oh. He's serious.

"They do," he says slowly, "but only because most people are asleep. They're out there shuffling through one day after another, waiting for life to start happening to them at some indeterminate point in the future. They tell themselves they'll finally take that dream trip once they get a promotion or pay off that credit card. Only they never get the promotion. They never pay off the credit card. Or if they do, they find some other arbitrary goalpost, then end up looking back on their lives forty years later and realizing they spent the whole thing wishing they were somewhere else. Doing something else. They sleepwalked through the best years they had and didn't notice until too late."

A cold prickle settles into my bones. It's like he's captured my deepest fears—things I haven't even dared articulate to myself—in a few ruthless sentences. "But not you? Everyone's asleep, but you're awake?"

"I *try* to be. I'm not saying I have it all figured out, just that life's happening to us all the time already. The way I see it, there's no such thing as tomorrow, because it's only ever *right now*. I'm only ever *right here*. So the best option is to make each moment count. To live inside it with everything I have. Which means if today's my last day, then yeah. I'll spend it just like this. Here. With you."

I stare at him for the hundredth time, only now...I don't see the face, or the hair, or the eyes. I see a man who isn't scattered or divided, but here in his entirety, and who doesn't need anything else.

Holy shit. No wonder he seems so sure of himself.

And no wonder he draws me like a magnet. Already, half of me has rushed into next month and boarded a plane to Athens. Meanwhile, the other half is busy worrying whether it would be easiest to live in my brother's shadow forever, the way my parents would prefer.

"Do you...?" I trail off, then try again, even though something in me curls tight at the question. "Do you think *I'm* asleep?"

Michael searches my face. "Maybe. But if so, you're in the process of waking up, and that's all that really matters. Because if there's no such thing as tomorrow, then there's no such thing as yesterday, either. The only thing that counts is what you do with your right now."

The words hit like a freight train. Between that and his casual approval of my innermost hopes, I feel like I'm staring in a brand-new direction I didn't even realize existed. Suddenly, I'm burning to explore the possibility of right now.

My pulse hurtles into overdrive. *What if I don't get out at Rosalie's house? What if—*

In my hand, my cell dings, scattering the thoughts like blown confetti. Kate's name pops up.

Crap. I should've texted her, but this drive has made it remarkably easy to forget.

I open her message, which consists of seventeen wordless question marks, and fire off a response.

Please don't hate me, and if my mother asks, I'm with you. But that guy from the fair is taking me. We're almost there.

Within seconds, a string of red-faced, bleep-mouthed emojis appears.

ARE YOU SERIOUS?!?!?!

I switch my phone to silent, but it still buzzes like an angry hornet.

I KNEW you were gonna do something crazy. Has he tried to kill you yet?

No, I type back. But there's still time.

Oh, HILARIOUS. Send me his information. At least I'll have some-one to tell the police about when they go looking for your body.

With a sigh, I pop the glove box open and rifle through, somehow certain Michael won't mind.

Sure enough, he watches my invasion with barely concealed amusement. "Can I help you with something?"

I dig out the Audi's registration papers and snap a picture. "Just sending this to Kate, in case she wants to steal your iden-tity later."

The corner of his mouth hitches upward. "Or have me ar-rested for kidnapping, you mean?"

I shrug, relieved to find the conversation back on solid ground. "That part's kind of up to you, isn't it?"

"She's protective, too?"

"Mmm-hmm. You can imagine how much my mother adores her." As I tuck the registration away, I spot something even better and pull it out. "Wow. Jackpot. Who keeps their driver's license in their glove box?"

His brow wrinkles. He studies the card as if he doesn't re-member stashing it there. "I do, apparently."

"But what happens if you're out somewhere and need to buy alcohol?"

"Trick question. No one ever *needs* to buy alcohol." Despite his easy answer, he stares at the flimsy rectangle as if itching to snatch it away.

It's the first sign of anything other than complete self-assurance, and I latch on to the possibility that he might not be as incredible as he appears. Anything to make the next month at Rosalie's feel as tempting as it did a few hours ago.

Angling the license away, I scan for clues. Apparently Mi-chael Bradley Drake is six foot three, weighs a hundred and eighty-five pounds, and has a birthday in February, two years before mine, which currently makes him twenty-five to my twenty-two. There's also an address in Seattle with an apartment number attached.

No surprises there. I move on to the picture.

The second I do, I know that's what he doesn't want me to see. He's younger here, his hair shorter, his cheeks fuller. But his expression...

He looks wounded. Haunted. Those blue-green eyes stare out of the frame as if asking how the world has dared hurt him so badly. Try as I might, I find no trace of the easygoing smiler of the past few hours.

Without thinking, I snap a picture and send that off, too. Then I hunt for the license's issue date—January, two years ago. "What happened to you?" I say softly. "Two and a half years ago?"

When I look up, a muscle feathers in Michael's jaw. He holds out a hand for the license, which he stares at for a moment before tucking it into his pocket. "Something I don't usually talk about."

"Oh. It's a secret?"

"No, it's just...painful." There's a bleak note in his voice—a hint of old, dark blood in the water, remnants of a wound that never quite healed. "I have to be in the right frame of mind to get through it. And with the right person."

An ache forms in my chest. I try to chase it off with a joke. "I guess we're stuck talking about the weather, then."

He doesn't laugh. "No, I'll tell you. I just... Don't repeat this, please. It's not something I share with just anyone."

That strikes me dumb, because I *am* just anyone.

But for whatever reason, Michael doesn't seem to think so. He soldiers on, looking raw and determined. "It had to do with a girl. My brother's fiancée."

"Oh." Irrational jealousy stabs through me. "You were in love with your brother's girlfriend?"

"No, no, nothing like that. I mean...Lily was incredible, in lots of ways. Pretty, like your friend Kate. Kindhearted. But she was so focused on ticking off the boxes people expected her to that she never stopped to wonder what she wanted for herself. Maybe that made her feel safe, letting others decide what she should dream about. And it's definitely why my brother adored her so much. She didn't demand a whole lot. Didn't mind making him her priority. Which is kind of his thing."

I frown, not at all certain of where this is going.

"Not that he didn't treat her well. He spoiled the shit out of her, actually. But then she…died." Michael's jaw works, as if he's chewing on something bitter and can't decide whether to spit it out or not. "Because of something I did. Lily died, and it was my fault."

"Oh. Oh…*god.*"

"It was an accident, but…it's something I can never make right. And trust me, I've tried. I'm *still* trying." His voice roughens, turning hollow and ancient. "But it's too late. She's gone, and nothing I do can ever be enough. I'm pretty sure my brother wishes I'd never been born."

Horror pools in my stomach. To be responsible for someone's death, even by accident…

"Holy shit," I say. "I'm so sorry."

"Thanks. It was…not a good time in my life. Hence the picture."

"Wow. I didn't mean to bring up bad memories." I wince at the paleness of my apology.

"It's okay. You didn't know. Though I wish you hadn't sent that photo to your friend."

Heat invades my throat. Why *did* I do that? I stare out the window, feeling as if I've betrayed Michael without meaning to.

The sting only burns hotter when I glimpse the suburban sprawl beyond the glass. When did we leave the forest behind? I hadn't even noticed.

I glance at the navigation: "Time to destination: 0:02."

My heart lurches. Two minutes, even though it's only ten forty-six. Michael has shaved a full twenty minutes off the trip, for which I should be grateful. Except silence pulses between us like a bruise. For a moment, I mourn the destroyed perfection of the drive, then tell myself it's better this way. Easier.

In my hand, my phone buzzes. Kate again.

That is...not what I expected him to look like. Obviously someone ran over his cat the day that picture was taken, but aside from that, goddamn.

Chest heavy, I type back, Yeah, no shit. Try sitting next to him for three hours and not drooling. It's harder than it sounds. Then I stash my cell away, because that's quite enough of that.

Michael coaxes the Audi to the curb. "Here you go."

Outside the window, a house awaits, no different than the half-dozen other brick ranch homes on the block. Try as I might, I can't find a single inviting thing about it.

I turn to him, words bubbling in my throat. I want so badly to wrap protective hands around the secret he's entrusted me with, but a wall has gone up behind his eyes and that perennial smile has finally failed.

I falter. On the navigation screen, the blue line marking my path has disappeared. There's nothing to guide me any longer, no arrow telling me which way to go.

"I guess I should get out now," I hear myself say.

His expression flickers. We stare at one another. Sweat breaks out on the small of my back. The Audi's clock ticks over to 10:50.

I weigh it all—my relentless need to see the world, the unrest simmering beneath my skin, the way my mother's grief has always bound me up in a box I didn't dare break free of.

Now is my chance. I only have to step out of the car.

Michael gives me a thin smile, as if he can read my inner

turmoil down to the letter. "Time to wake up," he says, soft as smoke.

Those simple words tilt the world back into focus. I know if I don't get out of this Audi right this second, I'll never make it to Greece.

So I unlatch my seat belt. Climb out. Every movement feels like a battle, but I retrieve my bag and peer down through the still-open door. "Bye, Michael. It definitely was interesting."

"Bye, Mina. I hope you tell me about Greece someday." He presses his lips together, as if trying not to say more. But I swear his eyes ask a question.

I hesitate, wishing I could stay and fall into those eyes. I want to put on scuba gear, for god's sake, and dive into that tropical expanse until I have nothing left to explore.

But if I take his number, email address, anything at all, I won't be able to help myself. I'll end up staying right here, the same way I always have.

I'll never know what the world would have offered me.

"Maybe," I say, though we both know I have no way to get in touch again. I have his address, but I resolve to delete my picture of his driver's license at the first opportunity.

As I close the Audi's door, I wonder if I'll regret this moment forever. But I don't turn back. Instead, I march up to Rosalie's door and ring the bell.

AFTER

Darlene swings open her front door and does a double take. Her snowy eyebrows climb her forehead as she regards the bundle in my arms.

"Hi." I rearrange my grip on the dog, earning myself a pitiful whine. "I'm so sorry to bother you on a Sunday, but she needs help, and I didn't know where else to go."

Darlene adjusts her glasses and beckons me inside. "Bother me? No, no, you just surprised me. Bring her here and let's see what we've got."

In the living room, I arrange the dog gingerly, aware that any jostling might drive a bone shard deeper. Her sides heave, but the sky-blue carpet provides a decent cushion, at least. "I found her hiding underneath my deck."

Darlene gets down beside me, somehow still limber, even at eighty-nine. She often says that her second passion in life—teaching aerobics—keeps her youthful, and I'm inclined to believe her.

"Did you see anything outside?" she says. "Another dog that might've attacked her, maybe? A bear?"

"No, nothing."

Darlene squeezes the dog's legs, prods her belly, pries her teeth apart and squints inside.

A lump grows in my throat. "Is it bad?" Now that our furious dash across town is over, I realize this poor, elderly dog is the first creature I'd spoken to in a week. She might resemble Penny in only the vaguest of ways, but I'd scale mountains for her regardless.

Anything that involves flipping death a giant middle finger.

"Hmm. Doesn't look like it." Darlene reaches between the dog's teeth and works a jagged stick free. Blood stains one end, but the moment it's out, the dog rolls onto her belly, her tongue lolling out like a banner.

I release a shaky exhale. Damn. Why didn't I think of that?

Darlene levers herself up—god, I really should start doing aerobics—and goes to her kitchen, which is really a continuation of the living room, separated only by a Formica counter and some scuffed wooden stools. She retrieves a box of chewy treats and gives the dog three, not seeming to care about the resulting shower of drool.

"She'll be fine." She peers at me. "But what about you? I haven't seen you in months. We've been missing you at the shelter."

I scrub my palms on my ratty pajama pants and avoid her pointed gaze. "Yeah, sorry. I just haven't been up for it."

Her lips thin. "That's understandable. But…are you all right? I saw your mom last month, and she said she can hardly get you on the phone anymore. She wasn't even sure if you were eating the food she left you."

I flinch. My mother's efforts haven't gone to waste; I've squirreled away every last casserole that's appeared on my doorstep, and now graduated to filling the chest freezer in the garage. The part about the phone calls is a stretch, though. My mother and I spoke dozens of times in the months after Michael died, when my heart felt as though it had fallen out through a hole in my stomach. All I'd wanted was for someone who understood grief to staunch the bleeding. I'd spent hours on the phone with my mother, hoping she would impart the secrets known only to those who've suffered the unimaginable and somehow carried on living.

Except it turned out there is no secret, only comrades united by loss, and eventually, I'd simply grown…tired of railing against the irrevocable. Of crying so hard I could barely get words out. So, fine, maybe I'd let the doorbell go unanswered a few times, and I might have let a call or two through to voicemail. But then August had rolled around, and contact had naturally dwindled, the same way it always does during my birthday month.

Darlene sighs. "Well, the next time I see her, I'll tell her you came by, put her mind at ease a little. Now, since you're here, why don't I grab you a beer?"

She tugs me up from the floor and steers me to one of the stools at the counter. I glance at the wall clock—a kitten whose minute and hour arms bat at a second hand with a ball of yarn at the tip. "It's ten in the morning. Can you really offer me alcohol this early?"

"I'll be ninety next month. I can do whatever I want."

That gets a wobbly laugh out of me. Darlene glances to where my hands tremble against the Formica, and I tuck them into my lap.

She rummages in her fridge as the dog munches away, then pops the top off a brown bottle and sets it down. "I have to say, I'd hoped you'd be feeling better by now."

I take a half-hearted sip. The cold beer settles heavy in my stomach. "Does anyone ever really feel better after their husband dies?"

It's an honest question, and Darlene weighs her answer accordingly. "I wouldn't know, myself. It's just…that year Margo

Fontenot died, when your parents took you away for the summer…you seemed better when you came back. I know what happened to that poor girl isn't the same, but however you managed then, I was hoping you'd find a similar kind of healing now."

I turn the bottle in place. It's true—going away that summer helped. Immeasurably. I'd spent the immediate months after Margo's death huddled in bed with the curtains drawn, barely stirring, barely eating. Eventually, my mother had insisted on a vacation, then packed up the car so we could drive to our summer cabin near Skykomish.

Where her intuition had proved correct. The magic of the woods had dispelled the dark fog of loss. The warm, lemony sunlight on my skin, the redolent scent of ancient woods in my nose… Being outside had stitched me back together, reconnected me to the world. Mother Nature had folded me into her embrace and breathed life into me again.

I don't say that to Darlene, though. Something about that experience feels fiercely personal, probably because the one time I tried to explain it to Michael, I sounded ridiculous. After our dog Penny had died, I'd brought up going to the cabin in Skykomish again. I'd wanted to see if the healing power of the woods could still soothe me the way it had when I was a teenager.

He'd frowned, told me we had a perfectly good forest in our backyard. *You can't run off into the woods and pretend real life doesn't exist, Mina. I mean, you can, but reality will still be waiting when you get back. At some point, you'll have to learn how to deal with it here.*

I pick at the bottle's label. He was right, of course. Which is why I've dutifully mourned him in Seagrove, in the same house we loved each other in. I've tried my best to honor his memory the way he would've wished.

"It's a good idea," I say faintly, for lack of anything else. "I'll think about it."

Darlene nods, but the set of her mouth tells me the lie hasn't escaped her notice. "I suppose that's all I can ask. Now, why don't we decide what to do with your friend here?"

I twist on my stool, grateful for the subject change. From the floor, the dog regards us with hopeful eyes. I'm guessing she'd devour the entire box of treats if given the chance.

"She hasn't got a collar, but I can scan her for a chip at the shelter tomorrow." Darlene comes around the counter. "If she doesn't have one, would you consider fostering her while we look for a new home?"

I pause. "Me?"

"Well, why not?"

As the dog and I lock eyes, warmth blooms in my belly. Maybe *that's* what I need. Not to run off to the woods, but to have some company. It's as decent an idea as any. "Why not?"

"Great. I'll let you know what I come up with."

We chat about nothing much as I polish off my beer. Before leaving, I get down on the carpet to snuggle the dog. "I'm glad you're okay," I murmur into her fur. She smells terrible, but my chest expands when I think of sharing my empty bed with her.

Not that any animal can replace a husband. No dog will ever dispel the memories of the way Michael's hair glistened in the morning light, or the long, slow inhale that always prefaced his surfacing from sleep. No pet can replace the treasured, quiet moments we spent in silence, our legs entwined, before the day's work inevitably drew us in opposite directions.

But even canine companionship beats the company of the crushing darkness that smothers me nightly now, its silence not tender, but taunting. I'm sick to death of lying in bed alone, obsessing over how I spent my last moment as Michael's wife.

I clear my throat and give the dog one last pat, then go to the door.

Darlene's eyes shine as she wraps me in a hug. "Sorry about

earlier. I hope you can forgive an old lady for worrying about her friend."

I squeeze back. "There's nothing to forgive. And I appreciate you caring. Really. I just wish I was more myself. But I'll get there. Eventually. I hope."

She nods and releases me. "If you need anything, you just let me know."

"Thanks," I murmur.

The thing is, I *would* ask, if I only knew what to ask for. But right now, even I don't know what I need.

Still, when I step out onto the welcome mat, I glance back, my gaze latching on to the dog and staying there until Darlene's door swings shut.

BEFORE

My cousin Patrick answers the door in a bathrobe.

At least I *think* it's my cousin, but he's not what I pictured. Lank brown hair falls past his ears while a toothpick juts from between his teeth. Eyes as small and dark as watermelon seeds slide over me, making me wish I'd worn a parka. Even though it's June.

Better yet, I wish I'd knocked on a different door.

"Mina Sutton?"

All my hopes of having rung the wrong doorbell evaporate. "Um…yeah. Hi. Are you Patrick? We spoke on the phone about—"

"Nah, I'm Randall, Patrick's friend. He said you were coming today, so I told him I'd get you set up. He's letting me crash here for a bit."

The back of my neck prickles. "Oh. Really? He didn't say anything about sharing the house."

"Yeah, it was pretty last-minute. I got evicted from my apartment and needed a place to stay. But don't worry, I won't be getting in your way."

I sidle back a step. Randall's grin suggests he'd like nothing more than to *get in my way*.

"Why don't you come in?" he says.

I peer past him into Rosalie's house, hesitant.

My eyes widen at what greets me. Mountains of clutter teeter on every available surface, like an episode of *Hoarders* come to life. And damn, Kate's right—it smells like cats. Ones that never get let outside.

My stomach drops. What is this? I agreed to sell off an estate, not dismantle years' worth of accumulated bric-a-brac.

Randall rolls his toothpick between his molars and grins. "Pat left some garbage bags in the kitchen. Gotta say, it looks like you've got your work cut out for you."

I gulp. Dear god. This is not what I pictured. At all. Not Randall, not the house—none of it.

"I think there's been a mistake." My voice thins to a wisp. "I agreed to do an estate sale. Not sort through trash."

Randall shrugs. "What's the difference?"

I chance another peek inside. In one corner of the room, a pile of discarded bottle caps avalanches onto the carpet. On a broken end table, a fish tank bookended by towering stacks of newspaper overflows with broken seashells. "Patrick needs a cleanup crew, not me. Tell him I'm sorry, but this isn't what I signed up for."

I turn away, praying Michael hasn't left yet.

"Wait, where're you going?" Randall's doughy fist clamps around my arm. "You can't just leave."

"Of course I can," I shrill. "Let me go!" I try to shake him off, but I'm tiny, and he very much *isn't*.

"No." Desperation seeps into his voice. "Patrick'll think I scared you off, and he'll kick me out, and then where will I go?"

"I don't know. Maybe you should take this job instead." Electricity surges in my muscles, but even when I funnel all my strength into making an escape, Randall's grip only tightens.

"Come on," he whines. "Do I look like I wanna sort through all this?"

Panic mounts. I pull harder, and all I can think is that Kate was right, only she suspected the wrong man, and the one I should've stayed in the car with must already be—

Here.

The smell of rain fills my nose. Michael appears from nowhere and yanks me free. He tows me backward and plants himself between me and the house like he intends to shield me from a bullet.

"What the fuck?" he growls. "She told you to let go, loud enough that I heard her from the car. What the hell're you doing?"

Randall throws up his hands. "Hey, man, it's cool. This your girlfriend? I didn't mean anything by it, if so."

Michael bares his teeth. "Does that mean you *did* mean something by it, if not?"

Randall pauses, confused. "Um...no?"

Michael's snarl only deepens, his eyes sparking like cinders. Nothing about the past three hours has suggested he had this kind of glorious anger inside him, yet nothing about it intimidates me. If anything, I just feel safe.

Randall steps outside. "Look, dude, she's supposed to—"

Michael jabs a finger at him. "If you so much as come near her, I'll turn that toothpick into a permanent part of your face."

Randall recoils, clearly at a loss.

Michael stands there, his back heaving. I step in to wrap a hand around his wrist. His fists are clenched, the muscles in his forearms standing out like cords. "Come on," I say. "He doesn't matter."

He swings around to look at me, his hair sliding over one eye. My heart skips. Damn, he's tall. Way taller than I realized, though I knew from his driver's license that he tops me by over a foot.

I just haven't stood next to him like this, up close.

"You're not staying here," he rumbles.

"No. Definitely not."

"Hey," Randall cuts in. "What am I supposed to tell—"

Michael flings out a finger. "I don't care. Just walk away, man. It's not our problem."

I don't look over to gauge Randall's reaction, but the front door clicks shut as Michael escorts me back toward the car.

I should breathe a sigh of relief, but he stops us by the Audi, staring at me with such focus that I can't breathe. If I called him arresting before, now he's something else entirely. The blush of sun on my cheeks and the hum of the lawnmower one block over fade to nothing. There's just me and him, this stranger who doesn't feel like a stranger at all, who just came to my rescue without hesitation.

"Are you okay?" he says.

"Yeah." Strangely, with him here, it's true. "Are *you*?"

"Well, I just told a man to walk away from me in front of his own house." He rolls his shoulders as if trying to shrug off his fury. "That's a new one. Reviews are mixed."

I crook a smile. "You also said you were going to turn his toothpick into a permanent part of his face. I have to say, I have no idea what that means."

"Me neither. But he looked like he was going to piss his pants when I said it, so I'm calling that one a win."

I giggle. It sounds odd, tinny, and I wonder if I'm panicking. If so, why do I feel so calm?

Michael flicks a narrowed gaze back at the house. "What is this place, anyway? You said you had family here, but when that guy grabbed you, you looked...*terrified*. You're not actually related to him, are you?"

"No. My great-aunt died a couple months ago, and her grandson hired me to auction off all her property. Only Patrick never mentioned that the house was a disaster. Or that his friend would be rooming with me. I was *supposed* to be staying here for the next month, earning enough for my ticket. But now..." I fumble for more. Nothing comes.

"Your ticket to Greece, you mean?"

"Yeah." My breathing turns ragged as the fantasy I came so close to touching recedes. "I have enough saved up to live in Athens for a while, just not enough to *get* there. And... Oh, god. I have no clue what to do now. Except text Patrick and tell him the job isn't something I can do."

Michael's eyebrows pull together. "Well, all you need is a ticket, right?" He yanks his phone from his back pocket, then starts typing and swiping with fervor.

"Yeah, but... What're you doing?"

"Booking you a flight. There's one from Sea-Tac at eleven eleven tonight, connecting through Heathrow. Will that do?"

I wonder if I've lost my mind, or if he has. "No, what? You can't do that. You can't just...*buy* me a plane ticket."

"Why not?"

"You don't even know me."

"The hell I don't." His fingers pause. When he glances up, something fierce glitters in his expression. "Besides, I'm not leaving you here with Toothpick Boy. Or letting you get into a situation with some other asshole like him."

"Put your phone away."

"Why," he says. Not a question, but a challenge.

"Because." I flail about for an explanation. "I have to *earn* it. Greece, this whole trip... None of it means anything if I don't make it happen on my own."

His jaw hardens, but a grudging respect flares in his eyes. "Well, damn." He stashes his phone. "What're our options, then?"

The *our* throws me. The whole insane, incredible situation throws me. In a matter of hours, this man has single-handedly prompted me to rethink my entire life, and now I can only blink up at him while he watches me expectantly.

"I don't understand you," I say.

"What?"

"*You.* I don't get it. I barely know you, but here you are taking me on road trips and rescuing me from aggressive jerks and trying to buy me international plane tickets. It's like everything Sarah and Brooke said was the complete opposite of the truth."

His eyes flare. "*Sarah?* And Brooke? How the hell do you know them?"

"I don't. I just met them for a second. Inside Seaside House, while I was looking for you."

"Huh." He blinks a few times. "I'm surprised you made it out to the parking lot if they got to you first. What'd they say?"

I bite my lip. "That you've been acting weird for the past month. Avoiding everyone."

His gaze slides away. "Uh-huh. Well, that's definitely true."

When he doesn't elaborate, I consider asking for more, but after what he shared in the car, that almost seems uncharitable.

"What else?" he asks.

"Um…that you're an asshole."

"Oh." He nods slowly. "Well, they're not wrong about that, either."

My breath spills out, and I edge closer. I don't know why, except that he anchors me somehow. "But you've been the exact opposite of an asshole."

"To *you.*" He curls one hand around my elbow and pulls— gently, almost hesitantly. "But you're different."

I try to hold on to logic, but I feel myself changing shape inside. "How can you say that? You've known me for a day."

"It'd be obvious to anyone with a brain." He exhales sharply. "I mean, I just tried to buy you a twenty-two-hundred-dollar plane ticket, and you *wouldn't let me.* Even if we ignore the entire car ride before that, that pretty much says it all."

My lips part on a drawn breath. God, he's so close, and so tall, and his smell makes my head spin. His fingers stroke my elbow, turning me fuzzy and electric inside. A hum builds in my center, as if I'm standing beneath a spool of high-voltage power lines and the current has sneaked beneath my skin.

"You asked why I've never left the country," I say. "And why my mother's so protective."

He stills. "I did."

The truth wells up. This time, it's easy. The easiest thing I've ever done. "It's because my brother died. On the day I was born. In Ireland."

Michael's breathing sharpens. "What?"

"Yeah. My mom was seven months pregnant with me. My brother, Jasper, was two. She and my dad had taken him to Europe, thinking they'd have one last big trip together before I was born. But Jasper got sick. Just fever and vomiting, at first, which my parents thought was food poisoning. But then he got worse. They finally took him to a clinic, but the doctor said it was a stomach bug and sent them away. Except Jasper just got sicker, and by the time everyone realized it was something more, his appendix had ruptured. They rushed him to the hospital, but...too late."

Michael's gaze bores into mine.

I swallow hard. "I guess it's rare for that to happen in kids that young, but my mom's convinced if we'd been here, the doctors would've caught it right away. Obviously, there's no way to tell. But who knows. Maybe she's right."

Michael's thumb circles my elbow, encouraging.

"My parents never really talk about the rest, but I'm guessing my mom went into shock, because I was born later that night. In the same hospital Jasper died in. The doctors say that's part of why I'm so small, because I was nine weeks premature. I was in the NICU for two months before my parents could finally bring me home. And ever since..."

His mouth tightens. "They've been terrified to leave the country? To let *you* leave the country?"

"Yeah." I blink away the sting in my eyes. I don't know if I've ever spoken about this so openly. "For a long time, I thought they'd get over it, but in tenth grade, one of my best friends did a foreign exchange program in Costa Rica and didn't come back. She was doing one of those rainforest zip line things and didn't clip her harness in the right way. She fell."

He does a slow, horrified blink.

"For my parents, that was absolute proof. Their terror come to life. And so I've never gone anywhere. I've just spent my life... Spent it..."

The corners of his mouth edge downward. "Shackled by other people's fear?"

Something twists inside my chest. "Yes. That. Exactly that."

"So you're a nomad at heart. But static by necessity."

I can't help it—I have to touch him. It's like something is pulling at me, commanding me to press a hand to his shirtfront. The thud of his heartbeat against my fingers feels like coming home, only to a house I've never set foot in before.

It's the weirdest thing, a brand of magic I've seen in movies but never thought actually existed. People don't feel this magnetic pull toward complete strangers.

But I do, and it's taking me by the hand, tugging me somewhere dangerous and lush and beautiful. As I stare into those turquoise depths, I decide I'm going to plunge headfirst into this ocean, if Michael lets me. At least until I figure out a way to get to Greece.

"Thank you," he says. "For trusting me with that."

I nod, marveling at just how superior that response is to the one I gave him.

His fingers come up to feather against my jaw. "I want to take you somewhere. Right now. Would you let me?"

Hesitation doesn't so much as stir. "Anywhere. Take me to the freaking moon."

His touch lingers, the silence more eloquent than any words. When we finally finish making some kind of pact with our eyes, Michael tosses my bag into the Audi again. We slide back into the air-conditioned safety of the car.

"Are you sure you don't want that plane ticket?" he says. "Because your entire life could change at eleven eleven tonight."

It's funny. An undercurrent of doubt has tainted most everything I've ever done, but now, it's gone quiet. Fallen asleep while I bared my secrets. "I hope it does. I'm just not sure I actually need to get on a plane for that to happen."

To my amazement, color sneaks into his cheeks.

Wow. He's blushing. I made Adonis blush.

"Okay, then." He clears his throat. "This is going to take a while, so we might not get back 'til late. But we can figure out what to do with you tomorrow."

"Tomorrow?" I laugh softly as a brand-new warmth unspools in my veins. "Haven't you heard? There's no such thing."

"Jesus. You minx." He sticks the key into the ignition. "You really are going to break my heart, aren't you?"

I smile as he accelerates back onto the interstate. Without a doubt, this has been the strangest day of my life, but I find myself wanting more. I want to drink down each minute, throw myself headlong into living and see where it takes me.

The freedom of it intoxicates me.

"I guess we'll see," I say, "won't we?"

BEFORE

I begin to suspect Michael's intentions after we leave Seattle behind, then Bellingham, yet the exit numbers along the I-5 continue to tick upward.

I text my mother that I'm safe—I'll give her details later, once I figure out what they are—then tuck my phone away and study the road ahead.

When a scant five miles of America remains, I fish my unused passport from my purse. My heart hammers so hard I'm surprised I can hear myself speak. "I'm guessing I'm going to need this?"

Michael's grin flashes—mischief and charm rolled into one. "Yep. That, and a bathing suit. Do you have one packed?"

"Will a bikini work?"

"A bikini." His husky voice edges toward hoarse. "Yep. That'll do."

Our gazes catch. I can almost see what he's thinking, because I'm thinking it, too, and it involves a whole lot of sweat and sliding, slippery skin. Hitched, breathless cries and slickened fingers.

Which means I've officially lost it. I've never been a one-

night-stand kind of girl, and that won't change now. Not even
for this breathtaking creature who just came to my rescue and
has apparently made it his mission to fulfill my most sacred,
lifelong dream. Today.

I fan myself with the passport's stiff blank pages. No choice
now but to change the subject with all the subtlety of a bull-
dozer. "You know, when I told you I'd dreamed about leaving
the country since I was a kid, I mean I've had actual dreams
about it, night after night. The kind I've always hated waking
up from. There's always this fleeting moment where I actually
believe I've gone trekking through a Brazilian jungle or joined
a bagpipe band in Scotland. But then I realize none of it's real,
and it always breaks my heart."

"Except it *will* be real." Unguarded glee fills Michael's eyes,
edging out the stark desire of a few moments ago. "In about
five minutes."

"I can't believe how excited you seem," I say.

"I can't believe I get to give you your first step outside the
country."

"I can't believe you *want to.* Why do you seem so giddy?"

"Because," he says, "it means you'll never forget me."

"I don't think I would have, anyway."

"I hope not. But this way, I get to be sure."

We don't say much after that. I scan the oncoming road like
a prisoner awaiting the guard's approach on release day. I feel
unbearably light inside, poised to fly. Finally, I spot a series
of bright signs along the roadside, announcing the gates of a
checkpoint—the entryway to another world.

Something touches my hand. When I look down, Michael's
long fingers weave through mine.

Fire floods my chest. I wonder if spontaneous combustion
is an actual thing. I'm guessing yes.

We pull up to the border station. Michael hands over his license and my passport, and after a few cursory questions from the border agent, we accelerate into British Columbia.

Just like that, it's done. I'm out. I'm free. I'm an international traveler, just like I've always wished.

My thoughts implode into a glittering cloud, and yet I don't look out the window, even as downtown Vancouver streaks past. I fixate on Michael's profile, tracing his pert nose and squared jaw. He's just given me something no one else ever has, and I'm afraid to blink. Afraid this will prove to be just one more neon, electric dream.

After a minute, or an hour, he squeezes my hand. "You have the most incredible look on your face right now. What're you thinking about?"

"Things I have no business thinking." A thin laugh escapes me. "Things that make no sense."

"No? Why not?"

"Because I only just met you." Briefly, I think of Kate's beloved women's magazines, filled with articles about how to ensnare men by acting mysterious and eternally hard-to-get. Somehow, I get the feeling that's unnecessary here.

Michael confirms it by saying, "Maybe you're thinking exactly what you should be."

"Maybe." I shift, full of a verve I don't quite know what to do with. "Except...I'm leaving. I'm going on an adventure."

"Not all adventures are geographical." He briefly releases the wheel to push his hair back, leaving his other hand safely entwined with mine. "Look, I'm not saying you shouldn't go. You should do everything you've spent years dreaming about. But I don't think living well has much to do with where you are. It's about the moments you create. And the fact that you can find beauty and meaning anywhere, if you look."

"That...might be the wisest thing I've ever heard anyone say."

"Maybe. Or maybe I have no idea what the hell I'm talking about. I'm sure it's one or the other."

I'm convinced he *does* know what he's talking about, but I don't get the chance to say so, because he arrows through a gap in oncoming traffic and onto a dirt pull-off. "Here we are."

When I look around, Canada steals my breath. We're perched on an overlook that faces the ocean. Majestic pines march down the hillside. Beyond the glittering span of water, mountainous islands burst from the sea, wreathed in myriad shades of green. Even the sky seems bluer here, full of buttery sunshine and fleecy, playful clouds.

"Wow," I say. "What is this place?"

"The Sea to Sky Highway."

"It's incredible."

"It is."

When I turn, Michael isn't watching the scenery. He's staring at me. "I would never ask you to stay," he says. "Not for my sake."

I freeze. "You wouldn't?"

"I'm not *that* selfish." His voice softens. "But I do want to ask you something else. Just...not here."

"Oh. Okay. Where, then?"

He gestures past the overlook. "Down there."

I nod, rendered mute by a spear of longing. Was I hoping he *would* ask me to stay? Do I even want to answer that question?

No. I'm leaving. This...*whatever* is only temporary.

Michael flashes a smile probably intended to reassure me. He gets out, fishes his swim trunks from his suitcase, and inconspicuously changes by his side of the car while I dutifully stare at the floor mat. Afterward, he strolls off to gaze at the water while I wriggle into my bikini in the front seat.

The whole time, my heart throbs. What could he possibly want? For me to keep in touch? Look him up when I get back?

Leaving my clothes puddled on the leather seat, I emerge wearing my tiny red two-piece and flip-flops. My long black hair tickles the small of my waist, but even though I'm half-naked, I pay no attention to the traffic whizzing past or the way the ocean breeze raises the hairs on my arms.

Michael turns at my approach. "Oh. Oh, wow."

I stand at the top of the hillside and let him stare, because the way he does it feels like a caress. His eyes sweep downward, darkening as they trace the line of my shoulder, the curve of my hip, the taper of my calves. He looks at every bit of me, then returns to my face. Hunger blazes in those sea-swept eyes.

Faint surprise stirs. I'm small in every way—short, fine boned, small breasted, narrow waisted. And while I don't dislike my tininess, it's Kate's brand of statuesque glamour that fills magazines and splashes across billboards.

Right now, though, I wouldn't trade the way Michael is looking at me for anything.

"Come on." He turns away. The roughness in his voice makes it sound like he's trying to control himself. Which I sincerely wish he wouldn't.

With a sigh, I follow him down the hillside, weaving between the pines. Michael offers a steadying hand, making sure I don't slip on the carpet of fallen needles. Halfway down, we reach a rock-ringed pool. A river jets over a stone outcropping, forming a waterfall complete with a ghostly, misted rainbow. Michael shucks his shoes at the water's edge, then pulls his shirt off and drapes it over a rock.

My mouth goes dry. He's so beautiful it's criminal. Long, smooth muscles come together like someone spent painstaking hours sculpting him that way. He has edges where most men don't, definition where I wouldn't have expected any.

When he turns, I zero in on the ridges of his abdomen and the sparkling silver chain resting against the impressive swell of his chest.

Dear god. If I ever go blind, I'd want this to be the last thing I see.

He gives me a smile—this one *does* look cocky—and leaps. A

splash swallows him up. He surfaces a moment later, whooping and laughing. Water streams from broad shoulders as he rakes back sopping golden hair.

"Come on in." He holds out his arms. "The water's fine. And by *fine*, I mean *absolutely freezing*."

I eye the crystalline pool. "Is that supposed to entice me?"

"Not really." He winks. "But I'll do my best to keep you warm. Hopefully that entices you a little."

Well. I can't refuse that. I doubt anyone could. I step to the edge, slip off my flip-flops, and jump.

The world turns to ice and darkness. Cold sears my skin, like wintry metal pressed in from all sides. But it only lasts a moment. By the time I surface, Michael is gathering me in his arms, heating my body with his.

An exhale pours out, one that involves my entire being. I wrap my legs around his waist and discover a brand-new feeling, a heady rush of newness mingled with a sense of fitting into the exact place I belong.

Michael cradles the nape of my neck and rests his forehead against mine. Droplets spangle his cheeks and make star points out of his eyelashes.

My heart delivers a few swift kicks against my rib cage. I want this man, I realize. In a relentless, painful way I have no prior experience with.

"Can you hold your breath for thirty seconds?" he says.

I blink. "I... What? Is that a joke?"

"Nope." His voice thrums with excitement, making me wonder if there's more to this place than just the pool. "Can you?"

"I think so." I mentally congratulate myself on sounding only halfway hesitant. "But does that mean I'm supposed to swim underneath something?"

"No. You're just supposed to hang on to me while *I* swim underneath something. That's it. I'll do all the work."

Images of waterlogged tunnels and dark, aquatic graves fill my mind. But Michael's zeal steals into me as our heartbeats press against one another. His eyes seem to ask a question.

I soak in the sight of him. Of Canada. And conviction blossoms—*this is the adventure.* Here, now. It's breathing this crisp, sea-drenched air, feeling the lap of icy water against my skin. It's the press of his strong body and the dance of sunlight on the waves below, the rushing song of the waterfall.

Life doesn't lie on the far side of an ocean. I don't need an airplane to get to it. It's all around me, all the time. I only have to *look*, to open my eyes.

The moment feels like drinking from a firehose, and for the first time in my life, I have no desire to be elsewhere.

I swear Michael sees what's happening, because he watches my face the same way a man might watch a budding sunrise. His eyes shine, reverent.

"What're you thinking?" he says.

My lips bend upward. "That I've been waiting my entire life for this exact moment."

His arms tighten around me. "So that's a yes?"

"It's a hell yes."

Delight glows in his face. "Take a deep breath, then."

I do. I fill my lungs with sunshine and his deep-forest smell and don't shut my eyes until the last possible second.

The water closes overhead. Michael pulls me into depths that grow even colder.

More than thirty seconds seem to pass. He guides us through the arctic void with swift, certain kicks. Stones scrape against my bare legs while my chest shouts for air, but all the while, I hold on tight.

I have no other choice. I've jumped. I've gone diving in head-first, and now I can only hang on and see where it takes me.

AFTER

The morning after I rescue the dog, Darlene rings my phone early.

I roll over and pluck the offending device from the bedside table, then wince against the brightness streaming through the windows. How can the sun possibly be so cheerful at this ungodly hour? Can't it show some respect for the fact that my life has been cut off at the knees?

"Hello?" I manage.

"Mina?" Darlene's voice wavers, making her sound eighty-nine, even if she doesn't look it. "I hope I didn't wake you."

"No," I lie.

"Oh, good. Well, I just got off the phone with your dog's owner. He's on his way to pick her up now. Apparently, Barley had been missing for three days. He was ecstatic that you'd found her. He made me promise to call and give you his undying thanks."

I try to smile, but my mouth doesn't respond. "Oh. Well, great. That's great."

Silence floats over the line. "Is it?"

"Of course." All the warmth in my body drains out, leaching into the empty sheets.

"Okay, but... You're sure you're all right?"

I force my lips into a curve, hoping the smile will sound more genuine than it feels. "I'm sure. I'm just glad she's going home. Thanks, Darlene."

After we hang up, I toss the phone aside and curl around my pillow. I feel as though someone could drop a pebble into me and it would keep on falling forever.

Which is ridiculous. It's just a dog. But this newest loss stacks atop the others, another domino placed on a teetering pile that threatens to come crashing down.

The hum of a car engine interrupts my pity-fest. Frowning, I work free of the sheets, then drag myself down the stairs to open the front door. It can't be my mother with another lasagna, not in August.

Sure enough, Kate's shiny black Suburban crunches to a stop in my driveway. She kills the engine, then climbs out carrying a bouquet of orange day lilies and one of those round plastic containers that serves as armor for store-bought cakes.

When she reaches my doorstep, her brown eyes catalog my rumpled hair and cracked lips. "Well, you're alive. That's something. Did you forget how to answer the phone?"

I give her a sheepish look. I did get the voicemail she left on my birthday, but not until three days later, and by then... Well, I don't know. I have no excuse for not calling her back.

"Sorry. I've been busy," I say, then wince, because it's so obviously a lie. Busy with what? Running until my toenails bleed? Reading Jane Austen into the early hours so I won't have to face the heroic act of sliding between the cold bedsheets alone? Writing articles for *Medical Devices Monthly*, which requires so little brainpower that I could do it with my eyes closed?

Rescuing dogs I'll never see again?

"Well, whatever's taking up your time, it's not working. You look like shit." Kate thrusts the bouquet at me. "I still love you, though. Happy belated birthday. I know your mom didn't wish you one, so here I am. Do you have coffee?"

With a half sigh, half chuckle, I usher her inside. Kate's a mother of two toddlers, ages one and three, and her patience, already dangerously low to begin with, has now plummeted to undetectable levels. If a cup of coffee can satisfy her, I'm happy to oblige.

Whatever it takes to convince her I don't need checking on. Even if I kinda-maybe do.

In the kitchen, I drop the lilies into a cut-crystal vase and fill two mugs from the French press. In honor of Kate's deep-seated aversion to calories, I leave her coffee black, though handing it over undoctored makes my tongue curl.

"Thanks." She deposits the cake onto the shiny granite island. New York cheesecake with cherries and whipped cream—my second-favorite dessert on earth, besides kettle corn, but it tempts me about as much as a plate of limp lettuce, because whipped cream always reminds me of Michael. Even now. I look away.

"Jesus, Mina." Kate leans in, sniffing. "When's the last time you showered?"

I clamber up onto one of the leather-and-chrome stools my husband once chose with such care. "Um…yesterday?"

Her eyes narrow.

"The day before? Maybe?"

She sighs, deep and heavy. Kate never used to sigh like that. She never used to sport dark circles under her eyes, either, or scrape her hair back into a yellow ponytail. She tells me she has to, though, or her kids will pull out fistfuls by the root.

Not that she doesn't still look fabulous. After two babies, god only knows how. Well, that's not true. I do know. She gets up at four thirty every morning and inflicts ninety minutes of cardio on herself while the rest of her family sleeps blissfully.

Her hard-earned slenderness aside, though, she looks lessened, somehow. I even spot two different mystery stains on her navy chiffon blouse. Very un-Kate-like.

"You kind of look like shit, too," I say. "Is everything all right? How're the kids? How's Tanner?"

She downs her coffee like she's shooting tequila. With palpable desperation. "Ha. The kids're…you know. Terrors. And Tanner's…Tanner. Always off playing computer chess while I'm cleaning up the *entire bag of flour* Hunter's exploded all over the couch or trying to stop Evelyn from eating pennies. I swear, it's like my husband has become just another human to keep alive. Sometimes I try to remember what it was like to desperately want to have sex with him all the time, and I just can't."

I nod in sympathy, though I can't actually empathize. I never stopped wanting to have sex with Michael all the time. Then again, I never cleaned up bags of flour while he hid in his office playing computer games, so maybe that has something to do with it.

Either way, I can't help but mourn the fact that while Kate once got starry-eyed when speaking Tanner's name, she now talks about him the same way she talks about her dog.

"But I didn't come here to whine," she says briskly. "I mean, I'm tired. Just…so damn tired, all the time. It's like no matter how fast I run, I never get anywhere. But that's a bullshit thing to complain about to *you*. Having a dead husband's got to be a thousand times harder than having a clueless, alive one."

I nod again, touched. Other people always dance around this subject, as if maybe I've forgotten about how my marriage ended and if they remind me, my grief will detonate all over them. *Mina Drake, land mine of hazardous emotion. Proceed with caution.*

But Kate has no problem speaking Michael's name aloud. She talks about him like he's just as real as he was. Like she's acknowledging that I have every right to feel the way I do.

"I'm worried about you," she says.

I fiddle with my coffee. Okay, so maybe this is going in a different direction today. "When are you not?"

"Well, never. But I'm extra worried these days. You're too skinny. Are you eating anything?"

I make a show of dumping in generous helpings of cream and sugar. "Does coffee count?"

"No. It definitely doesn't. And you never answer my calls anymore. Do you even talk to anyone? Ever? Because I tried emailing, too. Nothing."

I duck my head. "Yeah. I haven't checked in…um…a few months. Life's so much easier if I stay off the internet."

"Really," she says, flat. "How come?"

I stare into my cup. Kate knows exactly why I avoid the headlines and internet clickbait—for the same reason I shop at Seagrove's mom-and-pop grocery store, despite their failure to stock my favorite brand of kettle corn. At least there, I won't encounter the tabloids the larger supermarket plasters everywhere. I won't round a corner and risk confronting a face I'd rather forget. "Come on. You know."

Kate's scrutiny sharpens. "Is seeing Michael's brother *really* that hard? Because at this point, I have to wonder if that's just an excuse. I mean, you've never even met the guy."

A bitter laugh chokes me. I don't need to meet Grayson Drake to find the sight of him disturbing. "Maybe not, but you don't know what it's like to see an angry, tattooed version of your dead husband every other time you go out."

Her mouth twists. "Okay, maybe not. But I do know holing up here isn't doing you any favors."

"I'm fine. Really. I'm just waiting for the world to forget its fascination with my ex-brother-in-law."

"Then you're going to be stuck here a long time. Especially after this latest fiasco."

I wince. "Ugh. What's he done now?"

"Gone on another one of his benders." She waves a hand.

"Knocked out a guy in a nightclub, or something. Honestly, I didn't even read it this time. Just saw that he made the cover of *America Weekly* and *Celebrity Style*, looking as pissed off as always."

"Oh, wonderful." I sip at my coffee, then spit it back into the cup. In proving a point, I've rendered it undrinkably sweet. "Maybe this time, I'll finally get lucky and he'll do something he can't recover from."

Kate's look turns flinty. "You don't mean that."

I grumble. Of course I don't. But I *have* hated Michael's brother for fourteen years, ever since he and my husband collided in Seattle and everything changed.

It was bad enough when Grayson catapulted to fame three years ago. *National Geographic*'s gorgeous bad-boy photographer snapshotted himself just moments after being dug out of an almost-fatal avalanche on Mount Everest, and the picture took the world by storm. Within weeks, some nature network had snapped him up to host its newest wilderness show, which only lasted a season, but that didn't stop Michael and me from having to field endless questions. Now, with my husband gone, the questions have stopped, but the sordid life of Grayson Drake continues to resemble a never-ending car crash the public can't look away from. Watching him drink himself from one scandal to another while bouncing from one beautiful woman to the next has made it impossible for me to find peace.

"Look." Kate sets her coffee down and folds her arms. "All I'm saying is you can't stay miserable forever. It's been half a year. Don't you think it's time to rejoin the world of the living? At least a little?"

I run my forefinger around the rim of my cup. I *do* miss my old life with a ferocity that guts me, but excuses aside, I have this sense that if I go enjoy myself in a world without Michael in it, I'm accepting that somehow it's reasonable that one day my husband just ceased to exist.

It's not fucking reasonable, not in any capacity.

Besides, it turns out twenty-five-year-old Michael was wrong—there *is* such thing as yesterday. And sometimes yesterday grows so big, so ravenous, that it eats up not only right now, but tomorrow, too.

"I just...miss him." I spin my mug, wincing when milky coffee sloshes out. It's so hard to keep this stupid granite gleaming all the time, the way Michael liked. "So much that I'm drowning in it."

Kate's expression softens. "I get that. But can I be honest with you? Like, completely honest, best friend to best friend?"

I chuckle without humor. "Is that a real question? Because the Katelyn Archer I know would never ask." It's actually Katelyn O'Reilly now, but whatever. I'll never stop thinking of her by her maiden name.

"Okay then, here goes—I think you're wallowing. And to be fair, I probably would, too. But you're dwelling on the good parts of your marriage and forgetting the bad, and it's keeping you from moving on. Michael wasn't perfect, remember? You weren't even happy those last few years. You talked about divorce."

My stomach does a nauseating flip. I push my cup away, overcome by a sudden wish for Kate to leave. I don't want to think about the night I came in from a rainy ten-mile run and printed out divorce papers from a site online. Or about how that manila folder is still sitting underneath my bed, and how I haven't found the courage to throw it out because the simple act of unearthing it would make my wifely failings all too real.

I don't want to remember that I considered leaving the man I loved so desperately, even for a second.

My voice roughens. "I wouldn't have actually done it. I mean, yeah, our last few years together weren't great, but only because Michael wouldn't *go* anywhere. If I'd just gotten him away from work, convinced him to take a vacation again, we could've gone back to how things were. We would've—"

"Mina." Kate's brown eyes match her voice, soft and warm. "You realize your marriage wasn't about who you and Michael were during that first month together, right? Or that week in Hawaii, which, before you say anything, yes, I'm completely aware was the most magical week of your life, because you've told me ten thousand times. I mean, anyone can pull out the stops and act all incredible and sexy while avoiding real life. But what your marriage was *really* about was the day-to-day stuff. About all the time you spent here, in this house, with a guy who sent you running instead of talking things out. It's about the fact that Michael convinced you to move back to a town you'd escaped from, then buried himself up to his eyeballs in work."

I flinch. Kate has just dissected my eleven-year marriage with cold, clinical precision—not surprising, since cold, clinical precision is basically her specialty. But she's missing the bigger picture.

"You don't understand," I say. "I know it sounds so clichéd, but Michael was my soulmate. Things might've gotten hard, yeah, but I never stopped loving the man I first fell for. And that feeling hasn't gone away. I mean, I know he's gone. I think about that horrible box they handed me at the mortuary, how *heavy* it was. How when I got to the car, I couldn't figure out how to latch it into the front seat, and then it hit me that Michael's ashes didn't need a seat belt because he wasn't a person anymore. But my heart doesn't get it. It just keeps on trying to love him like he still exists. Part of me is missing, and meanwhile, I'm just…bleeding out, day after day, with no way to stop it."

Kate stays quiet. My throat thickens as words pour forth.

"I know you think I should go out more, but seeing Grayson only makes it worse. It's like…an *insult*. A slap in the face.

Like the universe took the wrong brother. Grayson has the life Michael still should, but he's so stuck and broken-hearted over a girl who died decades ago that he's just wasting it. I can't even begin to tell you how infuriating that is."

"That's awful," Kate murmurs. "But…do you really not see the problem here?"

"Problem? What problem?"

"You're judging Grayson for never getting over what's-her-name—"

"Lily." I frown. Kate knows the basics, but not Michael's involvement in her death. I've never shared that with anyone.

"Right. Lily. You're blaming him for never recovering, but here you are doing the exact same thing."

My nostrils flare. That's so untrue that I don't even know where to start. For one thing, Michael and I were married. For eleven years. And *I'm* not the one rampaging through the national media, punching out paparazzi and holing up in foreign hotel rooms for weeks at a time while refusing to talk to any—

Oh, god. I stare at Kate.

"Shit," I say. "You might actually be right."

She gives me a sorry-not-sorry smile. "Yeah, no shit. And what's more, I think you need to be honest with yourself. Which version of Michael are you so strung out over? The one you were actually married to? Or the one who drove you to Seattle fourteen years ago? Because that guy hasn't existed for years."

That last sentence sucker punches me. Michael changed; it's true. Shortly after we moved in together, he stopped reading every day. Stopped hiking and camping. Started wearing those damn button-ups all the time. As his paychecks swelled, architecture began to consume him.

Then, when Michael's coworker Ben convinced us to move to Seagrove so they could cofound a firm specializing in high-end coastal homes, the last vestiges of my free-spirited philosopher vanished. The open conversations gave way to lavish gifts and reliable Wednesday-night dinner dates at fancy restaurants. My husband began organizing his personal life like his professional one—everything bordered by straight lines, everything in its place.

Except the vivacious adventurer I fell for still existed, deep down. I know because when I finally succeeded in pulling Michael away from work, we tumbled straight back into the intoxicating synchronicity of those early days. In Hawaii, I fell in love with him all over again, hard enough that once we returned to real life, I managed to stomach four more years of missing a man who was right in front of me.

Except a vacation like that never happened again. I hate that that's where we ended.

The kitchen blurs. I swipe at my cheeks. "Sorry. I really should go for a run."

When I move to abandon my stool, Kate maneuvers me back with her crazy toddler-wrangling strength.

"No, you should fucking *not* go for a run. Jesus, Mina. Enough of that. Michael's gone. You don't have to bottle things up anymore. Just sit right here, bawl your eyes out, then eat this whole goddamn cheesecake in one sitting. *That's* what you should do." She's got her mom face on, the you'll-do-what-I-say-and-you'll-like-it expression usually reserved for her kids.

I study her through the haze. I could break down, here in my kitchen. But if I dribble tears all over the granite, it'll take at least half an hour to polish it again afterward, like Michael would want.

A jolt shoots through me. As if I'm watching from outside my body, a detached part of my mind turns that logic over. At what point did I become this someone else, this person who goes running instead of letting herself feel?

The moment stretches. Something hot and red writhes in my guts. I'm angry, I realize. At myself. At Michael. But most of all, I'm livid that he died. I want to punch life in its stupid, smarmy face, because for all that Kate's mostly right, she's gotten one thing wrong. The man I loved was still in there. I could've coaxed him back to me, if only I'd had more time. I would have broken through Michael's shell, jammed my fingers into the socket of the out-of-control power surge that first drew us together, and refused to let go. We would have lived our lives electrified, fighting for breath and grateful for every second.

But now we can't. That chance is gone, leaving me with nothing except a grayscale existence in which I haunt this perfect house day after day, chained by a grief that refuses to die.

I guess I'm that land mine after all, because I cry. Just normal tears at first, then great, wrenching sobs that scald my lungs.

Kate folds me in a hug. She smells like sour milk and expensive perfume, and I hold on for dear life.

When my shudders finally subside, she pulls back, her fingers combing through my unbrushed hair. "The thing is, Mina, you can do this. You've done it before, remember? Back when Margo died… Well, shit. You handled that so much better than I did."

I sniffle. I've never told her about how I found solace in the woods that summer. Kate, practical to a fault, would only side-eye my attempts to explain. Even Michael, who once revered the forest, outgrew his love of nature years ago.

I don't know a single person who would understand.

"I can't believe I'm saying this," Kate continues, "but maybe you need a vacation. Throw a dart at a map, even. Who cares. Just…get out of this awful house."

I peer around at my glass-and-steel castle. "You love this house."

She waggles her hand in a kinda-sorta gesture. "*Loved.* Past tense. And only because Michael was in it. It made sense on him, you know? But seeing you here alone, it just seems…sad, somehow. Sterile."

I look again, struck by the realization that nothing in here

belongs to me. Michael was the one who chose the white lac-
quered cabinets, the modular sofa, the sleek steel-wire chandelier. Not a single item reflects my tastes. It's almost like I'm an
absentee in my own home.

"You could start over," Kate says.

A prickly ball lodges in my throat. "What? Like, just forget
Michael existed?"

"I'm not saying *forget*. I'm saying move forward. Live your
life while you still have one."

I recoil at hearing my husband's long-ago ideas coming out of
Kate's mouth. Kate, who's never done anything other than exactly what she was supposed to and now has everything I don't.

"Maybe you should start dating again," she says gently.

I cringe. "That's over with."

"It might be good for you."

"Are you nuts? No. I mean, look at my mom. She never got
over what happened to my brother. And it's been almost forty
years. This is the same thing, Kate. If I even *tried* to fall in love
again..." I shudder. "Just no. It would be like a joke, compared
to the first time."

"Then don't compare it to the first time."

I level her with a look. "That part of my life is over. And
please don't bring it up again."

"Okay, fine." She deflates. "There probably aren't any guys
out there who're into bags of bones with nineties troll-doll
hair, anyway."

I flip her the bird.

She nudges the cheesecake. "Just promise me you'll eat something, at least, okay?"

I eye it for a long time. "Later," I finally say.

She sighs. "Liar."

"Really. I will."

"Okay. I'll hold my breath. Walk me out?"

In the driveway, I wrap her in a desperate hug. Just minutes ago, I wished for her to leave, but now I want to clutch at her leg and beg her to stay.

God, I'm a mess.

I hide the internal chaos behind a smile and watch the Suburban trundle off. Then I go to the mailbox. I haven't checked it in ages, and a giant stack has built up. A crisp mailer from the US Department of State sits right on top.

I grimace. My new passport. The one I only renewed because I'd been drinking that evening.

I have no idea what I was thinking.

Back in the house, I toss the pile on the counter and tote the unopened passport up to Michael's office. By his filing cabinet, I squint down at the envelope.

Throw a dart at a map. Start over.

Maybe I could have, once. But I'm a different person now, one who's made choices that can't be unmade. One whose yesterdays weigh too much to simply shrug off.

I open the file cabinet and shove the passport inside. I intend to go precisely nowhere. I'm staying right here, until I figure out how to manage this ravenous, gnawing grief, like any normal person would.

Except that's when I spot Michael's folder, tucked into the very back of the cabinet. The one I had no idea existed.

The one that explodes my entire life.

BEFORE

Just as my lungs spasm, Michael powers upward. The world brightens. My head breaks water. I gasp, hauling in fresh plumes of air.

We've surfaced inside a cave, but it's like no cave I've ever seen. Waterfalls pour in through gaps in the roof, along with moss-tinted spears of sunlight. Everywhere I look, water gushes over smooth white stone. Light refracts from a central pool, painting the grotto with dancing brilliance.

A sound of amazement slides from my lips. Michael tows me toward a pebbled beach, where he lays me beneath him and braces his weight on his forearms.

I can't decide where to look: at the myriad channels carved smooth by the water, or at the heart-stoppingly beautiful man inches from my face.

Within moments, Michael wins. Droplets trickle from his nose to splash against my forehead. My legs squeeze around him, locking our hips flush. When I feel him against me, a slow, excruciating dance starts up in the base of my stomach. A second heartbeat forms there, one that begs for him with every pulse.

Never in my life have I slept with someone I just met, but despite my earlier resolve, I decide I absolutely would right now. I'd let him have me here. I don't care about the freezing water or the illogic of it all.

But to my abject disappointment, he doesn't try for that. He just smiles his incredible smile and says, "What do you think?"

"I think Greece might actually be boring after this. This is the most magical thing I've ever seen."

"Worth it, then?"

"And then some."

"Perfect." He shifts, his bare stomach sliding against mine, which sends another pang lancing through me. "And now I have a question for you. As promised."

My breath falters. He looks serious again, even more so than when I first got into his car, which tells me my earlier suspicions were off the mark. This isn't about staying in touch, but something else entirely.

"I said I wouldn't ask you to stay," he says, "because I think it's incredible that you want to go. But I *will* ask you for time."

My heart catapults up my throat.

"Spend your month with me," he says, his earnestness stunning. "Go to bed with me at night. Wake up with me each day. You can get a job in Seattle, earn enough for your ticket, and in thirty days, I'll drive you to the airport myself. I won't say a word to stop you."

"You mean *live* with you? In your house?"

"It's a condo. But yeah."

A tingle starts in my temples. Despite the icy wavelets lapping at my legs and the rocks digging into my back, warmth suffuses me. "Have you ever lived with a girl before?"

"No. But I've never met you before."

I pause. "I'm not that special."

"You are," he says. "You know how I know?"

"How?"

"Because I've brought girls here before. A few times."

I frown.

"Hey, don't give me that look," he says, good-natured. "I just mean to the pool. You're the first one who's agreed to come in *here*. I kept hoping that someday, someone would. And look. Here you are."

My fingers creep up to brace against his shoulders. I study him long enough to decide I couldn't care less about his history or where this strange sorcery came from. I just know that if I go back to Seagrove, or, worse yet, let him buy me a ticket to Athens, I'll regret it for the rest of my life.

I open my mouth to say so, but Michael stops me.

"I have one condition, though."

I arc an eyebrow. "*You* have a condition? When you're the one propositioning me?"

"I'm not propositioning you. Yet."

I flush. "Still. Bold move."

"I'm kind of a bold guy, in case you haven't noticed. And yeah, there's a rule. No sex. Not until the month's over."

I wonder if I've heard him correctly. "You want to live with me but don't want to have sex with me?"

He chuckles and undulates his hips against mine. It makes me breathless. Mindless with want. "I think you can tell I want to have sex with you about as badly as I want my heart to keep beating."

"But?"

"But I've never asked a girl a question like this before, and if we do this, I want to know you. Really know you. And I want you to know me. I don't want you to be one of those weekend girls you accused me of having."

"It's not an accusation if it's true."

"Fine," he says. "But that's them. This is you. It's different."

I can't believe my ears. It sounds like punishment, being this close to him without reaching the kind of completion my body is screaming for. "Is this because you're terrible in bed and don't want me to find out?"

"I'm incredible in bed," he says. "And I'm probably going to regret this idiotic rule in about five minutes. I think I regret it right now. But it'll give me a chance to do things right. Because for once, I think I actually want to."

I consider. "Would you kiss me, at least?"

His attention drops to my mouth. "I'm absolutely going to kiss you. Before the day's over."

Heat coils in my belly. He stares and stares, but doesn't close the distance, and in the absence of his mouth on mine, everything else heightens. His fingertips feather against my shoulder, driving a shiver into my center. His bare chest surges against mine. And his firmest place of all still presses against me, the only separation his sopping shorts and my bikini. Every square inch of him proves so delicious that I find myself savoring the idea of this slow and delicate torture.

"You realize how crazy this is," I whisper. "Right?"

He lowers his head to my neck. "One hundred percent." His heated answer propels freezing droplets across my skin.

"But you want to do it anyway?"

"One thousand percent." His tongue darts out, claiming a bead of moisture.

Sensation rolls through me, leaving me quivering. "All right. Then let's live together. For a month. See what happens."

He sucks in a breath and raises his head. "Really?"

"Really."

"Jesus." He grins. "My heart's going about a million miles an hour right now. I feel like I just won the lottery."

I smile back, touched by his open vulnerability. He keeps surprising me with that. "Who knows? Maybe you did."

He laughs and climbs off me, then pulls me to my feet. We

manage to while away half the afternoon beneath the falling water, sifting through sparkling pebbles until our lips turn blue. When it's time to swim back, I cling to him again, stealing his heat and gifting him some of my own.

We surface in the hillside pool and float, nose to nose. Still, he doesn't kiss me.

I both love and hate this game, I decide. Mostly hate. I start counting the minutes, wondering how many I'll have to endure before he finally puts an end to my longing.

Back at the car, we sprawl on the Audi's hood while the sun bakes the wetness from our skin. After we discreetly change back into dry clothes, Michael points the car south.

"Where to now?" I ask.

He lifts my hand and kisses my fingers. The resulting zing reaches my marrow.

"Home," he says.

I smile at that word. *Home.*

Because the craziest thing is, I feel like I'm already there.

When Michael unlocks the door to his—*our*—Seattle condo, I do a double take.

Holy shit. This guy is loaded.

He ushers me into a wonderland of glass and concrete perched nineteen stories above the ground. A wall of windows overlooks the waterfront. Outside, lights glitter. Boats bob. Beyond the rim of the Pacific, a yellow flush warms the sky.

I soak it all in with widened eyes.

Michael stays close. "Well? What do you think?"

I spin a slow circle, feeling like I've strayed into that movie where the unsuspecting teenager finds out she's actually a princess, complete with her very own castle. "It's incredible. You *live* here?"

I expect him to puff with pride, but he gives me a sober look. "You like it?"

"I love it." When he doesn't answer, I frown. "But why do you look like you kind of wish I didn't?"

"Sorry. It's not that. It's just…you look natural here. Like you belong in a place like this."

"With you," I say, in hopes of chasing away the odd tension.

A ghostlike smile flits across his lips. "That's the hope."

Before I can respond, he turns and totes my purple bag through the door of what I can only presume is the bedroom.

Not quite ready to cross *that* threshold just yet, I wander, reminding myself that this must be strange for him. He's just moved in with a girl he met yesterday. Of course he'd need a moment to adjust.

I'll grant him as many as he needs.

The condo boasts an open layout—the kitchen flows into both dining and living room, where chrome floor lamps and sleek electronics bookend black leather sofas. On a granite-topped island, a stack of mail sits unopened, as if Michael has just returned from an extended absence.

My brow furrows as my conversation with Sarah and Brooke comes floating back. Michael can't have gone any-where recently—they made it clear he's spent the past month at the office. Moodier than usual, maybe, but *there*.

A thought occurs, and I surreptitiously flip through the mail. Maybe Michael's just gone through a breakup, and that's what has thrown him out of sorts at work. Maybe I'm not actually the first girl he's lived with, and that's why he looked so taken aback when we first walked in.

Maybe he's saving this mail for someone else.

But no. Every single envelope bears his name. With a quiet laugh at my own folly, I abandon the pile and venture into the living room to peruse the photographs on the walls. At first, the myriad photos of skyscrapers catch me off guard, consider-ing how uninterested Michael was in talking about his work. But he probably gets enough of it here, living in this gallery.

Or maybe he just realizes most people don't share the passion he clearly feels for buildings.

I'm busy pondering the possibilities when one photograph snags my attention, making me forget all the others. I sidestep the angular couch to get a closer look.

The picture shows a wide-open stretch of farmland in some place like Kansas or North Dakota. Ripened rows of wheat stretch away while overhead, the sky gathers like an angry bruise. From the raging purple clouds, a funnel descends, a chaotic finger reaching down to touch the orderly gold perfection of the fields.

I stare, glued there somehow. The picture radiates energy the same way a fire throws heat. I can practically smell the sulfurous tang of the storm, the restless heave of the wind.

When I blink, Michael is standing beside me. "You like this one?" His voice tightens, as if my answer holds significance.

I hesitate, not knowing what he expects. "I love it. I'm *in* love with it."

"Yeah? How come?"

"It's like…I'm there, in the calm before the storm. Like something dangerous and unstoppable is about to come turn the world upside down, and I'm caught in that moment, in the breath before a fall."

"I know that feeling." When his eyes meet mine, warmth fills them. Clearly, he's talking about something besides the photo. "I know it exactly."

My breath catches. "Do you?"

"Like a tornado's about to blast my life apart, and I'm probably going to love every second of it? Yeah."

The air heats between us. But instead of kissing me, he turns away.

Goddamn it.

I try to cool off by returning my attention to the photo. Only then do I catch the name inked in the corner. Grayson Drake.

My heart stutters. Grayson. *Drake.* That can only be the brother who wishes Michael had never been born. I step back, breaking the picture's gravitational pull. How badly have I screwed up?

Apparently, not much, because Michael makes a casual gesture toward the framed skyscrapers—spindly confections of glass and steel depicted in black and white. "What about these? Do they do it for you?"

Really, to me, the buildings are just that. Buildings. But I don't want to insult him, so I manage a somewhat sincere-sounding "They're great, too."

He laughs. "Not a fan of architecture, then?"

I shrug. "I'm not *not* a fan. I guess I've just never thought about it before."

He smiles, all forgiveness, and guides me to the couch by the windows, where two glasses of freshly poured red wine await.

I pounce on mine, realizing how ravenous and parched I am. On the way back from Canada, we stopped at a seaside oyster farm outside Bellingham, but for all that I love shellfish, it never satiates me for long.

"I was thinking about Italian for dinner." He flops down on the sofa beside me. "How do you feel about fettucine Alfredo?"

"At the moment? Deeply passionate." I sample the wine. It's divine—a Malbec, my second-favorite vintage after Cabernet.

"Perfect." Michael pulls out his phone, then delivers a practiced order to some restaurant whose menu he clearly knows by heart. He sets his cell on the table and slings a sculpted arm over the back of the couch, facing me with wine in hand. "So."

"So."

"We live together."

I twirl my glass. "We do. Which is crazy."

"It's balls-to-the-wall insane," he says. "And I like it."

I go quiet. In the face of his scrutiny, I feel shy suddenly, my tongue tied in knots.

I've never met a man who combines such unbridled intelligence with a raw thirst for living. And to find it all behind a face like *that*…it almost strikes me as unjust. Not only to every man who can't possibly live up to the standard Michael Drake has single-handedly set, but to me.

Now that I've met him, I can't imagine settling for anything less.

Every stupid college boyfriend I ever had fades to insignificance. None of them, I realize, really meant that much. They were only practice.

I lift my glass. "Let's toast."

"To what?"

I peek at him through my lashes. "To today."

He laughs. "Yes. Of course. What else?"

Our glasses clink. For the next half hour, we edge closer, titillating ourselves with fleeting touches and spirited conversation. When our food arrives, we pull apart, then devour the pasta, just to talk some more.

When it grows late, Michael turns off the lights, letting the dim orange glow from the harbor bathe the room. As he circles back toward the couch, I say, "Take off your shirt."

The smolder from outside backlights him, but I can still make out his one-sided smile. "What? Why? You're not trying to take advantage of me, are you?"

"No. Well, yes. Eventually. But for now, I just want to look at you."

His smile grows. He pulls off his black V-neck and tosses it to the floor. God, he's magnificent. I'm busy trying to get angry about it when he drops to the couch and prowls toward me on hands and knees.

I barely get my wineglass to the safety of the coffee table before he eases me back against the leather, nudging my knees apart with his hips.

My pulse skyrockets. He's everywhere—a living artwork of

muscle and skin, drenched in the storm-wild smell of woods. He comes so close that his hair brushes my forehead as he stares into my eyes.

"Hi," he whispers.

"Hi," I whisper back.

When he doesn't move, I clear my throat. "Not to complain, but I can't actually see your abs from this angle. Which was kind of the whole point."

He chuckles, low and sultry. Orange light caresses his face and kindles twin embers in his pupils. "I'll get up in three minutes."

I snake my arms upward and knead at the musculature of his back. "Three? That's oddly specific."

He swipes his phone from the coffee table. "Well, it's eleven ten right now. Which means your life is supposed to change in one minute. If you still want it to."

My breath stalls. I think of the jet that would have carried me away, taxiing down the runway as we speak, engines roaring, cabin lights dimmed in preparation for its leap into the sky.

I'd rather be pinned to this couch.

"I do," I manage. "I definitely do."

His fingers trail up the side of my neck and stroke the shell of my ear. I pant. It seems impossible that such innocent touches could affect me so profoundly, but I turn liquid, aching with his nearness.

"I'll do my best, then," he says.

The time on his screen ticks to 11:11. Somewhere southeast of us, a plane launches into the stratosphere, taking my pulse along with it. Michael tosses his phone onto the floor. Neither of us check to see if it's survived intact.

After the longest, hungriest moment of my life, he kisses me.

Except the word *kiss* doesn't do it justice. Energy snaps and sizzles, foreign in its intensity, and what Michael does to me, he does with his whole body.

He kisses me like he's starving for it, devouring, exploring, claiming. I love it. I want to erect an altar to this feeling. I rise to meet the demands of his mouth, savoring lips that seem to remake me on some molecular level.

Michael pairs the greedy force of the kiss with the tenderest of touches. His fingers brush across places most men don't bother with—the sensitive dip of my hip bone, the delicate valley of my elbow. He touches me in gentle worship, and all the while, the kiss remains savage, a fierce joining of questing lips.

He's a man of contrasts, even in this, and the juxtaposition of hard and soft, ferocious and tender, does something indescribable to me.

I'm floating. I'm flying. I'm coming apart in some unplanned way, and I chase the burning-down of myself until I become nothing but ashes.

When he finally pulls back, he says, "How was that? Sufficient?"

I almost toss back a flippant one-liner, but I don't want to diminish the fact that I'm no longer the same person I was three minutes ago. "It was mind-blowing. My brain might be lying on the floor somewhere. I'll have to go looking for it in a second."

With a smile, he tucks my hair behind my ear, then pulls me from the couch and leads me to the bedroom, where, as promised, we go to bed without anyone's underwear coming off.

The stardust remnants of the kiss still sizzle in my blood, though, and sleep hovers at arm's length. I turn on my side, studying Michael's face as he slips into slumber with his arm slung over my waist.

City-lit quiet floods the room. I marvel at what a single rise and fall of the sun can do. I've just moved in with a man I've known for a day, and not one single part of me wants to leave him tomorrow, even to go job hunting. Maybe I don't want to leave him at all, which is possibly even more inconceivable than moving to Athens for no reason.

My future shears into halves: life if I go, life if I stay. Far-flung vistas and adventure, or scorching kisses and soul-nourishing conversation.

Not that Michael has so much as mentioned the possibility of me staying. But it's creeping in already, tiptoeing through a back door in my mind, and I know that in thirty days, I *will* have to choose.

Which means I can only leap, one way or the other, and pray I make the right choice.

BEFORE

I decide I must be dreaming.

Yet days pass, and I continue to awaken in a nineteenth-floor palace beside a man who does things no boyfriend has before.

Every morning, Michael brings me coffee in bed. Then we head to work—him to his swanky architectural job, me to a temporary assignment collating loan data for a company that buys and sells mortgages, which is just as boring as it sounds. But boring doesn't matter, because in the evenings, we snuggle on the couch and watch campy horror movies other guys always made fun of me for adoring. Michael holds me close through all the tense parts, which he pretends is for my sake, but every time the villain pops out, he jumps, and I tease him relentlessly for it.

We kiss. We twine together in the orange dimness of the bedroom and talk until our eyelids get heavy.

We also don't have sex. Which I love.

And hate. Mostly hate.

On weekends, Michael introduces me to a Washington I've never seen. We hike the majestic, up-and-down trails of Mount

Rainier National Park while he teaches me to properly weight a pack and layer my clothing. We power up mountainsides, then lie in the sunshine and munch on dried fruit. Back at home, we curl on opposite ends of the couch, our freshly scrubbed feet touching while he reads his fifty pages and I write a travelogue about our hike.

One evening, Michael sets his book aside, then scoots around to my side and peeks at my computer screen. When I don't flinch, he raises a golden eyebrow. "You don't care if I read it?"

"No," I say, more distracted by his nearness than anything else. I'm aching to kiss him, but if I do, this paragraph will never get finished.

"I thought writers were private about their work."

"There's not much I'm private about." I gesture at my computer. "There's not even a password on this thing."

He snuggles closer, solid and tempting against my side. "So someone could just go poking through your email if they wanted?"

I chuckle. "There's only one 'someone' in this condo, and he's not pathetic enough to snoop."

"True." His gaze roves over my face. "I'd come up with something way more ingenious."

For a moment, we just stay like that, until I close the computer and stash it behind a throw pillow. God, I could stare into his eyes for hours. It's like floating in the ocean, except that I want to touch the ocean in extremely inappropriate ways.

He tucks a long strand of hair behind my ear. "No secrets, then?"

"Not here. What about you? Any closeted skeletons I should know about?"

He doesn't blink. "Nothing I won't tell you eventually."

I pause, wondering what exactly that means, but in another moment, he's kissing me. My arms wrap around him almost by themselves and, as predicted, the paragraph doesn't get done.

Some nights, we stay up late and blare Journey from the living room speakers while dancing around in our underwear. When I confess my unrepentant love for kettle corn, Michael invests in a home popper and experiments until he discovers the exact ratio of brown sugar and butter that makes me moan.

The first time it happens, he grins like a wolf. "I love that I just made that sound come out of your mouth. I can't wait to take a stab at it without any food involved."

I cram a fistful of popcorn into my mouth and waggle my eyebrows. "'Take a stab'? Are you being punny right now?"

"Maybe." He stalks across the kitchen and leans down to kiss me. Or pretends to. At the last second, he filches a piece of unchewed popcorn with his teeth.

"Hey!" I try to steal my treat back, but when that fails, I settle for retaliation. I surreptitiously fish an ice cube from the glass of Scotch he's just finished, lean up for my own fake kiss, and drop the frigid chunk down the back of his shirt.

He leaps away, bellowing and laughing. Within minutes, we're on the floor—concrete be damned—making out like teenagers, the popcorn forgotten.

Day by torturous day, I familiarize myself with every inch of Michael's body, except those inches I crave the most. I feel him against me often enough to know he's blessed in that department—because *of course* he is, he's ridiculous, which would annoy me if I wasn't so excited about it—but his fingers never stray past the waistband of my panties. He doesn't even take off my bra. Instead, he makes it his mission to discover erogenous zones I didn't know I had, sliding his lips along my rib cage, raking his fingernails over the tender expanse of my inner arm while exploring my mouth with his tongue.

I coil ever tighter. I'm like a tropical storm, spinning and swelling, drawing sustenance from the turquoise sea and yearning to make landfall, at which point I'll probably explode with enough force to annihilate everything in sight.

One evening in bed, I gasp against his lips. "I'm pretty sure the whole building's going to collapse when we finally get naked together. I've never wanted anyone so badly in my life."

He chuckles. "Just the building? I'll consider it a failure on my part if we don't level this entire block."

"Eleven days," I say.

"Eleven days." He dips his head to lap at the hollow of my neck, and I have to forcibly stop myself from tearing his boxers off.

A week later, we take a two-hour drive to a mountaintop observatory just to see what the night sky looks like beyond the bright dome of the city. Michael swings the Audi through one switchback curve after another and parks in the empty lot up top.

We emerge into the cool velvet evening. Overhead, some divine giant has sprayed frosty chips of crushed diamond across the sky with such enthusiasm that I can only stare upward, open-mouthed.

Michael cranes his head, too. We let glittering wonder flow into us. I feel simultaneously ageless and newly born, and utterly privileged to exist in a world that contains such majesty. In the darkness, Michael's hand finds mine.

"Holy shit," he says, after ten minutes of star-drenched silence. "There's an entire philosophy written up there."

My mouth curls. I love it when he gets reflective. "Really? And what're you reading, up there in the sky?"

"A whole book. About how infinitesimal we are. But also about how we're the exact opposite of tiny. I mean, think about it. No one else will ever experience this moment in this same way. Only you and me." His thumb draws circles on the back of my hand. "No other two people, not in the whole endless life of the universe, will stand on *this* mountaintop on *this* night, seeing *these* stars and holding each other's hands. It's a gift for us and no one else, ever. Which makes us anything but insignificant. It makes us infinite. It means we live entire lives full of moments that no other soul will experience. It makes us *giants*."

My attention veers from the sky to him. I would never have thought to look at it that way. Not in a million years. I stare up at his hopelessly beautiful face, my lips parted, my heart swelling to an impossible size.

And then, although I swear the moment can't get any more perfect, it does.

"Mina…" In the starlight, his eyes turn warm and expansive. "I'm desperately in love with you. I want you to know that."

"I'm desperately in love with you, too."

That's it. It's just…easy. True. A statement of fact that surprises nobody.

On the way home, Michael holds my hand atop the gearshift. I study his profile, wondering if I can possibly board that plane in four days.

I can't imagine it.

Not that this man is perfect. Nearly a month together has allowed me to ferret out some flaws, and in a way, Michael's coworkers weren't wrong. He's never an asshole to me, but he does reserve his charm for the handful of people he finds engaging—me, the chess-whiz doorman in our building, his friend Ben from work, who I went to school with once upon a time and seems to be the only person at Forsythe & Winter Michael truly respects.

Others don't get much from him. He's briskly courteous in public, but his patience wears thin when people find themselves confused by situations that seem straightforward to him, like when the girl at the grocery store fumbles to make change or the barista on our block misspells *Mina* as *Nemo* and spends a good five minutes calling the name of a cartoon fish before we realize it's *my* hazelnut latte that's ready. Then, Michael's words grow clipped enough that annoyance peeks through the polite facade.

He also doesn't need nearly as much sleep as I do. He stays up late and wakes up early. On weekdays, he reads his fifty pages in the morning, which grants me some extra time, but the condo doesn't offer enough in the way of sound dampening that I can continue to sleep while he clunks around making breakfast. So I nap after work. Otherwise, I'd fall to pieces, completely incapable of surviving on the five or six hours that somehow sustain him.

No one's perfect, though, and I don't expect even the incomparable Michael Drake to remake that rule. I actually like that he isn't Prince Charming.

I'd be suspicious otherwise.

After getting home from the observatory, we take our usual places on the couch and sip wine in the dark.

"I haven't bought my ticket yet," I say.

He sucks in a breath and sets his glass on the coffee table. It's hard to tell in the dimness, but I swear his hand shakes. "Why not? Are you not making enough at that mortgage place?"

"No, they're paying me fine. I'm just not sure I want to go anymore."

He leans close and cradles my cheek. "But you have to. It means so much more than just you getting on a plane. I know that. You do, too."

I pull back to get a better look at him, trying to fight the prickle invading my throat. "Are you saying you don't want me to stay?"

"No. God. I'd cut off my arm for you to stay. But…I wouldn't cut off yours. If that makes sense."

I shake my head. I wish I didn't understand him with such frustrating precision. I also wish I didn't suspect him of being right. "What if you came with me?"

He makes a pained sound and swings away. I feel his absence like a cold gust of winter.

"I can't, Mina."

"Can't? Why not? You must have plenty saved up, from what I can tell. And I know you'd have to quit, but…is your job really that irreplaceable? You barely talk about it. It doesn't seem like you even like it all that much."

He stares out the window, his profile lit by the glow from the harbor. "It's not that simple. I have…obligations."

I frown. *Obligations* sounds so unlike him that I can't imagine what that means. "To who?"

"My brother."

I blink, rapid-fire. "I thought you two didn't talk."

"We *didn't*." He rubs at his temples. "For almost a year after Lily died. But lately he's been…going through a hard time, and I've been helping him. Or trying to. We haven't actually seen each other yet, but we've been talking again over the past couple months. This might finally be my chance to fix things. I have to be here for it."

The past couple months. I'd almost forgotten Sarah's and Brooke's insistence about him behaving strangely, but this explains it. Finally.

I start to reach out. Except Michael withdraws in a way I'm not accustomed to, his shoulders hunching.

My heart softens. "Then you're right. You should stay, until things are back on solid ground. How long do you think that'll take? Six months? A year? I could wait. We could go after, when you're ready."

He stabs a hand through his hair, which flops right back over his forehead the moment he lets go. "But that's just it. That's what people always say. And then they never go. They never *live.* I can't let you fall into that trap for my sake. I just know if you don't go now…"

He doesn't finish, but he doesn't have to. When he looks up, his expression does it for him.

"When I brought you here," he says, "I knew you'd break my heart. And I'm prepared for that. I'm *okay* with it."

Something inside me snaps clean in two. "What if I'm not?"

His eyes grow suspiciously bright, even in the dark. I imagine a death-row convict on execution day would look exactly like he does right now.

"I won't pretend I'm noble enough to stop you from staying," he says. "But that's not what I actually *want* for you, Mina. I want you to go and spread your wings. All those dreams you had as a kid? I want every last one of them to come true."

I inhale sharply. "And you?"

"Will be right here. Hoping to fucking god that you come back to me once they do."

"Michael, I—"

"Don't." His forehead pleats. "Because I'm about a millisecond away from asking you to forget everything I just said. So don't answer. Just...think about it. Please. You don't have to decide anything yet. We still have four days."

Four days. It sounds like a blink. It sounds like an eternity. But I do know one thing. If I give myself to him, if we consummate this sublime fever dream, I won't ever tear myself away.

Later, in the bedroom, Michael murmurs in the dark. "Tell me something?"

My eyes are still open, pointed at the ceiling, and I turn my head. I'd thought he was asleep already. "Of course," I whisper back. "Anything."

"Would you still love me, without all this? The car, the condo, the job? The money? What if I was nobody? What if I had nothing?"

My brows knit. The question surprises me, but I *did* just ask him to torpedo his entire life for me.

"Let me make something clear." I nestle close, pressing a kiss to his smooth chest. "You could get fired, go broke, gain a hundred pounds, shave off all that gorgeous hair, and move into a cardboard box, and I wouldn't love you any less than I do right now."

He chuckles, low and warm and rough, which somehow wields enough power to make my stomach clench with desire.

"You're lying," he says, but pulls me closer. "The part about the hair's a dead giveaway."

I ponder that, wondering whether he has something to tell me. But by the time I decide to ask, he's already asleep.

AFTER

I stand amid the cold silence of Michael's office, staring at the unfamiliar folder at the back of the cabinet. Its jammed-in angle disrupts the order of the entire row, as if my husband stuffed it there in a fit of emotion. Except Michael didn't do fits of emotion.

I pull the thing out. I haven't checked the filing cabinet in months. I've barely even set foot in this room, because of all the places in our home, this one belonged most thoroughly to him. Somehow, the idea of dismantling it has felt like a permanent admission of defeat.

The folder has no label, but it weighs a ton. When I crack the cover, glossy clippings cascade out.

Shock punches all the air from my chest. Michael's face sears my eyes, only it isn't Michael. No, *this* man has a scar bisecting one eyebrow, visible even through the crystalline snow clinging to his stubbled cheeks and abundant lashes.

It's Grayson. My husband's identical twin. The man I didn't even know *was* an identical twin until I encountered this picture in the grocery store three years ago.

My breath shortens. Grayson stares out from the cover of *National Geographic*, his gaze as penetrating as it is tormented. He's clearly only just escaped the avalanche that buried him alive, and his golden brows crook together. And there's this...*thing* in his face. This horrible sort of longing, like he's just glimpsed death and hasn't decided yet whether to go chasing after it. His full lips are parted, frozen in the moment right before speaking, and I wonder, as I have a thousand times before, what he's about to say. What critical message he feels compelled to impart after having stood on—and been hauled back from—the brink of oblivion.

I toss the magazine to the floor as if it's burned me, but that still leaves a stack in my hands. There's a clipping from some gossip magazine. Then another, and another. Which makes no sense. Michael eternally avoided the subject of Grayson after the last time they saw each other in Seattle. He wouldn't have followed his brother's every step, even from afar.

Yet my fingers flip through picture after picture. Here's the man who looks so much like my husband, wearing a leather jacket Michael never would've been caught dead in. Here's Grayson on the deck of a yacht, glaring across the water at whoever's photographing him, one hand splayed over a bare chest so glorious it makes me hate myself for noticing. Inky lines feather out from beneath his fingers, but the photographer hasn't captured what he's hiding, and for all that I've avoided these awful articles, I know that will be the case for every photo here. No one has ever caught this particular tattoo on camera. Despite the speculation, only the women he's loved and inevitably left truly know what it is.

The images scorch themselves into my brain. Grayson, one arm draped over the handlebars of a motorcycle while he flips the camera the bird. Him in a nightclub, turning away from a woman who probably models for Victoria's Secret.

The photos abruptly end, and I find myself holding a stack of pages cut with exacting care from *National Geographic* itself.

Grayson's work.

My hands tremble, but try as I might, I can't stop flipping through. An African tribesman in traditional dress holds a cell phone aloft, searching for a signal beneath a full moon. An underground lake reflects the lush greenery of the jungle above. A school of a million silver fish bursts apart as a hungry seabird dive-bombs the water, its red beak gaping.

The pictures are like visual poetry, and I fling the pages away. They scatter to the floor.

My chest heaves. Amid the mess, a bundle of printer paper lies face down, and I bend to pick it up. For a moment, I can't understand what I'm looking at, because shouldn't these still be in the manila folder beneath my bed?

Except these aren't the divorce papers I hid away last year. *Those* had blurry splotches from where my wet hair had dripped onto the still-warm ink.

These are pristine. Crisply aligned and stapled together. And they're signed.

By Michael. In handwriting I know as intimately as my own voice.

My heart dies inside my chest. Just sputters out between one beat and the next, leaving me with a numb, lifeless lump beneath my ribs. What little spark remained has just been extinguished.

I hurl the divorce papers at the wall and walk out.

Downstairs, I find my cell phone. I have no idea what I intend to do with it until my disembodied fingers tap on my mother's name.

Normally I would never call in August, which she clearly knows, because she answers on the first ring. "Mina? Honey? What's wrong?"

I blink furiously. To my amazement, the force of habit proves even mightier than the jagged crack ravaging my soul. "Nothing, Mom. I'm fine. Hi."

"Hi." She releases a breath. "You scared me."

"Sorry. I know we…haven't talked in a while."

I don't state the obvious—that even though she and my dad live two miles away, we always maintain radio silence at this time of year. Even after nearly four decades, even after I've lost a husband, apparently, the anniversary month of my brother's death still throws my mother into a tailspin. Under normal circumstances, I'd honor her withdrawal and hold off calling until September.

These, however, are not normal circumstances.

"It's not your fault." Her tone softens. "I'm… Well. We both know how I get."

I close my eyes and clutch the phone until the plastic creaks, tethering myself to the timbre of her voice as if it has the power to coax something other than a gutting betrayal from what I've just seen.

"And I've been thinking about you." She sounds tentative, fumbling. "I've actually wondered if…maybe you…did something special last week?"

My eyes shoot open. For my mother, Jasper's death has forever marred the day I came into this world, a stain that no amount of time or distance has ever washed out. Back in my childhood, we never celebrated. While my friends all turned six, nine, thirteen, I got cake and balloons on my half birthday. I turned six and a half. Nine and a half. And, in a horrendous, fateful twist, thirty-six and a half on the day Michael died, ultimately leaving me with two cursed dates on opposite sides of the year.

Now this is the closest my mother's ever come to acknowledging my birthday. My real one, that is.

And so, because I feel compelled to reward her in some way,

I lie. "Yeah, Kate took me out for drinks. Then we got massages. It was great."

"Massages! How wonderful. At Woodhouse Day Spa?"

"Yeah, Woodhouse."

"Oh, I love it there. Jackie's my favorite. Such tiny hands, but so strong. Who was your therapist?"

"Um...Lance?" I say, then clamp my teeth around a curled forefinger, because *Lance* sounds more like a guitar-wielding YouTube star than a Seagrove masseuse who kneads out soreness while Tibetan chants waft in the background.

Clearly, my mother has the same thought, or maybe she knows all the therapists at Woodhouse by name, because her tone goes flat as roadkill. "You didn't go anywhere, did you?"

"Um...no. But I don't want you to worry. I'm fine, Mom, really."

"Are you?"

I fist a hand against my temple. I'm not fine. I am so much the exact fucking opposite of fine that I want to scream, but that would only terrify her.

"When's the last time you left the house?" she presses.

"I don't know, when's the last time *you* left the house?" I shoot back, then immediately regret it. "I'm sorry, that was shitty of me. I'm just...on edge. Which is actually why I called. Kate suggested I take a vacation, and I think she's right. I want to give myself a chance to heal, somewhere away from here."

My mother draws a sharp breath. "By yourself? But where would you go?"

Into the woods, I think, because I can't stand another second in this house. I no longer care if leaving betrays the man I loved so wholeheartedly. Because clearly, he betrayed me, too. By withdrawing. By sinking into his work.

By dying at thirty-nine after signing divorce papers he hadn't mustered the courage to use.

I swallow, hoping my tone won't give me away. "Don't worry,

nowhere crazy. I was hoping I could use the cabin. Being out in nature...helped me a lot the summer Margo died."

"Oh, the cabin. Well, it's wonderful that you want to go, but..."

My gut clenches. "But?"

"We sold it."

My stomach drops. "Sold it? When? Why didn't I know?"

"Dad and I just accepted the offer last week. We hadn't been there in a year, and I didn't think you had any interest anymore."

I stem a breath, but I can't argue. The cabin lies northeast of Seattle, in the wilderness near Skykomish—a long enough drive that I've only made the effort a handful of times in the past twenty years.

"Though you could still head up, if you wanted." Her tone turns hopeful. "The closing's not 'til next week. All our furniture's still there, and the movers aren't coming until Wednesday. You'd have four days."

"Then I absolutely want to go. Right now." Urgency ignites in my muscles. I dash for the stairs and vault upward two at a time. In my walk-in closet, I toss clothes into my ancient purple roller-bag. "Is the key still in the same place?"

"Yes, but...are you sure you're all right? Why does this sound so urgent?"

I mumble something about changes of scenery. My mother defaults to worrying mode again, but I don't have the mental energy to dig her out right now. I'm depleted, left with nothing but a scorching need to escape.

After hanging up, I stuff my laptop into my suitcase, then grab my running shoes and haul everything out to the garage. A four- or five-hour drive awaits, depending on Seattle's traffic, and it's already well past three.

Halfway through loading my Genesis, I stop. Michael's bullet-silver Porsche Cayman—his "splurge car," not the SUV he died in—sits beside mine, silently begging to escape the concrete confines of the garage.

I never drove the thing when he was alive. I always worried that if I went near it, I'd ding the bumper or spill something on the precious leather, which would've made him go quiet for days.

Now a wild edge of defiance pulses beneath my skin. I don't stop long enough to question it, just fling my things from the Genesis into the Cayman.

After exchanging my keys for Michael's, I gun the Porsche out into the driveway and execute a U-turn that makes the tires squeal.

My husband would've been horrified. Or proud. I can't decide which, and in the moment, I don't even care.

In the rearview mirror, the garage door descends, a guillotine marking the death of my nightmarish vigil inside a box of glass and steel.

God, Kate was right. Inside of a mile, I feel like I'm waking up. I have a purpose. A place to be. As Seagrove fades, the rush within me grows, joining the powerful roar of the Porsche's engine. The car strains and pulls, eager for open road.

Only after reaching the highway do I remember I'm not nearly as good a driver as Michael was. Still, I power through each forested curve, feeding the car throttle. The hungry engine takes it all and asks for more.

Then the memories awaken, twining up from the floorboards like living shadows. I remember that first drive with Michael, this particular hairpin turn, the way he handled the Audi like he'd been born in the driver's seat. I remember this gas station streaking past the window, the hitch-drop in my stomach as I tried to deny the allure of a man I suspected, even then, would change my life.

In hopes of banishing the ghosts, I fish out my phone and dictate a text, but after updating Kate, I still have four-plus hours to kill. Four hours to run the gauntlet of knife-bright memories that lurk around every corner.

So I command my phone to list my personal emails aloud. For months, I've avoided this, mostly because the endless platitudes from friends I haven't spoken to in years only fatigue me. But right now, I'll take what I can get.

Surprisingly, my strategy works, at least for a while. Until my phone announces a message that makes me jerk the Porsche right off the road.

The car screeches to a halt inches from a boulder. I barely register the close call, just stare at the marching trees beyond the windshield. "Repeat that," I command.

"You have an unopened email from Grayson Drake," my phone chirps. "Would you like me to read it?"

The cheery, robotic Australian voice I once selected on a whim does nothing to dispel the frost crystals forming in my bloodstream. *Grayson Drake.*

He didn't attend our wedding. Never sent Christmas cards. He had no involvement in our lives whatsoever, except on that terrible day I still think of as That One Time. After that, Michael asked me never to speak of him again.

And I didn't—except for once. Not that the silence changed much. Whatever happened between them that day, it was the spark that lit the fire of my husband changing. Which is why I hate Grayson and always will.

I didn't realize he even knew I existed.

Breath churning, I hit the hazards and snatch up my phone, which displays a message with a send date of two months ago and a single-word subject line: "Armistice."

Cold trickles down my spine. It's a word not many people would use, yet it hauls the weight of an entire history behind it. It's the pointed, terminal end of a long and painful war I'm left fighting even after one participant is gone.

I suck in the warm, stale air of the car and click.

Hi Mina,

I realize you probably have no desire to hear from me, and for understandable reasons. But with Michael gone, I find myself with a sense of unfinished business. I imagine you might feel the same way. Obviously, you have no obligation to grant me your time, but I'd like to meet for coffee sometime and put a few things to rest, if you're willing. I'd be happy to drive down to Seagrove. Please let me know.

Hope to see you soon,

Grayson

His phone number lurks optimistically beneath his signature. I barely look at it before pitching the phone down and pulling back out onto Highway 12.

For the next twenty minutes, my mind grinds in useless circles. Grayson's polite, apologetic tone baffles me, a glaring mismatch to the habitual drinker who flips off photographers and snubs lingerie models in nightclubs.

Ultimately, though, it doesn't matter whether I'm passing right through Seattle in a matter of hours. If Grayson thinks I'm going to call him, much less sit down for coffee, he has another thing coming.

I recite that like a mantra for the next three hours. By the time Seattle's outskirts jockey for space beyond the windshield, my resolve has hardened. In the stop-and-go traffic on the 405, I open my phone and swipe left to delete Grayson's message. Then I empty the trash folder, ensuring I can't change my mind.

Only later, as I nose the Porsche into the cabin's gravel driveway, does a heaviness descend between my shoulder blades like an ache.

I ignore it. In the fading light, I focus on the cabin's familiar brown siding and pine-green trim. In the background, the jagged, toothy mountains of the Wild Sky Wilderness rear up like the serrated fangs of some sleeping beast, their tips frosted with snow. The waning day catches on the glistening spires, splashing them with dusky, bloody crimson.

I pop open the car door. Outside, the crisp scent of pine mingles with the spice of the burbling creek, but even the evening's briskness can't clear my mind.

Grayson Drake. I can't believe he emailed me.

I grab my phone and slam the car door harder than necessary, then wander into the cabin's overgrown backyard. Beyond the swaying grass, the forest awaits, a tangle of gleaming blue shadows that seems to beckon.

A sense of familiarity enfolds me, as if this place has been waiting. As if it always knew I would someday need it again.

I shake myself. Time enough for that later. On the porch, I find the key beneath a carved wooden grizzly bear, and let myself in without unloading the car.

Inside, I zigzag through the shadowy living room to my old bedroom, where I curl up with the knitted afghan from the foot of the bed.

Within moments, my eyes drift shut. Hours later, I awaken to total darkness. The rush of the creek and the mournful sigh of wind-bent pines fill the night.

I feel for my phone and tap the screen, then jerk back: 11:11 p.m.

Ugh. Of all the minutes between dusk and dawn, it had to be that one.

Swallowing hard, I wait until 11:12 arrives, then open my email inbox. I don't scroll up or down, but stare at the place where Grayson's message was. For the first time, I admit that, of everyone I know—or don't know, as the case may be—he's the only person who might actually understand what this feels like. Who's loved someone so deeply that their death broke him to pieces.

But his message is gone. No matter how long my eyes scorch a hole in the screen, the email doesn't exist anymore.

And now it's too late to get it back.

BEFORE

During my last four days with Michael, we don't mention the possibility of me staying again. Yet he often gets a faraway look, as if arguing with himself, and sometimes, I catch such conflict in his eyes that my pulse skitters erratically in response.

Our kisses get deeper. Longer. Laced with desperation. Michael does everything short of tearing my underwear off, and I do everything short of tearing off his. We writhe and sweat and moan together until I nearly climax from the rock of his hips alone, but I stop myself. I want him inside me, that first time. I want everything he has to give, all at once.

It's torture.

At Michael's insistence, I put a price hold on a ticket to Athens, which reserves me the option to purchase at any point until departure. My assignment at the mortgage company has left me with enough to cover the cost, but I don't click Buy. Or Cancel. Because how do you decide which half of your heart to rip out?

On our last morning together, or maybe the first of many, I awaken to find a breakfast tray resting on the crisp white sheets.

Michael stands beside the bed in boxer briefs, a single red rose in hand. Backlit by the foggy morning, he looks like an angel who's accidentally tumbled to earth.

I sit up, my heart straining against my ribs. Maybe his name suits him, after all. At the very least, he's come swooping into my life like a miracle, and today, he'll finally, finally belong to me in all the ways I desire.

Except the longer I look, the more his smile looks wrong. An edge of despair sharpens that normally easy grin, as if he expects to have earth-shattering sex with me and watch me fly away afterward.

Which, of course, he does.

"I made your favorite," he says. "Eggs Benedict with bacon."

"Wow," I croak, my voice gritty. My eyes drop to his perfectly packaged...package. This moment has been a month in the making. "It's like you're trying to get laid, or something."

He gives me a knowing look and lays the rose on the breakfast tray. "You know, it took me three tries to get the hollandaise right. I had no idea eggs and butter could be so finicky when you mix them together. It's like they have some kind of feud going on."

He's striving for lightness, but he can't fool me. "Michael..."

"It's okay," he says briskly. "I'm okay. There's no tomorrow, remember? Just today."

I nod. Those magical words only sound sad right now.

He clears his throat. "Anyway. What time's your flight?"

I look away. I don't tell him I haven't actually booked anything, just have the option to. "Eight p.m."

"Okay." He lets go of a long breath. "Plenty of time. Eat up, and then I'm taking you somewhere."

Disappointment washes through me. "Taking me somewhere? But...wouldn't you like to do something else first?"

"What, were you expecting me to pounce on you the second you woke up?"

"I wouldn't say *expecting* it." I lick my lips. "More like desperately, shamelessly begging for it, inside my head."

"Really," he says, not a question.

"Really."

He stands there long enough that the air snaps and sizzles. The bulge of his boxer briefs grows decidedly bulgier, but instead of tackling me the way I long for, he only adjusts himself and backs up a step. "Don't ruin this. I have it all planned, and it's supposed to be memorable. Because if there's one thing I've learned from romantic comedies—and I think there might actually be only one—it's that."

I zero in on his impressive downstairs showing. "There's nothing in this room right now that isn't extremely memorable."

"You know, I'm starting to feel like you just want me for my body."

"That's a distinct possibility," I say.

His tongue sweeps out over his lower lip. I can see his mental scales tipping. I imagine the breakfast tray crashing to the floor, him on top of me, thrusting and claiming, each honed muscle sharp and perfect as he buries his body in mine.

Even in the feverish realm of imagination, it's almost too much. I have to press my thighs together in order to quiet the fluttering ache there.

Michael shakes himself, breaking the moment. "I have a *plan*, you minx. And it starts with breakfast. Don't mess it up."

I pout, but I have to admit the eggs look incredible. Hollandaise drenches half the plate, rousing an entirely different kind of hunger. "Fine. Food first. Then this secret place. Where you intend to...?"

"Tell you something." His voice drops. "About me. I have to get something straight before we go any further."

"Wait...what?" I frown. "That sounds ominous."

His smile looks watered-down. "I hope not."

"Okaaay." I draw the word out. "But it kind of makes it

sound like you've been keeping some giant secret this whole time."

Secret. Even the word tastes strange.

"No, not a secret. Consider this more of a full-disclosure, informed-consent kind of deal."

I climb out of bed, suddenly needing the reassurance of his touch more than anything else. Halfway to him, a thought occurs, and I freeze. "Is this about you having some kind of incurable STD?"

His lips twitch. "No. And it's really not all that earth-shattering. I promise. So just…enjoy your breakfast. I have a quick errand to run, and when I get back, I'll take you someplace special. And we'll talk. Then, if you decide you still want that goodbye gift we agreed on…" His perpetual grin struggles to the surface, and he almost seems like himself again, his familiar confidence burning off the tension the same way Seagrove's sun dissolves the ocean haze on summer mornings.

I go up on tiptoes to kiss him. The familiarity of his lips against mine convinces me that whatever he has to say, it won't change anything. "Then? Then what?"

His aged-bourbon voice turns to smoke and ash. "Then I'm going to fuck you like you've never been fucked before."

I succumb to a whole-body shiver, and when he smiles again, I smile back. Neither of us mentions what will happen afterward.

That can wait, I decide. Because right now, I want to be in this moment, here, with him, and nowhere else.

"Hurry back," I say.

AFTER

On my first morning at the cabin, my head is a mess.

I try to escape the chaos by wandering into the living room, but it doesn't look the way I remember. The knickknacks on the mantel have vanished, along with the bug-eyed owl clock on the wall. The wicker daybed and split-log table now sit on a perfect perpendicular to the ashless fireplace, and the knotty-pine-paneled walls gleam, no doubt recently polished to showcase the place for buyers.

The unfamiliar order makes me wish for the cozy, controlled mess of my childhood. That, at least, might have soothed this chaos inside my head, in which glossy magazine clippings fall and fall, never finding the floor. In which a stapled stack of printer paper flutters open to an inky signature that cracks my life in two. In which thoughtless ex-brothers-in-law send emails to—

My hand shoots out. Someone has folded the blanket over the daybed with military precision, and I yank it off. From there, I march into the kitchen, pull the silverware drawer halfway out, then crumple a dishtowel beside the sink. I retrieve my luggage from the car, splay my suitcase open near my bed, and leave the rumpled sheets untouched.

The acts of rebellion soothe me. Or delude me into feeling like I have some say in the fifty-car-pileup that is my life.

Either way, by the time I finish, my mind has quieted enough that I get through my morning ablutions and sling on my laptop bag. I have an article due for work, and I'll need to stock the cabin's cupboards for my four-day stay.

In the car, dirt road rushes past, then asphalt. Twenty minutes later, I park in an angled spot along Millbrook's Main Street outside Grounds for Dismissal Coffee. Pedestrians amble past. I watch them through the windshield, wondering how many have had their lives shattered at some point.

How did they manage to move forward? By running from their pain? Trying to forget it?

Starting over?

Why the hell isn't there an instruction manual for this?

Inside the coffee shop, I nestle into a plush armchair. My hazelnut latte sweetens my tongue as I autopilot through an article about continuous-delivery insulin pumps. The words fail to excite me—they're as dry and unappetizing as uncooked pasta—but the work gives me structure, so I keep slogging through, even though Michael's substantial life insurance payout means I could probably retire tomorrow.

I finally send off the article, then knock back the rest of my drink. Caffeine zings in my blood, prompting me to open my email's trash folder. A blank screen stares back. There's no recover button, no way to undo yesterday's impulsiveness. Unless...

An idea germinates. I nurture it, sit with it until I'm sure.

I pull out my phone and hunt through my contacts. Kate will have her kids up by now, so her tech-wizard husband—who just happens to work for the same mega-conglomerate that owns my email service—will be safely sequestered in his office.

Tanner answers on the first ring. "Uh...hi? Mina? Is that actually you?"

"Yep. Hi, Tanner. How's it going?"

He pauses. "Did you butt-dial me?"

I wince. We haven't spoken in months, and I'm aware of how classless it is to break radio silence in order to ask for a favor, but I'm not exactly flush with options. "No, I called you on purpose. And I'll apologize in advance, because I know I'm a jerk for asking, but I was hoping you could help me out. Could you maybe recover an email for me? I emptied my trash folder, but I needed something in there."

Silence. I brace, wondering if he'll hang up. I wouldn't blame him.

Except when he answers, interest warms his words. "It's possible," he says slowly. "How old was the email?"

My grip on the phone relaxes. Of course. This is the sort of thing Tanner thrives on. He likes puzzles. Challenges. For him, hunting down lost data probably equates to a spa day.

"Months," I say. "I'm not sure of the exact date, but it was from Grayson Drake."

Tanner doesn't seem to notice that I've named a minor celebrity. "Sure, sure. Do you know his email address?"

I bite my cheek. "I don't, sorry."

"That's okay, I can try with a name." He launches into a breezy explanation about server caches and backups that I understand roughly five percent of. Keys clack away in the background.

When his monologue ends, I say, "Sounds great. How long will that take?"

"A few days, probably. I might have to turn over a few stones, but I'll call you when I have something."

"Thanks, Tanner. I appreciate this more than I can say. At the very least, I owe you a bottle of something expensive. What's your favorite?"

He laughs softly. "Whatever Kate's in the mood for."

I smile. He might be oblivious sometimes, but he really does love my best friend.

After hanging up, I contemplate a second latte, but decide against it and instead skim the unread remainder of my email. After all, Kate had a point. I can only put off real life for so long.

Halfway through, the surrounding clink of silverware fades. Apparently, I've wasted my favor with Tanner, because Grayson sent me a second email, at least a month after the first. His name burns black on my screen, paired with another single-word subject line: "Appeal."

My pulse gathers speed, a boulder careening downhill.

Dear Mina,

First off, I don't blame you for not responding. After some reflection, I've realized how selfish it was for me to message you out of the blue asking something of you.

I know I have no right. None at all.

I've tried to imagine how Michael's death must have affected you. Obviously, he and I grew apart a long time ago, but I've still mourned him, and at times it's felt like an endless pouring out of the spirit that leaves me empty. I suspect that, for you, that's amplified by an order of magnitude, since you were married to him. In essence, I'm sorry I made demands of you when you're probably already overburdened.

Too bad no one's invented that "unsend" button yet.

If they had, I would've used it. But since we're still waiting on that, I'll just come out with this directly, instead of making vague, inconsiderate requests: I need to know you're okay. If nothing else, you're my brother's widow, and that means something to me, regardless of the issues Michael and I had.

I'll do my best to make a meeting worth your while. If you need something to cry on, I have not one, but two (!) available shoulders. Or, if you'd rather rage at the injustice of Michael's death, I'm not at all intimidated by expletives—shouted, snarled, or otherwise. As a last option, if you'd prefer to toss a cup of coffee in my face as retribution for my first message, not to mention everything else, I'll buy.

Pick one, or, if you're feeling really daring, all three.

Let me know.

Grayson

I read it three times.

Compared to the first, this message seems written by a different person. One who's clearly nothing like my husband, because he's done the exact opposite of urge me to go running. He's invited me to *feel*. To explode my land mine on purpose.

Moreover, he's owned up to the damage he did. To Michael. To *us*.

I fire out a response. I don't censor myself, the way I did with my husband those last few years. I just write what I feel and don't worry about how he'll take it.

Grayson,

You're right. Your first email did piss me off, though I'll admit that probably had more to do with me than you. Your second... not so much. But as tempting as I find the idea of dousing you with hot beverages (the important question being, of course, can I *actually* bear to waste a perfectly good hazelnut latte), I don't think I'm ready to meet someone who shares Michael's face just yet. Seeing you in National Geographic was weird enough (what a way to find out your husband has an identical twin!), so I can only imagine the effect face-to-face.

That said, we probably should talk. I'm at my family's cabin right now, where the cell service is spotty, so you're welcome to call the land line. (Bet you didn't even know those existed anymore.)

Keep the coffee offer on standby, though. Maybe the one with the expletives, too.

Mina

I add the cabin's number, then read what I've written. I almost sense a real live person behind the words, one with a heart that beats and everything. The woman I used to be peeks through, like a pinpoint of light shining through a tattered curtain.

I hit Send and bang my laptop closed.

Back in the Porsche, I navigate to the market on the outskirts of Millbrook. Town only consists of three stoplights, so the drive doesn't take long. In the parking lot, Michael's car attracts a few appreciative looks, and I return multiple friendly waves before rushing through my grocery shopping.

I tell myself I'm only in a hurry so I can go seek solace in the forest. But beneath the daydreams of towering trees and whispering wind, something else simmers, as well.

I don't examine it too closely. I'm not sure I actually want to know what it is, even as I speed through the checkout line and urge the Porsche ever faster on the drive back. The whole time, a hive's worth of bees buzzes in my stomach.

At the cabin, I'm only just slipping the key into the lock when inside, the landline rings.

BEFORE

Michael's "quick errand" lasts a long time.

In his absence, I savor my homemade breakfast, then shower. When I emerge steamy and dripping to call his name, only my own echo answers.

With a shrug, I blow-dry my hair and do my makeup, adding extra liner around my eyes to make the blue pop. I choose my sexiest underwear—a matching bra and thong in scalloped white lace—then a bright yellow T-shirt and cutoff jean shorts. This late in the game, I don't feel the need to impress Michael *that* much.

When another half hour passes, I don't worry. I find myself, as usual, in front of the tornado photograph. It enthralls me, making me wonder what kind of person can create an image this powerful. My mind conjures a man with emerald eyes, his brown hair flattened against his forehead by the encroaching storm.

What was Grayson thinking about, in that remote Kansas field? Did he read something profound into nature's destruction, like Michael did with the stars at the observatory that night? Or did the tornado simply remind him of his pain? Of Lily's loss?

When I finally tear myself away, the microwave clock reads 10:30. Two hours have passed. Frowning, I carry my cell phone to the windows, where I stare at the mist hanging over the ocean and tap Michael's name.

The call goes straight to voicemail, as if his phone isn't even powered on.

My heart shivers. For the first time, I wonder if something's wrong. Then, when two more hours crawl by and Michael still doesn't return, I *know* something's wrong.

Outside, dark clouds spit water that dribbles down the windowpanes. Inside, I pace. I call Michael a dozen more times, always with the same result.

Doubts invade my mind like thorny vines. I envision the man I love lying bloodied and broken, the victim of some senseless act of violence. I imagine the Audi careening off a bridge and dragging him into the black-water depths of the bay. I sense my entire world ending without my permission, and the horror of it nearly chokes me.

If only I'd told him I wanted to stay. If only I'd decided not to get on that stupid airplane, Michael wouldn't have gone wherever he went.

I will myself not to vomit. I clutch my phone until the casing creaks, begging the screen to light up with a call, anything.

When it finally dings with an incoming text, my knees buckle. But then I see Kate's name and fight to stay upright.

How're things in Seattle? I miss you. The new job's all right, but it would be a ton more fun if you were here to bitch to about the parts that suck. Anyway, I hope you're having a blast at Patrick's, and that you've got enough for that ticket by now.

The words blur. I realize that, throughout my month-long

delirium, I haven't thought about my best friend but a handful of times. In a haze, I type, I'm not actually at Patrick's. I moved in with Michael. I'm sorry, I completely forgot to tell you.

When my phone pings—once, twice, many more times—I set it aside and squint through the veil of rain in hopes of catching Michael passing along the waterfront. I would go out and search for him, except I have no idea where he went.

Acid coats my throat. The minutes skulk past, each one like the turn of a screw in one of those medieval torture devices that splinters people's bones in the slowest and most horrific way possible.

I wander through every room. I fruitlessly call Michael's phone. I cancel my held ticket to Athens, but even that fails to ease the thousand-pound weight in my chest.

At 5:00 p.m., I finally realize that, if and when he does return, I'm dressed completely inappropriately for the dreariness outside. For some reason, that seems important.

I shuffle into the bedroom and strip to my bra and thong. I stare unseeing at the paltry collection of clothes in the drawer Michael cleared out for me. Then I wonder what I'm doing, why I came in here. I can't remember.

The front door opens and closes.

All the blood in my body cascades inward. I race out to the main room, not caring that I'm in lingerie. Michael stands by the front door, his shirt clinging to his chest. Water plasters his hair to his face.

My head seems to detach from my body and float upward. He's safe. Soaked to the skin and jacketless, maybe, but *whole*.

"Um…" He studies my state of undress with widened eyes. "Hi."

I careen across the room and launch myself at him, clamping my legs around his waist and burying my face in his neck. "Hey."

He stiffens, enough to tell me that whatever happened today

was not pleasant, and I hug him tighter, my relief powerful enough to overcome his rigidity. To overcome anything.

"Holy shit, am I glad to see you." My lips press against his rain-soaked skin. "I was so terrified something had happened. There wasn't a single thing I wanted more than to see you walk through that door."

The second I say it, I realize Greece can wait. For now, maybe for always. I don't care, as long as I have him.

I pull back, cupping his face. He gazes up with rounded eyes, like he didn't expect me to go halfway out of my head with worry. He unbends some, though. His arms come up, his artist's fingers cupping my backside.

"I don't think anyone's ever been so happy to see me." He sounds surprised. Awed, even.

"Happy doesn't even cover it. I'm elated. Ecstatic. Euphoric. Probably a whole bunch of other e-words I can't think of right now, too."

"I'm so sorry, but—"

I push a finger against his lips. "I don't care. Explain later. Right now, I just want you to take my clothes off. Correction. I *need* you to take my clothes off."

His gaze drifts over the lacy scraps adorning my body. "You realize you're not actually wearing any?"

"Well, not technically. And I know you wanted the first time to be special, but I swear to god, if you don't pin me to something in the next five minutes, I'm going to lose my mind."

He hesitates. I wonder what on earth went so terrifically wrong today, but right now, I need to join with him, to wash away this frantic afternoon with the purity of his magic. I need to feel him, solid and alive, here in my arms.

"Please," I say. "I need you."

Reluctance still crowds his eyes, so I lower my lips to his, channeling all my love and longing into a kiss.

It starts slow, a tentative sampling that takes surprisingly long to deepen. I slip my tongue into his mouth, coaxing, teasing.

Begging.

Pleading.

Finally, something awakens inside him. His fingers clench, pressing into my bare ass. His tongue snakes into my mouth—sampling at first, then devouring.

There, I think. *There you are, my love.*

When I squeeze my legs tighter around him, his reticence melts away. I feel the moment our unification becomes inevitable. We come spiraling together, two stars that have circled for weeks, finally locking into orbit.

Michael groans as I feast on his mouth. He staggers over to the island and scatters the pile of mail he never gets to, then lays me on the granite and yanks me to the edge. The stone sucks enough warmth from my bare back to make me gasp, but somehow that only heightens the intensity rocketing toward my core.

Our movements turn frantic, electrified. We wrench at each other's clothes. His sopping shirt slaps onto the concrete, followed by his jeans and boxers, which he shucks in one hurried motion. My bra and thong quickly follow.

Bare and wet and splayed before him, I raise my head. My vision goes soft around the edges. I can't see anything but him, only him, naked and glorious and so damn beautiful that my heart takes a moment to smash to pieces inside my chest.

His sea-crystal eyes flush as he bends to explore me with his tongue. Rainwater drips from his hair, and I halfway expect the hiss of steam whenever the droplets hit my skin.

I moan. I melt. I burn for him, and when he finally, finally, *finally* closes his eyes and pushes inside me, it's like nothing I've ever felt. I've been starving for a month, and now he's filling me up, only he's somehow ending a thirst of years instead of weeks.

I buck my hips, abandoning myself to the oblivion of sensation. His hands clamp around my waist. He drives into me over and over until bright black heat blossoms behind my eyes and we both spangle apart into wondrous, glittering dust.

I... He...

Just...

Wow.

When I finally manage to remember what planet I'm on, I pry my eyelids open—first one, then the other. Michael lies half-collapsed on top of me. He raises his head, his expression incredulous.

"That was... I'm..." He straightens, clearly dazed. "Holy god. Who *are* you?"

I giggle. The sound comes out sticky and languid, just like the rest of me. "Mina. Your minx."

"Mina the minx." He speaks my name like he's tasting it. "I've never... Well, whatever that was, I've never done it before. Not like that."

My answering smile slips and slides across my face, too inebriated to truly catch hold, like I'm made of nothing but gelatin and satiation. No bones left in this body.

"We should probably talk," he says, "but the truth is, I really just want to do that again."

I raise an eyebrow. "What, right now?"

"Right now."

That rouses me. I trail a finger down his bare chest, and this time, that's all it takes.

In another moment, he's scooping me up and carrying me to the bedroom.

BEFORE

We have sex three more times.

It's different than I imagined. I expected tenderness. Long, searching looks and Michael whispering into my ear. I expected slow, sliding lovemaking that intensifies over hours.

But when he and I collide, it's primal. Raw. All his contrasts—the fierce gentleness, the soft hands and hard kisses—disappear, giving way to some driving force neither of us can fight. We crash together, burn each other up, then come apart and do it all over again.

The building doesn't quite shake to pieces, but almost, and Michael makes good on his promise. He fucks me like I've never been fucked before, until my neck can no longer hold up my head and I transform into a satisfied puddle on the mattress.

In the middle of the night, we finally pause long enough for me to ask, "What happened today?"

Michael lies with his head propped against the black leather headboard, his face luminous in the city light. One hand splays against his chest while the white top sheet tangles around his waist. He's silent for so long that I roll onto my side and prop my cheek on one hand, though that simple act saps the last of my reserves.

"Michael?"

He seems to weigh something. "Yeah," he says softly. "That's me."

"What happened today? When you disappeared?"

His jaw works as he grapples with some private decision.

Seconds tick by, and my stomach tightens. Whatever it is, I'm clearly not going to like it. I'm busy gearing up for something truly horrific when he says, "I got arrested."

I pause. "You...*what?*"

"Yeah. I spent the day in jail. I'm sorry. I didn't mean to scare you."

Confusion drags my lips downward. "But...arrested? For what?"

"Sheer stupidity, mostly." He sighs. "I was on the sidewalk this morning when some guy started yelling at this woman for taking his parking space. I mean, genuinely screaming at her. Got out of his car and everything. She was terrified, so I cut in, and before I knew it, he and I were swinging at each other. Someone called the cops, but the other guy insisted I'd started it, so we both got hauled off to jail. Then, when I got out, I didn't get my things back like I was supposed to. They kept my phone, my keys, my jacket, everything. I had to walk all the way here in the rain."

I gather enough energy to sit up. Michael's gaze flickers to my bare breasts, but I haul the sheet up, intent on clearing the air before we inevitably succumb to round five.

"Your necklace." I point to his bare chest. I should've noticed before, but I was...distracted. "It's gone."

He misses a beat, then glances down. "Oh. Yeah. They took it when they processed me. And I was so desperate to get home that I didn't argue when they didn't give it back."

For some reason, that infuriates me more than my own mental anguish. I loved the way that twisted-silver chain accentuated the angles of his chest. "That's bullshit. You should go down there first thing in the morning and—"

"It's fine," he says. "I'd rather just replace everything than tempt fate."

I blow out a breath. "Okay. Well, I guess you have a point."

He gives me a wan smile. And then I remember.

"What was your big secret, then?"

His smile falters. "My secret?"

"Yeah. The thing you wanted to tell me before we had sex."

Another silence unfurls as he searches my face.

My heart lurches. Maybe he hasn't been entirely up front with me, but he's never looked...*cagey* like this. Never purposely lied. But I have the unsettling sense that he wants to right now. That he's actively considering it.

I poke his muscled side. "You know you can tell me anything, right?"

He breaks from my gaze to look out the windows. "Yeah. It's just...humiliating. Like most secrets."

"Humiliating? Come on. You're talking to the same girl who said you could go broke, gain a hundred pounds, and lose your home, and she'd love you just the same."

He refocuses on me with intensity, as if seeing me anew. "That's quite a statement."

"It is," I murmur, holding his eyes. "And I meant it. I still do."

He chews on his hesitation a moment longer. Finally, he clears his throat. "Okay then, here goes. I'm an alcoholic. There. Now you know."

"Wait, what? No, you're not." The wheels in my mind grind. To be fair, Michael does like his Scotch and his wine. But I've only seen him tipsy enough to find everything hilarious, not to regret anything the next day. "You never have more than a couple drinks."

He makes a throaty sound. "When I say 'alcoholic,' I don't necessarily mean I drink too much. I mean I *want* to. I crave it. All the time."

"Oh. Okay." I pretend to understand, though in reality, I feel adrift. The sex we just had transformed me, but now this whole conversation feels off-kilter, as if something has knocked him for a loop. Something more than just a day spent in jail.

But I want to support him. And I'm burning with my own big decision. Maybe *that* will wield enough power to get us back on track. "We'll pour all our alcohol down the drain, then. I won't drink anymore, either, if that'll help. Booze isn't nearly as important to me as you are. Nothing is. Not even Greece."

He stills, as if already knowing what I'll say next.

"I finally decided, while you were gone." I swallow. "I'm not going. I'd rather stay with you. For today. And the today after that. And the today after that, too."

The darkness obscures his expression. "But…"

When he doesn't continue, I breathe, "What?"

"I thought this was it," he says. "I know you missed your flight today, but I figured we'd get you to the airport tomorrow."

A shiver rips through me. I roll atop him in a straddle, taking his face in my hands. "Is that what you want?" My shadow looms across him, hiding his face.

"I…"

I hold my breath for what feels like an eternity. The same helpless finality that paralyzed me earlier, when his phone wouldn't connect, comes rushing back.

"I *should*," he says.

"You shouldn't." My voice hitches. "I mean, I get that you think us being together will stop me from living. But it won't. Because this, right here, with you—it's the most alive I've ever been. There might've been a hole in me when we met, but you've filled it. And now that I know about this alcohol thing,

I can do the same for you. Compared to that, Greece means nothing. I'd rather be here. With you. *For* you."

His fingers come up to knead my bare thighs. I fold forward onto his chest, seeking the reassurance of his heartbeat.

"You'd do that?" he murmurs. "Just...change your plans? After I told you I have an addiction?"

"Of course." In an attempt to cross the unfamiliar distance, I invoke the same words he used at the observatory. "I'm desperately in love with you, after all. Addiction or no."

His chest rises and falls beneath my cheek. *God, please say something.*

When he doesn't, I rush to fill the quiet. "You've taken better care of me this past month than anyone else ever has. I want to stay, not just as your girlfriend, but as an accountability partner."

"Like an angel sitting on my shoulder?" he muses.

"Yes. Exactly. An angel." My fingertips graze his side through the sheet. "Who also happens to love having mind-blowing sex with you."

He's thinking. I can almost hear the tick of calculation echoing in his rib cage.

"Well, when you put it like that," he finally says, "it would probably be stupid of me to say no."

Tension bleeds out of me. I squeeze him tight. "Incredibly."

His arms snake around me, subduing my doubts. I *know* he wants me here; I felt it that night on the couch. He might have forced himself to say otherwise, but the intensity of his longing nearly overpowered me then.

Now guilt must plague him, hence his reserve. But maybe framing it this way will make it easier for him. I'm not staying because he's asked me to. It's because I love him, because we need each other. Because what we have far outweighs some harebrained jaunt across the sea.

"That's incredibly generous of you," he says.

I tilt my head up. The planes of his face gleam in the sodium

light, although the illumination doesn't brighten his eyes the
way it usually does.

"I try." I press a kiss to the underside of his jaw. My desire
for more sex has fled. I just want to put this bizarre day behind
us, wake up tomorrow, and go back to normal. I want Michael
to turn those open-ocean eyes on me again, the ones so clear
and deep I can see all the way to the bottom.

I want the shadows in his face to go away and never return.

He seems to sense as much, because he eases me off and pillows my head on his chest. His fingers run along the curve of
my shoulder in the silent dark. As his touch grows sluggish, I
catch hold of a nagging whisper in the back of my mind.

"Don't you get a phone call?"

He jerks, his chest muscles jumping beneath my cheek, telling me he was almost asleep. "What?"

"Don't they let you make a phone call, from jail? Why didn't
you call me?"

His fingers tighten around my shoulder. "I didn't know your
number by heart. The only one I could remember was…my
brother's."

"Oh. So… *Oh.*" Lightning flashes inside my head. Michael
talked to his brother. The one who still blames him for Lily's
death.

God, no wonder he's acting so strangely—all this remote-
ness is his reaction to Grayson, not me. "Did he have to come
bail you out?"

He stiffens. "Yeah."

"You saw him, then? In person?"

"Yeah."

All at once, I forgive him everything. I sling one arm around
his taut waist and tuck myself close. Once Michael recovers from
the shock of seeing the sibling who despises him, everything
will be fine. "I'm sorry. That must've been hard."

"It was. But then I came home, and you were waiting, and…I

think maybe this is exactly what I need. That you staying will make the difference for me."

The vulnerability underpinning those words breathes new life into me. "It will," I whisper. "And for me, too."

Just before I drift off, he says, "I haven't been able to talk to anyone about this in so long. I figured I never would."

I'm too far gone to ask what he means.

In the morning, Michael outsleeps me for the very first time—evidence of just how much yesterday cost him.

It feels strange, waking up beside him. I didn't even realize how much I'd come to relish the steaming coffee on the nightstand until it wasn't there.

But Michael deserves a reset, so I survey his peaceful face and the arm flung up beside his head—does he always sleep like that?—then decide to tend to him the way he so unfailingly tends to me.

I sneak into the kitchen and load the French press. While the coffee brews, I rifle through the cupboards in search of alcohol to pour out. Nothing. A quick peek into the recycling bin reveals three already-empty bottles.

I give them a poke. Huh. Michael must have dumped them yesterday, before he went out.

With a shrug, I locate his latest book and carry it to the bedroom along with his mug. It's Wednesday, and while he took a vacation day yesterday, he's scheduled to go back to work this morning. Still, he can probably squeeze in his fifty pages before leaving.

When I set his dual sustenance on the nightstand, he cracks open an eye. I pause, searching for...I don't know, exactly. Whatever went missing yesterday.

He smiles. Not with his usual wattage, but close. "Hey."

"Hey."

"If it isn't my live-in guardian angel," he says. "Come here."

The moment we touch, a spark flares and burns its way down to my center. Within minutes, we're locked together, sweating, writhing, colliding. Sounds emerge from my mouth I've never made before. The rest of the world falls away.

There's Michael, and there's me, and then, with him buried in me, there isn't even that anymore, just us together, a single entity that blazes with such ferocity that all else ceases to exist.

Afterward, Michael sits up and rolls his shoulders, his golden hair all askew. He looks sated, like a man made new by the act of losing himself. "I think I'll work from home today."

"Really? I didn't know you could do that."

"Not usually. But they won't mind if it's just this once." He reaches for his coffee, then grimaces on the first sip. He tries to mask the reaction, but I'm too focused on him to miss it.

"What?" I say from my tangled nest of sheets. "Don't you like it with sugar?"

"Not this much. But it's okay, I'll make another one. And can I use your phone? I'll replace mine this afternoon, but I need to let work know I won't be in."

I unlock my cell and hand it over before he totes my too-sweet offering to the kitchen. I overhear a brief conversation explaining he'll be available by email today. He putters around for a bit, then he's back, tossing my phone onto the mattress and sipping from a fresh mug.

He's stark naked, but I don't look down. I search his face, soaking in every flicker of those dark gold eyelashes.

My stomach sinks. Yesterday's distance is diminished, but still there. Some part of him has pulled back just enough to brush with outstretched fingertips, but not fold within my grasp.

Jesus, I think, catching myself. How unforgivably selfish to dwell on myself when this must be a thousand times harder for him. A woman once *died* because of him, and his relationship with his brother has fallen apart because of it. Now the reminder has left fresh, shadowed footprints all over him. Not to mention that this constitutes his first day of sobriety.

The least I can do is help him deal.

I gesture to his book. "Do you want to do your reading now?"

He glances at the nightstand, unmoved. "No. I'd much rather spend the day in bed. With you."

"Really?" That coaxes a smile from me. "Breaking the military routine? I didn't think I'd ever see the day."

He takes a long draft of coffee. "I happen to have a very good reason. And she's lying in my bed, looking incredibly sultry right now."

That revives my spirits, and I lift the sheet in invitation. He abandons his mug and crawls in, and at the moment of joining, I breathe a sigh, because by then, no space exists between us at all.

In the afternoon, someone knocks on our door.

We're on the couch, naked, having never actually made it into clothes at all, when Michael jerks up from kissing my belly button.

The knock comes again. "Who's that?" I say.

"I don't know." His eyebrows snap low over his eyes. "I'll go check. You stay here."

I frown. I can't imagine who would show up unannounced on a Wednesday afternoon, but I obediently hunker into the couch, hiding my nudity from whoever's in the hallway.

Michael grabs a throw pillow to shield himself with and goes to the door.

"Hey, Mr. Drake." I recognize the baritone boom of our downstairs doorman, the one who looks like a UFC champion but apparently obsesses over chess in his spare time. "Oh. Um...sorry. Should I...come back?"

"Hey, Juan." Michael sounds relieved. "No, it's fine. What can I do for you?"

"Sorry to disturb you, but..." Feet shuffle. "Your brother's in the lobby. I knew you were already up here, so I stopped him from getting into the elevator, but he's getting loud down there. Says he won't leave until he sees you. The manager wants to call the police, but I figured you should have the chance to deal with it first, if you want to."

A curse slips past Michael's lips. "Yeah. Give me a minute to get dressed, will you?"

Juan rumbles an affirmative. Michael closes the door and tosses the pillow aside. He strides to the bedroom, his bare soles slapping against the concrete.

I get up and follow.

By the dresser, he stabs one leg into a pair of jeans, then the other. With his tousled hair and swollen lips, he's clearly spent the day in the throes of passion, but he doesn't bother to hide it. "God, the last thing I need is for him to make a scene."

"What does he want?"

Michael drags a hand through his tangled hair and sighs. "It's... He sort of...asked me for a favor, yesterday."

I frown. "Favor? What favor?"

"It doesn't matter," he says. "It's not something I can do."

Something to do with Lily, I suspect, based on his evasiveness. "Would it help if I went down with you? For moral support?"

He shoots me a startled look while buttoning his jeans. "No. I don't want you getting dragged into my family drama."

"It's not dragging if I'm volunteering."

He shakes his head, then pulls on a T-shirt and angles past me. "No. Stay here. I'll only be a minute."

His parting words come so close to matching yesterday's that my heartbeat thickens, but I assure myself he won't disappear this time. While I wait, I don jeans and a vibrant yellow-and-purple top, then take up a post at the kitchen island.

Twenty minutes later, the condo door opens again.

I cry out. "Oh my god, what happened? Are you okay?"

Michael stalks in. One eye is swollen shut, his bottom lip split and bleeding. Red splatter-marks stain his white T-shirt. He prowls past me, clearly on some kind of mission.

It takes me a moment to realize he's aiming for the tornado picture.

He lifts the photograph off the wall, his movements so measured that I can only compare to that day outside Patrick's house. Then, he was angry. Gloriously so. Now, he's something worse. Eerily, perilously calm, so much so that I shiver.

"What're you doing?"

"Taking this down," he says, his voice perfectly even. "And throwing it away."

I press a hand to my chest. Something inside fractures at seeing him toss out the photograph I've spent the past month bonding with. "But *why*?"

Michael swings to look at me. A savage fire burns behind his eyes, as if his calm is just a facade. "Because Grayson took this, and he just punched me in the face. Repeatedly. At which point I told him I don't want to see him again. I don't want to see this picture, either. It was idiotic of me to put it up in the first place. I don't know what I was thinking."

I stare open-mouthed as the door clicks shut behind him. I swear I can feel the photograph careening down the trash chute at the end of the hall.

When Michael returns, he comes close. Air saws in and out of him, like he ran up to the nineteenth floor instead of taking the elevator. Except he stands so terribly, horribly still.

I lay a hand against his bloodied shirtfront, reassuring myself that he's in one piece, at least. "Let's get you cleaned up. In the shower?"

My offer takes the edge off the blaze in his eyes. Or eye, singular. One's swollen to a slit. "Fine."

I lead him to the bathroom. In the glass-walled shower, I sit him on the tiled bench and gingerly wipe away blood with a washcloth. He gazes up as the hot water works its way into him.

"What happened down there?" I say.

He snorts. "He *hit* me."

"Right, but why?"

His mouth twists. "You know, I actually thought he and I were making progress. But in the end, it's always the same story. Everything's always all about him. What I need is never actually going to matter to him."

I frown. "So he still hates you? Wishes you were dead?"

His uninjured eye narrows. "Is that what you think?"

"Well, yeah. That's what you told me. Last month, on the drive up from Seagrove. Remember?"

He doesn't answer, just studies me while I dab at his wounds. Not in that open, soul-deep way, but like he's searching for something specific.

My voice drops. "I just don't get it. Why would he punch you after bailing you out of jail? Is he still mad about what you did to Lily?"

It's the wrong thing to say. Despite the billowing steam, all the color drains from Michael's cheeks. He stares, stricken, as if I've just slapped him across the face.

My insides quiver. "Oh, god, that didn't come out right. I didn't mean to make it sound like you killed her."

I wince. I should just slap *myself* across the face, at this point. "You know what? That didn't come out right, either. I'm just going to shut up now."

Michael doesn't move. The thundering water wreathes us in fog, and I stand there, sickened by the sense that I've just broken him.

It certainly *looks* like I have. In the seawater depths of his eyes, a jagged crevasse yawns, an empty hurt so much greater than anything I suspected he had inside of him.

Which begs the question of how he could possibly have been

so openhearted with me all this time. Because now, peering down, I understand that some part of him is shattered. Smashed to bits.

Has Grayson inflicted all that damage since yesterday? Or did I simply miss it?

"Fuck your brother," I say, incapable of thinking of anything else.

A shutter descends, whisking Michael's pain from view. The reaction unsettles me, but he finally unfreezes. With infinite care, he sets the washcloth aside, then clasps my hands. Water tries to slip between our fingers, but I hang on.

"Promise me something." He sounds hoarser than usual, as if he's screamed himself raw, except he hasn't once raised his voice.

"Anything," I whisper, aghast at myself.

"Don't mention Grayson ever again. Or...her." Raw pain flashes across his features before he stows it away again. "Please. I just want to forget them both."

I nod, mute.

Michael stands up, then spins me around and pins my hands to the glass. He nips at the back of my neck, suckles on my earlobe, runs his fingers down my sides and up around the curves of my breasts.

This time, he's gentle enough that each touch feels like forgiveness. I welcome the absolution. Eventually, he nudges my legs apart, then clutches me close and eases into me, bringing our bodies flush. Every tender slide of flesh smooths the serrated silence, reshaping it into a blissful, coiling roar that heats me from the inside.

My eyes flutter shut. There's him. Wet, slippery heat. Nothing else matters.

His arms tighten around me as we both go over the edge.

Afterward, he dresses and leaves to buy a new phone. He makes me promise not to open the door, and while he doesn't say why, I know exactly who he's trying to protect me from.

In his absence, I grow restless, plagued by the sense that something fundamental has changed and that a man I've never met is responsible.

Eventually, I can stand the silence no longer. I take the elevator down to the basement, where I stand by the dumpster and glare at the wreckage of the tornado picture. It lies on a mountain of refuse, its glass shattered, its frame splintered, and yet the thing still makes a valiant attempt to hypnotize me.

Fuck you, Grayson Drake, I mentally shout. *You had no right.*

I repeat the words until fury replaces temptation, until the tornado and the field turn my stomach.

Back upstairs, Michael returns in the early evening. He goes straight to the bedroom and changes into a pair of slacks and a dark blue button-down. "I want to take you to dinner," he says. "Something nice."

I pause. We rarely, if ever, go out. "You don't want to order in?"

"No. This has been a day from hell. All I want to do now is eat lobster by candlelight with a beautiful woman. My woman."

I squint at him. "Even though you have a black eye?"

"Mostly *because* I have a black eye," he says, matter-of-fact.

My fingers twine as I hover in the doorway. I have nothing against fancy dinners, but spending an evening separated by a gulf of linen and silverware strikes me as an unlikely way to bridge this distance. I'd rather find our way back to the evenings spent entangled on the couch with delivered Italian, when nothing could penetrate our blissful bubble. When nothing mattered but *today*.

Michael must catch my hesitation, because his expression softens. He comes and cups my face. "Look, I know everything's strange, but it won't feel this way forever. You're staying. I won't drink anymore. From now on, we're going to eat expensive food and have lots of sex and just...take care of each other, okay?"

I gaze up. Those eyes hold mine, yet despite his assurances, they're more opaque than fathomless right now. "Things will go back to the way they were?" I prompt.

"Yes. Soon."

"Okay," I breathe. "Soon."

He kisses me, with enough heat that my misgivings melt away.

I change into a clingy dress that earns a look of approval. Downstairs, in the parking garage, the Audi sits in its usual spot. Michael tells me he picked it up from an impound lot today after getting a new key made at the dealership.

On the way to the restaurant, he drives with a firm ten-and-two grip. I try for a joke, though I already suspect my efforts to lighten the mood will prove futile. "Since when do you drive like an old lady?"

"Old lady?" He gives me a skeptical look. "What do you mean?"

"You look like you're worried you'll lose control at any second."

Instead of cracking a smile, he actually ponders. "Maybe it's time I took driving more seriously. It's not like there's no risk involved. And now I have something to protect."

Something to protect. The sentiment should soothe me, but I can't help wondering how long it will take for Michael's humor to return. His open, easy confidence.

Soon, I tell myself, settling back in the seat. He said soon, and he hasn't broken a promise to me yet.

Someday soon, everything will go back to the way it was.

AFTER

The cabin's telephone shrieks, rattling the glass of the front door. I fumble with my groceries, trying to maneuver the lock, but the key sticks.

The phone rings again. *Damn it.*

I drop my bags. Glass shatters, but I don't stop to assess the damage, just wrench open the door and beeline for the ancient rotary phone by the daybed, where I yank up the receiver mid-ring. "Hello?"

A long pause. The plastic digs into my ear. "Hi, Mina? It's Grayson. Grayson Drake."

His voice rolls through me, top to bottom.

Aged bourbon.

Smoky, oak-paneled rooms.

Breathless moans in the dark.

One minute, I'm standing. The next, I'm on the floor with my knees jammed together and my sneakers splayed to either side. I have no idea how I got that way, only that a wave has knocked me off my feet.

"Mina? Are you there?"

Oh, god. I clutch the phone with damp fingers. He sounds so much like Michael that I can't breathe.

"Is it my voice?" Concern swims in his tone. "Shit. This must be weird for you. Even my mother could never tell us apart on the phone."

"I am *not* talking to my dead husband right now," I hear myself say. "I'm not. You're someone else."

"Yes." His voice tightens.

"You're Grayson."

"Uh-huh."

"The photographer. Not an architect."

"That's right." Silence filters through the line. "Shit. I knew this was a bad idea. I just... Would it be better if I hung up?"

"No," I say. Then wonder how that word jumped out of me so fast. "Don't. Please."

"Okay." He's quiet. Something rustles in the background, and I picture him on a sofa somewhere in Seattle—scarred eyebrow, secret tattoo, and all.

That helps. Scar. Tattoos. Things Michael never had.

"The last thing I want to do is make this hard for you," he says.

"My husband's dead. It's already hard for me. Talking to you isn't going to change that." I bite my lip. I'm not actually convinced that's true—it's essentially the exact opposite of what I told Kate. But at this point, I have to know what this is about. And the longer I sit here, the more the galloping in my veins slows.

"Okay," he says. "If you're sure."

I try to wait out his silence, but he doesn't add more. Whatever he wants, it doesn't seem as though he's going to come out and say it.

"To be honest," I venture, "I'm surprised you got in touch. I didn't think you knew I existed."

He draws a long, pained breath. A dull thud sounds on the

line, followed by a silence taut enough to make me fidget. Maybe he's dropped the phone.

"Grayson?"

"Yeah." He answers immediately, his tone brittle. "Sorry, I'm here. Of course I knew you existed. If anything, your email made it sound like *you* didn't know about *me*."

I frown, wondering why he sounds so resentful of that. "I mean…I didn't, not really. Not before you got famous, at least."

Another long pause. "So Michael never…talked about me? Ever?"

"To be honest? No. He really didn't."

"Jesus Christ. That motherfucker. I shouldn't be so surprised. I really shouldn't."

My lungs inflate. Him swearing helps, too. Michael rarely did. "There's no need to get angry. After…what happened, I think it was too hard for him to talk about you. Too painful."

"So you don't know a thing about me, then."

"I do," I say slowly. "Sort of. I've seen pictures in magazines. Your stuff in *National Geographic*. It's kind of hard not to. And we used to have a photo on our wall. That you took. Of a tornado."

"Yeah, I gave that to Michael one year for Christmas. I couldn't afford anything better, at the time. What happened to it?"

I wince, realizing my use of the past tense has tipped him off. "He…uh…threw it out."

"Oh." More rustling. "In a fit of rage, I'm guessing?"

"Michael didn't really do fits of rage."

"You know what I mean. His version of rage, at least? Where he got all creepily calm?"

"Well…yeah."

He gives a broken chuckle. There's a rawness to it, a vulnerability that makes him sound nothing like the Michael of recent years.

It makes my belly clench, but indignation flares the moment I recover. "What about that is funny, exactly? You must realize he only got rid of that picture because you hurt him badly enough that he had to cut any reminders of you out of his life, right?"

He pauses. "You think *I* hurt *him*?"

"I know you did," I snap. He can't be serious, can he? *Michael* was the one who so desperately wanted to make peace, up until That One Time… "You know, I was there that day, when you bashed his face in. In Seattle. After you got him out of jail."

"After I got him out of jail," he repeats flatly.

"Don't tell me you don't remember."

"Oh, I remember. I'll never forget."

"Well, you wouldn't have known it, but I was upstairs in our condo that day. Which means I got to be the one to try to put him back together again afterward."

"Oh, yeah? And how did that go?"

I hesitate at the bluntly personal question. So much for small talk. Grayson has ventured straight into territory that drives a heated flush up the back of my neck. "Not that it's any of your business, but not well. Michael was never the same after that. I don't know what the hell you did that day, but it changed him."

This time, his laugh turns bitter, the bourbon laced with arsenic. "Oh, come on. *I* didn't change him. He was only ever himself. At least hold him accountable for his own actions."

I clamber up off the floor. At least ten miles' worth of frustration is suddenly bubbling up inside me, maybe eleven. I need to run hard enough and long enough to drain myself dry.

But the moment the thought forms, I catch myself. Damn. Kate was right. I've spent so much time bottling everything up that I don't know how to tackle things head-on anymore.

Luckily, there's another option. A man on the other end of the line who deserves my anger. "Do you want to know the truth?"

"Sure. Why not? I get the sense you're going to tell me anyway."

I bristle. "Yep. And here it is. Even though we've never met and I don't know the first thing about you, I've hated you for fourteen years based on that day. Maybe you're right, and that's unfair. Maybe Michael's the only one I can blame for...well, being Michael. But I know things would've gone differently if you hadn't shown up and attacked him out of the blue. And don't even try to deny that you were the one who picked that fight. I know it was your fault."

"I don't deny it," he shoots back. "But it wasn't out of the blue. Michael deserved every bit of what I did. He deserved worse, actually. Much worse."

My words come out in a deadly whisper. "He *got* much worse, eventually. In case you've forgotten."

Grayson inhales sharply, as if realizing what he's said. "Shit. You're right. I'm sorry. But...still. That doesn't mean I wouldn't hit him all over again, if I could."

My jaw works. Briefly, I consider hanging up. I already know he'll never call me again, so what does it matter?

Something stops me, though. In some ineffable way, it's a relief to talk to someone like this, without worrying about whether my next remark will widen the distance or close it. It feels so fucking good to let my anger out. To allow some color to burst inside me.

I spit words through gritted teeth. "Who holds a grudge against a dead man?"

"I do, apparently."

"Well, you sound like an asshole."

"Probably because I am."

His ready agreement throws me.

"But for what it's worth," he continues doggedly, "Michael hurt me, too. No one else has even come close to tearing me apart the way he did. You have no idea."

That stops my tongue. He sounds so...*earnest*, as if he finds his wounds exhausting but feels compelled to acknowledge them anyway. And then I remember.

Grayson lost Lily, just like I lost Michael. Only, unlike me, he had someone to blame.

Between one moment and the next, my anger sputters out. I sink onto the daybed, shame rising hot in my chest. How could I forget that I don't have a monopoly on this experience? That I'm not the only one who's struggled to rebuild after the worst has happened?

"I'm sorry." My voice shrinks. "You're right. I forgot that you've had your world end, too."

He sighs bitterly. "Maybe you do have an idea, then. Maybe you understand better than anyone else."

I go quiet. Even now, I have no idea how Lily died or whether Grayson has reason to find fault with my husband. I don't dare ask, either.

"Jesus," I say. "I have no idea why I gave you my phone number, then got ugly within ten seconds of answering."

"I do. Because you're angry. Obviously."

Try as I might, I detect no blame in his words. "You're right. I'm pissed. Pretty much at the whole world, at this point."

"Good. You should be."

My brows furrow. "Why do you say that?"

"Because life hasn't treated you all that well. And I'm not the only Drake who's an asshole. Michael wasn't exactly the poster child for selflessness."

"Michael was wonderful," I say. "At least, he used to be, before you bashed his face in. And after that, sometimes, too. He may have gotten…closed off, but he was always generous. And never cruel. Which means if he hurt you, he didn't mean to."

Grayson barks a laugh. "Oh, no. He knew exactly what he was doing. Trust me."

I frown. That almost makes it sound like Michael killed Lily on purpose. Which doesn't make the slightest bit of sense.

"You don't think he—" I hesitate. I've spent fourteen years keeping Lily's name locked behind my lips, and don't want to free it unless Grayson does first. "—took her from you on purpose, do you?"

He remains quiet for so long that I wonder if he's hung up. But I can still hear him breathing.

I tense. I recognize that silence, the signpost marking the point at which I've pushed too far. The weight of old habit settles on my shoulders. "Never mind. You don't have to answer that."

He sighs. "I do, though. I'm going to be honest with you, Mina. I'll answer every question you ask. Even if they're fucking nuclear, like that one."

My mouth opens. No sound comes out. It's such an un-Michael-like thing to say, and hearing it in my husband's voice only confuses me.

"So." Age-old pain saturates his words. "Yes. I do think he took her away on purpose."

Now it's my turn to deliver a heavy-breathing silence. What felt like solid ground a minute ago turns wobbly and sucking, the conversation like quicksand beneath my feet. Clearly, the bad blood between them runs deeper and darker than I knew.

Because if I'm hearing correctly, Grayson thinks my husband killed his fiancée intentionally.

Which is inconceivable. Michael might have had habits I didn't know about—like following his brother's every move and daydreaming about divorcing me—but he wasn't a killer. Nothing on this earth can possibly convince me otherwise.

I glance through the open door to where my groceries lie in a heap. "This conversation has gotten way off track," I murmur. "I know you didn't call so I could rip open wounds that healed decades ago."

"They never healed. But, that aside, this is exactly why I called. So you could say whatever you need to." His tone lightens. "I *did* offer to let you throw coffee in my face, remember? This is probably as close as it gets, over the phone."

Despite myself, that tugs a smile free. "But why? Why do you care? You don't even know me."

He pauses. "I want to make sure you're okay."

"I'm nobody to you."

"That's…not true. I realize you don't know *me*, apart from the shit you've read on the internet, but I know more about you than you realize."

I blink, rapid-fire. That could only be true if… "Are you saying you and Michael kept in touch?"

Another sigh bleeds out of him. "Just because he never talked *about* me doesn't mean he didn't talk *to* me."

"You mean you two actually spoke? *After* that day in Seattle?"

"Not often. But yes."

I flinch. Yesterday, I might have questioned his truthfulness. Today…

In my mind, magazine clippings and divorce papers spew from a never-ending folder of secrets. It seems I didn't know my husband half as well as I believed. "What do you know about me, exactly?"

"That you're a writer." Grayson's throaty rumble caresses my ear. "That you dreamed of writing creatively, but ended up doing articles for some medical magazine instead. Hmm, let's see… You wanted to travel, but it caused problems with your family, and life never really gave you the chance. What else? You're a runner, you love bright colors, you have this weird obsession with kettle corn. I have to admit, I don't understand the popcorn thing at all, but hey. There're worse habits."

"Oh. Wow." I sit back. It's a superficial evaluation, yet my estranged brother-in-law seems to have taken my measure more precisely than my husband did. He tried, but as the years passed, the ways in which we differed mystified him.

"Am I being creepy?"

"A little," I admit. "But also…I sound pathetic when you describe me that way. Like someone who never followed through in life. Someone who abandoned her dreams."

His voice gentles. "I didn't mean it like that."

Maybe not, but aside from disconcerting me, his assessment makes me view myself in a different light. One I don't find at all flattering.

So I deflect. Because that's the obvious next step. "Didn't anyone ever teach you to make small talk?"

"No," he says. "I mean, if you really want, I could probably muddle through, but I don't give a shit about the weather or whatever politician's currently embarrassing himself on social media. I care about you. How you're doing. Whether you're all right."

I swirl my finger into the spirals of the phone cord like I used to when I was a kid. "You don't have to. I mean, I get that we're technically related, but—"

"We're not related," he says, his voice hard.

I frown. *Okaaaaay, then.* "I just mean you don't owe me anything. Whatever mess Michael left behind when he died isn't yours to clean up. It's mine. Granted, I've been doing a piss-poor job so far, but hopefully that's about to change."

"Oh yeah? Are you going to therapy?"

I lift my gaze to the bay windows and examine the layer of shadow at the edge of the yard. "No. I'm going into the woods."

I have no idea why I actually say that, except that the passing squall of my anger has anchored me inside my own skin somehow, and honesty seems like a natural extension of that. Like I'm a storm cloud that's spit out all its lightning and subsided to an easy rain.

It feels surprisingly good.

"Into the woods," he repeats, clearly confused. "What does that mean?"

A half chuckle slips out. "You wouldn't understand."

"Try me."

I hesitate. For one crazy, incandescent moment, I consider confessing. I could tell Grayson about Margo's death and how I found solace in the woods at fifteen, if only because he absorbed my anger without batting an eyelash.

Except he'd bat one of those long, golden lashes at this. "Maybe some other time."

"Like when?"

"I don't know. You'd probably have to catch me in the right mood. Or very drunk."

"All right. Easy enough. I'll just call you a lot, until I get lucky."

I open my mouth, but say nothing. This is…not what I expected. At all. "You don't have to. Really. I'm okay." My voice quavers on the last two words.

Thankfully, Grayson doesn't know me well enough to catch it. "I know I don't have to," he says. "I *want* to."

This time, there's a hint of…supplication in his tone. Like he's searching for something and for some reason has decided I'm where he can find it. "Look," I say. "No matter what Michael's told you, you don't know me."

He hesitates. "I want to."

Something flits around inside my chest. Something that hasn't shown its face in so long that it takes me a full ten seconds to determine its identity.

When I do, I promptly squash the feeling flat. What is happening right now? This man isn't Michael. We aren't flirting. Grayson is not—and never will be—a substitute for the person I loved down to the roots of my soul.

It's just the voice. And the bizarre way in which he's talking to me as though there's no one else in the world he'd rather be on the phone with.

"I should go," I say.

He sighs. I can practically taste the frustration in it. "Was that too much?"

"Yes. Or no. I don't know. You're just…not what I expected. I've spent all these years hating you, but the person I was mad at was completely different, in my head."

"In what way?"

"I just thought… Well, I thought you were this ungrateful, angry mess."

"Fuck." He laughs, all gravel and smoke, and I have to close my eyes for a second. "And now you think I'm not?"

"I don't know. Are you?"

"Yes, Mina, I'm a mess. I'm fucked up and full of scars and have a special talent for pissing off most everyone I come in contact with."

My mouth twitches, unsure whether to bend up or down. I can't deny that his candor feels like a cool breeze against my skin.

"But also," he says, "I'm the kind of guy who'll go to the ends of the earth for the people I care about. Even if there aren't that many of them. And I'd like to think I manage to tell a decent joke now and then. And also…I'd really like to call you again. If you'll let me."

I go achingly still, feeling myself balanced on a knife's edge. On either side, the world plunges away toward shadowy black depths I can only guess at, and one wrong step will send me tumbling into the abyss.

I have the distinct feeling that letting Grayson Drake call me again would only be the first of many wrong steps.

But for so long, I've tried to make the right choices and only managed to circle back to the beginning. I'm no better off than I was fourteen years ago, when I sprinted across town trying to catch a ride with a stranger. Then, life was poised to open up for me, but since then, I've gone backward. Retreated behind the same lines that have marked my worn-down territory for decades.

I try to name a single risk I've taken since the day I got into Michael's car and come up blank. Because even staying with him amounted to playing it safe, in a way.

"All right," I say. "Call me again, if you really want to."

Air rushes out of him, as if he's been holding his breath. "Okay. Then we'll talk soon."

"Okay."

After we hang up, I stare at the phone. I have no idea what to think. Nothing about that lined up with my expectations.

Shaking my head, I go clean up the groceries, managing to salvage everything except a broken jelly jar and three eggs.

Once that's taken care of, I have nothing left to do but head into the woods.

BEFORE

For our first dance as a married couple, Michael insists on "Angel" by Aerosmith.

Neither of us knows how to dance, especially to something with such a brisk tempo, but he insists the lyrics remind him of me, so we sway together to Steven Tyler's melodic wailing. Behind me, my white gown swishes against the country club's parquet dance floor.

Our friends and family surround us, but their faces blur. I can't wrench my eyes from the blue-green ones I've been gazing into for three years now. As of two hours ago, this man is my *husband*. The person I'll spend my life with, for better or for worse, 'til death do us part.

Michael smiles down and my chest constricts. I can't believe we're married. Especially because, at times, I didn't know whether we would make it this far. The scars Grayson inflicted cut deep, enough that we almost didn't survive those rocky months of aftermath. I've had to adjust to a partner who's more serious. More reserved. Who goes quiet in the face of confrontation, because he's still in recovery from more than just alcohol.

But once I adapted, I realized Michael's love never wavered. He just shows it in different ways now, mostly by keeping me flush with everything I could possibly want—three-hundred-dollar running shoes that channel my inner Usain Bolt, a brand-new work computer with every possible accessory, flowers for no reason at all.

He takes care of me. I don't regret my choice.

I grin, then reach up to run my hands through his hair. He wears it short these days—always tidy, always precise—and gold strands slip through my fingers like satin. "So," I say. "We're married."

"We are."

"How do you feel?"

"Lucky." His smile deepens. "How do *you* feel?"

"Lucky."

The song reaches its final bars, and Michael swoops me into a dip. I almost shriek, but he manages to support my weight without me having to bring any grace into the mix.

To the delight of the crowd, he plants a kiss on me. People flood the dance floor as another song begins—something with a peppy beat that has everyone throwing their arms into the air.

Michael rights me. "I only know how to slow dance. Do you think anyone'll mind if I just do this all night?"

I lace my fingers behind his neck. "Don't tell me you're regretting not taking those lessons now?"

His mouth slants. "You know I wanted to."

I nod. I do know. Work has increasingly gobbled larger portions of his time. His high-end custom designs have people clamoring for his attention, and most days, I count myself lucky if he makes it home before seven.

But he works so hard for me. For us. So I do everything I can to support him.

Two guests emerge from the crowd and head our way. I recognize Michael's coworkers—Sarah, who gives me an exaggerated, open-mouthed wink, and Benny Gallagher, who's changed remarkably little since we went to school together back in Seagrove. He's still barrel-chested and ludicrously tall, with a mop of sandy hair, a perpetual sunburn, and a braying laugh that permeates the room.

Privately, I'll never stop likening him to the Jolly Green Giant after he painted himself green and donned a leaf skirt last Halloween, but of course I'd never say so.

"Congratufuckinglations!" Benny shouts. He plucks two champagne glasses from Sarah's hands and dangles them in our faces. "Are you two ready to party, or what?"

Michael's expression goes neutral, his grip tightening at my waist.

Which is my cue. He's been adamant about keeping his struggles with alcohol private, so I whisk the glasses away with a sheepish smile. "Thanks, Benny, but I'll fall flat on my face if we drink these now. I can barely stay upright as it is. Later?"

"Right, right. Later!" Benny laughs with enough gusto that I have to wonder how many glasses he's ingested himself. "Time enough to get wasted after Michael's big honeymoon surprise!"

Big surprise. A frisson of excitement rockets up my spine, and I shoot a glance at my newly minted husband. He's remained stubbornly silent on the subject of our honeymoon, but, for the first time in…well, *ever*, he's finagled a week-long absence from work.

Which means I'm in for something big. The overnight bag in the Audi outside has been packed accordingly, with my passport tucked safely in a bottom pocket. And if I've obsessively googled the best times to visit the Acropolis and what the ferry schedules from Athens to the island of Aegina look like, it's all in the name of being prepared.

I flash Benny a grin. "Surprise, hmm?" Somehow, I manage to keep my voice at a reasonable pitch. "Tell me more."

Michael cuts him a warning glance, and Benny mimes locking his mouth and throwing away the key.

Which, unsurprisingly, lasts for all of two nanoseconds. "You're gonna love it!" he booms, then waggles his eyebrows and tornadoes away with Sarah in tow.

My husband exhales and kisses my temple. "Thank god he didn't ruin it. And thank you for coming to my rescue. Again."

"No problem." I hold up the glasses. "I'll just go get rid of these. When I come back, you can tell me all about this *surprise*."

He chuckles. "Not a chance."

I weave across the packed dance floor to the bar, where I find Kate lecturing a fuzzy-cheeked bartender on the critical differences between tonic and soda water. He gazes at her with widened eyes, apparently too stunned to make whatever drink she's ordered.

I nudge her away with an elbow and deposit the champagne flutes in her hands. "Would you stop distracting the poor staff? There's a half-mile-long line behind you."

She pouts, then takes an experimental sip. "I wasn't *distracting* him. He was fascinated. He was hanging on my every word."

I laugh. "Yeah, because you look like Gisele Bündchen. Not because he cares about the hidden sugar content of tonic water."

"Well..." Kate's expression turns speculative. "Now that you mention it, I *did* catch him peeking down my cleavage. Which I'm blaming on you. Did you really have to pick something this low-cut?"

I give her a once-over. She looks stunning, in a violet A-line bridesmaid dress I chose specifically with her in mind. "I absolutely did. Because it's my wedding, and I get to be upstaged by my maid of honor if I want. Now do me a favor and disappear this booze, will you?"

She snorts, then drains an entire flute in one go. "You say that like you're trying to get rid of a body."

I shrug. "Just about."

"The things I do for you." Kate goes to work on the second drink, then makes a shooing motion. "Now go on. Dance with your shiny new husband."

I should do exactly that, but I linger. By this time tomorrow, my best friend will be back in Seagrove, and who knows when I'll see her again. "In a second. It's just so good to have you here. It's been way too long."

"It really has. Let's never go this long again, okay?" Kate sets her empties on a nearby table and wraps me in a hug. "And thanks for making me part of your special day. And congratulations. And I love you. And have a kick-ass honeymoon, wherever you're going."

The grin I bury in her shoulder might actually qualify as shit eating. "Oh, trust me. That's not going to be a problem."

Outside the banquet room windows, dusk deepens, turning Lake Washington a rich shade of indigo. On the far shore, the suburbs of Seattle glimmer.

Inside, we dance and eat and cut cake, but Michael glances at his watch with increasing frequency. Shortly after nine, he takes my hand and steers me through the party, bidding our guests good night. My father hugs us. My mother cries. Once everyone is sufficiently thanked, Michael leads me out to the Audi.

When we get on the freeway heading south, toward Sea-Tac, an entire flock of butterflies hatches inside my belly. By unspoken agreement, we haven't broached the subject of travel since I chose him. We've contented ourselves with a life of promotions and paychecks and all the necessary practicalities of adulthood.

But the daydreams have never strayed far from my mind. I've kept them near, like lit stars tucked in my back pocket. Old friends I might someday see again.

Michael grips the steering wheel, never straying from his customary ten-and-two. He sneaks a sidelong glance at me. "I've never seen you this excited before."

I giggle. I'm about to make an oblique reference to Europe when my cell phone rings. I fish around in my clutch purse. It's probably someone we missed on our way out, calling to see us off. But when I free the phone, the screen displays a bizarrely long string of numbers.

I frown. Someone's calling me from…Mongolia?

"What?" Michael scans my expression. "Who is it?"

"I don't know. A telemarketer, maybe? It says Mongolia. Are there call centers in Mongolia?"

"Mongolia?" His knuckles tighten around the wheel. "Really?"

I hesitate, momentarily thrown by the brittle edge in his tone. "That's what it says."

"Cancel it."

"Why?"

"Because." A muscle ticks in his jaw. "We don't need some salesman ruining our evening."

I nod and hit the red button, but a moment later, the phone rings again. This time, Michael grimaces and holds out his hand. I pass over the cell for him to answer.

"What?" he says.

I wince. No *hello*. Just a single word, flat and hostile, and even though I also detest cold calls with the fire of a thousand suns, pity flares when I consider the poor soul on the line. Whoever he is, he's probably just trying to feed his family. It's not his fault that we have no need for foreign-sourced prescription drugs or whatever telemarketers are peddling these days.

"Yes," Michael says, his voice cut from steel.

My frown deepens. Yes? Yes, what? *Do* we need foreign-sourced prescription drugs?

"Yep. Yes, of course." He glances over at me and pauses, then grimly announces, "Absolutely not."

I raise my eyebrows in question.

Telemarketer, he mouths, then turns his attention back to the road. "Are you *drunk*?"

The salesman apparently launches into something long-winded, because Michael stays quiet for agonizing moments.

"Look," he finally says. To my abject astonishment, he actually raises his voice. He hasn't done that in years. "Right now, you're interrupting my wedding night, and the last thing—"

I can't help it—I snatch the phone away. "Sorry," I say into it. "What my husband means to say is that we're busy being blissfully happy right now, and will be for the rest of our lives. Please don't call again."

I hang up before the telemarketer can respond and give Michael a significant look. "What on earth was that?"

He stares at me, then the phone. "Sorry. I don't know. I just… I've been planning this for a long time. I don't want anyone interrupting."

I blow out a breath. "What was he trying to sell you, anyway?"

Michael's gaze skitters away. "Who knows? He wasn't making a lot of sense."

"Did he actually speak English?"

"Yeah. But he sounded…confused."

"Weird," I say.

"Very."

Silence settles in the car. I turn my attention to the window, where reflective highway signs zoom out of the dark. I crane my head as one flies by, then sit up straight, the odd moment forgotten. "Wait. You missed the exit."

Michael blinks. "No, I didn't."

"For Sea-Tac? Yeah. It was a mile ago."

"What? No. We're not going to Sea-Tac."

My breath catches, but I manage to keep my expression composed. Even while every last butterfly in my stomach drops dead midflight.

It's a hotel.

An exceptionally beautiful hotel, composed of steel and glass and nestled within an old-growth forest halfway between Seattle and Seagrove.

Michael parks in a sparsely filled lot. The place sparkles like a lit jewel amid the shadowed woods. Gilded light streams from a towering array of windows, and in the lobby, a waterfall chandelier cascades from a soaring ceiling.

"Well?" Excitement suffuses Michael's voice. "What do you think?"

I peer through the windshield. "It's stunning," I manage.

Really, it's more than stunning. It's a superlative display of crisp, contemporary beauty, all the more striking given the lush backdrop of night-cloaked woods. It's just not what I expected.

"It's mine," he says, pride evident.

"It's... Wait, what?"

"It's mine." Michael makes a thick sound of pleasure. "Well, not *mine* mine. I don't own it. But I designed it."

My hand flutters to my chest as the ice beneath my sternum thaws. "You mean you *made* this?" I've never seen a Michael Drake original in person before.

"I did."

I take a beat to reassess. The hotel looks like something out of a travel brochure for royalty. I've never stayed anywhere like it. I've never even set foot near a place like this.

"The best part is, we're the only guests." Michael sounds downright gleeful now. "The hotel doesn't actually open 'til next month, but I negotiated a special condition in my contract. The owners are letting us stay for a week with a full staff on-site. We'll have a personal chef, two masseuses, a riding in-structor, a yoga teacher. Anything you want."

I falter on an inhale. He must have planned this ages ago. "You did this for me?"

"For my angel? Of course."

Guilt swamps me with such ferocity that I have to fight the urge to curl up on the floor mat in a fetal position. This is a far cry from Greece, but it clearly represents something intensely personal to Michael, and that's so much better.

"Let's go inside, okay?" His eyes glitter. "I'm dying to make an honest woman out of you."

I turn to him, so mired in shame over my own selfishness that I can only nod.

He pops his door open and skates around the car to do the same with mine. I follow him into the cool evening. The lace hem of my wedding dress snags on the asphalt, but I hardly notice and definitely don't care.

In the spacious lobby, a bevy of smiling staff lines up in greet-ing. The porter shows us to our room, where an expanse of pale marble and glass awaits. Sprays of fresh lilies occupy glossy vases in every corner. A mullioned screen affords a view of the bath-room, where a blue-lit Jacuzzi occupies a marble dais. Across from the king-size bed, a slider opens on a private patio, where a hot tub steams gently in the dark.

The place hits the same way our condo once did, only mul-tiplied by a thousand, and I have to forcibly pick my jaw up off the floor.

The porter leaves our luggage. When the door clicks shut, Michael beelines for the outdoor hot tub, loosening his bow tie and shedding his tuxedo on the way. Once naked, he strolls into the steaming water, then turns back and crooks a finger at me.

I stand there and survey him for a moment. I can't believe I'm married to a man who spoils me like this. I shouldn't need anything more.

I *don't*.

I reach back and tug my zipper down, letting the dress sigh down my body and pool at my feet. Next, I shed my stockings, then my shoes. I wriggle my toes, relishing the return of my circulation.

Michael scans me with hungry eyes. "Come here." His voice is gravel, making my belly clench.

This, at least, never changes. Whatever voltage flared between us on our kitchen island three years ago has yet to subside. I already know that when we touch, everything else will fade. We'll speak to each other in *our* language, the one that no amount of crossed wires can ever diminish.

I step into the tub. Michael welcomes me with eager hands and fervent kisses. The water siphons the aches from my body as I lose myself in the heady intoxication of joined lips.

He hoists me onto the corner of the tub and pushes me back against the smooth wood of the patio. My skin exhales steam into the darkness. Michael makes a drunken sound, then leans over me and closes his eyes.

I follow suit, letting my awareness narrow to a glut of heat and sensation. The lap of steaming water around my ankles, the power of his body surging into mine, the cool expanse of wood beneath my shoulder blades—pleasure crackles through me, drags me to a pinnacle, and flings me off the summit.

It's fast and ferocious, so very us.

When I float back to earth, my lashes part. Overhead, through the latticework of boughs, a canopy of glittering stars awaits.

"Look," I whisper, pointing upward.

Michael rests with his cheek pillowed against my chest, but obediently turns his head. "Hmm?"

Déjà vu flits against my consciousness. "The stars."

"Yeah." He returns his attention to me. "They're gorgeous."

My smile falters. I don't know why. I don't know what I expected him to say.

Thankfully, Michael eases us back into the water, dismissing the moment before I can dwell. We float for a while, him content to study the hotel's geometry, me content to watch him.

He catches me staring. "You like this place?"

"I love it." I smile.

"I'm glad," he says. "Because I've been thinking. How would you like to live in a house like this? Smaller, obviously, but in the same style?"

I blink. "You mean...sell the condo?"

"Yeah. We could buy some land, build something for ourselves. No more dog barking upstairs at 3:00 a.m. No more standing by the windows to get cell reception. No having to use the treadmill. You could go running in the woods every day, if you wanted."

"But...land in Seattle is exorbitant. Could we really afford that?"

"I wasn't thinking about Seattle, actually." His cadence remains steady, but I have the distinct impression that he's measuring each word in advance. "I was thinking about Seagrove."

My breath deserts me. *"Seagrove?"*

At my tone, Michael hoists his palms out of the water. "I know, I know. But hear me out. Ben Gallagher's leaving Forsythe & Winter, and he's asked me to go with him. He wants to start his own firm. He thinks that, with the demographic in Seagrove, we could make a killing. And I think he's right."

Seagrove. It should surprise me, but Benny *has* always said he'd move back. I just never thought he'd ask us to accompany him.

"It'd be good for us, Mina." Michael searches my face. "It'd take our income to a whole new level. And wouldn't you like being near Kate again? I mean, you cried when you saw her yesterday."

It's true. I did. It had been so long.

"You wouldn't have to miss her anymore," he continues. "You could just...hop in your car and go to her house for a visit."

My heart manages a frail beat. I do miss my best friend, every minute of every day, but I've never envisioned myself back home. I left that place for a reason. Maybe I didn't get quite as far as I intended, but I got out.

"Mina?" Michael prompts. "It's the kind of opportunity that won't come again."

I swallow thickly. "But wouldn't this just mean you working even longer hours than you already do?"

"At first, maybe. Yes." A cool note slides into his voice. "But once Ben and I got the firm off the ground, I could back off. A few years from now, I could be working less, not more."

That stops me short. Longing scorches up my throat. "You mean...we could take vacations together?"

He stills. "*This* is a vacation."

"I know, but...real ones."

He says nothing, and I grimace. I didn't mean to insult his generosity.

"Sorry," I say.

He nods. His expression remains smooth, but the air around him seems to thicken, as if he's diverting everything inward with such force that it's sucking the surrounding night along with it.

I bite my lip. Michael never gets angry. Never raises his voice. He just gets quiet, and normally, this marks the point at which I back off. I relent, because there's a whole continent inside of him that I no longer have access to. I haven't since That One Time, and I've learned to allow him the safety of that retreat.

But this is a big ask. Enough that I can't just drop it.

Maybe Michael senses as much, because he sighs and drags a hand down his face, leaving droplets clinging to his cheeks. "Look...if I said yes to vacations in a few years, would you say yes to moving?"

I hesitate. A duet of cricket song and swaying branches fills the quiet. The melody finds its way into the innermost sanctum of my heart, where I harbor desires too fragile to survive the light of day.

I could have more time with him. More opportunity to work past these walls, to get back to the people we would have been if Grayson hadn't driven a fist through everything we'd built.

Here in the dark, in the forest, with my husband at my side, I allow hope to flower. "You know what?" I say. "Yeah. I think I would."

Michael exhales sharply. "Really?"

I smile. "Really."

Michael grins, crushes me in a wet hug, and just like that, it's decided. We'll travel backward—in time, in geography, to where we first met. To the place where we first struck the spark that ultimately led us here.

And maybe, just maybe, history will repeat itself.

AFTER

With Grayson's phone call still heavy in my mind, I want nothing more than to walk straight off the cabin's porch and into the forest. But if Michael taught me one thing, back when we still spent time trekking up and down mountainsides, it's to never venture into the wilderness without three things: clothing warm enough to survive the night, a way to make fire, and a way to make light.

In the woods, he said, *you never know what'll happen. If something goes wrong, you might not find your way out again on your own schedule.*

The first two items are easy enough. I layer running shorts over leggings and stuff a waterproof shell into a backpack, then slip in two lighters and a water bottle.

Which leaves me in need of light. My battery-powered headlamp is still in a dusty drawer back in Seagrove, so I venture out to the dim one-car garage no one's ever made a habit of parking in and search for a substitute.

Here, too, evidence of my family's long ownership has vanished, but behind a stack of spare window screens, I find an overlooked red metal kerosene lamp. Wire loops circle the glass bulb in the middle. A rusty dial adjusts the wick up and down.

The lantern evokes memories of thunder-drenched summer nights, when the power went out and I played board games with my parents by lantern light. As a child, the flickering magic of those evenings intoxicated me. I always felt like we'd gone on an adventure, even though we hadn't set foot beyond the door.

Now the memories only push an ache against my ribs. I'll never have nights like that again, no giggle-soaked Monopoly matches with my own children. Not that I would have, anyway—Michael and I agreed early on that we didn't want kids, and witnessing Kate's struggles with motherhood has only confirmed that for me—but the other part, the husband I could cuddle up beside and haggle over Park Place with and pop kettle corn with... I thought I'd have him forever.

My eyes tingle. I blink away the sting and carry my reclaimed lantern outside. It's close to six o'clock, and while the shadows haven't yet fallen, the light has melted in that peculiar way that makes everything warmer and sharper and closer. In the yard, long grass the color of Michael's hair waves in the breeze. The saw-blade mountains gleam, their faces lifted toward the sun.

Between the two waits a tangle of deep green shadows. The trees seem to peer at me, friendly and remembering. Welcoming.

I cross the burbling creek that bisects the yard, and the world shifts. The sunlight retreats, plunging me into a realm of muted bird chatter, pungent wafts of evergreen, and blue shadows that lap against my skin like cool water. I swing the lantern at my side while pine needles crackle underfoot.

There's no trail, so I memorize landmarks. Most people don't realize how easy it is to get lost in the woods, but it can happen with little warning. Once, in Mount Rainier National Park, Michael and I stepped off the trail to find a picnic spot, then lost our bearings. He coached me through it, explaining how to use the surrounding topography to reason my way back in the right direction. Soon enough, we had our boots on the trail again.

At the memory, a whimper rises in my throat, and I clamp down on it until the urge passes.

God, I wish we'd stayed like that forever. I wish I'd had a life with the real Michael, the pure one. The man he would've been if he and Grayson had never torn each other's heart out.

I reach a clearing where the moss piles thicker, cloaking the fallen trunks with mantles of green. I arrange myself cross-legged with the lantern before me. Cast-off pine needles prick through my pants.

I heave a breath and peer around, feeling suddenly ridiculous. This place is beautiful, but what did I expect? That I would listen to the birds sing, maybe raise my face against the dappled light, and simply be *over* it?

Yet the longer I sit, breathing in concert with the forest, the more my splintered edges soften. This place is the exact opposite of my home in Seagrove. No spotless surfaces to polish to within an inch of their life. No chrome-plated appliances to advertise my washed-out reflection whether I like it or not.

Not a straight line or squared corner in sight. Just gentle beauty and the earthy lullaby of rustling pines.

A twig snaps, shattering the calm.

I rise, instinctually brandishing the lantern as if to ward off shadows. Yet daylight still lingers, so I force my arm back down and squint into the underbrush.

Branches rustle. Something large pushes fallen leaves aside. A moment later, a furred head emerges from a bush. A very *wide* furred head.

I stare into the bottomless dark eyes of a black bear.

My pulse hurtles into overdrive. I try to remember what Michael used to say—look the animal in the eye? Don't, so as not to seem like a threat? Shout? Stay quiet?

It's been so long that I can't remember. I only know I shouldn't flee.

The bear snuffles and paws at the ground. A silky cub totters to its side.

Blackened terror lurches through my veins, sending me staggering backward. This much, I *do* remember: the most dangerous bear in the forest is a mother with her young.

The bear lowers its head, and instinct takes over. I revert to the same thing that's saved me countless times before.

I run.

BEFORE

On our seven-year anniversary, I finally reach my breaking point.

It's already dark outside when I pull the steaks for our celebration dinner off the grill. Michael hasn't come downstairs yet, so I parse out the asparagus, set the table, and light two taper candles before pouring some bubbly cider.

My husband has a decade of sobriety behind him, which astonishes me when I realize how much time has passed. Ten years have gone so quickly, six and a half of them here in Seagrove. As expected, moving allowed Michael and Benny's business to explode, which has left us flush with financial comfort, and my husband couldn't be happier. He relishes the constant press of work. But I...

Well, I have no cause to complain. And now I write for a living, the way I always wanted, even if endlessly chronicling medical devices isn't exactly what I had in mind.

I put the finishing touches on the table. After one last glance at the hallway mirror to confirm my hair is properly curled and my little black dress tight in all the right places, I venture upstairs.

As usual, Michael is bent over his drafting table, his eyes fixed on whatever architectural wonder he's currently transcribing from his imagination. I clear my throat.

He looks up. "Hey."

"Hey. Dinner's ready."

"Great." He smiles in that muted way that tells me he's still miles away, in drafting mode. "I'll be right there."

Back downstairs, I wait so long that the steaks cool. I sigh when I think of how much the meat cost, but…oh, well. We can afford it, thanks to him.

Finally, Michael takes the chair across from me and drapes a spotless linen napkin over his lap. "This looks amazing. Thank you. And happy anniversary."

"Happy anniversary." I smile as we toast. Cidery sweetness fizzes on my tongue.

While we eat, we revisit all our usual topics—the amazing July weather, the dinner party we have planned with Kate and her new husband, the question of whether or not we should get a dog. I vote yes, Michael votes no. It would just be extra work, he says, for no real reason.

Ultimately, I let him win, because the conversation functions as more of a pressure-release valve than anything else. As a stand-in for discussing the one thing he can't buy me. Because I've already brought *that* up enough times, and it always ends with him sending me off on a run.

Over dessert, Michael sets an envelope on the table.

I stare. "I thought we agreed on no gifts," I squeak out.

"I couldn't help myself." He smiles. "You know how I feel about spoiling my angel."

I try to smother the thump in my veins, but this is no jewelry box. It's an *envelope*. The kind that just might have plane tickets inside.

I can't wait another moment. I snatch the envelope and tear it open, then whip out a...

...gift certificate. To a dog breeder. For a shockingly large sum. I turn it over a few times, my brow furrowed. "What's this?"

"What does it look like?"

"But...didn't you just say no dog?" I go hunting in the envelope again, but it's empty.

"It was a bluff, Mina." He looks concerned by my lack of enthusiasm. "I found a breeder here in Seagrove who's got a litter of purebred Labrador puppies we can choose from. We're scheduled to have a look tomorrow."

"A puppy? A purebred?" I fiddle with the paper. On the off chance Michael ever agreed, I pictured us going down to the animal shelter for a toothless, half-blind old mutt, the kind that needs love and snuggles in its twilight years.

Besides, Darlene could probably fund the shelter's efforts for half a year with a check this large.

Michael's face falls. "Is this not what you wanted?"

I tuck the certificate away. "I... When I said I wanted a dog, I meant one that needed a home."

He looks mystified by that. "Oh. Okay. Well, if you'd rather go to the shelter, we'll do that. I'll just call the breeder and tell her we had a change of heart."

I muster a smile. I love the idea of a stinky old dog lolling around on our pristine leather couches, but...

The hole the dog conversation fills yawns wider than ever.

Michael's brow pleats. "Why don't you look happy right now?"

Oh, god. I hate that I'm doing this. I pull my smile wider. "I *am* happy. Thank you."

When he searches my face, I know I haven't fooled him. For a moment, I have the strangest urge to go get him his pencil, because he's studying me the same way he studies his drafting board, as if he can design his way to the desired outcome. *Just adjust this angle over here, shift that wall to the left, and voilà. Everything in its place.*

His smoky voice turns rasping. "What's this really about, Mina?"

I tell myself to let it go. Then, for some reason, I don't. "To be honest, the dog thing has mostly been a way to distract myself."

"From?"

"Asking for what I really want."

"Which is?"

I clamp my teeth over my lip. Not today, of all days. I already know how this will end. "Never mind."

His mouth thins. "You want to go on vacation."

I push my asparagus around on my plate. "You said it, not me."

Michael sighs. "Is this ever going to stop coming up? You know what work is like for me."

"You asked for a few years, Michael," I blurt. "It's been *six and a half.*"

"Business is crazy right now."

"Business is always crazy right now. And what about the fact that Benny and Sarah spent Christmas in Tahiti last year? If he can leave, why can't you?"

"I've given you everything else. Everything you could possibly ask for."

I flinch, because he sounds hard-bitten and weary, as if he's done his utmost to make me happy and can't understand why it's not working.

I look around. I am happy, really. I *should* be. I couldn't ask for more than what's spread out before me—a beautiful house, if in the last place I thought I'd settle down, a beautiful husband, a beautiful *everything.* And yet…

I clear my throat. Crap. I can't seem to help myself. "Do you remember when we drove out to that observatory, back when we first met? The one outside Seattle?"

He blinks, long and slow.

The blankness in his eyes stabs at me. He can't have forgotten, can he? "Where you first told me you loved me?"

"Right." He sets his fork down. "What about it?"

"Well, I've been thinking about that. A lot." Endlessly, in fact, but I don't need to rub it in his face. I twist my napkin, then give up and toss it onto the table. "It keeps coming back to me. How you looked up at the stars and said what you did. My whole world shifted in that moment. It felt like we were the only two people in the world right then, and I keep thinking it's because we were out there being free together. Away from expectations. Just us and the sky and the world. And I miss that. I miss us, together, being like that."

His gaze slides away. As if he's uncomfortably aware that he's no longer the same man who stood on that mountaintop and read poetry in the stars. "That was a different life, Mina. A different me."

My heartbeat snags in my throat. "It doesn't have to be. If we just went somewhere, if we could get some distance from Washington, we could reconnect. The way we used to."

He huffs a humorless laugh. Something about it sounds hollow. Like I could reach across the table and my fingers would pass right through him.

"Things change." He keeps his tone measured, but underneath, emotion thrums, some caged reaction he refuses to grant me access to. "People change. This is me, now. This is our life. I don't know what more I can give you."

I ease back in my chair, at a loss. Of course he's changed. Ten years have changed me, too. But I can't help feeling like he's forgotten his own advice, like he's fallen *asleep*. That we both have.

How I long to wake up. To lure the Michael I fell in love with from the hibernation Grayson drove him into. I'm certain he's still in there, buried beneath the hurt. Somewhere under the work deadlines and haircuts and grocery runs.

"Are you ever going to let this go?" he says softly.

A shuddering breath steals out of me. "I don't think I can."

The moment it's out, I realize it's true. Underneath the shine and glamour of our life together, I've never forgotten that I gave up Greece for him. For this. And while I don't regret the sacrifice I made to build a life together, I always thought Michael would live out *some* version of my dream with me. Except he refuses. For years, it's been eating at me, and now there's no place left for my frustration to go except spilling across the table.

"Why don't you go somewhere with Kate?" he says, his voice taut. "Book a trip to Cancun or something?"

"I don't want to go with Kate," I force out. "I want..."

I grope to fill the blank as taunting possibilities cascade through my mind. I want to travel with *him*. I want him to wake up. I want him to wake me up, to stand under the stars again and hold my hand.

Michael closes his eyes, as if forcibly mastering himself. When he looks again, his gaze is calm. "Mina. Come here."

I hesitate, because I know, even before I circle toward him and his fingers go skimming up my bare thighs, what will happen next. One touch, and I melt into a puddle of want.

This never fails to distract me, and he knows it.

Sure enough, when he pulls at me, need takes over. I tear open his shirt, buttons flying, then yank down his zipper. He whisks my underwear off and I sink onto him right there at the dinner table, a mindless cry simmering out of me as two become one.

His artist's fingers hike my dress up and dig into my bare ass. I ride him hard, with a kind of desperation, my hips rolling as my back arches and my eyes fall closed.

Michael clutches at me. I rise and rise and rise inside until I crest somewhere in the stratosphere.

When I come to my senses again, limp and draped against him like a rag doll, I raise my head.

He looks up at me. "*This* is what we have, angel. This, and our house, and our life. Where we take care of each other. Forget the past."

"I can't," I murmur. "And none of this changes what I just said."

Alarm crowds his gaze, quickly masked.

"What I *really* want for our anniversary," I press, "is to go somewhere. With you."

A slow sigh bleeds out of him. "Fine. The Oregon coast, then? We could drive down next weekend and—"

"No." We did that last summer, and it wasn't enough. We only managed to bring all the same work—emails, Michael's conference calls, my lethally boring articles for *Medical Devices Monthly*—to a different place and do it there. "I want to go somewhere real. On an actual airplane. No half measures this time."

His muscles lock. I'm afraid to see what I've just done, so I concentrate on disentangling our bodies and snagging a clean napkin to stem the flow of him down my legs.

"I don't like flying," he says tightly.

I frown. He's never said that before, and when I finally meet his eyes, the shutter that has become so familiar has dropped into place.

"I didn't know that." Maybe I should chalk up his hesitation to a flying phobia and be done with it, but my mouth keeps on producing words. "But are you telling me that's it? We're just never going to go anywhere we can't get to in a car?"

Michael makes a noncommittal noise and tucks himself back in his pants, then stands to clear the dishes. He leaves me standing there with a napkin pressed between my legs and an awful, stony lump in my throat.

I try to fight it, but when he retreats to the sink at the island, I feel myself losing ground. Fear of flying or not, it feels like he's taking our night at the observatory and yanking it straight out of my hands—hands that have turned that memory over and over again in adoration.

He glances up from the dishes. "You'd feel better if you went for a run."

I don't want him to see how close I am to breaking, so I march upstairs, exchange my cocktail dress for running clothes, and pelt out into the night.

Even though it's nine o'clock and pitch black, I run until my lungs crack open and my teeth jar in their sockets.

When I finally stumble back inside, Michael has cleared off the dining table and polished the granite. The whole kitchen looks brand-new. But he hasn't gone to bed. A pool of light brightens the lawn out back, which means he's in his office. Again.

I mount the stairs. For once, the run hasn't taken enough out of me. For once, I refuse to back down.

I *can't*. I miss him too much.

In the doorway to his office, I prop my hands on my hips. Michael looks up, startled.

"I can't live like this," I announce. "I can't be married to someone who won't go anywhere with me. You promised we'd travel, and we haven't, so if your answer's still no, I'm finding us a couples therapist tomorrow."

His eyes widen. He blinks, apparently struck dumb by the fact that I've abandoned our script. Long moments pass, punctuated by the tick of his tabletop clock.

"Say something."

"I…" He swallows. "All right."

"All right like, 'Let's go to therapy'? Or all right like, 'Go ahead and book a ticket'?"

He pinches the bridge of his nose with the hand holding his pencil. "I mean, all right, book the tickets. Jesus, Mina. Just… Where're we going?"

I nearly choke. I can hardly believe my ears. *Greece,* I want to say, but I know that chance has come and gone. Best choose something that doesn't involve crossing international borders. Less to explain to my mother that way, too. "Hawaii."

"Okay," he says. "Then choose the dates and book us in first class. Put it all on the Mastercard."

My jaw slackens. Apparently we're both breaking form tonight, because for him to give me carte blanche to interfere with his work...

I don't dare complete the thought, even to myself. There's something about gift horses and mouths that suits this situation perfectly.

"Thank you," I say. "Wow. I love you so much." I turn to go. "Mina?"

I glance back to find him still swiveled toward me, his back to the desk. "Yeah?"

"I love you, too. You do know that, right?"

"I do."

A few beats of silence pass before he asks, "Do you still want the dog?"

"Yes." I smile. "I still want the dog."

A week later, we bring home a shaggy, twelve-year-old mutt with a coppery coat and wretched breath. The shelter warns us she'll have to take special pills for the rest of her life because of an issue with her kidneys—the reason her last family surrendered her, apparently—but I don't care. I'm in love even before she flops down beside my desk in the living room.

We name her Penny.

"Just don't let her up on the furniture," Michael says.

I reach over my chair arm to pat her head. "I don't think she could get onto the furniture if she tried."

He cracks a smile. "Good point. Maybe you were onto something with the whole no-puppy thing."

I smile back. "Maybe I was."

In the weeks that follow, things change. I no longer write in solitude—Penny keeps me company, stinky breath and all, and Michael starts getting up ridiculously early, like he used to. He even starts running again. I can tell by the shadows beneath his eyes that the late nights and early mornings are taking their toll, but when I ask why, he only flips his shirt up to display newly chiseled abs.

"We're going to the beach," he says. "Do I really have to explain?"

My stomach clenches. I would never call him chubby, but the eight-pack *had* slowly coalesced into something more like a two-pack. Now...well, he looks like he did at twenty-five.

Predictably, we end up having sex right then and there, him hoisting me up against the wall and driving himself into me until I unravel.

When he puts me down again, my knees make a reluctant agreement to keep holding me upright. "I think we need to do that every day on vacation," I slur. "Twice a day."

I expect a smile, but he gives me a serious look. Not his normal I'm-working-right-now-can-we-do-this-later look, but something else. "Actually, what do you think about no sex on vacation? Just you and me and...us staring at the stars together. Or however you described it."

"No sex?" A thoughtful note sneaks into my voice. "You mean like when we first met?"

A beat of silence passes. "Yeah. Exactly."

My ensuing rush of longing catches me off guard. I love having sex with him. Would crawl across a desert for it. But I can't deny that our first—and only—sexless month wielded a singular magic. One I've been trying to recapture for years. Maybe *this* is the key. It's certainly a strategy I haven't considered before.

"Okay," I say. "Let's do it. Or rather, not do it. For ten long, horny days. But only because you let me test-drive those new abs in advance."

His shoulders relax. A smile brightens his face. "You look so happy right now."

"I am," I say. "I really, really am."

"Because of the sex thing?"

"No. Because I'm finally going on an adventure." I lean up to steal a kiss. "And it's with you."

The morning of our flight, we drop Penny off at Kate's house. For the rest of the drive to Seattle, I wonder if I've gravely miscalculated. Michael's gotten quieter and quieter, and while I tell myself not to ask why, I eventually have to.

"I'm just nervous," he says. "About flying."

"Really? It's that bad?"

"Yeah. I hate airplanes."

"Huh." I study him. He looks pale. Sweaty.

I wonder how he could possibly fear flying but routinely guide this car through curves that statistically have a *way* higher likelihood of killing us than a measly airplane. "Is there anything I can do? Hold your hand while we take off, maybe? Bribe the captain to announce that it's your birthday?"

That earns me a lopsided smile. "It's okay. I'll be okay."

It doesn't seem that way, though. The closer we get, the tighter he winds, and as we make our way through security, I wonder if he'll implode.

At the gate, he keeps checking his phone without seeming to see it, and I can't keep my mouth shut any longer. "Is there a reason you hate flying so much? Something in particular?"

He jerks a glance at me, his cheeks ashen. "Um… I'm going to go to the bathroom. I'll be right back."

I stare after him, plagued by the sense that I've just touched on something forbidden. Something to do with Lily.

I smooth down my floral-print dress and consciously decide to let it go. Michael has conceded on both the dog *and* the vacation. The least I can do is let Lily and Grayson lie. Besides, this is supposed to be *our* time.

No tomorrows. No yesterdays, either.

Michael is gone for several minutes. When he comes back, he looks better. Astonishingly so. He's splashed water on his face, and his hair is wet in front, combed back with his fingers. The color in his cheeks has returned.

He comes close, stopping inches away. "Hi."

"Hi."

"Sorry about that. I just needed a minute. What were you saying?"

I gaze up. He's done such an admirable job of getting himself together that I lose myself to a heady whirlwind, the kind that robs me of breath and makes me wonder if someone has injected pure sunlight into my blood.

A moment later, I realize why.

Michael's looking at me like he *used* to. No shutters, no walls, just a wide-open aquamarine infinity. He stares at me like the rest of the world has faded. Like I'm the only woman he sees.

Someone announces our flight over the loudspeaker. People jostle to line up, but neither of us move.

Lily doesn't matter, I realize. Grayson doesn't, either. Nothing does, just us. Just this.

"Nothing important," I say. "Except that I love you madly."

Longing kindles in his eyes. He's probably already regretting the no-sex rule. "I love you, too. You have no idea."

My heart skips. "Oh yeah? Prove it."

"How?"

I smile slyly. "I'm sure you'll come up with something."

He gives me a considering look before we board the plane and settle in for the long flight to Oahu. During takeoff, he tenses, but when we level off at cruising altitude and the seat belt sign goes dark, he flips up the armrest and takes my hands.

"You want proof?"

"Desperately," I say.

"I love these fingers." He kisses each one. "The way they make that clacking noise when you type. How ordinary it sounds, except the words coming out are anything but."

Something catches in my throat. "You mean my medical articles?"

"No. Your travelogues."

I would startle if I didn't find the movement of his thumbs across the backs of my hands so soothing. I haven't written a travelogue in years, and had come to consider my long-ago dream of travel writing as taboo a subject as Lily. But maybe that's just me. Maybe *I'm* the one who locked up that fantasy and threw away the key.

His fingers trail up my arms, leaving electric ripples in their wake. "And I love these shoulders, the way they hunch up when you're brushing your teeth. Like you're worried someone's going to sneak up and steal your toothpaste."

I blink. Do I do that?

"And these ears." He fondles one lobe. "I love how this one's rounded at the tip, but the other one has the slightest point. It's subtle. But adorable. Like a secret someone can only discover if they're paying attention."

My breath dwindles. My god. It's just my ear, but lightning strikes my core, a direct hit.

"And these eyes." He tugs me close. "I could stare into them all day. All year. All my life."

For long moments, he does exactly that. I can't breathe. I just gaze back for some delirious amount of time measured in heartbeats instead of seconds.

"Do you believe me now?" he says.

A smile more genuine than any I've felt in months blossoms on my face. "I'm getting there. But you might have to keep this up. Until I'm fully convinced."

He chuckles. The sound slides into the base of my stomach and pulls everything tight, and I wonder how on earth I'm going to keep from ripping his clothes off for the next ten days. Because it's working. We've barely left the ground, but already, the freedom of hurtling through the sky, the promise of an island my feet have never touched before, these compliments, holy shit, these *compliments*—everything simmers in my blood, effervescent.

Michael laces his long fingers through mine. As our palms lock together, something clicks inside me, and I think, *This man was the right choice.*

And he always will be, as long as he's holding my hand.

AFTER

I run until the forest blurs. Fallen branches snatch at my feet. Only when my heart threatens to smash through my rib cage and my vision fades at the edges do I chance a look behind me.

Nothing but empty forest.

I stop and double over, clutching at my knees. An inane giggle erupts, then fades when I realize what I've done. I never should have run. Not from a *bear*.

I'm just lucky she didn't chase me. So purely, stupidly lucky.

When the tightness in my lungs eases, I raise my head. Shadows crowd the forest, longer and bluer than expected, and I rub at my arms. Damn. I have no idea where I am, and it's getting darker and colder by the minute. Which means I need to concentrate. Figure out how to get back to the cabin.

With a steadying breath, I unsling my backpack, then zip on my extra jacket and guzzle my entire bottle of water. I still remember Michael's process from all those years ago and perform a rough calculation—I entered the forest going north, then ran toward the setting sun, so now my house should lie…

I choose a southeastern bearing, then adjust fifteen degrees to the west, like he taught me. If I aim for the cabin and miss in the easterly direction, I'll enter open wilderness. But if I intentionally overshoot the other way, I'll run into the road at some point. Better to do that and walk back than risk wandering into miles of empty woods.

I set off, making enough noise to warn off foraging bears. How could I have forgotten they always come out around twilight?

Thankfully, I don't encounter anything larger than a squirrel, and after what feels like hours, the trees clear.

A strangled sigh works free as my boots bite into the graveled road. Early stars pierce the sky. Darkness seeps from the forest like spreading oil. I flick one of my lighters and flare the lantern, creating a sunshine bubble of brightness I carry into the falling dark.

By the time I stumble into the cabin, fatigue weights my limbs. I plunk the lantern onto the knotty-pine coffee table, build a fire, and collapse on the braided-rope rug. With my knees hugged to my chest, I gaze into the flames, wondering what would have happened if that bear had marked me as prey. Would anyone have found the leftovers afterward? Or would my parents have spent the rest of their lives wondering what had become of me?

Time slips by. I'm still staring into the orange glow when the phone rings.

I shake off my stupor. In town earlier, I emailed my mother to say I'd arrived safely, but she'll still want to hear for herself. After what just happened, I can't even blame her.

I carry the ringing phone to my haven between lantern and fire—the cord's plenty long enough to reach—then rearrange myself cross-legged and pick up. "Hey. Don't worry, I'm safe."

A pause crackles on the line. "Okay. Should I be relieved? Or concerned that you felt it necessary to answer that way?"

Air spirals from my lungs. It's Michael.

No. *No.* Not Michael. Grayson.

"Um…" I say, making no attempt to sound less guarded. "Hi. Sorry. I thought you were my mom."

"Well, that's better than who you thought I was last time. But you should give your mom my condolences. She probably doesn't enjoy sounding like a forty-year-old man."

I blink. I can't believe he just said that. Both parts. "You're not forty. You're thirty-nine."

"True." A low, silky laugh comes through. He sounds different this time. More relaxed. Less on edge. "I wish I could take the fact that you know that as a compliment, but…"

"Right." It's not *his* birthday I have memorized. "Why're you calling me?"

"Because I said I would?"

"Yeah, but that was like…six hours ago."

"Uh-huh. And?"

I wait, but apparently that's a serious question. "Don't you know you're supposed to wait three days to call a girl again? Or whatever the rule is?"

The moment the words come out, I want to stuff them back down my throat. This is not a courtship. Or anything remotely resembling one.

"No, I don't know that." Grayson sounds dubious. "Where'd you even hear that?"

"I thought it was common knowledge."

"It's not. And it doesn't make any sense. What's the point?"

"It's supposed to…" I trail off, frowning. What *is* the point? Who decided men should feign disinterest so no one will know how they really feel? And where does that end? With husbands compiling secret folders full of magazine clippings? Signing divorce papers without telling their wives? "I… Now you're confusing me."

"I wanted to call you," he says. "So I called you. I can't think of anything less confusing than that."

Well. Touché.

"Besides," he continues, "I was hoping you might've had a couple drinks and be in the right mood, this time."

I pause. "Right mood? For what?"

"Telling me about your secret mission in the woods. The one I'll never understand."

I go still inside. Memories of Margo float to the surface like silvery bubbles emerging from dark water.

"Mina?"

"Yeah. I'm here." I clutch the receiver until my knuckles go numb. The room seems to hold its breath, the firelit shadows and lemon scent of floor wax swirling together. Even the lantern's flame stills as if in waiting.

It strikes me then how alone I am here. This warm oasis is nothing but a pinprick, a fleck of light amid this darkened ocean of trees. As the weight of my isolation hits me, I realize I actually *want* to tell him. Want to share that part of myself with someone. I even want to know what he'll say back. Whether he's the kind of man who looks up at the stars and sees elegance, or whether he left that sense of wonder behind long ago.

Still, I shy away from baring myself to a stranger without taking the lay of the land first. "You know, I tried to explain it to Michael once, and he thought I was crazy. You'll probably think so, too."

"Nah. Nothing you could say would change my opinion of you."

"You can't know that."

"Yes, I can. Because I *already* think you're unhinged. You married my asshole brother. Indisputable proof that you're fucking nuts."

Despite myself, I chuckle. "Okay. *Maybe.* Maybe I'll tell you.

But only if I have that drink, and only if you tell me something about you first."

He draws a crisp breath. "Wow. I didn't think that would actually work."

I make a tsking sound Kate would be proud of. "Don't get ahead of yourself. It has to be something good. Not some throwaway confession like how you only eat the top parts of muffins or secretly have a thing for women who bowl."

He chuckles. "Nah. My bowling fetish and habit of dismembering baked goods are already public knowledge, anyway. I've got worse. Way worse."

My eyebrows creep upward. "Oh yeah?"

"Yeah. I've got a whole fucking dungeon of things no one knows about me. But if we're trading secrets, maybe you should tell me what yours is about. Just a general category, so I can see if I've got anything that matches up."

I fiddle with the phone cord. "Okay. But it's not a secret, really. It's more like... Have you ever felt like nature could heal you? Help get you through something traumatic?"

He's silent so long that I tense up. "*That's* what this is about?" he finally says.

"Maybe."

"Huh. You know what? Yeah, I've felt that way lots of times."

My breath catches. "You have?"

"Yep. One of those experiences even saved my life once, if you can believe that."

I sit up straighter. "Really?"

"Really. And I'll tell you all about it. But you should probably get that drink."

"Okay. But it'll take me a minute. Or two."

He doesn't hesitate. "Go ahead. It's not like I have anywhere to be."

"Shouldn't you, though?"

"Probably," he says. "But fuck it."

A strange energy catches hold of me as I set the receiver on the rug. In the kitchen, I dig out the paper cups I bought at the market and pour from my bottle of Cabernet—twist-off, since I assumed the corkscrew would be packed up. In the bedroom, I shuck my dirt-smeared clothes and don a garnet-colored off-the-shoulder cashmere sweater and black leggings, all the while wondering if Grayson will still be on the line when I get back. But I don't rush. Some rebellious part of me wonders how long he'll wait. At what point he'll deem his time too valuable for me to waste.

Michael would have told me to call him back.

But Grayson isn't Michael, because when I arrange the daybed's throw pillows into a cozy nest by the fire and climb in with my wine and the phone, he's still there.

"Hi," I say.

"Hi."

A long pause. That strange energy intensifies, zipping around like wasps in my bloodstream. I try to soothe it with a gulp of wine. "So. Tell me what happened to you."

Something clinks—ice in a glass, I think, which makes me wonder whether he's drinking water or something stronger.

"I've never told this story before," he says. "And it's about as personal as it gets. So if you're not up for that, say so now."

I smile into the receiver. "Personal is kind of the point."

"Okay. But don't say I didn't warn you."

I wiggle deeper into my pillows. The intensity of my brush with the bear slips away. There's only me here, soft and warm and bathed in firelight while the wine expands on my tongue and Grayson's smoky tenor purrs in my ear.

"This all happened in the Himalaya," he says. "A few years back."

"The Himalayas, you mean?"

"No," he says. "That's just a bastardized American way of saying it. People here get it wrong all the time, but in the local language, *Himalaya* is already pluralized. Saying *Himalayas* is kind of like saying *sheeps*. Or *mooses*."

I turn that tidbit over. Grayson might be a drinker and a self-proclaimed mess, but I forget that he's also an adventurer. That every stunning *National Geographic* photo represents a journey he's taken which I've only dreamed about. He's climbed mountains, dived oceans, watched the sun set over a thousand different horizons.

Amazing.

"Anyway," he says, "at the time, I was in a...dark place, in my life. One of the darkest I've ever been in. And I got sent to Nepal, on assignment. My job was to shoot these caves there that had only just been discovered. They were carved out of the cliff face a thousand years ago, but had lain untouched for centuries because they're so hard to get to. A ledge runs underneath, but there's no way to get to it without ropes."

I picture Grayson in climbing gear, scanning the rock face from beneath that scarred eyebrow while mountains jostle for space in a majestic sky. "Okay. Go on."

"It was just a normal day. A normal assignment. I climbed up while my partner waited below, and when I got onto the ledge, I unclipped so he could follow. But then I turned to look at the valley we'd hiked up from, and something happened. I had this...moment. This *episode*. It was like the whole world poured into me, all at once. The sky was so blue it hurt to look at, and those mountains... Christ, those mountains. There's something that happens, sometimes, in those high places, when the breeze rises on a clear day. The wind sweeps snow up off the summits, just shoots these fountains of sparks right into the sky. It's called spindrift."

A murmur catches in my throat. I've heard the word, but never knew what it meant.

"So there I was," he continues, "standing on this precipice in the middle of nowhere, and the whole world was laid out below me. The spindrift made it seem like the peaks were exhaling into the sky, and it all just looked so...weightless, you know? Like the mountains were about to let go of the earth and float up into the blue. The whole scene hit me right in the heart, and it felt like life was reminding me that no matter how fucked-up things get, there's always something beautiful somewhere, balancing it out."

"Wow." A delicate shiver dances through me. "You definitely understood the assignment."

He gives a soft laugh.

"Then what?" I say.

"Then I stood there and thought to myself, well, maybe that's all there is to it. Maybe I just need to let go, like these mountains. Maybe I need to stop hanging on to this thing that's slowly killing me. It was almost like I could hear something inside me, chanting it, over and over. *Let go, let go, let go.*"

I take a sip, but I'm too caught up to taste the wine. "And... that saved your life?"

"In the end, yeah."

"But how, exactly?"

Rustling fills the line, as if he's rearranging himself. "Because on that same trip, I climbed Everest, and what happened there had everything to do with those two words."

"Everest." Air rushes in through my teeth. "Where you were in that avalanche? Where you took that picture of yourself?"

"You've seen it?"

"Of course. I told you so already, in my email."

"Right," he says, momentarily gruff. "That's right. Then you probably know the story, or part of it. Except there's another part I never told anyone. And it's that right before the avalanche, I was still reliving that moment on the ledge. Just trudging along, hearing *let go, let go, let go* with every step. Because it felt like if I could just get to the top of that damn mountain, maybe I really could. Maybe I could finally let go of this thing that had been rotting inside me for years. Finally be free of it."

A pang twists in my chest. I know what *it* is without having to ask. Or rather, who. Lily. The woman whose death broke him in ways time has never reconciled.

"The point is," Grayson says, "when I heard the crack and saw all that snow, I did exactly what I was shouting at myself to do. I let go. *Physically.* I knew I couldn't outrun what was coming, so I threw down my axe. Ripped off my pack. Everything I could possibly let go of in those ten seconds went. And then the snow took me and I did my damnedest to swim upward, and when it was all over, I only ended up buried four feet down."

I make a horrified sound. I know the basics—he spent eleven minutes entombed in snow before his climbing partner dug him out. Eleven minutes in the dark, starving for air, not knowing whether he would live or die.

"Four feet's still plenty enough to kill you, but if I'd had all that gear weighing me down, it might've been more. I could've ended up ten feet down, and then Alex might not have gotten to me in time. As it was, I probably only had another few minutes. So in hindsight, yeah, that moment saved me. Those *words* did. And they never would've been in my head in the first place if not for that moment outside the caves."

The back of my neck prickles. This is already so much more significant than my story. "And after that? Did you manage to let go of the past, too?"

His gritty laugh warms my ear. "That? Fuck no. Here I am, three years later, still hanging on to all my bullshit. I doubt I'll ever figure *that* out. Living through an avalanche was easier. Way easier."

He goes quiet. In the silence, the pull of his breath comes and goes like a reassuring tide.

Or a turquoise ocean, my mind supplies.

I pass a hand over my eyes. How strange that I can picture

him so precisely when he has no clue who he's talking to. It's even stranger that I've spent well over a decade loving the hue of his hair, the angle of his nose, those delicate fingers. The sound of him breathing.

And the strangest thing of all? I feel like I know him. I can't tell if it's the voice, or the way he's just shared without trying to make himself sound noble, or something else entirely. But listening to him talk this way feels undeniably intimate, as if he's touching me on some deep level Michael learned to shy away from.

It emboldens me to say exactly what I'm thinking.

"There's something I want to know," I say. "Something I've wondered about ever since I saw that issue of *National Geographic*."

"Yeah? What's that?" His tone gains an edge, a sort of guarded hope I don't know what to make of.

"What were you thinking about? You'd almost just died, but it looks like you want to say something. Like you're trying to give someone a message."

He makes a pained sound. "Jesus." More ice clinking.

Probably not water, then.

"Nobody's ever asked me that before," he says. "People always want to know what it's like to be buried alive. What it feels like to drown on dry land. Whether I saw a light, did my life flash before my eyes, blah, blah, blah, all that crap. Nobody's ever asked what I wanted to say when I came back."

I flush, feeling suddenly ridiculous. "Right. Sorry. That's probably a stupid question. I'm sure you weren't thinking about anything but survival."

"No," he says quietly. "I did have something to say. It's just that out of the thousands of people who've seen that picture, you're the only one who's ever noticed."

I wait. My breath thins to nothing.

"The truth is…" I hear an audible, scraping swallow. "I was

thinking about *her*. How I'd never see her face again, never touch her skin, never wake up and breathe the smell of her hair. Never hear her laugh. Never piss her off by accident again, either. No matter how badly I wanted those things, it was impossible, and it didn't actually hit me until that avalanche did. And then I realized it was over, all of it, and all I could think of was how badly I wished I could get to her, wherever she was. Like…like I was fucking *drowning* in the need to tell her what she meant to me. I wanted to say, 'I love you, and you changed me, and you destroyed me, too, but I forgive you for that, and whether I die today or fifty years from now, it doesn't matter, I am who I am because of you.'"

He lets out a shuddering breath. More ice clinks.

"Does that answer your question?" he finally says.

I squeeze my eyes shut to stop a tear from sneaking out, then follow his example and partake in a hefty dose of wine.

It's a nonsensical reaction, this urge to cry over the depth of his love for some woman I've never even met. But there's something so wretchedly, tragically beautiful about his pain that I catch myself wishing someone would love me like that. So brightly that it burned them.

Because I suspect, on a cellular level I can't escape, that if *I* had died in that car wreck instead of Michael, he wouldn't have said about me what Grayson just did about Lily.

"Your turn," he says.

I take a few moments to collect myself. "You sound like a soldier who's just gone to battle and barely made it back."

He gives a dark chuckle. "That about sums it up. But don't change the subject. You managed to get two confessions out of me, so now I get your one. It's only fair."

It's more than fair, I almost say, because by the sound of it, he's just ripped his heart open and spilled the contents into my lap.

Telling him about Margo almost seems like cheating. "My story's not as intense as yours. Not even close."

"It doesn't have to be," he says softly. "It just has to mean something to you."

I swallow. "It does. It absolutely does. I just...don't know where to start."

"At the beginning." His voice strengthens, as if the subject change has granted him a reprieve. "You asked if nature has ever healed me, which means it's done that for you. So what did you need healing from?"

"Losing my best friend," I say, grateful for the straightforward question. I can do straightforward. "She died. In Costa Rica. When we were in tenth grade. And I wasn't okay after that. Not for a long time."

Silence comes through the line, giving me room to find my way. All the details Michael never asked for slide free—first in snipped-off pieces, then in long gushes. I tell Grayson about how much I adored Margo, how clever she was. I talk about the time we watched that Christmas movie where the boy licks a frozen flagpole, then rushed outside together to see if our tongues would really stick. I describe the time we learned to catch food in our mouths by tossing Cheerios across the room while shrieking with laughter. And our freshman year of high school, when Margo posted our school for sale on Craigslist, then lingered outside the office with me, eavesdropping on the bewildered staff as they muddled through one awkward phone conversation after another.

"When I found out she was never coming home, it was like someone had dropped me into the bottom of a well." I take another draft of wine. The bold, dry sting warms my throat. "I don't know how else to describe it. It was like I was watching my life happen through this tiny porthole overhead while everything around me was dark. I hid in my room for days at a time, not eating. My grades tanked. I lost a bunch of weight. I'm pretty sure my mom thought I was going to waste away."

Grayson grunts. "Grief. It's the most challenging emotion

in the human experience, isn't it? The hardest to deal with. You're not alone in that."

I pause. It's such a simple idea, but...I've never thought of it that way. "Yeah. You're absolutely right. And I was only fifteen, and I had no idea how to handle it. I was just spiraling, and my mom finally decided to pack up the car and bring me here for the summer. Try to snap me out of it."

"And being in the forest was the thing that finally helped," he says. Only the barest hint of a question mark softens the words, as if it's not a question at all.

"Yeah. It might sound silly, but...it felt natural, being here. Like forgiveness, and recovery. Like all the things people talk about finding in church, only I had to go outside to feel them. So I did. Every day. And by the end of the summer, I was better. Not great, but better. Margo being gone didn't hurt any less, but it was like I grew bigger and stronger, enough to handle it. If that makes sense."

"Perfect sense," he says. "You know, the Japanese have a word for what you're describing. *Shinrin-yoku*. It means something like...'forest bathing.' It's based around the idea that nature is therapeutic."

I stem a breath. "That's a thing?"

"It's a thing."

I swipe away the tears that sneaked out during my soliloquy about Margo. "How do you even know that?"

"I know a lot of things." He laughs. "Which is pretty ironic, considering that when it comes to this whole life business, I haven't the faintest fucking clue."

"I don't, either. At least that's how it feels, these days. I just hope being here will help me figure it out. Help me put myself back together."

"I hope so, too," he says, and sounds like he really means it.

For a few moments, I soak up the sound of him breathing. "You don't think it's stupid of me to come here? To 'forest bathe'?"

"You're talking to a guy who's built an entire career around chronicling nature's majesty. So no. I don't think it's stupid. At all."

We lapse into silence. The quiet settles over me like a blanket. I feel warmer than I have in hours. Months. Years, maybe.

"So, what now?" he finally says. "You're going into the woods tomorrow?"

"I did today, actually."

"Oh yeah? How'd that go?"

I reach for my cup again but find it empty. "Pretty well, actually. At least until the bear showed up."

"Bear?" he says. "Wait. *Bear?* What bear?"

"It's not a big deal," I hedge. "It was just a black bear. She came into the clearing I was in. With her cub. But it's fine. I'm fine."

"A mama? With her cub?" His tone sharpens, a complete departure from the smoky ease of earlier. "What'd you do? Put your arms up? Make yourself look big? You didn't look her in the eye, I hope?"

"Um…" I shrink into the pillows. Of course Mr. Nature Photographer Extraordinaire would know what to do. "Not exactly."

"You didn't run, did you?" His tone goes flat. "Tell me you didn't run."

"Okay," I say. "I won't."

When I don't elaborate, Grayson groans. "Really, Mina?"

I make a sound of protest. "I was too freaked out to think straight. I just…reacted. But it's fine. She didn't chase me."

He curses under his breath. "It's not *fine.* Someone should be there with you. Someone who can…" He makes a strangled sound.

"What?"

"Keep you safe."

I sit up. I don't think I'm imagining the panic edging his voice. As if he truly, genuinely *cares*.

"I want to see you," he says abruptly. "Face-to-face."

I frown. "What? You want to meet me?"

"Yes."

"When?"

"Right now. Where are you, exactly? This is a western Washington area code, so you can't be that far away."

I struggle to cobble together a response. "I'm up near Skykomish. It's an hour and a half from Seattle, at least."

"Okay, so it's ten thirty now," he says.

I shake my head. "This is crazy."

"No. My brother's widow is holed up in a cabin all by herself while a fucking bear prowls around outside, and meanwhile, I'm here, drinking Scotch and feeling sorry for myself and doing nothing even remotely useful. *That's* crazy."

For some reason, I latch on to the absolute least important part of that statement. "You're drinking Scotch?"

"Always."

I wince. I wish he hadn't named the same drink Michael once favored, but I have no doubt it's one of those twin things, since on a biological level, they're actually the same person. "How many have you had? Are you too drunk to drive?"

"This is my second, and I'm only halfway through, so no, I'm not drunk. And I'll put this glass down right now if you give me your address."

I cast about as though I might find someone here to tell me what to do. My gaze catches on the lantern, which still burns steadily, but it offers no answers.

Nothing here but an empty room—so empty I can feel the weight of it, dragging at my limbs.

"All right," I say, surprising myself, and rattle off the cabin's address.

A jangle sounds—car keys, I'm assuming. "Great. I'll see you in an hour."

"No. You won't get here until midnight. It's an hour and a half."

"Nah. Not the way I drive."

I start to caution him about the road's snaking curves, but it's too late. He's already hung up.

AFTER

While I wait for Grayson, the hum beneath my skin returns full force. I try to work it off by pacing, then, when that doesn't work, by downing more wine. As a last resort, I take the hottest shower I can tolerate. I decide I need to wash today's dirt off regardless, though I have trouble explaining why I put makeup on afterward.

I pace some more. The buzz rises to a fever pitch.

I am not, I think, *even remotely prepared to face a clone of my dead husband.*

But after sixty-seven minutes of agonizing anticipation, when a knock cuts through the percussive burble of the fire and I swing the door open to find six feet and three inches of man on my doorstep, my first thought is not that he looks like Michael.

Nope. He's even more attractive.

Grayson props one elbow against the doorframe and looks down with drawn brows. His hair is longer than Michael's ever was, the rich gold waves feathering against his cheekbones. The scar on his eyebrow glints in the firelight, and that, coupled with the leather jacket and dark jeans, gives him a faintly dangerous air, as if I've opened the door for a battle-worn tiger, already coiled and ready to pounce.

A tingle sweeps through me. Too late, I question the wisdom of allowing a stranger to drive out to my remote cabin in the middle of the night.

"Hi," I say.

"Hi." The furrow between Grayson's brows deepens. "Are you okay?"

I fiddle with my hair, tucking the ends behind my ears. "Should I not be?"

"I don't know. You tell me. I wasn't sure if you'd throw up. Or pass out."

I feel myself out. Neither seems imminent. "Do women often vomit when they first meet you? Or lose consciousness?"

The ghost of a smile touches his mouth. "I haven't gotten those reactions yet, no. But it's not every day that your husband's identical twin shows up."

I smooth down my sweater with both hands. "You know, I think I'm okay. You don't actually look like him. I mean, you do. But not as much as I expected."

He gives me a skeptical look. "People always say the opposite."

"No, really. Compared to Michael, you're much more..." *Raw*, I want to say, because a single glance tells me Grayson's past contains something cataclysmic. Unlike his brother, he wears his pain openly. It glitters there in the blue-green ice of his eyes, buried in plain view instead of behind a locked door.

"Good-looking?" he says hopefully.

The corners of my mouth curl. That, too, but I don't give him the satisfaction. "Wounded."

"Oh." He abandons his lean against the doorframe. "Well, shit. That's not what I was going for at all."

I step back. "Do you want to come in?"

"Yeah. Thanks." He ventures over the threshold, his eyes sweeping the room. I can't tell if he's cataloging the kitschy coziness or scanning for bears hiding behind the wicker furniture, but when he flips the lock and draws the latch chain, I suspect the latter.

"I don't think that's going to stop her if she really wants to get in," I say.

"Can't hurt."

"I guess not." A flush creeps into my cheeks. With him here, I suddenly have the urge to hide. He's so big, and so close, and… God, I'd forgotten how *tall* Michael was.

"Even if you're not going to puke," he says, "you do look like you could use a drink."

I wonder if that's code for *him* needing a drink, but decide it doesn't matter. My years of abstention with Michael were all about moral support, and I'm not the booze police. With a nod, I go to the kitchen and pour two cups this time.

I return to find Grayson standing by the fire.

The sight of him glaring down into the flames like he's contemplating some life-or-death decision stops me in my tracks. He's laid his jacket over the daybed, revealing a body that's honed and carved in ways even Michael's never was. I already knew from those photos, but seeing it in real time astonishes me. His dark green T-shirt accentuates his musculature and reveals two tattoos—a lion on his upper arm, inked in black except for sapphire eyes so vibrant they seem to glow, and some kind of Celtic knot work adorning the inside of his opposite forearm.

I shake myself and hand off the wine, which he reduces by half in a span of moments. "Cabernet," he says. "Nice. I always was a fan."

"Me, too. Sorry about the paper cups. It's all I have."

"No problem. Wine is wine."

"True." I nod at the tattoos. "What do those mean?"

He shrugs. "Nothing in particular. I just liked the way they looked."

I study the lion, which stares right back. Michael didn't have any tattoos. Neither do I, so I can't say from experience, but I've always assumed people have some deep meaning in mind when they get one. "None of your tattoos have any significance?"

"I didn't say that." His eyelids flicker. "One of them does."

I know without asking which one he means. The one he doesn't let anyone see.

My eyes stray to his chest. A few buttons adorn the neck of his shirt, only half of which are done up. The inky end of something oblong and pointed—a stylized leaf, maybe?—peeps at me from the curve of his pectoral muscle.

I tell myself to stop staring, but the urge to know more pushes questions against my lips. And from the way Grayson's watching me, intently and with half-hooded eyes, I have the strangest sense that if I asked, he'd strip off his shirt right now and let me see for myself.

Something flutters in my throat. I break from his gaze and carry my wine toward the daybed, then pause, realizing we can't both occupy it without touching. I turn back, at a loss.

Grayson's mouth quirks. "It's okay. I don't have any problem with the floor." He takes a cross-legged seat on the rug and gestures at my abandoned pillow nest. "Looks like you'd already gotten comfy down here, anyway."

I reclaim my earlier place, grateful for the four feet of empty air between us. "I can't believe you drove all the way up here in the middle of the night."

"I can't believe you let me."

I turn my cup around but don't drink. Maybe I shouldn't. I already seem to be making decisions I normally wouldn't. "It sounded like it was important to you."

"It was," he says.

"Why?"

He heaves a breath. "I already told you. I need to know you're okay. And I couldn't stand the idea of you getting mauled by some wild animal with no one around to help. I mean, I get why you came, but have you really thought this through? The wilderness isn't the kind of place you should go wandering in alone. At least not at twilight."

I glance toward the fire. Of course I haven't thought this through. My entire mission here has been borne of desperation. Of a need to do something other than take the same painful, lurching steps I've been attempting for months, none of which seem to have gotten me anywhere.

Best to be honest with myself about that. And with Grayson, after the way he's bared his soul.

"I don't have any kind of plan," I say. "And maybe I shouldn't have come. But I just couldn't spend another minute in that house."

"Look, I'm not saying this was a mistake." His tone softens. "I'd just feel a lot better if you had someone watching out for you. At least until you go back home."

Back home.

The words immobilize me. I can't imagine returning to Seagrove—sleeping in the same bed Michael and I once shared, reimprisoning myself among the trappings of a life that might never have been what I hoped for. I can't picture myself ever plucking those divorce papers off the floor without wanting to throw up.

I screw my eyes shut, blocking out the thoughts.

"Hey." Grayson's voice fills with smoky concern. "Where'd you go?"

"Somewhere bad," I say.

"Yeah. I can see that."

I open my eyes. He looks worried. Maybe because he's already emptied his cup.

"Here." I push my drink his way. "This is the last alcohol in the house. You can have it. I've already had two, anyway."

He doesn't look down. "I don't care about the wine."

"But you care about me." I mean it as a question, but somehow it comes out like a statement.

"Yes," he says.

"Because I'm your brother's wife?"

He hesitates. "No."

I give a faint shake of my head. "Then I don't get it."

"Get what?"

"This." I wave a hand. It hardly seems real. *Grayson Drake*—famous photographer, eternal bachelor, love-wrecked Romeo who outlived his Juliet—is sitting on my living room floor, watching me with a potent combination of vulnerability and concern.

But I haven't done anything to earn it. Not one thing to justify this level of interest.

"Why did you come, exactly?" I say. "You've driven all this way to make sure I'm all right, but… Well, it shouldn't matter to you. *I* shouldn't matter. There has to be something more. Some reason you're looking at me like that."

He stares, then drags a hand through his hair. "Wow. You really don't pull any punches, do you?"

"Do *you*?"

"No. So I can respect that." He picks up my wine without breaking eye contact and gulps half of it down. "You're really going to make me tell you?"

My heartbeat flickers faster. "I think I have to. Otherwise I'll just be dissecting everything you do, trying to figure it out."

He still doesn't look away, so I don't, either. Finally, he reaches into his back pocket, pulls out his cell phone, and flicks a few buttons. "This is the reason. What made me come."

I take the phone. The room retreats, the snap of the fire fading.

It's a picture. Of me. Standing on a beach in Hawaii, freshly emerged from the ocean, four years younger and four years happier. I remember the moment with perfect clarity—Michael and I had just gone swimming with sea turtles off Laniakea Beach. I'd never done anything like that before.

And haven't again since.

I cradle the phone close. It's not a terribly flattering photograph, even if thirty-three-year-old me does look pretty damn good in a bikini. I'd just pushed my snorkel gear onto my head, and a red mark from the mask indents my face. My hair pokes out around my ears, hopelessly in need of brushing after its encounter with the sea.

Yet I have to admit there's magic there. Joy shines from my face like light. I'm laughing, exploding with celebration over being alive, and somehow the feeling rises from the pixels in a way that hits me square in the chest.

Okay, so maybe Grayson did know who he was talking to. Except...

"I don't look like this anymore." I stare so long my throat thickens. "I don't feel like this anymore, either."

"You could," he says softly.

"No. That was another life."

"Bullshit. That was this one. And that girl? She's you. And the truth is..."

In the pause, I glance up.

He looks terrified, but keeps going. "The truth is...the woman in that picture takes my breath away. She's *radiant*. She isn't thinking about how she looks, or whether her photo's going on the internet someday. She doesn't care about getting her Christmas bonus or what's going to happen next year. None of that crap. She's just relishing a moment. She understands a secret other people don't, about how to live, and I want her to share it with me. I want her to whisper it in my ear."

I can't move. I can't even breathe. My attention dives to the photograph again—anywhere but the naked supplication in Grayson's face. The snapshot wavers, a taunting reminder of the person I used to be. The person I *could* have been.

Then I notice the heart icon at the bottom. It's filled in, meaning he's saved this to his favorites.

I pray for my voice to hold steady. "How many times have you looked at this?"

"A thousand," he rasps. "More."

I fight back my tears and swipe a button to display the picture's metadata. There's a date from four years ago and a line showing it was saved from a text message from Michael's phone number.

"I don't understand. Why would Michael send this to you?"

He laughs, low and humorless. "So I could torture myself with what I don't have."

"No. He would never—"

"He would." His voice is hard. Final. "He absolutely would."

I press my lips together, then decide to let that go. For now. I thrust his phone back. "Fine. So now you're here to…what? See if I'm still her? Because I can tell you right now I'm not."

"But you could be. In the right circumstances."

"Really? And what circumstances would those be?"

"With me," he says quietly. "At least, I think. Or not. That's what I'm here to find out."

"With *you*?" I try to absorb the enormity of that statement and fail. "You mean you came here to try and save me? Or is this about saving yourself?"

Something heated and steady burns in his gaze. "Both. I never said I wasn't a selfish bastard."

I shake my head, a wobbly denial. I have no idea what to say.

"The point is, Michael's the one who died, not you." When he glances down at his phone again, the unguarded tenderness in his face makes my lungs ache. "And even though you said on the phone you're okay, I could tell you were lying."

I fidget, but don't confirm the obvious.

"So," he continues, "you're right. Me coming here is about more than just making sure you don't get eaten by bears. It's about the fact that I'd never forgive myself if I didn't try to find the girl in this picture. If I let her fade away without even attempting to bring her back."

"Okay." My voice is rough. "Let's say you have a point. What exactly do you want from me? Right now?"

"In this exact moment?"

"In this exact moment."

His attention slides to my neck and downward, where my sweater cups the curve of my shoulder. "I don't think you want me to answer that."

A jolt shoots through me and settles low, pooling into something liquid and fiery.

Try as I might, I can't deny that his interest does something to me. I knew it on the phone, and now that he's here, it's like a living thing, curling and crackling between us.

Shaken, I scoot backward. The distance helps squash my traitorous response. Not that it's real, anyway. It's just my stupid brain getting confused, because of who he looks like. Or doesn't look like, as the case may be. "Aside from that. What do you want from me that I can actually give?"

"Just for you to spend time with me. We can go into the woods. Or not. Whatever you need."

"Spend time with you? As what? A friend?"

"Anything you want."

I weigh that. "How much time, exactly?"

"I've got a week. After that, I have to go out of the country, on assignment. I'll be in New Zealand for a while."

A bolt of longing joins the heat in my belly. I wonder if he has any idea what that statement means to me, that he managed to end up with the life I once dreamed of for myself.

He doesn't seem to. He just awaits my answer with innocent

eyes, as if it's perfectly normal to drop into a grieving widow's life and ask her to get to know her late husband's estranged twin brother.

Then again, it's not like I have much to lose. But a week is out of the question.

"Three days," I say.

"What? No. I can't work that fast. A week."

"*Three days*. Take it or leave it."

He thinks for a moment, then extends a hand. "Fine. Three days. During which time I'll do my best to make you smile like that again." He nods down at his phone. "And if I can't, you can tell me to get lost."

I hesitate. I'm afraid to touch him. Afraid of what it will mean, of what it might do to me. But when I tuck my palm into his grip, it turns out it's just a handshake. "Deal."

We break apart, him looking like he wants to say more, me wondering what I've just gotten myself into. The sensation of having walked this path before ties my gut in a knot.

"What?" Grayson says. "Why do you look so skeptical all of a sudden?"

"I just…have the craziest feeling you're about to say we should have a rule about no sex."

"No sex?" He somehow makes the words sound foreign. "What? Hell no. I'll gladly fuck you right now, here in front of the fire, if you want. It's not like I haven't imagined it enough times."

The knot of tension within me only ravels tighter. "Oh. You…have?" Shit. I sound like I'm dying of thirst. Like I haven't had a drop of water in three days.

Or six months.

"I can guarantee you'd enjoy every minute," he says. "And that there'd be a lot of them."

A squeak comes out of me. "Do me a favor."

"Yeah?"

"Don't say that again. Please."

His mouth turns down at the edges, then up, as if he can't decide whether to frown or smile. "So that's a no?"

"Definitely a no." I'm not foolish enough to think that sleeping with the twin of the man I'm still grieving wouldn't open a Pandora's box of problems best avoided.

I break from his gaze and focus on the battered red lantern, trying to banish the mental image he's conjured. Its flame glows, a steady star, and I force myself to think of the nights spent playing board games by its light, how I dreamed of doing the same thing with a partner, someday. "To be honest, I think I'd rather…"

Grayson leans in, his lips parted. "Yeah?"

"Play Monopoly."

He blinks, as if waiting for the punch line. "Play…Monopoly?"

"Mmm-hmm."

"Okay," he says slowly. "Not what I thought you were going to say."

I shrug. "You said we could do whatever I wanted."

His expression turns sly. "Okay. But I should warn you, I'm not a gentleman. I won't just let you win. And I call dibs on the shoe."

A smile stirs. "Perfect. I like the dog, anyway."

"Great. Just one condition. We play for more than money."

I brace myself for something sexual. "Like?"

"Secrets. Well, not *secrets*. I won't ask anything invasive. But every time you pay me rent, you also have to answer a question. Same goes for me."

I process that. "Like Truth or Dare? But without the dares?"

He grins. It's open and boyish, affording a glimpse of the man he might have been if Lily had never died, if he and Michael had never had a falling-out that burned so hot it left them both blackened and scarred. "Exactly."

"Huh," I say. "That sounds…surprisingly fun, actually."

"Sometimes I manage to come up with a good idea." His tone plays at modesty, but he looks profoundly pleased with himself.

Thankfully, the cabin's Monopoly board hasn't gone the way of our other belongings. I find it wedged in the bottom of the TV cupboard, right where it's always been. After blowing a layer of dust off the top, Grayson and I stretch out on our stomachs and dole out the prescribed stacks of colorful paper money.

He indeed proves ruthless, buying up one property after another, building houses the second he's able, mortgaging and unmortgaging like a pro. Still, I win the first question.

I rest my chin on fisted hands and watch the firelight play over his face. "How about…where'd you get that scar on your eyebrow?"

He looks startled, but recovers in moments. "That's easy. Riding a bike."

"Oh. That's it?"

"Yep."

I deflate. I'd imagined a bar fight. Or maybe a jilted husband taking a golf club to him after finding him in bed with the cheating wife.

Not that I would've preferred that. But my mental image of six-year-old Grayson cartwheeling over the handlebars of a bicycle doesn't have quite the same impact.

"My turn," he says, when I land on Tennessee Avenue. "Tell me about your first kiss."

I freeze. Damn. Why is his question so much better than mine? "That depends," I say.

He frowns. "How can it possibly depend?"

I fidget with my token, turning the dog around on its orange rectangle. "Do you want to know about the first time my lips touched someone else's lips? Or the first time a guy *meant* to kiss me?"

"Well, now I really need to hear this." He ponders. "First time your lips touched."

Old habit makes me clamp down on the answer, but the curiosity on his face soon frees my tongue. God, I haven't thought about this in years. I doubt Michael would have approved. "It happened when I was fourteen. Margo dared me to pretend to drown in the town pool, and the lifeguard pulled me out."

He stares. "The... Wait, what?"

I duck my head. "Yeah. The lifeguard. He was in the grade ahead of us, and I'd had a crush on him for like, three years. Margo was so sick of hearing about it that she came up with this cockamamie plan to get him to kiss me. Which, looking back, I realize was not even remotely okay. But Margo had this...effect on people. Being around her made you braver than you really were."

Grayson's eyes slit like he's trying to decide whether I'm joking. "So this kid pulled you out of the water and gave you mouth-to-mouth? I thought that only worked in movies."

Heat scalds my cheeks. "Yeah. I'm ashamed of it now. I probably scared him half to death. I even found out later that he'd had a crush on me, too. He was trying to work up the nerve to do something about it, but after the pool thing, I was so embarrassed that I took off running every time I saw him in the hallway. So I guess, in the end, I got what I deserved. Which was nothing."

"Well, damn. That still might be the most badass first-kiss story of all time."

My lips spread into a startled smile. Not the reaction I was expecting, but I'll take it. "Your turn."

Minutes slide into hours. When the fire dies, we play on by lantern light. I learn that Grayson's favorite country is Egypt, that he used to be penniless before he started working for *National Geographic* and hated being poor because it made him feel like a failure compared to Michael, that despite his many conquests, he's never slept with a married woman—"Come on, I have *some* morals"—and has a lifelong phobia of injuring himself and not being able to climb mountains anymore.

"Really?" I say. "Why's that so important?"

He glances sidelong at the dying embers. "I think it's because mountain climbing is one of the only things I can actually control. I mean, look at me."

I do, though I've been doing little else all evening.

"I'm somehow forty years old," he continues, "entirely against my will."

"You're thirty-nine."

A smile tugs at the corner of his mouth. "Okay, *almost* forty. A number I never imagined I'd actually reach. I especially never imagined being forty and lonely, but I can't seem to fix that, either. So the mountain-climbing thing, it's kind of like a consolation for me."

"Because it's the only battle you can actually win?"

"Yeah. Exactly." He dips his chin affirmatively. "You get it."

"I *think* so. It sort of sounds like me and running."

A line appears between his brows. "How so?"

I hesitate, but the evening's honesty permeates the air. "When I was with Michael, running was a way to...distract myself. To convince myself I was happy when sometimes I really just wanted to scream."

His eyes flare. He looks more than a little disturbed by that confession. "Why on earth would you have wanted to scream? And more importantly, why wouldn't you have?"

"Because," I say, "half of being married is just keeping the peace."

"That...doesn't sound right."

"What would you know? You've never done it."

He doesn't flinch, but the look on his face gives the impression that he has. "Is that what you've spent the last fourteen years doing, Mina? Keeping the peace?"

I pick at my fingernails. The question worms its way into my gut. My first instinct is to shy away, but something about the way Grayson's watching me makes me wonder.

Did I spent the entirety of my marriage so in love with what could've been—with what I'd only touched in those first heady weeks, and then in the briefest of snatches—that I never stopped to examine what I actually had? Have I spent the last six months mourning a man who ceased to exist long before he died?

"I don't know," I say honestly. It won't help to reiterate that I've always blamed Grayson for Michael's distance, that I devoted an enormous slice of my life to trying to undo the damage he caused.

Because I have the sneaking suspicion that he might be right. He was never responsible for that. *Michael* was.

"I don't know much," Grayson says. "But I do know you shouldn't tame yourself for other people's sake. If you want to scream, scream. And if you want to do something else…do that, too." When his attention drops to my mouth, I suspect we've strayed onto an entirely different subject.

Heat shoots across my cheeks. "Maybe you're right," I say hurriedly. "But if so, that also means you shouldn't have to climb mountains just to feel like you have some say in your own life."

Thankfully, he doesn't call my bluff on the subject change. "True. But you know it's a lot easier to dispense sage advice than to take it, right?"

I snicker. The crisp tension in the air softens.

"Besides," he says, "mountain climbing keeps me fit. And I'd prefer not to dislike what I see in the mirror every day."

"Well, that sounds impossible."

"Oh? Why's that?"

Okay, maybe this direction isn't any better, but I can't seem to stop myself. "Come on. Look at you over there, with all your muscles. You look like sin. You could probably spend the next year being a couch potato and still drive women crazy."

I swear his chest puffs out, even though he's lying down. "You think I look like sin?"

"I do."

"Is that a good thing?"

I pause. "I'm ninety-nine percent sure it's the exact opposite of a good thing."

He cracks a smile, and what could be the most awkward of moments instead turns into us trading goofy grins. "For the record," he says, "I think you're gorgeous, too. In case you hadn't realized."

"Well, thanks. Not as much as I used to be, though."

"Every bit as much as you used to be. Based on that picture, I mean." His eyes heat. I don't know why I compared them to ice at first. Warm, tropical waves tickle at my toes, inviting me to step in. "Maybe a little too skinny right now, but we can fix that. I'll bring you a cheeseburger tomorrow. Two cheeseburgers, if you let me win."

My self-consciousness dissolves. We laugh, and then I roll and land on Park Place, setting my dog next to one of his hotels.

"Damn." I inventory my assets, but even if I mortgage everything, I don't have enough.

"Game, set, match," he says. "And now I get one last question. The one I've been saving."

I push all my money across the board. He takes it, his fingers brushing mine.

I snatch my hand away. "Um… Yeah. Shoot."

"I want to know what your favorite moment is. Ever. In your whole life."

My eyes widen. What a question.

Memories clamor over one another, mostly involving Michael—the moment I walked up to his car and first saw his face, the time I opened my eyes in that underground cave in Canada. The first time I had him inside me. The night we lay in midnight waves in Hawaii and just talked, every word a thread stitching us together.

But none of those quite measure up.

I clear my throat. "Once, when me and Michael first met, we drove out to this mountaintop observatory. Not too far from here, actually. When we got out, he looked at the sky and said something about how tiny we are, but how our smallness also makes us everlasting. I remember holding his hand while this indescribable feeling came over me."

Grayson studies my face. "What feeling?"

"Like"—I chew at my lip—"one of those Magic Eye pictures I loved as a kid. The whole world seemed to snap into focus, and life made sense in a way it never had before. I could *feel* how us standing there was a gift for us alone, forever until the end of time, never to be experienced by anyone else. In that moment, I knew life wasn't about tomorrow or yesterday, because those aren't real anyway. It's just about what we do with our right here, right now."

He draws a shaky breath.

I do, too. "God, I haven't felt like that in so long. But I did then, and it was intoxicating, and illuminating, and…and…"

My voice withers in the face of Grayson's fierce frown.

"Shit," he says. "I didn't mean to make you cry."

I look down. A few tears glisten on the pale green game board. I sit up, scrubbing at my cheeks and making fervent wishes for more wine. "Sorry. It's just… The truth is, I felt like my whole life was decided right then. And then it turned out so different from what I expected. So very fucking different."

"I know the feeling," he says gently.

I nod. I don't doubt he does. I've intentionally avoided questions about Lily all evening, but for a moment, it's like her ghost is here with us, a silent ship passing in the depths of his gaze.

"Would a hug help?" he says.

I gather my knees to my chest. "No. It's fine. I'm fine."

"Okay." Skepticism weights his voice. "Just tell me what you need."

"Some sleep, I think. It's almost four, anyway."

He nods, then starts packing everything away.

I watch, struck by how competent he looks just cleaning up a board game. I wonder if his hands move with that same swift confidence when he takes a picture, and if he wore this same determined expression when he photographed that tornado.

"But maybe," I venture, "you could tuck me in?"

When his fingers still around the stack of yellow hundreds, I rush to clarify.

"I don't mean in a naked way, just that it would be nice if you laid down with me for a minute. Maybe tell me a story about one of the places you've been to."

"Sure." He clears his throat, though it doesn't do much to smooth the roughness there. "I can do that."

"Thanks. And hey. Looks like you turned out to be a gentleman, after all."

Long seconds pass. "That's definitely not the word I would use."

In my bedroom, I close my door to change into my pajamas, then let Grayson in and crawl under the covers. He flips off the light, plunging us into the freedom of darkness. When he lowers himself onto my bed, the mattress dips, but somehow it feels more like a weight lifting than settling.

I consider scooting against the wall, but after that Monopoly game, I feel closer to him than I have to anyone in a long time.

Screw it, I decide. Life is short.

So I cuddle into his side, nestling my cheek against the hard plane of his chest. I try not to notice how well I fit. I do, however, note the arm that curls around me, the fingers that play shyly with the small of my back.

"Which country do you want to hear about?" he asks.

I wonder whether I'm imagining the quaver in his voice. "How about your favorite? Egypt."

"Egypt." His tone turns reverent, like he's tasting each letter. I *am* imagining it, clearly. "Good choice."

My lashes drift against my cheeks as he paints me pictures with smoke-soaked words. He talks about bright, dusty plazas and the organized chaos of men herding goats across barren, sandy roads. About the particular sweetness of the way water smells in the desert. He tells me about stone temples glowing pink at sunset and the impossible awe of tracing millennia-old hieroglyphics with bare fingertips.

I drink it up. I can *feel* the weight of history, the majesty of the pyramids, the kiss of a Saharan breeze against my skin.

"I'd like to go," I say in the darkness. "Someday."

"You should." He rolls toward me, cupping one hand against my cheek, and I coil tight, knowing I don't have the strength to refuse him if he tries to kiss me right now.

But he just tucks my hair behind my ear and says, "Good night, Mina."

"Good night," I whisper back.

"Will you be all right by yourself?"

I know what he's asking—about my safety, but also whether I want him to stay. "I'll be fine."

"Okay." He swallows audibly. "Is there a way to lock the door behind me?"

"Yeah. The key's under the grizzly."

The mattress springs back, and he goes without another word. A minute later, the engine of something throaty and powerful ignites in the driveway.

Long after the sound of gravel beneath tires fades away, I lie in the dark with open eyes, wishing I'd asked him to stay.

BEFORE

I spot the necklace while out for a walk in downtown Oahu.

The twisted silver chain glints in a jewelry shop window, and I stop to press my fingers against the glass. The necklace is spare, simple. A perfect twin of the one Michael lost the day he went to jail.

The traffic and salt-soaked sunshine fade, the tropical breeze giving way to the scent of kettle corn. I think back to those nights in our condo in Seattle, which inevitably ended with me and Michael making out on the couch or whispering in the dark. I can still feel the way the chain tangled around my fingertips when I swept my hand over the broad planes of his chest.

My arm falls from the window. God, that feels like so long ago. I don't even remember the last time we used that corn popper, only that we brought it to Seagrove when we moved. I shoved it into the cabinet next to the dishwasher and don't think it's strayed from that spot even once.

I start to walk away from the window, then stop, unable to

make my feet carry me any farther. Five minutes later, I walk out of the jewelry store with a bag in hand.

Back at the hotel, I find my husband on our patio overlooking the Pacific, catching up on emails. Beside his computer, a virgin piña colada sweats in a tall glass.

The flower-rich breeze ruffles his close-cropped hair. Usually, I would never interrupt him while he's working, but here...

I sneak up behind him, set the bag down, and drape my hands over his eyes. "Guess who?"

I feel him smile, the apples of his cheeks plumping against my hands. "My favorite person in the whole world?"

"Nope," I whisper in his ear. "Just your wife."

When I let go, he snaps the computer closed and spins his chair around to face me. I climb on, straddling him. The effect is instantaneous, though I can't say what gets me more hot and bothered—the willingness with which he abandons his work, or the way his hands clamp around my waist.

"I got you something," I say, breathy.

"Did you?" His thumbs draw circles around my hip bones— something he knows I love but never takes the time for anymore. "Let me guess. Is it wet? And smooth? And tastes just a little bit like honey?"

My eyes squeeze shut as his fingers skim up my sides. It's hard to believe he hasn't kissed me once, and yet the way he's touching me conveys something deeper than lust. It's reverence. Worship.

Still, if he wants to pin me to the bed so we can toast the demise of our six-day run of celibacy afterward, I don't think I can refuse. "You know, I think it's exactly those things."

"Oh, good." His hands drop. "Because I was just sitting here, wondering how I could convince someone to bring me another piña colada."

I open my eyes to find him grinning up at me. "A piña colada," I say tonelessly. "You're a bastard."

"And you love it. Now what'd you really get me?"

WHEN WE HAD FOREVER

I study him through slitted lashes. Fine. If he wants to play, we'll play. "You have to let me put it on you to find out."

He splays out in the chair like a starfish. "Be my guest."

I lean down to pluck the chain from its bag. All the while, I wriggle and buck, grinding against him until he stiffens beneath me.

"There we go." I fasten the clasp, all innocence, and pull back.

His eyelids have dropped to half-mast. "You minx. You know you're evil, right?"

"No," I say. "*You* are. This whole abstinence thing was your idea."

"Was it?"

I brace my hands on his shoulders. He's on the brink of recanting—I can tell by his parted lips and the liquid shimmer in his eyes.

But his self-control proves unconquerable, because he sighs and cups my chin. "I think resisting you might actually be the hardest thing I've ever done."

For a moment, I consider begging, but a worm of doubt wriggles in the back of my mind. Without his drafting table here to distract him, this week has been every bit as intoxicating as our first. Maybe even more so, since now I don't have to worry about whether he's mine or not.

He is, now and forever.

What will happen once we resume our habit of devouring each other on every available surface?

"I can see that." I climb off, casting a pointed smile at the impressive tent in his shorts. "But you're right. A deal's a deal."

A shadow crosses his face. He brings his hands up to play with the chain. "Yeah. And look—at least I get this fancy consolation prize. Though I'm surprised you remembered."

"How could I forget?"

"It was forever ago."

"Ten years isn't *that* long. Do you like it?"

He holds the necklace out and looks down. When he smiles, the clouded moment passes. "I love it. I'll treasure it forever."

For the rest of our vacation, he wears it day and night—in the ocean, in the shower, during a tandem parasail that makes the beach shrink to a ribbon and leaves me wondering whether I detest heights or wish I could grow wings.

He only takes the necklace off once. The night before we leave, we amble down to the beach in our bathing suits at sunset. Michael sits on the sand and draws me down next to him. The ocean sighs and nibbles at our toes. Palm fronds chatter behind us. We say nothing as the sky kaleidoscopes from rose to lavender to indigo.

One by one, the stars unveil themselves. I halfway expect Michael to get up and walk off, but he seems content to watch the evolving majesty of the oncoming night. The silence deepens, rich and wide and welcoming, and I lace my fingers through his. He squeezes.

I don't know how long we sit like that, watching the stars. Hours, maybe.

"Fuck," he finally breathes. "Would you look at that? There must be billions of them."

My heart cracks open and hinges wide, admitting a rush of ocean-filled night and undiluted love for the man beside me. Michael hasn't cursed in…years, probably, and that alone betrays the depth of what he's feeling.

"Do you see that one, there?" He points skyward with his free hand, leaving the other folded around mine. Sandy grit abrades our palms, but I don't care.

I follow his finger. Michael has singled out a purple-hued star, brighter than the rest. "I see."

"That one's my favorite."

I laugh. "You have a favorite? Out of billions?"

"Absolutely." He turns to fix me with his gaze, and my breath dwindles. "It's hands-down my favorite, and the most amazing thing about it is, I'd know it anywhere. I could be in...I don't know, Mexico. Timbuktu. I could be halfway across the planet and still look up and find *that* exact star, and say, 'Oh look, there she is.' Because distance doesn't matter. Time doesn't matter. Even in the daytime, when I can't see it, *that* doesn't matter, either, because that star is still there, still burning so brightly because it just can't help itself. Still outshining all the others."

An awed sound slips out. My chest works like a bellows.

"You understand what I'm saying, right?"

"I think so," I whisper.

"It's you," he says. "You're my star. My one in seven billion."

I can't stop myself. I reach out.

He grabs for me at the same time, and we go tipping into the sand together, his fingers in my hair, my hands fastened to his sides like I can hang on to him forever, like I can live in this *exact* moment until the sun goes dark.

His face hovers inches from mine. His skin feels like scalding silk beneath my fingertips. His rib cage expands and contracts, expands and contracts, its urgent rhythm a perfect counterpoint to the naked longing in his eyes.

"I want to kiss you so badly right now," he says.

I inhale. *Do it*, I try to say, but a rogue wave chooses that moment to crest over us, drenching us with cold water and gritty sand. Michael bellows in surprise and I roll away, laughing and not quite sorry for the excuse to draw out this potent magic that much longer. When I sit up and push my sopping hair out of my eyes, a flash of white tumbles in the receding wave, and I reach for it. When I brush the sand off, I find a gleaming puka shell in my palm, complete with a hole punched through the middle.

I hold it out. "Here. Here's your kiss. A reminder that you're my one in seven billion, too."

He gives me a wry smile, then takes the shell, handling it as though the fate of the universe depends on him keeping it safe. He takes off his necklace, threads the puka on, and refastens the clasp. The shell rests below the hollow of his throat, the perfect accessory to that beautiful chest.

"I'm never going to take this off."

"You'd better not," I say.

But the following afternoon, just before our jet takes off, when I weave my fingers through his in an attempt to ease his anxieties, I frown. The top few buttons of his dress shirt, which has already made a reappearance in preparation for our return to normality, are undone. In the gap, his tanned skin is smooth and bare.

My fingers tighten around his. "What happened to your necklace?"

"What?" His free hand gropes at his neck, and his eyes flare. "Oh. Crap. It must've come off in the ocean this morning. Damn it. I'm sorry."

I try to shrug it off, but the sting of my wasted gift lances deep, spurred by the fact that Michael is already slipping away again. I can *feel* it. As we taxi onto the runway, he tugs his hand away and starts fiddling with his phone. When I glance sidelong, I see him swiping through pictures of our vacation. "What're you doing?"

"Nothing." He brings up a shot of me after our turtle swim, taps a few buttons, then pockets the phone and faces the window. "Just seeing if there're any good ones in here."

"Are there?"

"A few."

He sounds casual, but in a forced way, and something in the set of his shoulders puts him as far away from me as the moon. It seems the pictures are just that already—pictures. Yesterdays that have nothing to do with our right now.

"Are you nervous again?" I hate my pleading tone. "About flying?"

"Yeah," he admits. "I hate this part. And to be honest, I really, really don't want to go home."

That last part breathes hope into me. "Nothing has to change, you know. We could still be the people we were here."

When he finally looks at me again, I see everything I need to know—a stony hopelessness etched into every line of his face.

Nothing will change. We'll go home and resume the same routine we drifted into years ago. He may have put work aside for ten whole days, but he can't resist its siren song any longer.

"I wish it worked that way," he says.

"It could," I whisper.

His mouth twists. "Tell me something."

"What?"

He waits so long that my stomach churns. "Are you happy? With me?"

The churn intensifies, but I muffle it with a smile. "Of course. I love you. I'd marry you all over again, if I could." *If only so I could have this one vacation.*

"Are you sure?" he says. "Because I really need to know. You don't ever think about the past? Wish you'd done it differently?"

I frown. He never talks like this.

In the pause, I consider admitting everything. How, for all that he's given me the world, I wish he would buy me less and give me more of himself. How I mourn the easy vulnerability that came so naturally to him, back before Grayson ruined him.

How, at times, I've wondered what my life would've been like if I'd gotten on that plane to Greece, or what chasing the travel-writer dream would have amounted to.

Except I really *would* trade it all over again for more weeks like this one.

So I tell him half the truth, if only as a way of asking him not to close me out again. Especially because I know now, beyond a shadow of a doubt, that the man I fell in love with still exists. He's been staring into my eyes all week. "No. No one else could ever make me as happy as you do. And our life together, how hard you work to take care of me…that means everything. *You* mean everything, Michael."

It's my last-ditch attempt to close the widening gap. To catch hold of this version of him and force him to stay. But he only nods and goes silent, his broad shoulders walling me out as he turns his attention to the window again.

Stung, I face forward and jab at my screen until a movie about ninjas comes on.

I watch the film without really seeing it. The whole time, I think about the necklace. How apt its loss is as a metaphor for our marriage.

Here I am, giving myself, offering him something precious, and he's just…letting it slip away.

We don't speak for the rest of the flight. Only after we land in Seattle and he freshens up in the bathroom does he finally relax enough to start a conversation.

On the drive home, I try to blame his fear of flying for the silent interlude. But our sex that night, for once, does nothing for me. It's mechanical and joyless, and I can't figure out how ten days' worth of volcanic buildup could possibly end with such a fizzle.

It does, though. And in the morning, Michael's side of the bed is empty. He's already in his office; I can hear the purposeful scratch of pencil against paper, even from down the hall.

I stare at the ceiling, trying to decipher the tangle inside my chest. Defeat and hope war for dominance, and I feel myself arrive at a turning point.

I can give up, or I can keep going. Keep trying.

Eventually, the mental dust settles. The answer seems achingly clear.

Michael's brother might have scarred him all those years ago, but that didn't snuff out the spark that first drew us together. Hawaii has proved that I still have a chance at having it all—

our life here, *plus* the incomparable man who watched the stars on the beach with me.

I just need to find a way to reach him again.

I'll spend the rest of my life trying, if I have to.

AFTER

On my second morning at the cabin, the world beyond the windows looks different. Sunlight has polished the swaying grass to a gilded shine, and the sky stretches, somehow broader than yesterday. Even the birdsong sounds brighter. Clearer.

I perch on the edge of my bed and marvel. It's amazing what a change of scenery and a few hours of decent sleep can accomplish.

I spend the morning bustling around, making scrambled eggs and strawberry French toast, then surprise myself by devouring every bite. At noon, I'm busy scrubbing out the pan when the phone rings. I zip into the living room, but my shoulders droop when I answer. "Oh, hey, Mom."

"Hey, sweetie. How're you doing? Are you okay?"

"Yeah." A reluctant smile digs into my cheek. "I'm okay."

While she chatters away, I survey last night's mess. Weirdly, the sight of the extinguished lantern—along with the new ashes in the fireplace and the empty cups littering the hearth—almost makes me feel as though I haven't lied.

We discuss the cabin: what needs to be done before the closing, whether the new owners will use the place themselves or list it on Airbnb. But my mind drifts. By the time my parents sign over ownership, my three days with Grayson will be up.

God, that man. He seemed so optimistic last night, so hopeful that he could resurrect a girl who wilted to nothingness long ago. Meanwhile, the most I'd hoped to find here was strength, like I did with Margo. Still, the way I looked in that picture from Hawaii—

"Mina? Are you there?"

I jerk back to reality. "Sorry, what?"

Worry threads through my mother's tone. "Are you *sure* you're all right? You seem distracted."

"Yeah, I'm fine. Sorry. Just haven't had any coffee yet."

I spend another few minutes soothing her. Once we hang up, I stare at the quiet phone, my heartbeat pattering, then scold myself for behaving like a teenager with a crush. If there *is* one rule I actually believe in, it's that women should never wait on men to call. Not even grieving widows with strange affinities for their ex-brothers-in-law. So I pack my laptop into the Porsche and head for town, parking once again at Grounds for Dismissal.

On the way in, I step aside for two twenty-somethings with dewy skin and hot coffees in their hands.

"I heard he was *here*," one bubbles to her friend, "in Millbrook. Can you believe it? Devina saw him at the Shell station this morning. She said he was driving some kind of car she'd never even seen before."

I linger, holding the door for them. I would've done it anyway, but I don't *hate* the chance to eavesdrop, considering I know exactly who they're talking about.

"I wonder if he's staying at the Roadside Inn," says the other. "He must be, if Devina saw him at the Shell."

I exhale hard. Damn. I didn't even think about the challenges of finding a hotel room at 4:30 a.m. in a town like this. I hope Grayson didn't actually get stuck at the Roadside. All the rooms there smell like cigarettes.

What was I thinking, letting him leave?

The first girl smiles at me in passing before turning back to her friend. "Totally. So you wanna go stake out the Burger Shack across the street?"

"Oh, yeah. I just have to find my lipstick first, the one that makes me look like…"

Their voices fade as they waltz down the sidewalk. I quell a grin and head inside for a hazelnut latte, then curl into an armchair by the windows and open my computer.

I tell myself I'm here to get a head start on my next article, but the truth is an idea drifted into my head this morning while talking to my mother. One so nascent and fragile that I fear acknowledging it directly might pop it like a gleaming soap bubble.

So I don't think about what I'm doing, even as I bring up a fresh Word document and begin to type.

Once upon a time, I ran away from my own life, into the forest. You see, my husband had just died, and…

It's just an experiment, and at first, I can't even say what will come of it, because the words arrive in halting bursts. But soon, they gather momentum. Vines of black blossom across the screen.

It's like wrenching open a tap that had previously rusted shut. For so many years, I've pushed away the words I've *wanted* to write. Sentences have appeared in my head sometimes, usually in the shower—luscious turns of phrase to capture the feel of a new-to-me but ancient city, or a field of sunlit wildflowers waving in welcome.

I always shrugged them off along with the hot water. Let them slip down the drain like slivers of spent soap.

But maybe they never truly left, because now I breathe them onto the page. I craft lines about starglow filtering through pine needles and how lantern light makes a beloved childhood haven look warmer and more welcoming than any other place in the world. I write about the unique loneliness of trapping yourself in a place you once shared with someone long after they're gone, and how sometimes a change of scenery equals so much more than just a geographical shift—it's a breaking down of mental walls, a reclamation of your own sovereignty.

When I finish, my empty mug has grown cold and my chest rises and falls like I've run a marathon. I glance at my phone. Nearly three o'clock, though it feels like only minutes have passed.

I do a quick scroll through the pages. They're special. The most honest ones I've ever produced. I snick my computer closed and look up. And freeze.

The opposite armchair no longer sits empty, as it did when I arrived. An incredibly large, incredibly beautiful man sits there, wearing a leather jacket and a rapt expression.

"Hi," Grayson says.

I set my computer on the tiny table between us—slowly, like he's caught me doing something illicit. "Hi. How long have you been there?"

"Half an hour, maybe." His long fingers wrap around a mug as empty as mine.

"Doing what?" I say, all caution.

"Watching you write."

My mouth goes dry. I want to be surprised that he knows what I was doing, but I'm…not. "Sounds boring."

"It wasn't. It was riveting, actually."

"Riveting?" I echo.

"Yeah. Your face. It was luminous."

Luminous. My fingers dig into the chair arms. My god, this man is going to make me do something I'll regret, using words like that. "How'd you find me?"

He chuckles. "This town is the size of a postage stamp. And Michael's car doesn't exactly blend in."

"Right." I clear my throat and look away, only to find the girls from earlier out on the sidewalk, peering in through the window.

Thank god. Something harmless to talk about. "Looks like you attracted an audience."

Grayson twists around, waves at his admirers, and turns back. "Yeah, that happens sometimes."

The girls flush and cover their mouths. One returns his wave, even though he's not looking anymore.

"Does that bother you?" I tilt my head. I don't know how I would feel about strangers habitually following me around.

"Not really." He shrugs. "It's usually innocent, even if they're expecting someone different than who I actually am. I only get annoyed when people take pictures of me without asking. Or when women try to fix me—when they decide I'm some kind of problem that needs solving, and they're the answer."

I nod, recalling the photo of him cold-shouldering that model in the nightclub. Strangely, I understand that so much better after having met him. "You never know. Maybe someday one of them *will* be the answer."

He crooks a half smile. "Maybe. But that one probably won't give me the time of day."

I snort. Delicately. "You know you could have any woman you want, right?"

He sets his empty cup down, the leather creaking. "Not *any* woman," he says, holding my eyes.

I turn that over, wondering if that's part of the allure. I'm certainly no pushover, which might be why he finds me so intriguing. But I'm only so reticent because of losing Michael, which makes Grayson...what? A broken man who loves other broken things? Or a normal, red-blooded male who relishes a challenge? "Well, you could have the ones out on the sidewalk, at least."

He scoffs. "They're children. And I don't just mean because of their age."

I look again. The girls are fresh-faced, pretty, with the bright eyes of those life hasn't yet managed to discourage. They have years and years of possibility ahead of them, and they know it.

He drums his fingers against his knee. "Can you really imagine me with someone like that? Actually try to picture it. I'll wait."

My attention drifts back to him, taking in the scars—both inner and outer—and the wry, pained twist of his mouth. The stains of a past that seem to cling to his skin.

"No," I say. "You're right. It'd be like pairing a tiger with a kitten. It'd only end up with something carnivorous happening."

"Then there you go." The bitter tilt of his lips relaxes. "And now that we've cleared that up, how about those cheeseburgers I promised?"

I chuff a laugh. My hand sneaks to my midsection, which still bulges from my lavish breakfast. Hours have passed, but my stomach has grown unaccustomed to such generosity, and I don't have room for anything else just yet. "How about later? Tonight?"

"That's perfect, actually. I have some work stuff to take care of, and I'd like to switch hotels, but I can come by around seven."

"Great." My tone comes out even, but underneath, my heartbeat accelerates. I almost tell him he can stay at the cabin. Almost. But the invitation gets stuck just south of my Adam's apple.

"I'll see you later." Grayson stands. He sounds so damn casual, the bastard. He swipes up my empty mug and totes it to the bussing bin along with his.

It's a small thing, done with the sort of thoughtless automaticity that makes me suspect he doesn't even notice he's gone out of his way to make my life easier.

But *I* notice, and I'm still thinking about it when he pauses out on the sidewalk to chat with his admirers. They bat their eyelashes. One digs in her handbag for a copy of some gossip magazine I've successfully managed to avoid seeing, then hands it over along with a Sharpie. Grayson runs a hand through his shamelessly beautiful hair, which I decide is completely unfair to them, the poor things, then autographs whatever page details his latest debacle.

While he does it, he looks up through the window and holds my eyes. And winks.

My stomach clenches. Jesus. I'm definitely going to do something reckless if he keeps that up. The urge gathers strength inside me, heady and delicious and wicked.

I lower my gaze to the fruit icon on my computer until the feeling passes. When I look again, Grayson is zooming off in something red and aerodynamic. Like Devina, I don't recognize it. A Lotus, maybe?

Whatever. It doesn't matter. Michael was the one who loved expensive things, not me.

Outside, the girls tilt their heads together for a quick conference, then come into the shop. As the jangling bell over the door quiets, they walk right up to me.

"Hi," one says. "Sorry to bother you, but…do you know him?"

I can't help but smile at her directness. "Yeah, I do."

Her hazel eyes round. "Wow. How?"

I glance around. It's late in the day for coffee, and now it's only me, these girls, and an older woman reading a book. I have no reason to avoid the truth for a measly three people. "I married his twin brother. That's all."

"Whoa," says the second. "Twin like, identical twin?"

"Yep."

Now they both look impressed. "You're married to a guy that looks like Grayson Drake?"

A needle twists in my chest. "I was. He died."

"Oh. Oh my god. I'm so sorry. That must've been really hard." They go quiet, but not in that alarmed, what-did-I-just-say way that strangers usually retreat to. Instead, they crook their brows as if they can't believe life could be so cruel.

I decide I like them. "It's okay. I mean, you're right, it was hard. It's still hard. But life goes on and...you survive, you know?"

One nods, though I can tell she doesn't appreciate the full gravity of what I'm saying. I hope she never has to.

"Well, we just wanted to come inside and tell you he likes you. It was super obvious, even from outside."

I sit back a fraction. "You think?"

"Definitely," says the second. "I mean, it makes sense. You're really pretty. And also, we're incredibly jealous."

I laugh at her friendly tone, but when my amusement subsides, the smile left over feels tattered around the edges. They make it sound so easy. *You're really pretty, so he likes you.*

What I wouldn't give for life to be that simple again.

"Thanks," I say. "But even just being around him feels weird, honestly."

"What? Why?"

"Because. I was married to his identical twin. Who *died*."

They look at me like I've sprouted another head.

"So?" says one.

"Girl," says the second, "I don't mean to be disrespectful or anything, but you'd have to be out of your mind not to pursue that. Who cares what the situation is?"

I blink. "Erm...I do?"

"Then you're definitely overthinking it."

I ease back in my chair. Huh. That attitude is so…blithely optimistic. So egocentrically youthful, too, but maybe that's not a bad thing.

And really, so what if Grayson resembles Michael? From what I can tell, the similarities end at the surface. And it's not like I owe my husband eternal celibacy. He's gone, and I'm… not. Besides, if that folder I found is any indication, he might not have stuck around much longer, anyway. "You know, you might have a point."

"Yeah, no kidding. Just…send Grayson our way if you decide you've got better things going on, all right? It was really nice to meet you."

"You, too."

They walk off, glancing back once from the sidewalk to wave.

I watch until they disappear, then snap open my computer again. Blithe optimism. I could probably use some of that in my life.

I pull up a browser and navigate to my favorite website, Travelique.com. I've visited it more times than I can count, always to salivate over the travel journalism and photo spreads of far-flung places. Typically, Travelique doesn't feature stories about domestic destinations like Washington, but they publish articles with an outdoorsy bent, and it can't hurt to try.

I find an email address for submissions, then type out a message and attach my article—if that's what it even is—about searching for solace in the forest.

I hit Send before I can talk myself out of it.

That done, I pack everything away, breeze out onto the sidewalk, and duck into Michael's car.

At the cabin, I toss all my things onto the daybed, then pull on my running shoes and venture back outside. On the porch, I close my eyes and tilt my face to the sun. Warmth presses against my cheeks like adoring hands.

I bask. I can't remember the last time I stood like this, just enjoying a moment.

It feels damn good, and when I run, it feels *different*. Like a celebration instead of an escape. I fly down the gravel road, eating up the miles.

Ever since Michael's death, I've shied away from our happiest memories, but today, I let them in. As the sun-warmed trees flicker past, I think of the way meeting him brought me to Technicolor life, how my heart expanded to fill my entire body when we swam to that underground cave in Canada. I recall the radiance of that last starlit night in Hawaii—not spent making love or even kissing, but just existing together, wholehearted. I even relive the wash of wonder that flooded me at the observatory all those years ago, when I looked into those sea-deep eyes and knew I had no desire to ever love anyone else.

Those moments are gone forever, never to be repeated. Somehow, though, the surrounding forest makes that certainty more bearable. And for the first time, I consider that, instead of being unfortunate enough to have lost so much, maybe I'm lucky to have ever had it in the first place.

When I finally make it back to the cabin and step into a steaming shower, the spray seems to rinse off so much more than sweat and dirt. It's like my head is breaking water for the first time in half a year. I chase the feeling. I take a draft of the air I've missed so intensely and hold it in my lungs.

Afterward, I look in the mirror. Really look. Kate and Grayson are right—I've gotten too skinny, but I still find pleasure in the way my eyes catch the afternoon light and my hair skims my jawline.

The coffee-shop girls weren't lying. I'm pretty.

I'd forgotten that.

I play it up, dusting blush on my cheeks, layering shadow and liner around my eyes. When I finish, I smile at what I see, then blow-dry my hair to a glossy black shine. I slip into a wine-red, close-fitting tank top and clingy dark pants.

It's partly for Grayson. I can't lie to myself about that. But it's also for me. It's everything I wrote in that article—a declaration, a statement about my independence.

I'm here. I survived. I still matter.

Maybe I should start acting like it.

I complete my ensemble with dangly earrings and head into the living room. While laying a fire, I think of what I told Kate, about how I'll never fall in love again. How I *can't*.

That still feels true, and I'm okay with that. But just because I can't fall in love again doesn't mean I've joined a convent.

I consider calling my best friend and telling her so, but ultimately decide against it. She'll only talk some sense into me, and I don't actually want her to.

Because for once, today strikes me as an excellent day to do something I'll ultimately regret.

AFTER

Grayson shows up bearing gifts—a brown paper bag that smells like an overworked fryer, a bottle of Scotch, and more Cabernet, to be exact.

"Grease and alcohol," I say when I swing the door open. "It's like you're trying to charm me."

He does an obvious double take. "Wow. Yes. I am. Though if I'd known you were going to answer the door looking like that, I would've brought you the whole damn cow. The whole damn liquor store, too."

A flutter races up my spine. How does he do that? I say something innocuous, and he escalates it with no apparent effort.

I do my utmost to sound unaffected. "Actually, kettle corn would've been the likeliest way to get results. But now you know."

His eyes rove. "Now I know."

The words sound completely different in his throaty purr, and I succumb to a full-body shiver. Great. We've exchanged roughly ten sentences and I can already tell I'm playing with fire.

Some irredeemable part of me decides that means I should pull the door open wider. "Would you like to come in?"

"Hell yes," he says.

Yep. Definitely in trouble.

Inside, I lead Grayson to the kitchen, where he sets down the food while I pull paper cups from the cupboard. "Sorry I don't have any glass—"

When I turn, he's standing close, hemming me against the counter with a wall of muscle and sparking eyes. Whatever I was about to say evaporates.

"You look incredible," he says.

I take the flimsiest of breaths. "Thanks. So do you."

"I want to touch you."

He says it just like that, hoarse and heated, and makes no move to step away.

I pretend my heartbeat hasn't taken up residence in the roof of my mouth. "Is it the eyeliner? Wow. I guess I know now why this stuff costs forty bucks a tube."

He chuffs, not quite a chuckle. "No. I wanted to touch you earlier, at the coffee shop. I was dying to, actually. But I wasn't sure you wanted that. And we had an audience. Now we don't."

My mind gears up for some tired calculation about what will happen if I agree. But the machinery sputters out before it truly gets started, because for once, I don't actually care to think. I just want to *feel*.

As if in slow motion, I set the cups aside and reach for his chest. A breath hisses from between his teeth at the contact.

His heartbeat slams against my palm like a fist on a door, demanding entry. His hands come up to cage me against the counter. The leathery musk of his jacket hits me, undercut with a note of…something I can't quite identify. Whatever it is, it makes my stomach melt into a delicious surge of heat.

"Tell me to stop," he says. "Say one word, and I'll leave you alone."

I hold his gaze and lift my chin. And say nothing.

His oceanic eyes heat to a simmer. When he bends down, I expect him to kiss me, but he angles past and presses his lips to my neck.

Wet warmth hits my skin. A mewl of surrender sneaks out as he tongues the shivery spot below my ear. My back arches. He kisses and sucks, gentle enough not to leave a mark, but firm enough to send my rationality draining into the floor.

I clutch at his shirt and fist my other hand into the glossy temptation of his hair. He resists without even seeming to. No matter how desperately I try to pull him closer, the pressure of his mouth remains steady, a torture of nips and soft, sliding heat.

It's exquisite. Excruciating. I close my eyes and come within a hairbreadth of asking him to hoist me onto the counter and splay me open right here. It's been so long. Far, far too long, and I can already feel the gathering electricity at the base of my spine that means I'll fall apart in moments.

But I want this beautiful torment to last. Because who knows when I'll feel it again? When I'll indulge like this?

Maybe never. Once I give in, Grayson will undoubtedly find some new conquest—maybe a mountain, maybe a woman— which suits me fine. It'll save me from having to cut him loose myself.

He kisses his way down my neck and slides his tongue along the exposed half of my collarbone. When he pulls away, he leaves me draped against the counter like a limp rag.

"Is that it?" I say weakly.

"For now." His tongue sweeps out over his bottom lip, as if gathering up my taste. "I'm hungry, first. For food. And I owe you a rematch."

"A rematch?"

"At Monopoly."

"Monopoly," I say, apparently incapable of doing anything except parroting his words back to him.

A slow, sultry smile claims his mouth. He knows exactly what he's doing, the jerk. "Oh, come on, don't look so disappointed. We could play for clothes this time, instead of secrets. If you want."

"As in...strip Monopoly?"

"Mmm-hmm."

I straighten. My fingers have left his hair a tousled golden mess, and his mystery tattoo peeks out at me again.

The quiet flames of curiosity ignite beneath my skin, clearing my mind. "Actually...I like that idea. A lot."

With a grin, he reaches past my shoulder to grab some paper plates. "I had a feeling you might."

Like before, we sit by the fire, but this feels different. Last night, we were exploring one another, feeling each other out. Tonight, we trade smoldering glances that have nothing to do with the heat pouring from the hearth and everything to do with the fact that we're two adults who already know exactly how this evening will end.

Our fingers brush as we whittle down the fries. The cheeseburgers disappear, too, and when we push the plates aside, Grayson stretches out on his side to take pulls of Scotch while I sip at my wine.

He hasn't shed his jacket. Dots of perspiration glisten at his hairline.

I imagine catching one in my mouth, how the prickle of salt would blossom on my tongue. "Aren't you hot in that?"

"I'm roasting. But I don't have all that many clothes on, and I fully intend to get you naked first."

My stomach clenches like a fist. I bury my face in my wine, trying to hide the hitch of my breath.

His smile turns lazy, leonine. Clearly, he sees right through me. "Now, are you ready for the dessert I brought?"

My gaze slips down his chest and beyond. I already know

what enormous pleasure lies in store for me. And when I say enormous, I do mean—

"Hey." He snaps his fingers and points to his face. "Eyes up here. I'm not a piece of meat, you know. And I didn't mean *that*."

The burn of embarrassment saturates my cheeks. If he only knew. "Right. Sorry."

"As I was saying, I brought you something. Do you have enough room for it?"

My face only flares brighter. "You'll really need to find another way to phrase that."

When his eyes round, I realize I've managed to throw *him* off-balance, for once. "I have a treat for you," he says. "The kind that goes in your mouth."

I shake my head, wordless.

"Jesus Christ. Does your mind *live* in the gutter? I'm just going to go get it." He plunks down his drink and disappears out the front door. A minute later, he reappears toting a plastic bag from Morton's, the mom-and-pop grocery in Millbrook. He marches past.

I stay seated until the rush of blood in my cheeks fades. When Grayson starts banging around in the kitchen, I pluck up my wine and go to the doorway.

"What on earth are you doing?"

He crouches before an open cabinet and reaches toward the back for the sole remaining pot. "I'm *trying* to cook. But your kitchen isn't making it easy. Why's this place so barren?"

"Because we're selling the house."

He glances over his shoulder, his scarred eyebrow skewing upward. "Really?"

"Yeah. By this time next week, I'll be back in Seagrove, and this place'll belong to someone else."

He sets his scavenged pot on the stove. "Ah. So *that's* why you wouldn't give me more time?"

"No." I tip the last of the wine into my mouth and trash

the cup. I don't even need another drink. Something far more potent than alcohol zips around in my veins. "I wouldn't give you more time because I didn't feel like it."

It's something I never would have said to Michael, but it just comes right out, like breathing. I don't even brace for the fall-out. And I don't think I'm imagining the answering approval on Grayson's face.

"You seem…different today," he says.

"I *feel* different." I don't know if it's him, or this place, but part of me is…unstretching. Flowering into the kind of woman who insists on finding double entendres where they don't exist and getting excited about strip Monopoly.

I don't even recognize myself.

No, that's not right. I do. Except the girl wearing my skin today feels like a younger, lighter version of anyone I've ever been before. Maybe she's who I would've grown into if my brother hadn't died. Or if I'd gone off to Greece instead of getting married.

"I like this side of you," Grayson says.

"Me, too."

He holds my eyes for a moment, then unpacks the grocery bag. After igniting the burner, he melts together butter and brown sugar, and—

No way.

"You've got to be kidding," I say. "Are you doing what I think you're doing?"

He pours in a clatter of corn kernels, then covers the pot and shakes. "If you think I'm making you kettle corn, then yes. I am."

His oh-so-casual tone renders me speechless. When I finally find my voice again, I say, "I've never seen anyone do it that way before."

"Well, I've never made it like this. But I did watch a You-Tube video this afternoon, which is basically the same thing. No guarantees on quality, though."

He jostles the pan with the same focus he directed toward boxing up the game last night. His muscled shoulders bunch and roll, visible even through his jacket, and it seems impossible to me that someone with such an abundance of power—enough to get him up the tallest mountain in the world, for god's sake—would harness it for something like this.

But he has, and the realization carves out a home beneath my skin. This isn't one of those grand gestures Michael made so freely—no bouquet of hothouse roses in December, no twinkling diamond tennis bracelet or candlelit evening at a five-star restaurant.

No, this is *personal.*

I step fully into the room. "Why on earth didn't you say something earlier, when I told you that you should've brought this *exact thing?*"

He slides a smile my way—mischievous, prideful. "Because I wanted to see the look on your face. Which, as it turns out, was one hundred percent worth it."

A tender barb catches in my throat. One hand sneaks up to play with an earring, as if giving my fingers something to do will quell this swell of emotion.

I have no idea what to do with this man.

I thought I did, but...

Sex, I tell myself. *Just have mind-blowing sex with him, maybe for a day, maybe two. Then he'll jet off to New Zealand, and you can go home and get on with your life.*

"What?" he says. "Why are you looking at me like that?"

"It's nothing." I play at a smile. The gunfire pop of exploding kernels ricochets off the yellowed linoleum. "I just can't wait for my dessert."

And then, because I don't want him to see how deeply the simple act of him making popcorn has affected me, I add, "Both of them."

★ ★ ★

By the time we polish off the kettle corn, I've managed to get myself back on track. I think.

The tide of golden light beyond the windows fades to a gleam. Grayson adds a few logs to the fire before freeing the Monopoly box, then sets the lantern back on the table. "Can we light this?"

"Sure. But why? The fire's plenty bright."

He stares at the battered old thing, his expression indecipherable. "I just like it. Something about it reminds me of you."

"Of *me*? A lantern reminds you of a girl you just met?"

"Yeah, why not? I mean, look at it. It's seen some things. Been around the block a few times. But its color hasn't faded, just gotten a little scratched up. And it still burns as brightly as ever. It might not be new, but it's every bit as strong as the day it was made."

I scoff. "I think you're giving me too much credit."

He plucks the lighter off the coffee table, then raises the lantern's glass to ignite the wick. "I think you're not giving yourself enough."

"Maybe." I lay out the game. "But if so, I'm not the only one."

He squints. "Which means what, exactly?"

"I'm just saying…" I trail off. What *am* I getting at? "You burn bright. Brighter than anyone I've ever met, maybe."

He gives me a long look. There's a depth there, one begging to be explored. "You know, for years, I thought I'd destroyed myself. I *knew* I had, actually. I had nothing to offer anyone. But now…I don't know. Maybe you're right. Maybe there's more to me than I've let myself believe."

The moment stretches, tightens. Something in my chest tightens along with it.

Sex, I tell myself. *Just sex.*

"I'm"—I clear my throat—"going to go put on some socks."

He smirks. The charged tension dissipates. "Socks? As in two extra pieces of clothing? You've already decided to cheat, I see."

"No, it's not that. I'm just cold."

"Bullshit. You're flushed."

"It's the wine," I say. It's definitely not. "Besides, you still have your jacket on. Which makes me no more of a cheater than you."

"Fine," he says. "Go ahead, then. I'm still going to win."

I stick out my tongue and go to the bedroom. When I finish up and pad back to the fire, I find Grayson lying on his stomach with his chin propped on one fist. My feet break into a sweat the moment the heat touches me.

"Are you ready?" he says.

Damn. Talk about a loaded question. Unsure of what might emerge if I open my mouth, I plop down on my belly, snatch up the dice, and roll.

We play. His jacket comes off first, but after that, the tide turns. For my opening gambit, I pluck out an earring and set it on the coffee table.

"No way," he says. "Jewelry doesn't count."

I arch an eyebrow. "Says who?"

"Says me."

"Nuh-uh. You can't just make up rules like that after we've started."

His eyes narrow, but when I flutter my lashes in a show of innocence, he relents. "Fine. But *earrings* count as one article, singular. And you have to answer a question, too."

I consider. He drives a hard bargain, but I still have a trick up my sleeve. One that'll get me much further than the jewelry. "Okay. What do you want to know?" I stack my other earring atop its twin.

"What were you writing today? At the coffee shop?"

I still. I should've seen that coming from a mile off. I don't mind telling him, though. I even include the part where I submitted the article to Travelique.

As I explain, his eyes glint, growing ever warmer as the twilight from the window fades and the fire glow takes over. "Is that who you'd write for, in a perfect world?"

"Definitely. I've always loved their content. I don't know if you've ever been on their website, but—"

"I have. I did a project for them once, actually."

My teeth snap together. "You did?"

"Yeah. They've been bugging me to do another one ever since, but I've been so swamped with *Nat Geo* that I haven't gotten around to it. They're great to work with, though. Really accommodating. If you want, I can drop Siobhan a line and tell her you're a friend. You having the same last name might make her wonder, but she'll probably do you a favor if I ask nicely."

My fingers flutter against the base of my throat. Briefly, I wonder whether I should insist on succeeding on my own merit, but I'm not twenty-two anymore, and I've been around long enough to realize writing's a brutal business. A nobody like me needs all the help she can get. "You'd do that? For me?"

"I'd do—" He bites his lip. Changes course. "Yeah. Sure. I'll call her tomorrow."

"Thank you," I say. "I mean, *thank you* thank you. This is…" I cast around for more.

His lips cock into a smile. "This is…what? A writer at a loss for words?"

"This is…extraordinarily kind of you," I enunciate. "A staggering and unprecedented demonstration of generosity." Then, more normally, "I don't know how I can ever repay you."

"You're going to repay me in about ten minutes."

I shift, but no amount of rearranging will calm the sudden flutter his confidence evokes. He's doing it again.

"Maybe five," he says.

A tiny, eager sound climbs up my throat, and our eyes lock. His fill with a naked, scorching desire that carves a smoking path down my middle.

And then there's no pretending anymore. No stalling. The entire room heats, melting to a liquid swirl of supple light and blue-green eyes that make me go soft around the edges.

Grayson licks his lips and tosses the dice. And lands on Marvin Gardens. Which belongs to me.

He's already left his shoes and socks by the door, but instead of peeling off his shirt like I expect, he stands up and shucks his jeans, revealing bright red boxer briefs and long, muscled legs. His quads are so defined that they curve inward above his kneecaps, two halves of an inverted heart.

My god. Between that and the bulge...

I don't know what to do with my eyes, so I just leave them where they are. Screw it. It's not like *he* would look away.

With a knowing smile, he sits back down—cross-legged this time, probably so he can taunt me with the visual feast. "Your turn."

I tame the tremble in my fingers long enough to roll, then land on his property, of course. Baltic Avenue. Damn. I've always mocked those cheap purple ones, but not now.

When I don't move, he asks, "Do you need help with that sock?"

I roll off my stomach and mirror his sit. "Actually, yes." Extending a leg over the board, I set my foot in his lap.

He takes hold of me and frowns, clearly realizing by touch alone that something isn't right. Sure enough, when he peels off my sock, another one awaits underneath.

His brow crinkles. "What the hell? How many of these are you wearing?"

I lift a shoulder, let it drop. "Five pairs. Give or take."

"Shit," he breathes, respect blazing in his eyes. "I'm screwed."

"Yes," I say. "You absolutely are."

Instead of giving my foot back, he circles my ankle with his fingers. "I should've known you'd play dirty."

My breathing gathers speed. "I *told* you I was putting on socks. I just didn't say how many. And you didn't ask."

His smile spreads like a slow pour of honey. "You minx."

For half a heartbeat, I stumble over the fact that Michael used to call me that. But a moment later, the thought loses form.

The man sitting across from me is nothing like my husband. Maybe he used to be, back when they were young and hadn't broken each other yet, but now...

Nothing about Grayson reminds me of the man I spent fourteen years with. Only of the kind of openhearted man I *wish* Michael had been. The one I thought I saw, but who went into hiding before I could be sure.

Grayson's fingers inch upward, catching at my socks and tugging them off. He tosses the pile aside, then pulls my other foot into his lap and frees that one, too.

"You just took nine things off me." I sound breathy, my protest about as powerful as ten-second-old tea. "Who's playing dirty now?"

"I'm just leveling the playing field."

"You're cheating. At least give me one thing in exchange."

"Fine." His eyes glimmer. "Boxers or shirt?"

Boxers or shirt. My mouth goes as dry as the Sahara. I can barely get my answer out. "Shirt."

A half smile digs into his cheek. He pushes my legs apart, then rises onto his knees and pulls his shirt over his head.

It's like one of those art-gallery scenes in movies. The ones where someone whips a drape off a masterpiece and earns a gasp from the entire crowd.

Grayson Drake is so beautiful it makes my eyes water. There's a sort of...ruthlessness to him, too, his muscles so crisply defined that the firelight etches shadowed lines across his skin.

He must run like a demon to look like that, I think. I can see it in my mind's eye—him pushing himself to the point of punishment, sprinting after something he'll never actually catch. Something that escaped him a long time ago.

He drops onto his hands and knees and stalks toward me. The symphonic grace of all those ridges and angles shifting in concert steals my ability to think.

He flings the game board aside. I don't look to see where it ends up. There's just a clatter of plastic and paper, and then he's prowling through the buffer zone between us like it doesn't exist.

I barely have the wherewithal to scan the tattoo inked over his heart before he reaches me. One arm wraps tight, lowering me to the floor beneath him.

I gasp. I'm falling, falling and falling and he's there with me and then I'm flat on my back with my legs hitched up around his waist while his lips dive down to fasten against my neck again and I can't breathe, I can't see, I can't do anything but keep on falling, straight through the floor, all the while wondering if I'll ever stop. Grayson's hand twines in my hair until my scalp pulls tight, and when I grind my hips upward in entreaty, he groans, a hot exhale against my ear.

"Grayson..." My hands trail up his bare sides, encountering one rippled ridge after another.

He suckles at my throat until I rasp out a moan, then raises his head to look at me. His pupils are shot wide, little pools of infinity beneath a scar that gleams silver.

"Mina." He makes my name into a roughened, delicious offering. "I could spend all night listening to you say my name like that. Do it again."

"Grayson."

"Mmm. Again."

"Grayson. Gray— *Oh.*"

Between our bodies, his fingers hitch into my waistband. Wordless, I raise my bottom and shimmy free. He tosses my pants away somewhere near the game board.

That done, he pulls my shirt up over my head. I help him with that, too, and then I'm lying there, pinned, protected by nothing but a few scraps of black lace and the red-hot glow igniting in the thousand different places my skin presses against his. I'm aching, fluttering, drunk with the feel of him firm and flush against me.

"Do I get a question now, too?" I manage to whisper. "Since I won?"

"Of course." He stares down like he's falling into me. "Anything."

"Your tattoo... What language is that?"

The hand in my hair ravels tighter. "Arabic."

I cling to my last remaining sliver of sanity. "Oh. You got a tattoo in Egypt?"

"No, Tunisia."

I scan the foreign characters emblazoned over his heart. Whatever they spell, it's short, a single word at most. "What does it say?"

"It's...a name."

"Whose?" I don't know why I ask. I already know. Lily's.

The fingers on my hip tighten. "Does it really matter right now?"

I drag my eyes back up to his. Strangely, it does. It's part of what makes him so painfully beautiful—this unguarded brokenness, all the ways in which his past has wrecked him, none of which he bothers to hide.

"Kiss me," I say.

"Fucking hell," he growls. "I thought you'd never ask."

When he bends and slants his mouth across mine, the world dissolves into glittering darkness.

It's so...different.

Where my husband was a frantic, lightning-storm crackle, Grayson kisses like he's filling a years-deep hole drop by drop. His tongue sweeps against mine in long, worshipful strokes. The

Scotch makes him taste as smoky as he sounds, like a spreading flame consuming the dark.

I kiss him back. A wave builds and builds, a tsunami that tugs at something rooted so far down I can't tell where it ends. I finally admit, then, what I've been avoiding all evening.

This is not just sex. I *trust* him. He hasn't once rolled the shutters down. He hasn't closed me out. He's let all his jagged edges show, and that makes me feel safer here in this vast, empty forest than I ever did in my fortress of glass.

I bury one hand in his hair and skim the other down his backside.

His tongue plunges deeper, a slow and inevitable devouring. I open as fully as I can. Yet it's so much more than just my legs widening to accept his weight or my lips parting to welcome him in. It's a baring of myself, an offering up of my shadows in exchange for everything he's allowed me to see. It's a *recognition*.

No kittens here, after all. Just a pair of battle-bruised, still-fighting tigers, willingly engulfing each other while the world dims to a crackling glow behind us.

He releases my mouth. His hair drags against my neck as swollen lips kiss a path toward my chest, where his teeth tease me right through my bra.

My spine bows. He tugs the fabric aside and sweeps the peak of my nipple into his mouth, drawing a luscious sound of unraveling from my lips.

I slip my hands into his boxers and clutch at his ass, grinding my pelvis upward in a mindless demand for completion. He submits, if only partly. His hand strays downward, cupping between my legs, where his thumb draws maddening circles right through my panties, in a place that makes me want to hit the ceiling.

I cry out and hold him tighter. He levers upward and kisses me again, stealing one gasp after another from my lips as his fingers flick aside the narrow strip of fabric and slip into me. I tilt my hips up, giving him access, and I coil and burn and forget myself and care about nothing but the way he feels around me, in me, murmuring my own name into my mouth.

Just when I worry he'll bring me over the edge too early, his hand retreats to the curve of my waist. I ache with the sudden emptiness.

He pulls back and looks me in the face. "Fuck," he says. "I've dreamed about this for so long. You have no idea."

I gaze down my cheeks at him, not bothering to fight the drunken weight of my half-slitted lids. If he drags this out any longer, I might actually die. "You don't have to talk."

"I know," he says. "But I want you to know…this isn't just me trying to get into your pants."

"It's fine, if it is."

"No, it's… I'm…"

A frown steals in from around the fringes of my bliss. He looks so…resolute. Like he has something to accomplish before we go any further. "You're what? Why're you looking at me like that?"

"Because." He studies me from inches away, his attention jumping from one of my eyes to the other. All the depth from earlier is back, but this time, it's like it has no bottom. "The truth is, I'm so in love with you I don't know what to do. I'm so fucking in love with you it hurts."

"You…wait, *what?*"

"You heard me."

It's like he's flung a bucket of ice water straight at my face. I snatch my hands free and scramble backward, laying one palm against his chest to press him away. "You don't mean that."

He cringes. "Oh, god. I'm sorry. Shit. I wasn't trying to scare you. I just needed you to know."

"What, that you're somehow in love with me? Even though we just met?"

"Jesus, don't say it like that. Like it's ridiculous. And it's a little more complicated than—"

"No. It's not. I mean, I get that you've looked at my picture on your phone a few times, but that doesn't mean you understand me well enough to be *able* to be in love with me. I think you're...getting confused."

"You're pissed," he says.

"No. I'm freaked out. I mean, is *this* why your girlfriends never last? Because whenever you get a new one into bed, you profess your love?"

"Damn it." He retreats, pinching between his eyes. "I'm doing this all wrong."

"Is there a right way to tell someone you've known for two days that you're in love with them?"

"Yes," he says. "It's just not like *this*. I even told myself to wait. To make sure you were okay, first. But you seemed better today, and then...I honestly didn't think you'd still react to me this way."

All the blood in my veins drains away. A horrible, weighted quiet descends. "What do you mean, *still*?"

"Oh, Christ." He springs up and paces tight circles. Enough energy pours off him to make the room feel bathed in daylight. "Why the hell did I think this was a good idea? You're going to hate me once I tell you. I can tell by your face you're never going to talk to me again."

My mouth tightens. I clamber to my feet, unwilling to grant him the upper hand by letting him tower over me, even though he still does. "Can you *please* explain what's happening right now?"

He stops pacing. One hand dives into his hair, making the fringed ends stick up through his fingers. "I'm too much of a coward to say it. Just...look in my jacket."

"What?"

"My jacket pocket. There's something in there you need to see."

I open my mouth. Close it again. And while I don't consciously decide to move, my feet propel me toward our discarded clothes, where I slip a hand into his coat. Cold metal meets my palm.

I pull the thing out and stare.

"What the hell is this," I say, only it's not a question, because I know exactly what I'm holding. A twisted silver chain, complete with the very same puka shell I once plucked from the sand in Oahu.

"I've been carrying that around for four years," he says. "I've tried to get rid of it. Even managed to throw it away a few times. But I always ended up diving through the trash afterward, so I eventually gave up trying."

My eyes snap up. "Why would Michael have given this to you?"

"He didn't." He swallows. Hard. "You did."

"What."

"Yeah. You...sat in my lap and put that chain around my neck. I'll never forget it."

All the air in my lungs billows out. I have the sudden, blinding urge to throw the necklace into the fire, but instead, I tilt my palm and let it clatter to the floor. "What are you saying? That *you* went to Hawaii with me? Not Michael?"

"Yeah." He stands before the darkened bay window in nothing but his boxers, and for all his athletic surety, he looks as lost as a person possibly could. "The thing is, I've...known you a long time, Mina. Not just two days."

My jaw locks. "No. That's impossible. What about your tattoos? Your scar?"

"None of them are very old."

A keening cry slices up my throat. "You told me you got that scar riding a bike."

"I *did*." His brows tent upward. "But you didn't ask for details. If you had, I would've told you I meant a motorcycle. In Tibet. Three years ago. And that I wrecked the bike because I was drunk. And I was drunk because I was trying to stop thinking about you."

My eyes prickle. Shit. *Do not cry. Do not cry.* "What? Why?"

"Why was I thinking about you?"

"No, why would you have gone to Hawaii? Why would Michael have agreed to that? Because he must have, for you to pull that off. To switch with him like that."

"Yeah, he did."

"*Why?* So he could spend that time working?"

"No."

"Then what?" I'm screeching now, but I don't care. "Why would Michael send his twin off to frolic with his wife on the beach? To stay up all night watching the stars with her? To tell her he loves her, for god's sake? That she's one in seven fucking billion? What could possibly make him *okay* with that?"

Grayson steps closer, but I splay out a hand, warning him off. "Don't you fucking touch me."

"I'm sorry. I won't." If heartbreak were a sound, his voice would capture it exactly. "And I'll tell you everything. Just... please understand it wasn't my idea. Michael just called me out of the blue one day, in a panic. Well, not a *panic* panic, you know how he was. But he sounded stressed, which I knew was the equivalent of World War Three for him, and he said he'd made you a promise he couldn't keep. Except if he broke it, you'd never forgive him. He said he had no choice but to ask for my help, and even then, he tried not to let you down. He really did. He had me wait in the bathroom at the airport, and I honestly didn't think I was getting on that plane until he texted me at the last minute, saying he couldn't make himself do it. Then he came in and gave me his clothes and his phone, and... Well. You know the rest. You were there."

I stumble backward. One hand finds the knotted-wool blanket on the daybed purely by feel. I draw it up, hiding my skin.

I feel like I'm choking. God, that trip. That magical, intoxicating whirlwind I clung to for so many years. How many times did I forgive Michael his distance—yet again—because of the searing warmth of that week? How many times did I tell myself the man I'd fallen in love with still existed, that our vacation was definitive proof? How many times did I reassure myself that if I only tried hard enough, I could *get* to him?

How long did I spend chasing the wrong man?

My knees buckle, dumping me hard onto the cushions.

"I'm sorry, Mina. I'm so, so sorry."

I look at him helplessly. "The one time I was actually happy, it was you?"

"No," he says in a rush. "You were happy at home. With Michael."

"No, I wasn't."

Oh, god. I've never said that out loud before. Not even in the privacy of my own head. But here it is, finally, and now I want to shout it. Scream it at the sky.

"Yes, you were." Panic laces his words. "I asked you on the plane, when we left Oahu. I know you probably don't remember, but you said—"

"I know what I said." I pass a hand over my eyes. That conversation plays entirely differently now, in my head. "But I didn't actually mean it. I mean, what I said was true. *In Hawaii*. But not at home. I just thought if I pretended, maybe the person you'd been on that trip would come back to Seagrove with me. It was…my way of asking you to stay. Or something."

He blanches. "I didn't take it that way. I thought… Fuck. I know it must not seem like it now, but all I've ever wanted was for you to be happy."

A gnarled laugh leaps from my throat. "And you thought that'd be best accomplished by lying to me?"

He winces. "I never actually lied. I made sure not to."

"I don't care," I say. "That's just a technicality. It doesn't mean you're not an asshole."

"I know. Believe me, I know."

My god. I should have trusted him on that. He told me so himself. "So that no-sex rule Michael and I had in Hawaii? That was the real reason why?"

"Yes," he murmurs. "That was why."

"You didn't even *kiss* me on that trip."

His eyes plead with me. "No. The only reason I did right now is because you asked me to. You knew it was me and you wanted that."

I go quiet. The urge to cry has passed, but something worse has taken its place. Where the room felt so safe and certain a minute ago, now I feel lost inside it, just a wandering speck floating between these wide-apart walls.

"What else do you want to know?" he begs.

I laugh, but it sounds desolate. Not like my laugh at all. "I don't know, why don't you tell me when you first fell in love with me? Was it when we spent that night on the beach? When we swam with the turtles? Or maybe that dinner in Kona, when I kept my feet in your lap under the tablecloth all evening, just so we'd be touching?"

"No. None of those."

"Then when?"

When he folds his bottom lip under his teeth, the floor drops away. I know, with absolute certainty, that whatever he's about to say will make this even worse.

"I can't pinpoint a moment." If he looked broken before, now he's shattered. "But when I look back on my stupid, fucked-up mess of a life, everything changed from the first moment I saw you. You just came walking by, threw a pie at me, and I was never the same again."

I don't move. Neither does he. Silence fills my ears to overflowing, and in the quiet, I can *hear* myself break, a soft little snap that reverberates for miles.

"That was *you*? At the fair?"

"Yeah. That was me."

Roughly a century creaks by. "But you told me your name was Michael."

"I didn't, actually." Desperation surges in his voice. "That old lady said that. I just didn't correct her. Look, I can explain. Because up until the other day, I thought you *knew*. All these years, I thought you knew you'd met me first. Michael said he'd told you. It wasn't until your email the other day that I realized he'd lied. That you barely knew I existed."

Another alien laugh tumbles out. "Oh, so this is all a dead man's fault? How convenient."

He flinches. "I know how it looks. And I should've told you everything on the phone. But you told me you hated me, and I knew if I explained, you'd hang up and that would be the end of it."

"That should've been what happened," I spit out.

"You're right. And I have no excuse for coming here. I mean, I *did* genuinely want to make sure you were okay, but the rest was selfish. I just thought that if maybe you got to know me, if I could *show* you the real me..." His Adam's apple bobs up and down.

I stare. "Then what? What did you think would happen, Grayson?"

"Maybe you wouldn't tell me to fuck off, once you knew."

For long moments, I say nothing, my entire being reduced to a whirl of hurt. "Just tell me one more thing."

"Anything." He sounds raspy. Ground down. "Ask me anything."

"How many times have we had sex? You and I? How badly did the two of you trick me?"

His eyes widen, as if he wasn't expecting that. "Zero. You and I, we've never... I mean, this would've been the first..."

He trails off. Wisely, I decide.

"Look," he says, "I know how overwhelming this must seem, but there's so much more. I can explain."

"Explain? How, by blaming everything on Michael?" Cold whispers slither through me, reminders of all the secrets my husband kept. But *this*... Even Michael couldn't have stooped so low. "Because if that's all you have to say, I don't want to hear it."

Grayson grimaces. "But he—"

"Right," I say. "Get out."

"Mina, I—"

"No. Get out. This is my house, and you're not welcome in it anymore, and I swear if you don't walk out that door right now, *I* will. I'll drive back to Seagrove and this will be the last time you ever see me."

The color drains from his face. I've struck a nerve. A deep one.

I scrounge up the strength to stand and go to where our clothes lie on the floor. I pick up everything and toss it at his feet, including the necklace. I don't want to touch it again. "Get dressed and get out."

"I will, if that's what you need right now. But please, Mina..." A horrible, shuddering exhale leaves him. "You might not want to hear it now, but you deserve to know the whole story."

"It sounds like I already do." I turn my back and pull the blanket tighter. "You're a liar. And you left me fourteen years ago. The end. Now leave me alone."

He must waver, because only the chatter of the fire breaks the silence. But eventually, fabric slides over flesh. Leather creaks as he pulls on his jacket.

It takes an eternity. A hundred eternities. I don't turn to see whether he puts on the necklace. I don't want to know.

When he finishes, he says, "Come see me, once the shock wears off. Please. I'm staying at the Flying Dutchman."

"Maybe," I say, if only to get him out the door quicker.

"I'll wait for you." He sounds wrecked, the smolder in his voice extinguished. "However long it takes."

With that, he pulls open the door. I don't turn, just stare out through the bay window. I hear the carved grizzly scrape against the porch, then the scratch of the key turning in the lock.

Heavy footsteps thump down the steps and disappear. In the yard, headlights slice through the blackness and fade.

The whole time, my eyes never move. The reflection of the lantern flame shimmers on the windowpane, but I squint past it into the breathing dark, where the trees whisper.

I doubt even they can help me this time.

BEFORE

We bury Penny in the backyard, in the same spot she and I lounged in on sunny summer days when I spread out a picnic blanket and did my writing on the grass.

Today is not one of those days. It's exceptionally gloomy, even for January, and the dismal wet glistens on the freshly turned earth of her grave. Yet I find the dreariness comforting, like even the sky realizes it should cry for her.

Which almost makes up for the fact that Michael doesn't. He stands quiet, his mouth a pale, slanted line. Rain drips from his newly shorn hair and darkens the starched collar peeking from his raincoat.

He's already told me he feels strange having a funeral for a dog, so I perform the roles of both priest and bereaved myself. While the clouds mourn overhead, I talk about how Penny spent ninety percent of our year and a half together asleep, how I loved the galumphy exhale she made whenever she lay down. How I even loved her terrible smell. I talk about the charm of her missing teeth and how much I looked forward to the way

she always held up one paw when we came home, as if in greet-
ing. Most of all, I talk about how glad I am that we were able
to give her some comfort at the end of her life.

Michael blinks hard at regular intervals. I laugh and cry, all
the while wondering if his silence means he's feeling too much
or not enough.

Later, over dinner, I tell him I've made us another appointment with Darlene.

He sets his fork down, perfectly perpendicular to his plate,
as if he's drafting walls and angles, even here. "Why would we
go to the shelter again?"

"To find our next Penny. I mean, not another *Penny*, obviously. That'd be weird if we named two dogs the same—"

"I don't want another pet."

I stop, my brow creasing. "What? Why?"

"I just don't."

I frown. "But Penny was so easy. She was hardly any work,
aside from her pills. And I was always the one to give them to her.
I mean, don't you miss her? Doesn't the house feel empty now?"

"I do," he admits. "And it does. But I don't want another
dog." He resumes cutting his chicken parmigiana into disturb-
ingly uniform bites.

I watch his cutlery rise and fall. "Come on. If you're going
to veto it completely, at least tell me why."

He sighs, and I know if I press, I won't get any answer at all.

With clenched teeth, I push my chicken around my plate.
The scrape of metal against porcelain fills the silence.

"I just can't stand it when things die," he finally says. "When
they leave me."

I pause. "Even dogs?"

"Even dogs."

I sit back, wondering what that really means. Whether this
has something to do with Lily and his brother or whether he
just resents change.

"I get that," I say. "But can we at least talk about it? Maybe not now, but later, once things aren't so fresh?"

"I really don't want to." Something flashes in his eyes—a rubbed-raw wound, there and then gone. But it's enough for me to know.

Too much. He's feeling too much. And now, since he can't go for the bottle, he'll retreat to the only place he finds solace. In approximately three, two...

Michael crumples his linen napkin beside his plate. "I have a lot of work to finish. Do you need help cleaning up?"

"No. Thanks. But it's already seven thirty. Can't work wait?"

"I really need to get this done," he says. "Maybe you'd feel better if you went for a run?"

Then he's gone.

After clearing the dishes, I venture out into the dark. I run and run and run. The pound of rubber against asphalt clears my head. When I return, Michael waits at the front door.

He holds out a hand as I shuck off my squelchy shoes. "Come on. I made you a bath. With bubbles. And candles. And I got you this a while back. I've just been waiting for the right time." He presses a silky black jewelry box into my hand.

I swallow the retort that springs to my tongue, because I recognize this for what it is: a peace offering. An apology that doesn't require the discomfort of words.

I thumb open the box lid and my breath catches. Nestled inside is a delicate necklace with a gold disk rimmed by tiny diamonds. *Penny* is engraved in the center.

I glance up, my eyes welling. "It's beautiful."

"I really do miss her," he says.

I nod, knowing this is the most he can give right now. It's enough. It has to be.

With a worn smile, I fasten Penny's token around my neck and let Michael lead me upstairs. While he pulls off my wet things and drops them onto the tile, I pop open the buttons of his dress shirt.

In the bath, I climb onto him and let his slippery fingers guide my hips into a rhythm, slower than our usual, so as not to send soapsuds spilling across the floor. The whole time, I watch his closed eyes, his knitted brow. It's like he's speaking with his voice, too, instead of just his body.

I'm only saying I don't want another dog because I'm so crushed, he tells me. *Penny dying hurt infinitely more than I expected, and I'm sorry, but I don't ever want to go through that pain again.*

"It's okay," I murmur, prompting him to clutch me closer. "It's okay. I understand, and I won't push."

When that dark, sucking heat finally spills through me and the tremors subside, I nestle against his chest while he runs his fingers up and down my back. The bathwater has cooled to lukewarm, but I don't care. I just want to stay like this.

"I'm sorry," he says, his lips in my hair.

"Me, too," I murmur.

"Do you feel better now?"

I smile against his chest. "Always."

And it's true. Because by the time we go to bed and he pulls me against him, I feel as though we ended up having a conversation, after all.

AFTER

After Grayson's confession, I don't sleep. Or if I do, I can't tell—the hours ebb and flow without any logic stitching them together. When I first check my phone at eleven eleven, the familiar numbers jab an angry red shock wave through me, but a moment later, the screen reads 3:12. Then hours pass, but a tap of my finger only shows 3:41.

Nothing makes sense.

Grayson and Michael. Michael and Grayson. They blur together in my head—two separate men I thought were one. And yet I can't understand how I ever could have missed the difference. Even if I didn't know they were identical twins.

I writhe from one sleepless position to another. The sheets twist around my legs.

God, no wonder I failed to coax Michael into opening up. For years, I tried. And tried. I never gave up on my mission of squeezing blood from a stone, because I believed I'd done it before. But the man who'd bled so much for me in the beginning, who'd stained my hands red with his honesty, was not the same one I married. In trying to change Michael, I may as well have gone to war with the ocean.

I wonder when he and Grayson switched places.

That much, at least, I can approximate. It happened around the time Michael...no, Grayson?...went to jail. Even then, I noticed the shift. I just misinterpreted the reason.

And afterward, I spent years blaming Grayson for the fight that made Michael "change." But really, Michael never changed. Now I realize he was actually amazingly consistent, from the day we met until the day he died. He was quiet. Serious. Tormented by all the things he kept buried.

As I lie in the dark, my thoughts devolve into nonsense again. What was that fight in Seattle really about, then? And how does Lily fit into all this? Who killed her? Who *loved* her? Was it the same man?

At four thirty-four, I finally give up. My eyelids ache for sleep, but I fling off the covers, pull on a bathrobe, and shuffle to the kitchen, then flip on the overhead bulb. Anemic light tints the room a sickly green, informing me that I have ground coffee but no way to brew it. The French press is already packed up, and the lack of caffeine, coupled with the lack of sleep, compounds into something I can no longer fight.

I sink onto the chilled linoleum and cry.

A tidal wave pours out—grief for a husband I never truly knew, heartbreak that Michael spent his life trapped behind a wall of silence, outrage over my own lost trust. I weep for all the ways in which the three of us wounded one another without even trying.

And I cry because, underneath it all, some diseased part of me insists that the man I've loved for nearly half my life, the one I would have burned down buildings and leveled cities for, never died at all.

I only thought he did.

I hate that I can even formulate that thought right now.

When I finally exhaust my supply of tears, I drag myself up and into the living room. Last night's mess still litters the floor—Monopoly pieces are scattered everywhere, paper plates stacked haphazardly on the hearth.

Firelight-soaked memories bombard me. I was lying right there, in that spot, when Grayson kissed me. When he touched me. And I sat over there while he explained. While he tried to blame all this on my—

I spin away, making a beeline for my bedroom, where I shed my bathrobe and pull on clothes. On the way back through the living room, I keep my eyes fixed on the front door. I pause only long enough to snatch my car keys off the coffee table.

On the porch, cold rushes against my skin. Beyond the trees, the roots of the sky blush with the stirrings of day. Droplets coat the grass, refracting starlight like tiny globes of ice.

Yet even the sorcerous beauty of the outdoors can't soothe me. I need to move, to put distance between me and the chaos inside my head. The chaos inside my living room, too.

In the car, I blast the heat and crank the stereo, trying to lose myself in a wailing country ballad about a man's beloved lost dog. I head for Millbrook, hoping Grounds for Dismissal will have opened by now. Mile after mile, the double-yellow line burns in my vision.

In town, the streets lie empty, but my heart leaps when I find the coffee shop's windows aglow. Inside, I order a hazelnut latte and tuck myself into a corner with my cell phone.

Kate must be awake, even though it's early. In the olden days, before she had kids, she might even have texted me already, but parenthood means our communication has grown sporadic.

God, what I wouldn't give to have her sitting across from me right now. I type out a message.

I miss your face. So, so much.

Within moments, she pings me back.

What, the one only a mother could love?

A photo pops up: a selfie taken while on the treadmill. Red splotches mar her skin, and rivulets of sweat have carried the remnants of last night's mascara into the creases beneath her eyes. Loose hair dangles around her face, spilling from a messy topknot half-soaked in perspiration.

Despite myself, I chuckle. The sound resonates oddly in the empty shop, and the barista startles before going back to grinding coffee beans.

Yep, that's the one, I write, followed by a string of heart emojis.

My phone dings again.

You know, as my friend, you're now morally obligated to burn that picture. Or throw your phone in the ocean. Your choice.

With a hollow smile, I suck down the rest of my latte and consign the empty cup to the bussing bin, then make my way back to the Porsche. I drive without purpose until the sky blossoms with color. Finally, I head for the cabin, my belly warm with coffee. Or maybe that's just rage.

Still, as Millbrook fades behind me, the urge to jerk the Porsche around grows. Not because I want to see Grayson. I'd rather pull over on a hillside, wedge myself beneath the wheels, and allow myself to be slowly run over than let him lie to me again.

Yet I can't stop thinking about what he might say. About the way his heart cracked inside his voice last night. About what it felt like to kiss him, to melt with him in the firelight.

And, long before that, what it felt like to stand on a starlit mountaintop, holding his hand, and understand that each mo-

ment here on earth amounts to both the smallest and mighti-
est of things.

"Damn it," I say, then punch the steering wheel. I don't do
it hard, but the horn sounds, startling a magpie from the roadside bramble into the peach-bright sky.

I watch it fade to a speck. I'm not entirely sure I want to
know how else Michael and Grayson deceived me. But maybe,
at the end of the day, I owe the boy from the mountaintop that
much.

By the time I pull into the cabin's driveway and kill the engine, I've formulated a plan. I'll let Grayson say his piece—just
go, hear him out, don't touch him, and be done with it.

Once I know everything, *then* I'll decide whether to speak
to him ever again. Because informed decisions, after all, are
always the best ones.

Right?

AFTER

I don't bother to make myself presentable. After an unsatisfying nap filled with fitful half dreams, I shower, gather my hair into a bristly ponytail, and pull on electric-blue leggings and a vivid orange top. The colors war with one another, but who cares? Not me.

I eat lunch. Or breakfast. Or dinner. Or whatever the hell it is.

By the time I climb into the car again, the sun graces the horizon, and I glance in the rearview mirror as I turn the key. Puffy, bloodshot eyes stare back, but that doesn't stop me from hitting the gas.

Near town, just as I cross into my service zone, my phone rings. I pull off onto the roadside. Not because I want to delay the inevitable. Okay, maybe. But I also prefer not to break the law. "Hello?"

"Hey, Mina? It's Tanner. I've got something for you. Sort of. Sorry it took so long."

I stare blankly through the windshield before finally remembering the favor I asked him for. That seems like years ago. "Oh, wow. I completely forgot. I'm so sorry you ended up going to all that trouble."

"It was no trouble," he says. "At least, it won't be, if all you want is this email from May. Is it that one? Or the one from fourteen years ago?"

Silence stretches between us.

"Fourteen years ago?" I echo.

"Yeah. You weren't sure of the send date, so I didn't limit my search, and two deleted messages came up. One from a Grayson Drake in May, but also an older one, from you."

A buzz fills the space between my ears. I never sent Grayson an email. Not fourteen years ago, at least. "*From* me? Are you sure?"

"Yep."

"What does it say?"

He hesitates. "Is that the one you want recovered?"

"Yes," I say, without thinking.

Tanner sighs. "Well, damn. I was afraid of that. To be honest, I'm not sure I can actually retrieve it, it's so old. And it looks like it was deleted on your end the day it was sent. But if you give me more time, I can try to get my hands on it. Just don't expect much."

Deleted the day it was sent. I blink, sifting through possibilities, none of which make sense. Fourteen years ago, Grayson existed as nothing more than a concept to me.

"Mina?"

I startle. "Yeah. Sorry. I'd…really appreciate it if you could get that message back. There's no rush, and if anyone can do it, it's you. You're a wizard."

He chuckles, pleased. "I'll see what I can do. Anything for Kate's best friend."

I hang up and ease back onto the road, my head spinning. There must be some kind of explanation. Even if I can't think of one right now.

At Grayson's hotel, I park and venture through a door marked

Lobby, which amounts to little more than a plain room with a check-in counter and a coffee station. A proprietor with salt-and-pepper hair watches a Bollywood musical on TV. The vibrant singing makes me feel like I've wandered into the wrong place. Everyone on the screen is so happy. So beautiful and perfect. Not to mention really damn good at dancing.

"Can I help you?" he says.

I turn away from the beaming smiles on television. "Yeah, I'm looking for Grayson Drake, but I'm not sure which room he's in. Could you give me the number?"

The man does a head wobble that might mean yes, might mean no. "I'm sorry, but I cannot tell you unless you are family. Please understand."

He looks deeply apologetic, and I *do* understand, given Grayson's notoriety. But I have absolutely zero desire to stand around in the parking lot waiting or, worse, shouting his name, so I plunk down my driver's license.

"I am family, actually. I'm his wife. Mina Drake. See? Same last name."

The man peers down.

In the silence, I drum my nails against the Formica. *Jesus. I could've said sister. I really could've said sister.*

"My apologies." He pushes a key with a wooden fob at me. "Room seventeen."

I pause. I didn't ask for access, but…what the hell, why not? I grab the key and head back outside.

Room seventeen awaits around the corner, at the far end of the lot. The curtains are drawn, but light leaks out from underneath, and I spot that sinful-looking red thing parked near the door.

My stomach tangles, but I knock before I can second-guess myself. When no one answers, I contemplate the key, then decide Grayson's wife wouldn't stand around waiting, anyway, and let myself in.

Inside, the room proves cozy and clean, if not overly luxurious. A brown, geometric-patterned rug complements a crisp white bed and two upholstered chairs. A desk lamp casts a warm net of light. Across from the bed lies a closed bathroom door; the waterfall roar of a shower drums through from the other side.

I try not to visualize too much of what's happening in there and restrict myself to poking around out here, where it's safe. On the bedside table, I find an antique-looking book with a fabric cover. Dante's *Divine Comedy*. Not just *Inferno*, like most people read, but all three volumes. I wish I didn't find that choice so compelling.

I flip to where Grayson has marked his place with a dog-eared fold. Page three hundred. When I sift through, I find a straightened crease on page two hundred and fifty, another on page two hundred, another on—

With a shudder, I snap the book shut and toss it down. Which leads me to the desk, where a laptop and a ridiculously expensive camera jockey for space. The camera looks freshly disassembled, as if Grayson has just returned from an extended photo session. His laptop lies open, sleeping. Curiosity prompts me to scribble a finger across the tracking pad.

The screen flares. An array of snapshots greets me, all taken somewhere nearby, in the woods.

I sink into the swivel chair, clicking from one to another as if lured. The photos are magnificent. Living, pulsing slices of a world both timeless and untouched. I can almost hear the burble of birdcall, the trickle of streams underfoot. One picture seizes my attention and hangs on. In it, trees arc high overhead, bathing the forest with sapphire shadows. Above the latticed canopy, the sky appears to have caught fire. Light pours through the branches in rivers, *waterfalls*, even, filling up the frame, reaching and reaching for the forest floor but never quite making it.

I stare until the space between my ribs hollows out. The light raining through the trees sifts in to fill that up, too.

How beautiful must a man be inside, I wonder, *in order to see the world this way?*

Somewhere to my left, a door opens. I hadn't noticed the shower turn off, but now the creak of a carpet-clad floorboard warns me, followed by a sharp intake of breath.

Briefly, I consider snapping the laptop closed, but I can't bear to disrespect the photo that way, so I leave the evidence of my snooping as-is and swivel the chair.

The sight of Grayson hits me like a bullet to the chest. Not because he's half-naked, towel clad, and glistening—he is, but I barely see that, because I can't get past the look on his face. Someone's smashed hope, dread, and adoration all together, tossed them into the oven to bake, then pulled them out again still raw and unfinished.

"Hi," he says.

"Hi."

"I wasn't sure if you'd come."

I drag my teeth over my bottom lip. "I decided I should at least hear what you had to say."

"Oh," he says. "Good. That's good."

Neither of us seems to know what to do next. He tucks his towel tighter, then takes a few halting steps to where his suitcase lies by the bed. "Um…do you mind if I put on some pants?"

"Go ahead." I tent a hand around my eyes and angle away.

Clothes rustle. The towel thumps against the rug. "Okay. I'm decent."

I look again to find him wearing a pair of black joggers with white stripes down the sides. No shirt. I wonder if that's part of some diabolical strategy, but if so, I'm not about to be swayed by the swathes of tattooed muscle and ropy sinew he's putting on dis—

Okay. I'm getting distracted.

Grayson takes a seat on the edge of the bed. I spin the desk chair to face him, close enough that I could reach out if I wanted.

Which I absolutely don't.

"I'm sorry." He clears his throat. Crystal droplets spangle his chest and cheeks, each one competing for attention in the overly cheerful lamplight. "It's the first and last thing I'll say, because I want you to know that above all else. I'm so sorry, Mina. I never meant to lie to you, or hurt you. I know I've made some terrible choices—*really* terrible choices—but they were never malicious. And I never had anything but love for you. I still have nothing but love for you."

I gulp against a prickly throat. "You'll forgive me if I find that a little hard to believe."

"I know." He finger-combs his wet hair back. A few strands fall right back down to kiss the end of his nose. "So I'll try to explain in a way that makes sense. I just don't know where to start."

I consider. Not at the beginning. I've already deduced that much myself—namely that Grayson came to Seagrove on a work retreat, just not *his* work retreat. It must have been Michael's, because Brooke and Sarah and everyone else at Forsythe & Winter thought that's who he was. He was using Michael's name. Driving Michael's car. Living Michael's life.

"How about you tell me why you were impersonating your brother when we met?"

He nods, short and precise, as if in relief. "That's easy. Because Michael was in rehab, and he didn't want anyone at work to know. He'd only been at Forsythe & Winter for two years, but he'd already made a name for himself—big-shot architect with big-shot potential, that kind of thing. He had a lot to live up to. But his drinking had gotten bad enough that he had to do something about it, and he wasn't the kind of person who could bear to show weakness. So instead of asking for personal time, he came to me."

I frown. "Okay. Go on."

He sighs. "At the time, I was just this broke, hungry kid who liked to take pictures. I had nowhere to be, and I would've done anything to fix things between us. So when he asked me to pose as him for a couple months, I jumped on it. All I had to do was show up at his office, be a dick like he would've, and pretend to know what the hell I was talking about. Which was surprisingly easy, considering I know nothing about architecture. Meanwhile, Michael did all the actual work, from his treatment center."

I nod along, taken aback only by how much sense that makes. I recognize Michael's reasoning all over it. And what Sarah and Brooke said all those years ago about him acting strange... "Why the hell didn't you tell me that, though? When I got in the car with you?"

Grayson's mouth pulls into a wistful curve. "I tried."

I glower. "You're supposed to be telling me the truth right now."

"I am, I am. I promise." He raises his hands, fingers spread. "I was going to give you the whole story right then and there. But then you asked if I was Michael, and I asked whether you'd still come to Seattle if not. At which point you tried to get out. So I did lie, at least a little bit, just that once. Because I really, really didn't want you to get out, Mina. Believe it or not, I already knew. I already fucking knew you were going to break my heart, and I was such a cocky bastard I thought everything would turn out fine. I was looking forward to it, actually. I thought it might be fun."

"And was it? Fun?"

His hands flop into his lap. "No. It was horrible. Zero out of five stars. Would not recommend."

The glimmer of humor eases me into the conversation. Maybe I can do this, after all. "Okay. So you were young and hopeful. Keep going."

"I don't know about hopeful." He scoffs. "More like arrogant. If I could go back and slap twenty-five-year-old Grayson, I would."

"No, don't. He was charming," I say faintly, then mash my lips together. Am I...*defending* him?

"He was an idiot." His tone grows clipped. "He was still young enough and stupid enough to know everything, and he thought he'd already overcome life's biggest challenge. He figured he'd been knocked down and gotten right back up again. He had absolutely no idea how wrong he was."

"What had knocked you down?"

He pierces me with a look. "You know."

"Right. Lily." When my lips finally shape her name, it's like letting go of a weight I've been carrying around for a decade and a half. "You loved her a lot, didn't you?"

"What?" He braces his hands on his thighs and frowns. "No. *Michael* did. I explained that to you. When we met."

I flick my head a few times, trying to clear the haze. I remember coming across Grayson's license in the Audi's glove box, but... No, that was *Michael's* wretched pain captured on film. Which means... "You're telling me my husband had a fiancée? A woman he was supposed to marry before me? Who died? Because he never mentioned that, not once."

His eyebrows crook. "Probably because he realized I'd already told you the story from the other way around. So he couldn't, really. Not to mention he wasn't exactly the most forthcoming guy in the world."

I sit back like he's just knocked the wind out of me. That... can't be right. "But if Michael was supposed to marry Lily, does that mean she died because of you?"

"Yeah," he says. "Like I told you in the car that day."

"*You* killed her?"

He flinches. I consider rephrasing, but this isn't the time for pulling punches. It's time for us to drag every ugly, cringing truth into the light.

"In a way," he says, "you could say we both did."

"How? How'd she die?"

"We…had an airplane."

I nod. Somehow, I knew this would have something to do with it.

"Michael funded it, but I built it. Which worked out—he had the money, I had the time. And we both loved to fly. Cars, planes, whatever. If it went fast, we liked it. Except when I built us that plane, I put the boost pump switch in a different place than he was used to. In our first one, it'd been on the panel. In the second, I put it on the joystick. But I forgot to tell him about the change. And one day when he and Lily headed down to Oregon for the weekend, the mechanical pump failed. Which shouldn't have been that big of a deal. They would've been fine if he'd just found the damn switch. But he didn't. He looked all over and didn't know where it was, and they crashed. He lived. She died."

Silence blossoms between my ears. So much of that has gone right over my head. "You're a pilot?"

"Was. I haven't flown since Lily died."

"And you built a plane? Just *built* a plane? Like that's a normal thing that people do?"

"It's really not that hard."

I gape at him. "And Michael was a pilot, too."

"Yes."

"Who crashed. And killed somebody. Which is why he was so terrified to fly."

He gives me a sad, spare smile, and waits for me to sort the facts into their proper columns and rows.

"I don't know anything about airplanes," I eventually say. "But it seems like…if Michael was the one flying, shouldn't he have, I don't know, figured out where everything was before takeoff? Isn't there a checklist, or something?"

Grayson laces his fingers between his knees. "There is. At least there's *supposed* to be. And you could argue that it was his fault for skipping it. But if I'd just put the stupid button in the place he was used to, none of it would've happened. Lily would still be alive. Michael never would've blamed me for the crash. He never would've started drinking, never would've started hating me so much... So many things could've been avoided."

"And you and I never would've met."

A sharp, blue-green glitter leaps in his eyes. "No. And trust me, I've already tortured myself into circles with that one. A million times."

"Okay. But I still don't understand why you didn't tell me who you were, once we got to Seattle."

His look turns rueful. "That's even easier. Because I wanted to impress you. I saw your reaction when you walked into Michael's condo. That place wowed you."

I think back. I would've been too self-righteous to admit it at the time, but... "Okay, yeah, it did. But that had nothing to do with why you became the love of my life."

He stems a breath, and my gut clenches when I realize what I've said. But he moves on, leaving it blessedly alone.

"I *was* going to tell you." His burnt rasp tugs at something inside me. "That last day. I was going to take you to my real apartment, the one with the taped-up Ansel Adams posters and the twin bed with the busted spring. I was going to explain everything, make love to you if you'd've let me, then put you on a plane to Greece."

Pieces click together in my head. "You mean *that* was the big secret? The thing you were going to tell me before we slept together?"

"That was it."

I press my lips together and drag a breath through my nose.

That line Michael fed me about being an alcoholic…true, but also a lie. "Except you went to jail that day."

"Yeah. Though Michael must've told you the story inside-out. It took me forever to figure out what was happening, what he'd said to you. But yeah, I got into a fight trying to defend some woman I didn't even know, and when I got booked, all I could think about was making sure you still caught your flight. Michael was checking out of his program that day, which was where I'd gone. To pick him up. But instead, I had to use my phone call to explain everything to him, and he *promised* me, Mina. Even though things were still terrible between us, I'd just done him this two-month-long favor, and he said he'd walk to the condo if he had to. Find a way to get you to Sea-Tac. And at first, I had no way to know he hadn't done that, because I didn't get released until the next day."

I worry at my lip with my teeth. "But when you did get out? Why didn't you call me?"

His gaze softens. "I did. Right away. But you want to know what happened? What still happens?"

I lean forward. I can't seem to help myself. "What?"

"I'll show you. Do you have your phone?"

I dig around in the side pocket of my leggings and pull out my cell. Grayson plucks his off the bedside table, then tilts his screen toward me and punches buttons.

"You know my number by heart." My frown fills my voice.

"I do. *Now.* Not then." He clicks Call and puts it on speaker. It goes straight to voicemail.

I watch my screen the whole time. Nothing.

"At first, I thought it was because you were on the plane." Grayson tosses his phone aside. "But it kept happening even after you should've landed, and I finally started wondering if maybe Michael had done something. If he'd gotten ahold of your phone and blocked me. Made it so I *couldn't* call you."

"I… No. He wouldn't have. He wasn't like that." I shake

my head, even as warmth drains from my cheeks. The morning after we first went to bed together, he called in to work. From *my phone.*

I don't know why I still remember that.

Grayson watches my face. "Have you ever checked your blocked numbers? Even once?"

I glance down. My hands tremble, but I unlock my phone and navigate to the blacklist. There's only one entry. No contact name, just a phone number with a Seattle area code.

One I didn't put there. I've never blocked anyone in my life.

"That's you?" My question sounds tiny. Shrill.

"That's me." He reaches over, clicks Unblock, and releases a long exhale. "I have to say, I've been wanting to do that for fourteen years."

"But you still could've reached me." My words come out small, stunted. "From another phone. Don't even try to pretend like this somehow kept us apart."

"No, you're right. Although I wasn't thinking clearly that first day. When I realized I couldn't reach you, I went straight to the condo. Except Juan refused to let me up, and when Michael came down..." His jaw hardens. He glances down, curling one fist into the opposite palm. "I knew. The second I saw him, I just knew. I could *smell* you on him. And I completely lost my shit. That whole month you and I had spent together, all that waiting... I've hit my fair share of guys in my life, but never like that. Never, ever like that."

I do a quick calculation and try to keep my chin from trembling. "Oh, god. This means..."

He tenses. "What?"

I swallow, my throat raw. "I had sex with Michael like *five minutes* after I met him. Five actual minutes."

He winces and closes his eyes. I suspect if Michael were here right now, Grayson would hit him all over again—back from the dead or not. "He shouldn't have done that to you."

"No. Well, I *did* kind of throw myself at him. And beg. In my underwear. I was just so relieved you'd come home. That you were okay."

"All he had to do was tell you his name," he grinds out.

That draws a hiss from me. "All *you* had to do was tell me *yours.* Or pick up a freaking phone that belonged to someone else."

He averts his gaze, as if he can't bear to meet my eyes. "I know. But I couldn't, not then. Because that day, I went to jail for the second time."

My jaw slackens. "What? Why? For beating Michael up?"

"Yeah. And those charges took a lot longer to sort out, because I'd just done the same thing the day before, at least in the law's eyes. I was in for over a month that time. And while I was there, Michael came to see me."

My chest rises and falls, its tempo building. Until a few days ago, I'd never thought of my husband as conniving. Or manipulative. But it seems I had no idea who I was married to. "What did he say?"

Grayson recoils from the icy venom in my tone, but I don't have the wherewithal to tell him it's not him I'm angriest at right now. "That he'd told you everything. That you'd slept with him knowing who he was. That you hated me for not being up front with you and that *you'd* blocked my number. That you never wanted to see me again."

Silence floods the room. "And what? You just...*believed* him?"

"Not at first. But it was the exact thing I'd been so afraid of. And it fucked me up, Mina. Screwed with my head. But that wasn't all. Michael told me I'd taken Lily from him, and it was only right that I let him have you."

I gape. I can't picture my own husband speaking about me that way.

"Shit," he says. "I know that probably sounds so messed up. But for what it's worth, I don't think he meant it like you were an item to barter. It was more like he thought he deserved you more than I did, because I'd been about to let you go. He said if I actually loved you, I would've asked you to stay, and the fact that *he* hadn't let you go proved you belonged in Seattle. I think, in his mind, you were going to save him from landing back in rehab, and after how much I'd hurt him, I owed him that. The *world* owed him that."

"You should've told him to fuck off," I scrape out, wishing I could unhear this story. And yet I can slot it right in among the strangeness of the day I met the man who would become my husband. Because it fits.

"I *did* tell him to fuck off," he says. "Multiple times. But right before he left the visiting room, he told me to check my email when I got out, because that would explain everything. So that's exactly what I did. The officer kept telling me to clear out, and I remember standing there just staring at this message you'd sent, because it was the worst thing I'd ever read. It was my whole life ending, right there in black and white." His eyes flick up and catch mine. I feel the impact down in my marrow. "I deleted it right then. I didn't want it to exist. Which means I can't prove any of this now. I can only tell you the truth and hope you'll believe me."

My vision blurs. A fourteen-year-old email. From me to him, just like Tanner said.

Really, Michael could have sent one so easily. I never set a password on my laptop, just left the thing lying all over the condo. "What did it say? The parts you remember, at least?"

"Oh, I remember every word." He shivers and closes his eyes. His voice drops. "'Dear Grayson. Forgive me for doing this by email, but I don't want to see your face after you spent the last month impersonating your brother. Thankfully, the real Michael was kind enough to tell me the truth. He's been kind about everything, actually. And after having a few weeks to think about it, I've decided to make a go at things with him. I shouldn't have to tell you I deserve a man who's honest from the beginning.'"

Grayson makes parentheses with his hands around that last line, and I recoil. I use parentheses in email all the time. Which Michael would have discovered if he'd gone snooping through my outbox.

"'Our time together was nice,'" Grayson continues. "'And I'll always think of it fondly. But remember when I said you could go broke, gain a hundred pounds, and lose your home, and I wouldn't stop loving you? Well, I should've qualified that with the one thing that *would* matter. Because it was you lying to me.'"

A broken sound slips out. I repeated that to Michael—the real Michael—the day I met him.

That fucking asshole.

The world tilts, the tapestry of my life coming unraveled in a hundred places at once. Even if I wanted to doubt Grayson's truthfulness, the carven line between his brows and the wobble in his voice would convince me.

He scrapes in a breath and soldiers on. "'If you care for me, you'll stay away. This will be the last time we communicate, though I wish you the best. Hopefully you'll treat the next girl better than you treated me. Take care of yourself. Mina.'"

Seconds crawl over my skin while I sit unmoving. "I didn't write that."

His eyes snap open. "No. But I thought you had. I mean, the part about me going broke and gaining a hundred pounds… I don't even understand how Michael did that. But he made absolutely sure I believed that message had come from you."

I make a pained sound. "So you left."

"Yeah. You'd *asked* me to. I had no other choice. And I was so young and dumb that I thought maybe I could find another you somewhere. You'd ripped my heart out, but I tried anyway. I went all over the place. Looked for you in every backwater village and remote jungle I could find. I climbed mountains on the other side of the fucking world looking for you. And by the time I figured out that you were never, ever going to be there, three years had gone by, and you were getting married."

A wretched whimper coalesces in my chest.

"And then I called you," he says, hollow. "From Mongolia. I was in Ulaanbaatar, and I'd drunk way too much because of what day it was, and I couldn't hold back anymore. I was going to beg, Mina. I had this whole speech mapped out, about how if Michael ever did anything to make you question his love, make you feel...*kept*, I'd be waiting. I'd swoop in and take care of you, even if I couldn't buy you all the shit that he did. Except then he answered your phone. I asked if you knew who was calling, and he told me yes, you did, then I asked if I could talk to you, and he said no. And then you came on the line, and..."

I press a fist to my mouth. "Told you never to call again." I nearly choke on the words. "I didn't know. I *didn't know*. Michael told me you were a telemarketer."

"I figured that out," he says. "Like, last week. But at the time...you sounded happy. You sounded like you didn't need me. Much less want me. So I spent another seven years stumbling around the world trying to find some reprieve. Then, one day from out of the blue, Michael called me about Hawaii. Which I know I shouldn't have agreed to. But I'd spent the last decade pining away for this woman who wanted nothing to do with me, and things had never felt even remotely over. I just thought that if maybe I could see you one more time, I could finally be done with it. I could prove to myself that we'd both changed, that the magic was gone. I could put everything in the fucking ground where it belonged. But the second I saw you at Sea-Tac..." He presses his palms into his eyes. "I was fucked. Royally, completely fucked. It was *worse* than the first time I saw you. Like ten years apart had made me love you more, not less."

"And then we had that incredible vacation together," I say, partly to myself. "And somehow I never noticed you weren't actually my husband."

"Yeah. Michael made sure you didn't. He got in shape before you left, then made me cut my hair and wear those stupid khakis."

"That picture of me on the beach," I murmur. "*You* took that. And sent it to yourself from Michael's phone. While we were on the plane."

"Yeah. I remember that right then, I was absolutely fucking dying inside. I knew how much that picture was going to hurt to look at later, but I sent it anyway. Because really, I just wanted to stay there with you forever. Except I couldn't. You hated me, and I knew if I told you who I was, it would ruin the last moments we'd ever have together."

"And the necklace?"

"I pretended to lose it. So I wouldn't have to hand it over to Michael once we landed. I still had my first one, actually, but after that, I only cared about the one you'd given me. Not that I've been able to wear it since the whole Everest thing. I always worried that if you saw it on TV or someone took a picture of me with it on… Well. If you ever found out about Hawaii, I wanted it to be from me. I *needed* it to be from me."

I nod. Not that I forgive him—none of this is that easy. But I can't ignore the desperation saturating his every word. And god, he could have slept with me so easily.

Like Michael did.

But Grayson didn't even kiss me on that trip. Instead, he stayed up with me all night. Stared into my eyes and told me he loved me in a thousand different ways. Called me his one in seven billion.

"After Hawaii was when I really fell apart," he says softly. "I got a bunch of tattoos, started drinking too much, crashed my bike in Tibet. Went to Everest, got caught in an avalanche, almost died. And even then, all I could think about was the fact that I was never going to see you again. Because for some reason, saying goodbye to you the second time was so much worse than the first. Maybe because I was old enough to realize you were it for me, forever. And I'd fucked it all up, and you hated me, and you were happy with my brother. And I had to respect your wishes by staying away."

"But I *wasn't* happy," I whisper. "Not really."

"I realize that. Now." Grayson's voice hitches. "I wish I had then. I would've done everything differently."

Jesus. I'm a mess. He is, too. I can see it on his face, and I'm raw inside, breaking beneath the burden of all those lonely, squandered years. But I reach out, very gently, and take his hand.

He runs a thumb over my fingers. I sense no hope in the touch. Just a despairing sort of apology. "When Michael died, I told myself it didn't change anything. But deep down, I kept hoping that maybe enough time had passed for you to forgive me. Or at least let me back in your life, if only as a friend. So I caved and sent you that email. Except when you wrote back saying you'd only found out I was Michael's twin three years ago…"

I squeeze his fingers. No wonder his emails sounded so apologetic.

"I always knew he was a selfish motherfucker, but even he couldn't have done something that messed-up. Or so I thought. I had to call you to be sure. I had to hear you tell me yourself that we'd never met." All the emotion drains from his voice, as if Michael's betrayal has bled him dry. "I may have punched a wall. While we were talking."

I turn over the hand I'm holding and suck in a breath. In the lamplight, faint bruises outline his knuckles. That thud. I thought he'd dropped the phone.

"I know I should've told you everything then," he says. "But I had to see you, Mina. I felt like I was going to die if I didn't."

At the very least, I had to be sure you were okay. And, if I'm honest, I think part of me thought that maybe… Maybe…" He looks away, his eyes bright.

"Maybe?" I say gently.

"Nothing. You had every right to react the way you did." He blinks furiously. "Back in my twenties, I was so convinced there was no such thing as yesterday, but now I know better. I get that we can't start over. I can never undo what's happened, or fix the fact that I could've done right by you and didn't. But I *am* sorry. If I could live my life all over again, I'd do it completely differently. I just hate that I'll never have the chance."

I don't speak. I can't. The truth crowds in, pressing all the air from my body. Grayson traces the tendons of my hand, but absently, as if in his mind, I've already gotten up and left.

Breaking the silence requires all the breath in my lungs. "The way you felt about me never changed?"

He looks up. His eyes gleam like a knife's edge, the agony there so sharp and bright it slices into me, too. "Never."

"Even now? I mean, do you even recognize me anymore? The girl you fell in love with was a completely different person."

"Yes, Mina." He sounds hollow. Scraped raw. "I recognize you. I'd know you anywhere. I think the bigger question is, do you recognize *me*?"

I look. Really look. He never used to have all these razor edges, and this version of him possesses a hardened, sinewy power that makes him look so much older than the boy from the Canadian fairy cave.

But I do recognize him. I'd know him anywhere. Maybe I recognized him from the first moment I answered the phone.

"You're different now," I whisper. "But yes. It's still you."

His mouth curls. I had no idea smiles could look so sad. "I hope you know I would've scaled that building and come through a nineteenth-story window for you, if I'd thought it would help. The only thing that could've kept me away from you was…well, you. Which I guess Michael knew."

My throat thickens. "I guess so."

We sit in silence. I roll the truth around in my hands until I've mapped the exact size and shape of Michael's treachery. It's breathtaking in its magnitude. My husband broke us. Stole years from us. Thieved me for himself without my knowledge. And Grayson's right—Michael *kept* me. Like a pet. Or an angel on his shoulder, one he caged with pretty things and broken promises. Meanwhile, the man in front of me had always intended to let me fly.

Grayson gazes at me with naked regret. Something wakens inside me, pushing against the underside of my ribs, trying to get to him. So much has changed, and yet the same eyes that once pleaded with me inside an enchanted cave plead with me now, all these years later.

"I just need you to explain one last thing," I say.

"Of course," he rasps.

My eyes stray to the script inked over his heart. "If that's not Lily's name, whose is it?"

He breathes in hard, then lifts the hand he's holding, pries my fingers apart, and presses my palm to his chest. Each searing black letter brands itself into my flesh. "It's yours. Of course it's yours."

A tiny, broken sound flees my throat. "You mean all this time? All this falling apart you've done in front of the whole world? Because I thought—"

"No. It wasn't about Lily. It was always about you. Always." He lets go of my hand and exhales, long and shuddering and low, like a man ravaged. And of all the things that've come out of his mouth, *that's* what undoes me.

One minute, I'm in the chair. A heartbeat later, I'm on the bed, straddling him, tipping him back onto the mattress.

He freezes, his eyes wide, like he doesn't understand how I got to him so fast, or that I got to him at all. "Mina?"

My hands press against his chest. "I don't want to talk anymore. I just want…"

He waits, his breath coming in ragged bursts. "What? What do you want?"

The thing beneath my ribs swells to a throb. "To stop missing you, I think. I've spent half my life missing you. And right now, I just want to know what it feels like not to."

His eyes flare wider. "Are you asking me to—"

"Yes." I pour everything inside me into that single word. Every last one of those aching, lonely nights when I ran out into the dark, searching for something I didn't even understand I'd lost. "Please."

He stares up, but in another second, he lets go. I catch the exact moment when his eyes darken and his lips part. The point at which he understands what I need from him and decides to give it.

His arms lock around me, pulling me down. Our lips crash together. I kiss him like I'm starving for it, like I'll die if I don't fill myself with the taste of him, with his smell—that incredible smell, the one I caught in the kitchen last night and should have recognized, because it's the same deep-forest rainstorm it's always been.

He rolls me beneath him, feasting on my mouth. We aren't gentle this time. My fingers scrabble against the ridges of his back. He releases my lips and sucks at my neck—god, that feels like it'll leave a mark, and I hope it does—then tears at my clothes like they've offended him. My orange top hits the rug, followed by my leggings. I rip at my bra and panties myself.

He rears back and stares down as I lie naked and spread beneath him. He's breathing so hard I can't hear myself think, but I don't want to, anyway.

If I did, it would only be about how right he is—there's no

starting over, no fixing all the things that went wrong. The sun will rise tomorrow and everything will still be smashed to pieces. I'll still have fourteen years' worth of secrets and betrayals to shoulder. The past will still weigh enough to crush me.

But, for maybe the first time since a girl stood on a mountaintop and let a boy convince her they both were giants, I don't care. What Michael stole from me, I'm taking back. I'm seizing a moment, a *right now* no one can rob me of, if only this once.

All my yesterdays will still be waiting for me tomorrow.

I curl my fingertips into Grayson's waistband, hunting for the boxers underneath. Nothing meets my touch except smooth, hot skin. My eyes flare. "You're not wearing any underwear. Why are you not wearing underwear?"

He raises an eyebrow, managing to look simultaneously provocative and uncertain. "Um...irrational optimism?"

Well, isn't he just full of impressive choices. Ever so slowly, I draw his pants down and take him in my hands.

He makes a primal sound and curls forward, catching himself with an arm propped beside my head. His breath fans across my cheek, heated and quivering, as he kicks his pants all the way off. The whole time I touch him, he looks at me. Straight on, catching me up in that ocean of his, even while my hands coax a strangled sound of pleasure from him.

My breath picks up tempo, keeping time with my fingers. This is so different. Michael always closed his eyes. But Grayson keeps his wide open.

He finally takes my hands and pulls my wrists up over my head, pressing them into the bed. My whole body comes alive, the skin over my rib cage pulling taut as he stretches me lengthwise.

He dips his head and paints whorls of flame against my neck with his tongue. He explores the base of my throat, the ridge of my clavicle, follows the swell of my breast and pulls my nipple into his mouth.

A stab of heated lightning shoots down into my center. Grayson drives it ever deeper. His tongue works at me while his free hand trails down my side, featherlight. His thumb lands against my hip bone and draws tender circles in the spot I love best. The spot I now realize Michael never found.

A wanton moan climbs from my throat, and I throw my head back. The contrast between his forceful mouth and deft fingers spills an ache through me, one that gathers into a fluttering beat between my thighs.

"Kiss me," I gasp.

He climbs my body and crushes his mouth to mine again. He kisses me with a brutal honesty I absorb like sustenance. I let my knees fall wider, let him pinion me to the mattress while our tongues write a story with one another and heat surges in my veins.

A dark, delicious yearning takes over, a whole bottomless pit of it, a craving I might never be rid of. I kiss him harder, stealing as much of his taste as I can, wrapping my legs around his waist and pulling him closer until his length nudges at my entrance. I tilt my hips up, inviting.

"Are you sure?" he says into my mouth.

I open my eyes to find him still watching me. When I tug my wrists against his iron grip, he holds me fast, the muscles of his arm standing out like ropes.

I nip at his bottom lip. "What, is fourteen years not long enough?"

His pupils change, swallowing up the lamplight. Devouring it. "It's too long," he says. The roughest three words ever spoken. "Way too fucking long."

"Then yes. I'm sure."

"Oh, thank fuck," he breathes.

With excruciating slowness, he pushes into me, in and in and in, and I whimper and arch my back, all the while holding his eyes as if he's commanding me to. It *feels* like he is.

He seats himself deep and stays there. A shiver tears through him and continues straight on into me.

Fuck. I could die like this. In rapture. I would welcome it.

"Am I hurting you?" he says.

I scrape together enough air to answer, even though I'm melting inside. "Just for a second. And only in the best of ways. Don't stop."

He makes a sound of anguished pleasure and pulls back, then pushes in again, torturing me with his exquisite self-control. I can't help but chase him upward every time he retreats, all the while making gasping, begging sounds. I try to free my hands, try to *get* to him, but he holds me in place, working up to his rhythm with maddening leisure.

When he finally gets there, it's every bit as consuming as I want it to be. Like he's dismantling me from the inside. He releases my wrists and I clutch at him, stabbing greedy fingers through his wet hair. His breath spurts hot against my neck. And still, he never closes his eyes.

He rolls his hips, driving into me. Faster. Harder.

I moan. The room is falling apart. Or maybe I'm falling into myself and taking him with me, because as I drown in the feel of him, I know I've never once had anyone fill me up this way. No one has ever surrendered with me like this.

God, I've missed him. My whole adult life, I've missed him without even realizing it, and now he's finally here.

My fingertips dig into the back of his shoulder as he pushes a rising crash of pleasure through me. I spiral inward, wound tighter with every touch. Hands. Mouth. Wet hair pressed against my forehead. The fresh, deep forest in my nose. A warm, tropical ocean, filling me up. Heat, heat, heat.

It's almost too much, yet I wonder if it will ever be enough.

And then I'm coming apart, bursting into the darkness like a star, only he's there to catch all the pieces, because he's holding me tight, so tight as he makes a sound that steals all the beauty in this world and presses it into a single moment, into this one hoarse cry coming out of his mouth.

We burn together and when the flames die back and his corded muscles unlock, I lie in the circle of his arms. Blissful ripples ebb and flow beneath my skin.

"Fucking hell." He's limp beside me, his face pressed into the mattress, his words muffled. "You had me so convinced I was going to die without ever getting to do that."

When I say nothing, he raises his head. His dreamy smile drains away as he catches my expression. "But…this doesn't mean what I want it to, does it?"

A pang slices right down the center of my chest. "I don't see how it can." There's no putting the pieces back together. No starting over. There never is. I've known that much for years.

Grayson musters a smile that can't quite mask the desolation behind it.

"But you can ask me again in the morning." I reach for him. "Technically, I do owe you this one last day."

His breath hitches as I pull his face to mine.

We have sex once more, this time long and sliding and slow, slow, slow, and he looks at me the whole time again, as if he's memorizing every lash and the exact hue of my eyes, like he's storing up every whimpered note he pulls from my throat.

When the wave crests and I come beautifully undone, he whispers in my ear. "All this time, I've loved you."

I clutch him tighter, afraid to open my mouth, afraid of what lies behind my lips.

Afterward, he closes his eyes without turning off the light. I let it be and watch him sleep. I think it's the first time I've seen him like this, lost to the world, not so much sleeping as he is drifting back in time, the lines of his brow smoothed by the innocence of unconsciousness. He looks vulnerable. Trusting. Unbroken.

And I hate—*hate*—that I'll have to ruin it all tomorrow.

AFTER

I wake before dawn.

At some point in the night, Grayson has turned off the lamp, and I lie in the blackness, thinking.

Yesterday broke me—sliced me open and pulled my guts out. But it remade me, too. It answered a question I've been asking myself for fourteen years.

I regret nothing.

Yet as I roll onto my side, trying to tether myself to the sound of Grayson's breathing, I become acutely conscious of every wound gouged into me. Of every bloodied furrow left by Michael's lies. The enormity of his deceit tears through me, as deafening as a stampede and even more destructive.

I can hardly comprehend what I've lost. Or whether I can ever heal.

Beside me, Grayson murmurs in his sleep. Not so much with words as with drowsy male sounds, but it's still enough to send the blood in my veins veering off course. I imagine him waking and turning those oceanic eyes on me, the sheer depth of *wanting* they'll hold. I imagine him asking me what happens next.

The answer he wants exists somewhere, buried deep—some naive sliver of me that wants to lie here forever, in this unfamiliar bed that somehow feels like home. But I can't actually reach it. Too much stands in the way, a thorny bramble of lies and betrayals that tear at my flesh.

The hotel room's shadows thicken, trying to pin me to the mattress, so I ease from bed and gather my clothes. My body aches in all the ways a woman's does after she's been skillfully taken apart and put back together again, but each movement only proves how much more the rest of me hurts.

My heart. My soul.

I slip from the room. In the parking lot, I cringe at the Porsche's full-throated roar and back out as quickly as possible. On the way to the cabin, I fixate on the glittering curtain overhead. The dash clock reads 4:30—an hour until sunrise.

Out in the darkness, bears are probably rooting through the underbrush, but the forest calls to me, promising solace. Comfort. One last chance to retreat, to make sense of this.

Because really, this *is* my last chance. My four days here are up.

Time to go home.

The thought makes my skin prickle, and when I reach the cabin, I don't stop to consider. I just layer a jacket over yesterday's clothes and snatch the lantern from the living room without acknowledging the Monopoly money still papering the floor.

Outside, in the yard, the woods stretch like a beckoning tunnel. Starlight whirls above the treetops, but I aim for the shadows, letting the indigo trees fold me into their embrace.

The glow of my lantern bathes the massive trunks. The scene looks like Grayson's photograph in reverse—light stretches up and up, never quite reaching the high dome of the forest. I steal through on quiet feet, not sure why I feel compelled to honor the silence, but doing it anyway. Nothing moves. Pine needles crunch underfoot, sending bursts of green into my nostrils.

In a clearing, I set down my lantern and unfurl on my back in the chilled moss, my gaze seeking the sky. Stars wink down through the sighing branches like benevolent, knowing eyes.

We see you, they seem to say. *You are not alone.*

I lie there, feeling like a stranger inside my own body. Nothing was what I thought. My life, my marriage… Fourteen years of memories attempt to rearrange themselves. Each snapshot moment looks different now, its angles subtly unfamiliar, like a long-lost friend greeted after a long absence, whose face has now changed.

Once upon a time, a thousand years ago, Michael's hand curled around mine, stopped me from getting out of a car. Except it wasn't Michael at all. That was *Grayson*. Grayson whose necklace glinted against his skin. It was his smell I wanted to drown in. His secrets, told without hesitation. *He* was the one who rescued me from Patrick's house.

Michael only came after. Now I think of him at our condo in Seattle, bloodied and bruised, and his selfish agreement when I asked to stay. I consider the lies he hid behind a wall of silence. The secrets, the scars he left behind.

A despairing laugh bubbles up. God, how many years did I spend wishing he wouldn't shut down at the first sign of emotion? That he'd invite me to feel instead of sending me off on a run?

Now someone's asking me to do exactly that, and I can't manage it. Because in the end, they both lied. They both broke my heart. And some things, once shattered, can never be stitched back together.

Apparently, Michael knew that even better than I do, because once upon a time, when the woman he loved died because of him, he built his walls and stayed behind them. He surrounded himself with what had proved safest—order. Routine. And then I came along and offered to help police the boundaries of the box he'd corralled himself into.

Of course he said yes.

A branch snaps. I jerk my head up. For a moment, silence greets me, then something moves in the underbrush. Something big.

I bound upright and raise the lantern. It can't be the same damn bear, can it?

Except Grayson emerges from the twilit vault of the forest, his hair a mess. "Mina? What the hell are you doing out here?"

I lower the lantern, the rush of my pulse subsiding, although I might actually have preferred the bear. "Me? What're *you* doing? Did you come out here after me?"

"You were gone," he says, his tone defensive, his expression haunted. "And I…"

I wait, but he doesn't continue, just swallows and glances to the side, as if he can't bear to meet my eyes, though he never once looked away last night.

"You what?" I prompt.

He swallows. "I had a dream. That you…disappeared. Forever. And then I woke up, and you weren't there, and…" He contemplates the distance. "I just needed to see. Needed to make sure you were okay."

I search for words. I know we have to talk. Obviously we do, but I don't know what the hell I'm supposed to say. Leaving before he woke up already sent a clear enough message.

"Just come back with me," he says. "Please? This is no place to be at twilight. Not unless you want to run into that mama bear again."

Okay, maybe he has a point. I glance around, but there are just trees and more trees, and nothing overhead but a scrap of velvet sky. As mired in my thoughts as I was, I didn't pay an ounce of attention on my way here. "Fine. But we're lost."

"Not really." Grayson turns a circle, inspecting the forest, the stars, the ground. He still doesn't look at me. The set of his shoulders gives me the impression he doesn't want to.

Finally, he points. "It's this way."

I scan the dark beyond his finger. "How do you know?"

He cuts me a look.

I press my lips together. Of course. *He* taught me how to orienteer. Not Michael.

We set off. Unsurprisingly, Grayson delivers us straight to my backyard. The cabin glows in the budding dawn. In the driveway, his red whatever-it-is sits parked at a cockeyed angle, as if he arrived in a hurry.

"Thanks." I catch at his arm. "For getting me home."

He pulls away. He's wearing a T-shirt, presumably chosen in haste, and rubs at his pebbled arms. "You *know* the woods are dangerous at this hour."

I flinch and attempt to swallow the shame in my throat. "Yeah. I just…didn't know what else to do. Where else to go. I needed to process. Alone."

He sighs and shoves his hands into his pockets. "And? Did you? Process?"

I waver. "Not really. But we should still talk. Do you want to come inside?"

He aims a glance at the cabin, then away. I can almost see him figuring that the evidence of our night by the fire still litters the room. "Not really."

"Okay." I shuffle my feet. "In your car, maybe?"

"Fine," he says.

"Fine."

We make for the driveway. I set the lantern down and climb into his race car. Grayson hunches in the driver's seat, his muscles taut as he glares at the steering wheel.

"A stick shift?" I say, in a futile attempt to lighten the mood. "I didn't know anyone actually drove these anymore. Looks complicated."

He stares at me like I've committed a mortal sin. "That's what you want to talk about? Really?"

I pause. "No. I just... Sorry. It's just that nothing I have to say is going to be what you want to hear."

He grunts. "Yeah, I figured as much. It's fine."

When he doesn't continue, I bury my face in my hands. "It's *not*, though. This is all too much to handle. I mean, Michael dying was bad. Really bad. But now I've found out my whole life has been a charade. That the guy I married was essentially a stranger. Not to mention a manipulative asshole. And the one I actually loved lied to me. Do you have any idea what that feels like? How confusing that is? How *hurtful*?"

His eyes darken. "I never meant to hurt you, Mina. Ever. Like I said last night."

"You know what? I actually believe you. But that doesn't change the fact that you did, anyway. Which almost makes it worse."

He goes quiet, gears turning behind his eyes.

"And the craziest thing is," I continue, "that despite it all, I still love you. I'm so fucking in love with you it hurts." I laugh hollowly, unable to imagine a sadder way to echo his words back to him.

He blinks, rapid-fire.

"But it's all twisted up," I say. "Mangled. Like a fork someone's pulled out of the disposal. It's not...functional."

"I'm not asking for it to be." He grimaces. "I know it's too late. I knew it last night. Even if I hadn't, when I woke up and you weren't there..." He bites down on the rest.

I look away. Silence piles between us.

"So what now?" I finally ask.

He makes a bitter sound. "You tell me. You're in charge here. What I want doesn't factor into this."

I consider, but it's like reaching for something that isn't there. "What *do* you want, though?"

He squeezes the bridge of his nose. "It doesn't matter. And you don't want to hear it. Trust me."

"Just tell me. Please."

He drops his hand with a humorless laugh and stares through the windshield. "You really want to know? Well, shit...where do I start? Really, I just want to carry you into that cabin and tear all your clothes off again. I want to make love to you in front of the fire and hear you say my name the whole time. My *real* name. I want to make you make that little squeaking moan again. I want to do that a million times. And then I want to bring you with me to New Zealand, and let you choose which assignment I take after that, and after that. Take you wherever you want to go. I want to wake up and see your face every morning and make you coffee while you sleep in like a teenager, and I want to beat you at Monopoly over and over again and cook you kettle corn that's three times too sweet because that's the way you like it and... I don't know. Get a fucking dog with you, or something. *That's* what I want."

I topple back in my seat like he's pushed me. "Would the dog be old?"

His brow knits. "I guess?"

"And smelly?"

"Sure. Why not."

I don't say anything. I can almost see it—us leading a normal life, like two people who just met and fell in love and didn't have an ocean's worth of lies and lost chances between them.

But we aren't those people. We never will be.

Grayson sighs. "But I know that isn't what should actually happen."

My breath catches. "What should happen?"

"You should go home." He doesn't miss a beat. "And put the pieces back together. Live your life. Do the things that make you happy. Forget about Michael. He wasn't worthy of you, anyway. And he's definitely not deserving enough to keep you from moving on. I'm not, either."

Tears prickle behind my eyes, but I hold them in check. "You make it sound so easy."

"Yeah, well, it's not. It's the hardest thing you'll ever do. I get that. But remember when you asked if I still recognize you? I said I do, and it's true. And the Mina I see is strong. Strong enough to get through anything."

"I don't feel strong," I say faintly. I feel like someone who's just been emotionally filleted.

"Bullshit. You are. You always have been. Look how much whining and feeling sorry for myself I've done, and in the meantime, you've survived so much worse than I have. But you're still here. Because you're like that lantern, Mina. You glow. You endure. So go home, and get past this. And be happy."

Get past this. The words catch beneath my breastbone. "But what does that mean for you?"

"I don't know. Maybe it's time I tried taking my own advice. Maybe I need to do what I decided in Nepal and let go."

My stomach shrinks to a hard, aching marble. "Of me?"

He shrugs stiffly. "Of my obsession with you, maybe. I've always thought the only thing I've ever done right in my life is love you. That it was my only redeeming quality. But I think... maybe I need to figure out who I am without you. Because right now I have no idea. It's like I've spent half my life running. Toward you. Away from you. Shit, half the time I can't even tell the difference."

My breath dies. He might as well have cut my chest open and let my heart squelch out onto the floor mat.

Except he's right. "I have no way to argue with that."

"Well, damn it." He fiddles with the steering wheel. "I was kind of hoping you would."

"I don't." My throat burns. "But I *am* sorry. For it to end this way."

He exhales and slides down in the seat. "It's okay. You promised me three days, and that's what I got. I might've gotten my hopes up for a minute, but I never really expected anything else. And the truth is I could never be with you, anyway."

"What?" My brows snap together. "Why not?"

"Because you're clearly not a fan of manual transmissions."

When I say nothing, he catches my eye. The silence stretches. "That was a joke," he says.

"Oh." I know he's trying to downplay the significance of what's happening, or maybe trying to let me off easy, but I can't muster up a chuckle.

"Great." He sighs. "Well, on that note, I'm not leaving until you do."

"What? Why not?"

"Because," he says, "I really don't feel like abandoning you out here. With the bears."

My fingers twine in my lap. I realize I need to get out of the car, but this feels so horrifically final. "I still have to clean the cabin, though. The movers are coming today."

"Okay. Why don't you pack up and put all your luggage on the porch? I can load Michael's car for you while you finish up."

"It's not Michael's car anymore. It's mine."

He gives me a quizzical look. Fair enough, since I have no idea why I said that. It's like I'm just trying to keep him here longer.

"Don't mind me," I say. "That sounds good. Thanks for the help."

He leaps out as if he can't get away from me fast enough. I get out, too. Once in the cabin, I tidy the evidence of my brief tenancy, stacking my suitcase and other belongings outside for Grayson to deal with. His footsteps thump against the porch. I give the furniture a cursory wipe-down, lock up, and stash the key beneath the grizzly.

Before I know it, Grayson is helping me into the Porsche.

I start the engine and look up at him through the open window, struck by the mirror image of that day in Seagrove, when I stood beside his car and caught my very first glimpse of him.

He took my breath away that day. And somehow, for all that my heart is splintering into shards right now, I feel like he's finally giving it back to me, all these years later.

"Bye, Mina." Grayson leans in through the window and kisses me, softly, with tenderness instead of heat. It only lasts a second. "I love you. Always."

I don't have the chance to respond. In another moment, he climbs into his car.

I shift into Drive and ease my foot onto the gas. Tears burst out before I even clear the driveway. In the rearview mirror, the sun crests over the trees.

Only when my sobs finally quiet do I look over at the passenger seat and realize what Grayson has sent with me. I accidentally left it beside his car, but there sits the red lantern, tucked between bags of groceries. As Seagrove looms closer, I glance at it a dozen times or more.

Every time, it feels as though Grayson's gentle lips are pressed to mine all over again.

I wonder how long it will take me to forget what they feel like.

BEFORE

It's just another afternoon. Just another grocery run, sandwiched between clothing donation drop-offs and pickup of this week's dry cleaning.

The grocery store's fluorescent lights fizz overhead. I inch forward in the checkout line as my mind plods along, calculating the time it will take to get the groceries and dry cleaning home. I still need to get my car to the auto shop before it closes.

Not that my Genesis has issues, but Michael trailed me out to the garage this morning, asking whether Sven had checked over the car recently. My husband insists on regular visits to the most overpriced garage in Seagrove, apparently because Sven does a twenty-four-point "vehicle safety inspection" the other places don't offer.

Which I don't exactly love. The visits always leave me carless for an entire day. But there are worse things Michael could obsess about besides my safety, so I humor him, though I do wish he hadn't chosen today to ask. I have an article due this week about a new eye irrigation lens that will provide an alternative to the standard Morgan. I can always push it until tomorrow, though, provided I can hold my enthusiasm at bay for that long.

The woman in front of me pays, and I push my cart forward. As always, I strike a deal with myself: if I don't glance at the magazine rack, I can have a bowl of kettle corn after dinner.

I make the same bargain every time. I've never confessed to Michael, but it takes concerted effort to keep myself from devouring the color-soaked covers with headlines like "Best Caribbean Islands to Get Lost On" or "Where to Go, Month by Month."

Today proves more difficult than usual. I wedge my cart into the lane and stack groceries onto the conveyor belt while the magazines stare a heated hole in my back.

I set down a gallon of milk and try to decide on tonight's dinner. Instead, I end up wondering who exactly pens those headlines. My mind conjures an image of a woman in a French hotel room, emerging onto her balcony with a coffee in hand while birds twitter all around.

Which is stupid. Travel writing can't possibly be that glamorous. In reality, those people probably have lives filled with misplaced baggage and delayed flights, with whole-body sunburns and precious keepsakes lost on buses.

I transfer a container of organic strawberries. I should count myself lucky that I never went to Greece. I hate sunburns. Better that I ended up with the *Medical Devices Monthly* gig, which I can do from the comfort of my living room.

Soon, I run out of groceries, and my attention settles on the conveyor belt. Whirr and stop. Whirr and stop. The cashier scans each item with marked disinterest.

Oh, for god's sake. Who am I kidding? I turn to the magazine rack.

Heat slams into my chest, like someone has punched me in the lungs with a molten fist. It takes at least five seconds to figure out why. I stare at the displayed issue of *National Geographic*, my mouth agape.

What is my husband doing on the cover, coated in snow and with a fake scar on his eyebrow? And why does he look so...so...

A high-pitched sound invades the quiet. It takes a moment to realize it's coming from me. I clamp my mouth shut and snatch the magazine. Crisp yellow words run along the bottom.

"Grayson Drake Defies Death at Everest."

My trembling hands rattle the pages. What? *What?*

No matter how long I stare, the headline doesn't change. And I finally realize this isn't my husband at all, but his brother.

His *identical twin*, apparently.

Blood bellows in my ears as I roll up the magazine and shove past my cart. My shirt catches on the candy rack, making a box of bubble gum smack onto the tile, but I don't stop. The cashier hollers. I turn just long enough to fish a twenty from my purse and push it across the counter, leaving my groceries behind.

In the car, I toss the magazine onto the passenger seat. The engine's roar adds to the hurricane inside my skull. Every time I glance over, the familiar face of a stranger stares back. And every time, it absolutely guts me.

I stomp the gas pedal harder. I don't understand the violence of my reaction. But it is. Violent. That aqua stare turns me inside out, pulling each nerve ending up to the surface.

The tachometer tips into the red. Rain lashes against the windshield. God, I never once pictured the man who upended our lives this way. I imagined Michael's stoicism pasted onto different features. Instead, Grayson's features are the same, but the open pain in his eyes? His beseeching expression?

Utterly different.

At home, I barrel up the stairs and into Michael's office. He jerks up from his desk, surprise splashed across his features. "Mina, what're you—"

"What the hell is this?" I brandish the magazine.

He freezes. His gaze travels from *National Geographic* to me and back again. In the silence, raindrops scrabble against the windowpanes.

I shove the magazine closer, as if he doesn't understand what he's seeing. "You never once thought to tell me that your brother's your identical twin?"

His eyes flick to mine, unreadable. Meanwhile, my heart tries to climb out of my body using my throat as a ladder.

"No," he finally says. "It doesn't matter."

I give the magazine a shake. Of course it matters. It matters so much I can hardly breathe. I just...can't find the words to explain why. "Why on earth would you have lied about this?"

"I *didn't*," he says. "I just didn't bring it up. Why would I have?"

I stand unmoving, locked in a mute battle with the fury scalding my throat.

Michael sighs and sets down his pencil. "What do you want me to say?"

"I don't know," I shrill. "How about the truth?"

"You know the truth. I didn't volunteer that he's my twin because it doesn't matter. What my brother looks like has no impact on our lives whatsoever."

My whole body trembles. I try to find a flaw in that logic and fail spectacularly.

"Mina." Michael watches me with steady eyes. He's utterly in control of himself. Always so unbelievably *controlled*. "Why are you so upset?"

"Because." My voice cracks. "This whole time, there's been another you, walking around out in the world somewhere? That's so...*wrong*. I should've known."

"He's not another me. At all. He's nothing like me."

There's a catch in his voice, a hint of some vastness buried beneath the measured words, and I latch on. "Oh, no? And what's so unbelievably different? What's made him not even worth talking about?"

Heavy seconds tick by. I hold my breath, knowing I'm skirting dangerously close to lines I agreed not to cross a decade ago. But I can't seem to let this go.

"I don't want to talk about this," he says softly.

"You never do," I snap. "You never want to talk about anything. Nothing real, anyway."

His lashes flicker. Barely. "Angel. Why don't you come here?"

"No," I bite out, already knowing exactly what will happen if I cross this room. If he thinks he can just fuck me into submission, he…might actually be right. So I command my feet to meld with the floor. "Don't do that. Don't distract me that way."

Michael waits, but when I don't move, he heaves a breath and scrubs his palms on his slacks. "Okay, you really want to know what Grayson's like? He's…selfish. Impetuous. Violent. Not the kind of person you'd want around. There."

"But he can't be all bad. You cared about him, once."

Michael makes an indecipherable sound. "Yeah, when I was a kid. Because I didn't know any better."

I hope for more, but my husband never elaborates if he doesn't have to. He just turns impenetrable like this, locks me out of whatever inner turmoil he's trying to hide. And yet, when I squint, I glimpse a sliver of that same depth I saw that day in Seattle—a world of pain piled up behind his eyes.

Not for the first time, or even the hundredth, I curse Grayson Drake to hell and back. If only Michael would let me *in*.

"I know I agreed not to talk about him," I say, quieter this time. "But I think I need to understand what happened between you two."

Another long pause. He props his hands on his knees. "Fine. I'll tell you, this *once*. Never again. And promise me, Mina, you won't go looking for him. He has no place in our lives.

All he ever does is take, and he's taken more than enough from me already."

"Okay," I say slowly.

"Promise me," he repeats. "You won't contact him, all right?"

I frown. That would never have crossed my mind. "I promise."

Michael lets go of an exhale and scrubs at his forehead. "Okay. The thing is, my brother's a bastard. He always has been. It just took me a long time to figure that out."

I lower the magazine. Now that he's agreed to talk, I almost want to stop him, because the effort involved alarms me. Sweat beads at his hairline while the apple of his throat scrapes up and down.

"When we were kids," he forces out, "Grayson...took everything for himself. All the attention. All our parents' time. Which was incredibly insulting, because he was always getting in trouble. Always breaking the rules. Meanwhile, I did exactly what I was supposed to and got ignored for it. Even in school, everyone liked him better. He was always the popular one, even though he spent half his time in detention."

I swallow. The sound carries over the drumming rain.

"He was always hogging the spotlight." Michael's voice roughens. "Asking out the girls he knew I liked. Using up all the oxygen in the room. Taking my share of *everything*. But I loved him anyway. He was my brother. So I forgave him. Over and over."

"That sounds hard," I murmur.

"It was. And after that last time..." Michael stops, glances around. His tone hardens, businesslike. "Well, look what I have now. Money, success. Stability. You. In the end, I won."

I frown. It's not a competition, but he continues before I can say so.

"Seattle was just the day I'd had enough. I finally told him he couldn't take from me anymore, that I was putting myself first. Which he couldn't stand. And..." Michael glances away again as if searching the room for an escape route. "Well. That's all there is."

"That's it?"

"That's it."

I waver. This vague attempt at an explanation does nothing to explain why Michael changed so drastically that day. It is, however, much more than I usually get, and judging by the way his chest heaves beneath his shirt, it's cost him dearly to give it to me.

Still, the magazine drags at my hand like a hundred-pound-weight. I glance at the cover, from which imploring eyes plead with me in silence. Then at my husband. His brow smooths. He's already locked himself back up, thrown away the key.

I inspect the magazine again. Then my husband.

The primordial mess of emotion within me burbles, and a half-formed suspicion heaves free of the muck. It's so misshapen and horrific I can scarcely find the words to acknowledge it, and yet...

"You would tell me, right?" For once, I achieve the same deliberate calmness he wields so adeptly. Not that I'm calm inside. There, I'm anything but. "If there was a...mix-up with you two, right? If things had gotten crossed somehow?"

He frowns. "Angel? What're you asking me?"

My molars lock together. What the hell *am* I asking? Am I so tragically desperate to unlock the secret of that week in Hawaii that I'm conjuring up conspiracies out of thin air?

Michael watches me with concern. When I say nothing, he abandons his desk and crosses the room, coming close enough to tip my face up.

"Are you feeling all right?" He presses a palm to my forehead. "You're not getting sick, are you? Is *that* what this is all about?"

"I..." I lift my gaze and stare into the same eyes I looked into on our wedding day. My husband gazes back with all the flat, unruffled calm of a windless sea.

All at once, my internal turmoil collapses into a low red pulse of shame. What the hell is wrong with me? He's never lied. Never betrayed me, never once come home smelling like perfume or with lipstick on his collar. No, he's built me this palace and would build me another if I asked. He's wined and dined me and kept me from wanting for anything. In Hawaii, he made my dreams come true, and someday, he'll do it again.

I shove my inchoate accusations into a strongbox, padlock the lid, and shove the whole thing down, down, down where it belongs.

"Sorry," I stammer out. "I—I don't know what got into me. I shouldn't have freaked out like that."

"It's okay." He drops a kiss on my forehead, then wraps me in a hug. "Seeing someone who looked like me but wasn't shocked you. It would've shocked anyone. Why don't we take your mind off it by going to dinner? Valenti's, maybe? It'll give you an excuse to wear that little red thing I got you last week, and we can order the lobster bisque you love so much."

I hesitate. "You hate the lobster bisque."

"Yes. But I love you."

The last remnants of my inner fire fizzle out. I burrow against his shoulder, already picturing us at our usual linen-draped table in the corner, gazing out at the sea as the sunset tints the water pink.

"We'll leave around seven?" Michael says. "That'll give you time for a run."

"Okay." I clear my throat and disentangle myself, leaving him to finish his work.

Downstairs, in the kitchen, I brave a glance at the magazine still clutched in my hand. Michael is right—what his brother looks like has nothing to do with us.

Yet as I stare, an ache as wide as the ocean opens inside my chest. Those eyes. And that expression. It's like Grayson's on the verge of saying something. Like he's the kind of person who *wants* to talk.

The internal strongbox rattles and thumps. I shove it deeper. There goes my overactive imagination, assigning meaning where there is none, connecting dots in such a grotesque manner that I'm ashamed I could even *consider* something like that.

With a sound of disgust, I pop the trash can lid and stuff the magazine to the bottom, then go to the front hall to pull on my running shoes. I sprint out into the rain.

This will all be okay. Ten miles from now, I will have forgotten all about this.

And not a moment too soon.

AFTER

After my return to Seagrove, a day passes. Then another. None of them blunts the chaos of emotion bubbling inside me. Or the way I miss Grayson so badly I can barely breathe.

But on the third day, in the midst of brushing my teeth, when I glance up and catch my reflection, a tiny, awed sound slips from my throat. I barely recognize the person in the mirror. That's no defeated widow staring back, but a woman with a fighting spark in her blue eyes.

Shaken, I steal down the stairs, make coffee, and pull on my running shoes.

September has dawned cool and mist laden, and I jog my usual route. But instead of trying to outpace the memories, I lean into them today. I trail my fingers across Michael's years of silence, then the fluorescent moments with Grayson—Grayson, who I met at a fair one day, who drove me to Canada and showed me how to open my eyes. Grayson, who once convinced me nothing could trump the power of now.

I let myself *remember*. And through it all, I keep going.

When I get home, I finally unpack the Porsche. Mostly to get the lantern, which I set on my glass work desk in the living room.

I light it. Even though it's daytime.

Really, I just want to see it glow.

The next morning, I get an email from Travelique.

I sit at my desk, my heart a blur inside my chest. Siobhan Monroe—senior editor, apparently—wants to run my article as part of a collaborative feature with a "noted photographer." She doesn't give a name, but she doesn't have to.

I try to calm the flurry of my pulse. That night at Grayson's hotel—he must've taken those pictures right before I showed up. Purely for my sake.

Thinking about him hurts, but it also leaves an echo of warmth behind. I can't figure out what that means. If anything.

Eventually, I give up trying and simply yield to the hum in my blood. This offer is a victory. A stepping stone toward building a life on my own terms.

I print out the Travelique contract, then sign it and send it back. They're not offering much, but Siobhan's email hints that if the article does well, she'll be interested in more.

I text Kate the good news.

Within minutes, my best friend responds that she's on her way with "skinny celebration margaritas." It's not even noon, and I don't know what skinny celebration margaritas are, but by the time I open the front door, I'm convinced they're the only thing that will do.

A refreshingly put-together-looking Kate stands on my welcome mat, brandishing a bottle. Her brown eyes widen as they travel up and down. Up again. Down again. "What the hell? What happened to you? I just saw you a week and a half ago."

I raise an eyebrow. I honestly have no idea what she sees. "What do you mean?"

"You've gained weight. In a good way. And there's something different about you. Also in a good way? I think? Or not? And..." She trails off, her attention fastening on my neck. "Oh my god. You have a hickey. Why do you have a hickey?"

My hand flutters to my throat. This is one distinct disadvantage to having chin-length hair.

"What *happened*?" she demands.

I shuffle my feet, which only wastes time, because of course I'm going to tell her. "Um...Grayson Drake happened?"

She stares, her hand loosening around her gift. Since I have precisely zero replacement skinny celebration margaritas in the house, I swipe the bottle before it smashes all over my welcome mat.

"Mina," she whispers, eyes round. "Did you have sex with your brother?"

"My brother's dead, Kate. So no. But if you're asking whether I had sex with my former *brother-in-law*, who is now no longer my brother-in-law, or, in fact, related to me in any way, then yes. I did. And that's just the tip of the iceberg. No, it's like, a *glimpse* of the tip of the iceberg. From forty miles away."

"Holy shit," she says. "You're so lucky I brought booze. Tell me everything."

As we suck down our margaritas, which turn out to be even tastier than anticipated, I spill the whole story.

Kate's eyes get wider and wider. By the time I finish, her mouth hangs open. Spots of color burn on her cheeks. "Please tell me you made all this up."

"I wish."

"You mean Michael lied to you? For years? *Tricked* you? And then just...never confessed?"

I hesitate, even though there's only one answer. "Seems that way."

She flops back against the couch arm, a hand pressed to her

chest. "Wow. I've heard some stories in my life, but this one takes the cake. Shit. I'd murder Michael myself, if he wasn't already dead."

I bark a laugh, even though nothing she says surprises me anymore.

"At least you're being rational about everything, though."

"Am I?" Absently, I swirl my straw around in my glass. "Being rational?"

"Yeah. I mean, I know Grayson's sinfully hot and all that, and it sounds like he genuinely believes he loves you, but he practically comes with a warning label that says 'emotionally unavailable.' Even if he didn't, you obviously can't date Michael's twin."

"No. Obviously not. But wait, you think he's sinfully hot? You've never said that before."

Kate straightens and sucks her drink so forcefully that the burble echoes off all the glass and steel. We're probably the opposite of classy to use straws like this, but I found them left over from a tropical-themed dinner party Michael and I once had and couldn't resist. They're the fun kind—brightly colored and with lots of curlicues.

"Come on," she says. "Everyone thinks that."

"Did you think Michael was sinfully hot, too?"

"Ew." Her nose wrinkles. "No. Don't be gross."

"You do realize they're *identical*, right?"

"No. No way. It's all about presentation."

Okay. I leave that alone, especially since I agree. Besides, I can tell that Kate considers Michael's role in this the only one of interest. To her, Grayson is no more than some bad-boy celebrity with an unrequited decade-and-a-half-long crush.

And why wouldn't he be? *She* doesn't wake up from dreams of kissing him in the firelight. She doesn't know that looking into his eyes felt like being in the exact place I belong.

She didn't fall in love with him on a mountaintop fourteen years ago.

I push back the flush battling for real estate on my cheeks. "Enough about me, though. How're things with Tanner? The kids?"

She gives me a narrow look but takes the bait. "Pretty good, actually. Tanner's babysitting right now, can you believe that?"

I guzzle half my drink. "I don't think it's called *babysitting* if they're his kids. That he helped make. And who he's obligated to keep alive in order to perpetuate his own DNA."

"Hmm. Good point. And Evelyn and Hunter are probably swallowing everything in the medicine cabinet as we speak while their dad plays a vicious game of computer chess against some dude named Boris in Russia, but hey. I'll take what I can get."

Amazingly, that makes me laugh. Even more amazingly, it feels good. Natural.

"You know what?" I say. "Forget Michael. And Grayson. Why don't we go out? Like, *out* out. To an actual restaurant. Or a bar. Talk to some people we don't know."

Kate's eyes round. "Excuse me?"

I repeat myself.

"Um…exactly who are you and what have you done with my best friend?"

I flash a rueful smile. God, she's been so loyal, all these months when I had nothing to give back. I owe her so much. "I guess we'll call me Mina two-point-oh. But I just happen to have Mina one-point-oh's credit card, so I'm buying. Sucks to be her."

Over the weekend, I list everything in the house for sale.

The red lantern keeps its place of honor beside my computer, but everything else—the black leather sofas, the chrome lamps, the glass tables—goes. I refurnish with one exhausting spree through the West Elm store in Seattle, which I've always loved but could never convince Michael to visit. The whole time, I'm on high alert, awaiting a familiar whiff of forest and rain.

I don't run into Grayson, though. It's a big city, and he's probably in New Zealand, anyway.

Back in Seagrove, I open a bottle of wine and try to drink enough to forget how much I just spent. It doesn't work. Mostly, I just go to bed wondering if I've made a gigantic mistake.

But when everything arrives and my home fills with light, bright fabrics and warm wood, I suddenly live in a different house. *My* house, complete with pops of color in the form of vibrant purple throw pillows and actual artwork on the walls instead of grayscale pictures of buildings.

Not a prison, but a haven. Lit by lantern light.

The only room I leave untouched is Michael's office, where the divorce papers and magazine clippings still cover the floor.

I don't know which intimidates me more, so I never once open the door.

BEFORE

The summer after Michael turns thirty-eight, he disappears.

Only for an hour, but it's utterly unlike him, and we're supposed to attend the opening of Seagrove's newest art gallery tonight. It's the kind of event my husband loves: an excuse to dress lavishly and converse with glittering people in hushed, reverent tones while nibbling at carefully crafted hors d'oeuvres. In all honesty, I've been looking forward to it, too. I don't often get him away from work so early in the day.

I've donned a slinky dress and blow-dried my hair, but he's nowhere to be found. He left for his annual physical hours ago, and I can't imagine a doctor's appointment taking this long.

I call him. When he doesn't answer, I pull up our location-sharing app. Since that day in Seattle, I've dreaded not being able to get in touch, though I've only had to use this thing once or twice.

Michael's blue dot pulses steadily on the map, and my fingers tighten around the phone.

He's in a place he absolutely should not be.

Inside of a minute, I'm zooming from the driveway. The greenery blurs past. This must be some kind of mistake. A glitch in the software. Or maybe Michael got a flat tire and had to pull over.

But when I round the last bend, my heart capsizes. Michael's BMW X7 sits parked outside the liquor store, right beside the door.

I slot my Genesis in beside it, my palms slick. My husband has been sober for thirteen years. I can't imagine what would have the power to make that change.

I leap from the car, then pause. Michael sits in the BMW's driver's seat, his face as pale as a full moon. He stares off, not seeing me, not even seeing the liquor store, from what I can tell.

I circle to his passenger side and test the door. It's unlocked. I climb in.

"Michael?"

His gaze swivels to me, much too slowly. Something's definitely wrong. His cheeks have a greenish cast that ties my guts in a knot.

"I didn't go inside," he says tonelessly. "I wanted to, but I didn't. I was hoping you'd come and stop me."

I gulp. "Okay. Good. That's good. But what're you doing here? What *happened*?"

He doesn't answer. He's looking at me, but also *not* looking at me, somehow.

"Was it something at your appointment?" I venture. Still nothing. "Michael? You're scaring me."

"I haven't been fair to you," he blurts from nowhere.

That rocks me back in the seat. "What?"

"I haven't…" He trails off, shakes his head. "Nothing. I'm just…not feeling well. I think I might throw up. Can we go home?"

The tightness in my belly eases. Food poisoning would explain that greenish tint and the sheen on his forehead. I got sick with it a few months ago and spent the evening curled around the toilet bowl, so delirious I swore I heard the jingle of Penny's collar, even though she's been gone for years.

"Of course," I say. "Here, come around to this side. I'll drive."

At home, I tuck Michael into bed with a glass of water he doesn't drink, then go downstairs to whip up some soup in hopes of easing his stomach. But by the time I head back upstairs with a bowl, he's asleep, even though it's only 7:00 p.m.

I watch him from the doorway. He doesn't stir, and in the end, I leave him be.

The following week, Kate's daughter is born.

My best friend texts me three days later. **Meet Evelyn!** The picture shows Kate on her couch with a squashed-face infant nestled against her chest. Dark circles hang beneath her eyes, but her smile looks genuine.

She's beautiful, I write back, because she really is. **And you did it, warrior woman!**

I did, she texts. **And thank god it's over. Margaritas at Tequila Mockingbird tonight? I could really use an hour of non-mom time.**

I hesitate, not sure new mothers are supposed to get drunk three days after giving birth. Then again, what would I know? Besides, Kate has told me she's going straight to formula this time—after a months-long odyssey with her son, Hunter, that involved multiple lactation consultants, excruciating nipple pain, and lots and lots of late-night tears, she's given up on breastfeeding completely. And she deserves to celebrate not having an entire extra human kicking around inside her rib cage anymore.

So I mount the stairs to Michael's office. Ever since the liquor-store incident, he hasn't been himself. Several times, I've caught him staring out the windows instead of working, and he points haunted eyes at me over the dinner table, as if his innermost thoughts disturb him.

Yet whenever I ask what's wrong, he shakes himself and gives me a smile. "Nothing."

"Hey," I say from the doorway. "Would you mind if I went out with Kate tonight?"

He glances up from his desk. "Sure. Will you need a ride later?"

I pause. I know he's asking whether I plan on drinking. By unspoken agreement, I never do when he's around, but I *have* indulged a few times with Kate over the years. "I don't know. Can I call you if I do?"

"Of course," he says, his tone mild, as if everything is perfectly fine. Maybe it is. "Whatever you need, angel."

At dinner, I do indeed end up having margaritas. Four, to be exact, which all hit at once the moment I stand up from the table.

I stumble. Kate slings a steadying arm around my shoulders as we make our way to the parking lot. Tanner, in a surprising show of competence, has managed to get both kids into the car in order to come pick us up, and I breathe a sigh of relief at not having to call my husband.

Whatever's going on with him, I don't want to think about it right now.

"How's Operation Vacation coming along?" Kate slurs in my ear. "Have you convinced Michael to get on a plane again yet?"

I would flinch if I hadn't drunk so much. As it is, I just hiccup. The lights of the restaurant twinkle and weave in the darkness. "Still working on it."

I don't feel like admitting the rest: that three-plus years post-Hawaii, I've nearly given up trying. Instead, I've come to accept that this is my life. I have a good husband, a good home, the best of friends.

It would be selfish to ask for more.

Tanner pulls up in the Suburban. He waves through the

windshield and puts a finger to his lips, indicating the kids are asleep.

"Come on," I say. "Our knight in shining armor is here."

Kate climbs in back, cramming herself between the two car seats. After a few clumsy attempts, I manage to hoist myself into the passenger seat and fasten my seat belt.

On the way to my house, Kate starts to cry. Normally, I would startle—my best friend rarely succumbs to tears—but between the alcohol and the postpartum hormones, I figure this is probably par for the course.

"She's so beautiful," Kate burbles between sobs. "I can't believe we *made* her. How mind-blowing is that?"

When Tanner pulls up to my door, I blow silent kisses toward the back seat so as not to wake the babies, then clamber out. Even from the driveway, I catch the wash of yellow illuminating the backyard. Michael is in his office.

I sneak inside and wobble up the stairs to our bedroom, where I run a toothbrush over my teeth, splash water on my face, and collapse into bed without even changing into pajamas.

I would say good night, if I weren't so spectacularly drunk. Even in my inebriated state, I realize that rubbing my intoxication in Michael's face would be incredibly cruel.

The world does a slow, nauseating spin, and I drift, not entirely certain whether I'm awake or dreaming. Eventually, a strong arm slips around my waist. A weight settles on the bed.

My eyelids flutter. It's dark, though I don't remember turning off the lamp. Did I? What time is it? It could be ten at night or five in the morning. I can't even tell if I'm in my bedroom or some amorphous dreamscape.

"Are you awake?" a voice says in my ear.

It sounds like Michael, and yet it doesn't. Something deep and broken drags beneath the words.

"I love you." Warm breath sifts against my ear.

I can't gather the energy to reply. My limbs feel heavy, my head fuzzy inside.

"I hope you know it's for my own reasons," the voice continues. "Even if you've never really loved me."

I freeze. Everything inside me quiets. I do love him. Of course I do. What kind of bizarre dream is this?

"I've tried to make you." The arm around me curls tighter. "I really have. But now I wonder if maybe I shouldn't have. If I should've let you go a long time ago."

Let me go?

"I just…needed you," he says. "I still do. What would've happened if you hadn't stopped me from going into the store that day?"

I open my mouth, or try to, but nothing comes out.

And in another moment, the dream fades. It spins off into silken, swaying darkness, taking me with it.

In the morning, my head feels like someone has taken a sledgehammer to the inside of my skull.

I drag myself upright with a wince. The clock on Michael's nightstand reads nearly eleven, and I hang my legs over the bedside before braving a walk across the room. God, I haven't been this hungover since college.

I tame my snarled hair and force some ibuprofen down my throat, then venture out of the bedroom. To my surprise, Michael's office is empty.

I find him downstairs, in the kitchen. The heavy scent of frying bacon and syrupy French toast saturates the air.

He's cooking. And *whistling*.

I collapse on a stool at the island and squint. "I didn't know you could whistle."

With a flourish, Michael serves up a heaping plate. His eyes twinkle. "Well, now you do. How're you feeling?"

"Great." The mere word threatens to split my head open. "Why're you so chipper?"

His smile widens. "Because my doctor called this morning. And it's good news."

I look down at the food, then up at him. He watches me, expectant, his expression more open than it's been all week.

"What good news?"

"My biopsy results came back. Benign. No cancer."

"Biopsy?" I shake my head, wondering if hangovers can cause auditory hallucinations. "What biopsy?"

"Dr. Maraida found a lump last week. On my testicle. I had to go do an ultrasound and get a giant needle poked into me. But it turns out it was nothing. Just a scare."

I sit motionless. "You thought you had cancer? And didn't tell me?"

"I didn't want to worry you."

I gape. "I'm your wife. It's my job to worry when, you know…something important happens."

He doesn't shrink from the accusation in my tone. It seems to roll off him like so much water down a duck's back. "I wanted to spare you, Mina. It wouldn't have made any sense for us both to be miserable. Not unless there was something to actually be miserable about."

I pause, weighing that. Last night's dream floats back to me in hazy snatches. "Is that why…?"

He waits, his head tilted.

My cheeks tingle. I had to have been asleep. Michael never talks like that. And yet… "I had the strangest dream last night."

He doesn't blink. "About?"

"It was you, I think. Or someone who sounded like you. You got in bed and told me all these things about what you should've done, like… Like you regretted stuff."

His expression turns thoughtful, but I discern no recognition on his face. "Just a nightmare. This whole thing has just been a horrible nightmare, and now it's over."

I search for a response. I can't believe he'd shoulder something like this for an entire week without telling me. And yet somehow, I'm not surprised.

"You know, I've been thinking," Michael says. "Maybe we could take a vacation. Go back to Hawaii."

Everything rushes away, the smell of the food fading. Even the hammering in my head quiets. My body fills with heat as the old daydreams come flooding back with a strength that makes me dizzy.

"Hawaii?" I could spend another night on the beach with him. I could hold that man in my arms again. "Really?"

"Sure. I could ask my doctor for some Xanax. That'd make the flight easier, don't you think? I'll just take so much I won't even notice getting on the plane. And we'll have even more fun this time."

"That would be impossible," I say automatically.

Michael's smile flickers, but soon recovers. "Let's do it."

"Okay," I whisper, all thoughts of cancer scares and foggy dreams forgotten. God, I love him. More than ever.

Except the trip never happens. For months, Michael resists my efforts to pin down a date, and when I finally do, a crisis at work forces him to reschedule.

Then, in February, less than two weeks after his thirty-ninth birthday, I get a phone call.

One that changes everything.

AFTER

In the weeks after I get home, Kate does her best to nurture me through the Grayson incident, like she did right after Michael died. She brings over kettle corn and marathons *Lucifer* on Netflix with me. She alternates with my mother to leave dinner on my doorstep every week, which is incredibly thoughtful, but really, I don't need caring for this time. Each passing day only solidifies my conviction that what happened with Grayson at the cabin changed me. Or maybe it helped me to change myself.

Maybe those aren't actually two different things.

I light the lantern nightly. It illuminates a place inside me that does more than admit he was right. It believes him, for my own sake.

I *am* strong. Which means someday, I'll think about him and Michael without dissolving into pain and doubt.

Someday, I'll open that damn office door.

I take up hiking again.

I pull all my gear out of the storage closet and acquaint myself with the trails that crisscross the mountains around Seagrove. Out in the woods, summer makes a slow surrender to autumn. I soak up September's sunshine and watch the squirrels stash acorns for winter.

I revel in the beauty of the woods, and even though it's not the cabin, forest bathing proves almost as restorative as it did when I was fifteen.

One evening at the end of September, just moments after I send off a medical article, the old, haunting question returns.

At what moment did I cease to be a wife?

It floats up from my subconsciousness, almost tentative at first. Yet I reach out and grab hold. Examine it from every angle.

And promptly decide that shouldn't be the question at all, because I never belonged to Michael the way I did to Grayson. Of course I didn't receive some cosmic broadcast from the universe at the moment of his death. I'm no longer sure that what I was doing right then even matters.

No, when I sift back through the years, the event around which my life pivoted didn't pass unnoticed, after all. I spent it in front of the windows of Michael's condo, frantically calling what I thought was his phone, so choked with fear that I couldn't have swallowed a grain of rice if I'd tried.

Because I knew. Somehow, some way, I *felt* Grayson leave my life.

I sit back in my desk chair, the knowledge hollowing out my stomach. Everything changed for me not in the bathtub, but in front of a rain-streaked windowpane in Seattle, and I spent the next fourteen years besieged by a longing I had no way to understand.

Which means maybe I never really ceased to be a wife.

Maybe I never truly was one in the first place. At least, not the way I thought.

★ ★ ★

At the beginning of October, my Travelique article goes to print, then goes viral. Two weeks later, Siobhan Monroe calls to ask if I can come up to Seattle to discuss the "future direction" of my career. She barely finishes asking before a *yes* bursts from my lips.

When the day arrives the following week, I make the long drive to Seattle and parallel park outside the Travelique headquarters. I can't help but notice that Grayson and I once lived a mere five blocks from here.

Michael and I did, too, of course. For far longer. But it's that month with Grayson that carves out space in my thoughts, and to my surprise, I let it.

Inside, I punch the elevator button for the sixteenth floor and emerge into a sleek office space done in hues of greige that showcase the stunning photography and article reprints decorating the walls.

Front and center, behind the receptionist, hangs the photo Grayson took in Millbrook. The same one that stopped my heart that night in his hotel room. The same one that went to print with the article I wrote, which garnered more views in its first week than any other story in the site's history.

"Mina Drake?" says the boy behind the desk. He's barely twenty, with dyed rainbow hair that makes me want to ask for his stylist's card.

"Yep," I say. "I'm here for my one-o'clock with Siobhan."

"Absolutely. Right this way."

He presses a bottle of water into my hand and leads me to a corner office. A slender Black woman in a gray-and-white geometric sheath dress rises to extend her hand over the desk.

"It's so nice to meet you in person, Mina." She waves me into a seat and settles back, her fingers tented.

I mirror her smile, then fight the urge to smooth my hair and pull at my white ruched dress shirt. Siobhan is stunning,

with lush lips and the kind of bone structure people write poetry about. Her hair is cropped short, barely there at all, but
somehow that only makes her beauty more obvious.

"It's nice to meet you, too," I say. "Thanks for inviting me.
This place is amazing."

For long moments, she sizes me up, her overt interest clearly
more than just professional curiosity. I find myself wondering
if she and Grayson ever...

Ugh. I twist off the bottle cap and swig some water. Jealousy
is not a good look. On anyone.

"As you know, your story knocked it out of the park," she
says, her assessment apparently complete. "I'll admit, I thought
we were taking a chance on it, and I might not have agreed
if your...colleague hadn't offered to collaborate, but what you
wrote seems to have hit all the right notes. We've had a flood
of responses, and from what our readers have said, they're hungry for a different kind of travel journalism. Not just where to
go and what to do, but *why*. Why do we wander? What are we
looking for out there? Is it more about something we're looking for in ourselves?"

My pasted-on smile stabilizes into something more genuine.
She gets it. She read my writing and she gets it.

"I think," she continues, "you'd be exactly the right person
to explore those questions."

My breath catches. Is she saying...? "Well, I'd love to try.
I've got plenty more where that first piece came from."

"I'm glad." Her eyes sparkle. "Because we're offering you an
ongoing position. But we'd like you to venture further afield,
this time. We'd start by sending you to Greece, if you'd be
open to it. Next month."

Everything stops. Behind her, seagulls wheel between the
skyscrapers, but I swear they're flying in slow motion. "Greece?"

She measures my reaction with dark-eyed curiosity. "Yes.

And I'll be honest—that's not an arbitrary choice. Grayson said it'd be the place most likely to get you to say yes."

My throat works. Time seems to trickle backward. Warm, turquoise waves rearrange the sand beneath my feet while somewhere far away, a circle closes. I almost feel like I'm twenty-two again, staring the world in the face. Only this time...

"I'll get on that plane tomorrow, if you want me to," I say. "And thank you. This is... Well, in all honesty, it's something I've dreamed about since I was a little girl."

Siobhan's eyes crinkle at the corners. "Grayson said you'd say that. He also said the photo collaboration would have to be a one-time thing, because you wouldn't want to work with him going forward. Forgive my curiosity, but between that and the shared last name, I have to ask. Are you and he—"

"No," I blurt, then reconsider. "And yes. Whatever you're about to ask, the answer's both no and yes."

She taps her fingernails against the desk. "I see." Oddly enough, I get the sense that she actually does.

I shift in the chair, emboldened by my victory. "If you'll forgive *my* curiosity, are you asking because this has...personal meaning for you?"

She laughs, silver and musical. "I have a bit of a soft spot for him, that's all. I've always taken a shine to people with his kind of candor. Truth be told, I *have* tried to play matchmaker for him a few times, but I think I see now why it's never worked." With a smile, she moves on, asking if I have questions about the job.

I do, of course. Dozens. By the time I leave her office, we're chuckling together like two old friends, and when I get back to the car, all I can do is grin like an idiot.

There is one downside, of course. Telling my parents. My mother, specifically.

But since August—and the anniversary of my brother's death— has safely given way to October, I at least have the confidence to invite her over instead of letting her leave yet another casserole on the doorstep. She hasn't seen my house yet, anyway, and I want to show her the transformation.

She arrives on a rainy Sunday afternoon as I'm putting the finishing touches on a late lunch. I greet her in the entryway as she shakes out her umbrella. "Hi, sweetie."

"Hey, Mom. Here, let me take your coat."

She frowns as I stash her jacket in the front closet. "You look…different. Are you okay?"

"Of course. You know I'm always…" I stop. Back up. "Actually, you know what? Things are kind of complicated right now. The truth is a lot has happened. Stuff you don't know about. And I'm still trying to figure out what it all means for me."

She leans her umbrella against the wall. Rainwater trickles onto the tile, but I don't care about the ensuing puddle. Michael would have, but I don't.

"Do you want to talk about it?" she says.

I give her a warm smile. "Actually, you know what? Yeah. I do."

I tell her everything. All the yearning I've stoppered up since childhood finally comes spilling free like a river bursting through a dam.

I start with my childhood dreams of other countries, how they filled me with a potent combination of longing and terror, because I always feared what chasing my hopes would mean for her. I admit that I walked away crushed when she and my dad shot down my foreign-exchange idea in college, and that the most sacred, secret chambers of my heart have always pulsed with hopes of becoming a travel writer. I tell her about my ill-fated attempt to move to Greece at twenty-two, why I ended up staying more out of fear than anything else. Which brings us to now, when my former brother-in-law has helped engineer the kind of fantasy job offer I'll only get one chance at.

"It's like my whole life has come full circle, Mom. And this time, if I don't go, I'll never forgive myself."

She sits silent, tears streaming down her face. The waterworks started somewhere around the part where I decided to stay with Michael instead of going to Athens, and they haven't let up.

"Oh, sweetheart," she says, her voice breaking. She twists her wedding ring around her finger, over and over.

I don't quite know what to do, so I clasp her hand over the polished knotty-pine dining table. We've finished our market salads and pushed the plates aside, and she dabs at her cheeks with one of the linen napkins that's survived my purge.

"You must hate me," she says. "All these years, I've held you back."

"No, no, Mom." I squeeze her fingers. "That's not what I'm getting at, not at all. I'm saying I've held *myself* back. I'm the one who never got on that plane. Who never told you what I really wanted. I settled for a life that felt too small for me and insisted on telling myself it was fine. None of that was you. I just fed my fears with yours. Nothing more."

She sniffs. Her blue eyes are shot through with red, her black hair mussed. She looks so much like me, only flooded with guilt and, beneath that…relief?

As if we've needed to do this for a long time.

"I think you should take the job," she says.

My breath stops. "You…do? Because I've been so stressed out that you'll only worry while I'm gone."

"I'll worry myself sick." She smiles gamely. Her makeup is a mess. "But you're an adult. Plenty old enough to make your own decisions. That hasn't been my job for a long time. My job is just to help you be happy. That's all a mother wants for her children, anyway. I'm sorry if I didn't make that clear enough while you were growing up."

I sit back, a telltale burn creeping up my throat. I can't cry, too. Then she'll start all over again, and we'll never stop. "Wow. That's not the reaction I was expecting."

Her smile turns rueful. "No?"

"No."

"I just wish you'd trusted me enough to tell me this before. But I know why you didn't."

For a moment, neither of us speaks. Oddly, the silence feels more like a gift than anything else. My mom clears her throat.

"Have you spoken to this Grayson of yours? Thanked him for getting you the offer?"

I try to cover my reaction, but her eyes track the way my hands dive into my lap. "No. I really don't want to."

"Why not?"

"There's...a lot more to the story, Mom. With him. You wouldn't even believe me if I told you."

"I bet I would," she says.

As it turns out, she's right, though she makes me explain some parts two or three times. I skip all the sexy bits, but aside from that, I confess everything, from how I accidentally fell in love with two different brothers to the way they switched places in Hawaii. I talk about Michael's gaslighting and Grayson's emails, how the truth finally came out at the cabin, how confusing and crushing I've found the whole thing.

When I finish, she gathers the dishes and goes to the sink, where she hand-washes each one and sets it in the dish rack.

I keep my seat at the table. "Aren't you going to say anything?"

"Shh," she says. "I'm thinking."

Well, that's more than Kate did. Something winds tight, some inner piece of me that craves her approval, even though, as she's pointed out, I'm an adult, and I can't say exactly what I want her to approve *of*.

Still, the feeling makes me restless enough to drive me out of my seat and toward the sliding doors to the deck, where I stare out through the panes. The forest blurs in a misty panorama of silver.

Dishes clatter. The water snaps off. Finally, my mother appears and hands over a freshly opened seltzer water. The can sucks the warmth from my palm.

"I think you should call him," she says.

I almost drop her offering. "What? Why? There's nothing to say."

"Isn't there?" There's a strangeness in her voice, a gentle sort of leading, as if she knows something I don't.

"No," I say. "If we talk again, it'll only make things messier. And I can't go back to that. Not when this is finally starting to make some sense."

She cocks her head. She's wiped off the mascara mess, and now appears as an older, wiser version of myself. "I'll just say this one thing, then, and that's that I've never seen you glow the way you did just now. When you were talking about him, every time you said his name, you had this look on your face. Like you were suddenly more alive than you ever were with Michael."

I hide the purse of my lips with a swig of fizzy water. "Mom. He *lied to me*. Then and now."

She sighs, tucks my hair back behind my ear. "And then he told you the truth. And I've been overprotective all your life, but here we are, and now I'm going to do better. We all mess up, sweetheart. And then we learn. All of us are growing up, all the time, and I don't think there's a person in this world who doesn't deserve a second chance."

A second chance. I can't believe I'm hearing this from my mother, of all people. "But *you* never had a second chance. After Jasper died, you were never the same. Some things cut too deep to ever recover from." I clamp my teeth together. I can't believe I even went there.

She doesn't fall apart, though. Tears only pool in her eyes. "No, I was never the same. I never will be again. But I could've done a better job than I did. I could've..." She glances down, away.

"What?"

A lifetime passes while she considers. "Celebrated your birthday."

That jars me. I didn't know she realized how much that bothered me.

"I should have," she continues.

I take a mile-long breath. "You still could, you know. If you want to. Next year. My half birthday's kind of ruined forever, anyway."

She glances up, her smile shy. "Maybe I could take you to Woodhouse? We could get massages. Then go to lunch. Something fancy."

I gape. And then I'm crying, too, and she starts all over again, and within moments, I'm sobbing on her shoulder like a little kid with a skinned knee, my arms thrown around her neck.

When we finally pull apart, I say, "You'll tell Dad? About Greece? Why I have to go?"

"Of course."

"What will he think?"

My mother pauses. "Probably whatever I tell him to think."

I giggle, which ends on a hiccup. How saucy of her.

By the door, she fiddles with her umbrella and takes one last look around. "What you've done here is incredible."

I help her with her coat. "You like it?"

"I love it. I'll be honest, I never really understood this place before. But now I think I do."

I nod. I couldn't have said it better myself.

"And, Mina?" She turns back in the open doorway, framed by the silken wet outside. "You were right before. You can never start over. But that doesn't mean you can't start new."

She leaves me standing there, blinking, my head awhirl.

That doesn't mean you can't start new.

From the lips of my own mother, who has more reason to cling to the past than anyone I know.

AFTER

On a gray morning in November, a week before I leave for Greece, I think about Michael without hurting.

I'm at my desk in the living room, penning a medical article—my practical side has decided not to quit until this travel job starts paying the bills—when my mind drifts. I gaze past my computer, recalling the time Michael sneaked up and laid an open-mouthed kiss against my neck. We'd fought about Paris earlier. I wanted to go; he didn't. He'd spent an hour holed up in his office, then came downstairs and apologized with his hands, his tongue. He'd bent me over the desk and confessed his regrets the same way he always did. I'd cried out and arched against him and asked for more. And he'd given it. He'd always given me that.

Rain trickles down the windowpanes. Rivulets seem to collect in my mind, reflecting truths I've never bothered to look at too closely.

Michael and I had off-the-charts sexual chemistry—we really did—from the very first moment he tossed me onto our kitchen island in Seattle and lost himself in me. But neither of us ever learned what the other really needed. How to truly connect.

Now I roll my chair back. Michael's office seems to whisper, luring me toward the stairs. My footfalls echo, a drumbeat leading me onward.

Upstairs, I push the door wide.

Cold silence lies thick in the office. Clippings carpet the floor. I gather up the divorce papers first, pausing on the page stained by my husband's signature.

Now that I'm looking at them up close, the letters look shaky. Smaller than Michael's usual. I trace the loops of ink and wonder, for the first time, if maybe he signed these not out of cruelty, but guilt. Could he possibly have understood what I'm only just now discovering?

That we were never right for each other? That we were living half a life? That despite all he stole from me—fourteen years, the life I always wanted—I was never truly his, at least not in the way I believed?

A thought occurs to me, and I check the date beside his signature—seven months before he died.

Sure enough, when I dig into the filing cabinet for his medical records, I come up with a biopsy report dated three days later. Which means Michael signed these during that week he thought he had cancer.

I squeeze my eyes shut and hug the papers to my chest. The best I can figure is that in the beginning, he kept me for himself, not only as an accountability partner in his battle with alcohol, but as some kind of trophy—tangible proof of his triumph over the man who'd overshadowed him and, in his mind, taken Lily. Eventually, Michael came to care for me, but deep down, he *knew* he'd done wrong. He never would've signed these if he hadn't.

With a held breath, I set the papers aside and gather the magazine clippings.

They look so different this time. Grayson appears no less tormented, but now I see myself in the shadows behind his eyes and the lines around his mouth. I see a man for whom grief and love are the same thing.

I take the stack downstairs and set it beside the lit lantern. The topmost picture shows Grayson on that yacht, shirtless and scowling, one hand splayed over his chest as if to keep my name safely against his skin.

My name, branded on his heart.

My throat thickens. I find my phone on the desk and open my contacts list. I saved his number that night in Millbrook, after he unblocked himself. I click the message icon.

I miss you, I type. Still. Always.

My thumb hovers over the send button. I go over the message twenty times.

The words are true. The deepest, most terrifying ones I have inside me. But another set of words runs through my mind, too—the last ones Grayson spoke to me at the cabin.

I need to figure out who I am without you. Because right now, I have no idea.

In the end, I hit Delete, then go upstairs to get my passport.

AFTER

The night before I leave, Kate arrives with gifts: a wide-brimmed straw sun hat and a DVD of *Captain Corelli's Mandolin*.

In the living room, I grip her in a hard hug, then plop the hat onto my head and examine the movie. "A DVD? Wow. I didn't know these still existed. I'm not sure I actually have a way to play this."

Kate shrugs. "No worries. We can always stream it, if not."

"Okay. But why this one? Didn't you once tell me that Nicolas Cage looks like a basset hound?"

"Yes. Because he does. But read the back. It's about two people having lots of sex. In Greece. Basically the exact thing you'll be doing by this time next week."

I give the synopsis a skeptical once-over. "You realize this is a war movie, right?"

"Oh," she says. "Hmm. I guess we can skip to the naked parts, then."

I snicker. "Works for me."

Ten minutes later, we've established that I definitely do not own a DVD player and are in the midst of googling which streaming service to use when my phone rings. A picture of my mother on a long-ago trip to Idaho flashes on the caller ID.

"Hold on." I hand the TV remote to Kate. "Hello?"

"Mina?" My mother sounds breathless.

"Hey, Mom. What's up? Are you okay?"

"Yes, sweetie, I'm fine. I just wanted to know if you'd seen it yet."

I frown. "Seen what?"

"That Grayson of yours. On TV."

Grayson. His name lands like a blow to the chest. Kate must notice, because she pauses her scrolling and mouths, *What?*

I wave away her question and hunker into the couch. "Mom, what're you talking about?"

"Grayson. He's on TV. Dad was playing around with the Netflix, and—"

"Just Netflix, Mom. 'Dad was playing around with Netflix.' It sounds weird when you put an article in front of it." I wince when I hear myself. Jesus. Talk about stalling.

She makes an exasperated shut-up-now-dear noise. "Fine. Dad was playing around with *Netflix*, and we saw a picture of Michael. So we clicked on it, but it was that Grayson of yours. Doing an interview."

A distant part of me registers surprise. Grayson may have had his stint on TV, but doesn't do interviews. He's friendly enough to starstruck girls outside coffee shops, but he doesn't volunteer anything he doesn't have to. "Please don't call him that. He's not mine. In any sense of the word. And who cares if he was on TV again? You already knew he was famous. It's nothing new."

Her voice softens. "No, but I think you should watch this. It's about you."

Everything drains away, leaving me with a head full of silver static. "What?"

"It's about you," she repeats, her patience infinite. "The whole interview. He didn't say your name, but...*I* knew who he meant."

I glance over at Kate, who's graduated to frowning with her whole body. She holds up her hands in a *WTF?* gesture.

"Just watch it, sweetheart," my mother says. "It's some show called *Celebrity Confessions.*"

"Okay. I'll think about it," I hear myself say.

The moment we hang up, I ask Kate if she has any idea what my mother's talking about.

"*Celebrity Confessions?*" Her nose wrinkles. "Ew. No. That show's so trashy."

"No kidding. Did you have any idea Grayson even went on it?"

"None. I've been ignoring him. Like you."

I chew on my lip. I haven't been ignoring him, exactly. Just trying to move past this, the way he wanted.

"But do you...maybe...want to watch it?" She sounds cautious.

"I think I might have to," I say slowly. "It'll only drive me crazy if I don't."

"Oh, thank god." Her tone changes in an instant. "Because I'd never hear the end of it if Tanner caught me watching that garbage at home."

She jabs a few buttons and brings up *Celebrity Confessions.* Within seconds, a familiar name pops up in the episode summary.

My heart bucks even before Kate hits Play. She tucks her legs underneath her and leans toward the screen, as if she's forgotten everything else.

The moment Grayson appears, I forget, too.

God, he's gorgeous. I hadn't remembered just how much. He's wearing his usual fitted T-shirt and leather jacket, and in the soft-focus lighting of the set, his hair throws its own gold-dark glow. It's grown, too, just enough to notice. He lounges in an armchair with one ankle slung over the opposite knee, and the way his lashes fan across his cheeks when he looks down is nothing short of sultry. And...

I force back a whimper. He's wearing the puka shell necklace.

"Hot damn." Kate speaks my innermost thoughts aloud. "It's like he somehow got even prettier. I can't believe you slept with *that*. I think I might actually hate you a little."

"Don't bother," I murmur, though my idiotic brain insists on offering up delirious, rapturous memories of having him inside me. I shiver, then lock the images behind a closed door. "It was a one-time thing."

Well, a two-time thing. In one night. But I don't remind her.

The camera pans to the hostess, a naturally pretty, girl-next-door brunette named Desiree. She has a way of getting famous people to open up, disarming them as if she's everyone's best friend, until they end up confessing their deepest secrets and crying on camera. It's practically a rite of passage for Hollywood's elite—*Oh, she went on* Celebrity Confessions *and didn't sob? She must be tough as nails.*

"We're here tonight with Grayson Drake, one of America's most famous—or infamous, depending who you ask—photographers," Desiree announces. "Many know him as the mountaineer who nearly died on Everest, or the host of *World Safari*. But tonight, in what will be his first-ever televised interview, we'll dig deeper, into the life and mind of a man who's remained a mystery until now. Welcome to the confession booth, Grayson."

He grins in a way that makes my stomach clamp around a kernel of heat. "Thanks. Glad to be here, Desiree."

She starts mildly enough, leading him through questions about the avalanche and his eleven minutes spent buried in the snow. No surprise there, because she always starts gently. She boils her frogs slowly, heating the water by degrees, until it's too late for them to jump out.

Soon enough, she steers the conversation toward a question

that feels entirely natural, though I know she must have planned it long beforehand. "Tell us, Grayson. What would you consider your biggest regret in life?"

My entire body tenses. I know what his answer would've been three months ago, but by now, it might have changed.

"That," he says, "is a very long story."

"Which is exactly why we're here," Desiree croons.

His fingers come up to play with the puka shell, flicking it back and forth. "It has to do with a girl."

"It always does, doesn't it? Why don't you tell us about her?"

Grayson casts Desiree a knowing look but doesn't back away from the question. Not that I'd expect him to. Avoidance was always Michael's forte, not his.

Still, I don't quite expect what comes next. His eyes darken to emerald while his voice turns husky. And he tells the whole damn story. Just lays himself bare in front of the world.

He glides over some parts and embellishes others in such a way that no one will ever figure out who I am, but his massaging of the facts does nothing to obscure the underlying truth. He talks about me with reverence. With a tender adoration that nearly topples me.

It's a story about a woman who swept him off his feet and shaped his life, about how she broke his heart and he deserved it. But he still wouldn't trade that pain for anything, because it proves they're still connected. That they always will be.

Halfway through, the unbelievable happens. Desiree reaches for the tissues universally reserved for her guests.

Grayson pauses, uncertain. He reaches over the tiny table between their chairs and pats her arm awkwardly. "Was it something I said?"

"It absolutely was," she says with a tearful smile. "Although I think I speak for romantics everywhere when I say we all hope to be on the receiving end of that *something you said*, someday. To be that precious to someone."

His brows quirk. "That's a good word, actually. Precious. That's exactly what she is to me. No matter what went wrong, she'll never be anything else."

The feeling in my gut blossoms into an ache. I try to inhale against the pain, but I seem to have stopped breathing a long time ago.

"I have to ask, why now?" Desiree dabs at her somehow still-perfect makeup. "You've notoriously avoided interviews ever since *National Geographic* first launched you into the public eye, so what's changed?"

Grayson sits back and runs a hand through his hair. "Mostly, I've finally made peace with all this. And I've decided people should learn from me. From everything I did wrong. The thing is, I should've told this woman everything. I've thought a lot about why I didn't, and it's because deep down, I was afraid. So the moral of the story is, don't be. Don't worry about whether you're enough for someone, or whether you deserve them. Fuck all that. That's for them to decide, anyway, not you."

"Wise words," Desiree says.

"I think so. But I didn't understand them at twenty-five, and I made a stupid decision, then covered it up with the kind of ridiculous confidence you only have when you're young. And look where I ended up. Without her. Which is okay, really. For the first time in my life, it's okay. Mostly because it has to be. And also because I'm happy knowing she's gotten a chance at the dream she always wanted. But she deserved more from me. She deserved fearlessness. So to everyone watching, be fearless. If you love someone, don't hide yourself. Throw yourself into it with your whole heart, your whole being. Anything else is a waste of time."

Desiree sniffles into her tissue. "And if she's watching right now? What would you tell her?"

His mouth curves. "She's not watching. Zero percent chance."

My fingers curl around the cushion and squeeze.

"But if she is?" Desiree presses. "What's the single most fearless thing you could say to her?"

He gives her a sidelong smile, as if he sees the trap she's constructed using his own words but doesn't mind walking into it. His gaze shifts toward the camera.

I lean in so far I nearly swan-dive off the couch. Kate does, too.

"Probably the same thing I wanted to tell her after the avalanche. The thing is, she's already heard it. She just didn't know I was talking to her, at the time." His chest rises and falls as those insanely beautiful eyes stare right into me.

Desiree smooths down her skirt. "Go ahead."

"I love you like crazy," Grayson tells me. "Meeting you changed me, and it broke me, but I wouldn't change it for anything. Because...and here's the part you don't know...it healed me, too. Knowing everything turned out okay for you, that helps me sleep at night. And I'll always have the memories we made together. Not that I don't wish we could make more. I'd kill to make more. But if this is all we ever get, it's okay. *I'm* okay. Even as bad as it hurts, it was worth every minute. You were worth any price."

Complete silence. Grayson holds my eyes for a flurry of heartbeats, then eases back. For a brief second, I think he's going to need the tissues after all, but then he winks at Desiree, who laughs.

"I think I'm going to give you my husband's number," she jokes.

He laughs. It's a sound I haven't heard in fourteen years, not like this. And I see he really does look at ease with himself, his hands slung together in his lap, his smile comfortable.

"Well," Desiree says, bringing the interview back around, "I think this might be one of the most honest episodes we've ever filmed. And after those closing remarks, I'm sure most of the world will be waiting to see what happens with your mystery girl."

Grayson casually pulls his phone from his pocket. "Probably nothing. But on the off chance that she texts me, I'll warn you right now that I'm walking off this set and letting you wrap things up on your own."

They trade a few more lines of banter. Even after the screen flicks back to the home page for *Celebrity Confessions*, I continue to stare.

He seems different. Maybe because we've both come to grips with the truth, or because he's finally realized his own worth, but whatever the cause, something inside him has untwisted.

Something untwists in me, too. My past cleaves into separate threads no longer intertwined.

Michael and Grayson. Two radically different people who mean entirely different things to me.

The process that has slowly been taking place for months finally reaches stillness, the last shock wave of an earthquake dying away. On one side, there's my love for Michael, soft and sad and forever broken. On the other, my love for Grayson, a firestorm of depth and possibilities.

Never the twain shall meet.

I open my mouth and turn to Kate. And stop. "Oh my god. You're crying. Why're you crying? You didn't even cry at *Pearl Harbor*."

Silent tears pour down her cheeks. "Why're you *not*?"

I blink. "Because that wasn't sad, Kate. That was the opposite of sad."

"Maybe for you."

After a stunned moment, I dash to the kitchen for one of those ever-handy linen napkins and come back to fold her in my arms. She blows her nose, her hair tickling my chin. I hang on and rub her back. "What's going on? Is this about Tanner?"

"Not exactly." Her tears dry up, but her voice wobbles. "I mean, I don't want you to think any less of him."

"It's okay. I'm your friend. I'm not here to judge, just listen. You can tell me anything."

She snuggles deeper. "It's not him, really. It's just that…as a wife, and a mother, you just give and give and give. To your husband. Your kids. They never see that you're always pouring yourself out to keep them afloat, because to them, it's normal. Business as usual. All that effort is invisible to them, and in a way, it makes you invisible, too. But, Mina. To *that guy*, you're not invisible. Oh my god. You're all he freaking sees. And I can't tell you what I wouldn't give to be that noticed by someone. To be that *significant*."

I try to cram all that into my head.

She pulls back, dragging the napkin across a nose as bright as a cherry. "I swear to god if you don't text Grayson right now, I'm going to do it for you."

When I don't move, she lunges for my phone, but I snatch it off the coffee table and hold it out of reach. "What are you even talking about? Didn't you say he and I had no future?"

"Yeah. I definitely did." She eyes the phone as if calculating the best angle to pounce from. "And, listen, I was definitely wrong. Because I've never seen a guy be that honest before. I didn't even know they could be. I mean, you didn't tell me, Mina. You didn't tell me he was like *that*."

"I'm pretty sure I did. Or tried to. Not that it matters. I'm going to Greece tomorrow, remember? Besides, he's probably in Namibia right now, or something."

"Who gives a shit? For once in your life, for once in *my* life, can we just agree that you should take a chance?"

I hesitate. "But after everything that's happened…"

"What?" she says combatively. "Is there actually an end to that sentence that's worth saying out loud?"

I search my mind. My heart. *After everything that's happened…*

The completion of my tectonic shift seems to have opened a new path inside me. I chase it down into the black, only to arrive not in darkness, but warmth.

After everything that's happened, Grayson Drake still means more to me than I can measure. He still feels *right*. And while he may not have been entirely honest at times, he's been more open with me than anyone else.

While my mother hid her pain, Grayson bared his without hesitation.

Michael told me to go running. Grayson told me to go to Greece.

Kate talked sense into me. But Grayson made me feel again. He gave me the dignity of an apology, an explanation. Another chance at Greece. The list goes on.

"Goddamn it," I say. "You know what? You're right. I'm totally, stupidly, ridiculously in love with him and I really don't care about anything else."

She eyes my phone. "Then do it."

I do. I bring up his contact info and fire off a text.

I have something to tell you. And I want to say it to your face.

A minute crawls by. Bubbles pop up, telling me he's writing back. I suck in an anticipatory breath. Hopefully not in Namibia, then.

I wait. And wait.

"Well?" Kate prompts. "What'd he say?"

"Nothing." On my screen, the bubbles disappear. I frown. "He didn't say anything."

"Did he read it?"

"I think so."

"Well, he probably passed out. I bet he's lying on the floor right now, trying to figure out whether he died and went to heaven."

My frown deepens. Somehow, I don't think so. Oh, god. What if he's reconsidered? That episode could have been recorded months ago. Plenty of time for things to change.

"Hey." Kate tries for lightness, but when my phone remains silent, she can't mask the tension in her voice. "Come on, let's have some wine. He'll answer eventually."

He doesn't, though. We drink an entire bottle of Merlot and watch *Captain Corelli's Mandolin* while my phone taunts me with utter silence.

By the time two hours have passed, my heart is falling apart at the seams. I can't accept that now that I've finally, *finally* figured out how to move forward, it's too late.

"Don't worry," Kate says gently. "Maybe he's asleep. There's no way he won't text back."

I startle, realizing the movie has ended. What even happened? Maybe the guy and the girl ended up together. Maybe everybody died. I have no idea.

"I should go to bed," I say. What I actually mean is, *You should go home to your husband so I can cry alone in the bathtub.*

Kate seems to sense as much, but she knows me well enough not to argue. "Okay. But you'll text me from Greece, right? Let me know you're okay?"

"Yeah. Sure."

She lingers for a few minutes, concern etched between her brows while she helps me tidy up. The whole time, I swallow repeatedly, trying to stave off tears.

I walk Kate to the door, where she gathers her coat. The lines around her eyes tighten.

"What?" I say cautiously.

She hesitates. "I honestly wasn't sure whether I should give this to you, and now I'm even less sure. But Tanner asked me to." She fishes a crisp envelope from her jacket pocket. "It's your email. He said it was like a one-in-a-million chance that he was even able to get it, but here you go. Apparently you owe him a bottle of Riesling."

I stare, then snatch the thing and rip it open.

"Does it say what Grayson said it did?" Kate asks while I scan the print.

"Exactly," I breathe. Not a comma out of place. Or a parenthesis.

I almost wad up Michael's treacherous, life-altering words, but giving in to anger feels like granting him power. Like letting his lies govern my life, still. And I'm better than that.

So I stuff the paper into the envelope and hand it back. "I don't want this. But tell Tanner thank you. And I'll buy him that bottle when I get back."

She pulls me in and squeezes. I rest against her shoulder, stealing a moment of comfort. God, I'll miss her.

"Have fun out there," she murmurs into my hair.

A sniffle escapes me. I knew Grayson had told me the truth that night, but the cold, hard evidence makes me wish I'd processed what that meant sooner. Before he'd changed his mind.

"Thanks," I say roughly. "I will."

"And have lots and lots of sex," she tacks on as I turn away.

"Yep. Bye." I turn away so she won't see me fall apart. I'm halfway to the kitchen, just pulling out my phone again and shriveling inside when I glimpse the time—eleven eleven, will the universe never quit mocking me?—when Kate says, "Oh. *Oh.*"

Irrational hope spikes through me. I stash my phone and back up. Kate hovers just inside the open doorway, motionless.

Sure enough, she's staring at Grayson, who stands on my welcome mat with his hands jammed in his pockets and rain dripping from his hair.

AFTER

My heart goes crashing into the roof of my mouth. "Hi," I manage.

Grayson just stands there for a few heartbeats. "Hi," he finally says. Orphaned hope fills his voice.

Kate shoots me a look over her shoulder. "I'm just...gonna go, okay?"

"Yeah. Um...okay."

She hesitates in the entryway, seemingly intimidated by the way he fills up the entire doorframe "I'm Kate, by the way."

His gaze flickers toward her. "Yeah. We've met."

"Oh. Right. Well, guess we'll catch up later. Or something." She slips past him, aims a slack-jawed glance from behind his back while dramatically fanning her face, then jumps into her Suburban and peels out.

I drift over the threshold and out into the rain. Icy rivulets stream down my back, but I barely feel the cold.

"You're getting wet," Grayson says, but makes no move to stop me.

"I am." I edge closer. The force of his scent and his gaze hit me at the same time, a double dose of intensity that arrows into me and just keeps on going. "How're you even here right now? It's a three-hour drive. I texted you two and a half hours ago."

"I drive fast." He clears his throat, looking more unsure than I thought possible. "And your message gave me extra motivation."

Despite the rain, heat splashes across my cheeks. "But why didn't you tell me you were coming?"

"Well, I'd like to say it's because I'm altogether that confident. But you said you wanted to see me, and the truth is I didn't want to give you a chance to change your mind."

"I wouldn't have."

"Oh. Okay, then." He pushes his sopping hair out of his face. Light sparks in those unforgettable eyes. It looks a lot like yearning. "You had something to say?"

"I did." I balance there, caught in a moment that seems to funnel my life back onto its charted course. Finally. I'm a soaring bird, stabilizing on an updraft. A ship righting itself in the current.

I reach for his saturated shirtfront. It doesn't feel like three months have passed since I stood with him like this. It feels like I've always been right here, one half of this perfect circle. Which makes what comes next feel absurdly natural. "I'm desperately in love with you. I want you to know that."

Grayson's whole body stills. "I'm desperately in love with you, too."

That's it. It's just...easy. True. A statement of fact that surprises nobody.

Well, maybe it surprises him, because he leans down, searching my eyes like he can't quite believe it. "Does this mean you forgive me?"

"Yes," I breathe.

An exhale gusts out through his nose. "And...we can start over?" he says huskily.

I tug him closer. The wet darkness falls away as the world whittles down to this single question. Grayson waits, his gaze the same one from that night on the mountaintop. And from earlier tonight, when he told me he loved me through the TV.

"I can't start over," I say. "But for you, I can start new. If that's what you want."

He closes his eyes for a moment. Opens them. "Fuck yes, that's what I want."

And then we're kissing. Falling into each other like we've crossed an ocean of years to arrive at this place. I go up on tiptoes and fasten my arms around his neck while he folds me against the length of his body. Every ridge and valley of him, every press of his fingers against my hip and in my hair, feels like home.

I'm lost. Found. Everything at once.

Ours tongues tangle. I sigh into his mouth, losing myself in the way he tastes like he's been waiting all this time, like his longing has been crouching inside of him for months, growing into something breathtaking and unstoppable.

"Take me inside." I cling to him, soaked through and shivering.

In another moment, he's hoisting me up, wrapping my legs around his waist and carrying me in. He slams the front door with his foot. "Where's your room?" The shine of his eyes deepens by the moment.

I can barely fit the word in between my cantering heartbeats. "Upstairs."

He carries me up. We pull off each other's wet things and burrow into my brand-new king-size bed, naked. Grayson nestles on his side and tugs me against his chest.

I press my face against his wet skin, then kiss his tattoos and breathe in his woodsy richness. When our eyes meet again, a sense of completion flows into me, of absolute belonging.

My breath hitches. God, I was right when I told Kate I would never fall in love again. Because what I feel right now has been living inside me for all of these years. It may change, sharpen, flow into different forms, but I will never not love this man.

"I hope you never stop looking at me like that," I say.

Grayson rolls onto his back and pulls me with him, staring up while I straddle him. "I don't plan to."

We stay like that, bodies pressed together, eyes locked. He reaches up and traces my jawline as if reassuring himself I'm his. That this is real.

"Hold still." He scoots to the edge of the bed without dislodging me and fishes his phone from his pants, then aims the camera upward. The shutter snaps.

A smile graces my lips. "What're you doing?"

He turns the screen my way. "Capturing a moment," he says softly. "And look. It's the best picture I've ever taken. The most beautiful thing I've ever seen."

In the photo, I gaze down, eyes soft and brimming with love.

"You'd better not stop looking at me like that, either," Grayson says.

I take his phone and set it on the bedside table. "I don't plan to."

He pulls me down against him, chest to chest. "You know, I'd ask you to prove it, if we weren't in Michael's bed right now."

"It's not Michael's. It's mine. Everything in this house is brand-new."

He pauses. "You mean you haven't christened this thing yet?"

"No. Or any of the other furniture in this house. I was waiting for you, I think. It just took me a while to actually figure that out."

"Well." His fingers drift into my hair, twining in my wet locks. "I was waiting for you, too. And we have a big job ahead of us, from the sound of it. Maybe we should get started."

I make a thick sound of pleasure as he kisses me.

It starts slow. And stays slow. It lasts and lasts, stretching into something ageless and powerful and pure. Our hands rove, exploring wet skin, teasing and claiming and worshipping. We kiss and slide into each other until I lose track of where I stop and he begins.

When I finally come rocketing apart, he crushes me close, his lips locked against mine as I cry my pleasure into his mouth.

Afterward, he tucks my head into the crook of his arm and traces the rise of my ribs with one finger. "You've gained weight. You look beautiful. Healthy."

I smile. My eyelids feel too heavy to open. "Thanks. I'd like to say I fixed myself, but I think you healed me, too. Not just the other way around, like you said."

His fingers pause. "You saw the show?"

"I did."

"What'd you think?"

I wriggle, prompting him to resume his caress. "It made me finally realize how I felt. And that I should text you. So, mission accomplished?"

"Wow. I was about ninety percent sure you'd never speak to me again."

"That's only because you one hundred percent don't know me."

He chuffs a laugh. "The hell I don't."

I pry my weighted lids open. For long moments, we stare at one another, the silence overflowing with a thousand words we don't need to speak aloud.

Finally, I say, "I'm going to Greece tomorrow."

He smiles. Actually smiles. "For Travelique?"

"Yeah. They want me to do an extended series on finding yourself in the Mediterranean. Which Siobhan told me had everything to do with you. I don't know how I'll ever repay you for that."

"You repaid me about five minutes ago," he says. "But you can repay me again in five more, if you want."

I snuggle closer. "I do want."

He laughs. "Okay. Just give me a second to recover."

"No rush." Smiling, I trace my tattooed name with one finger, underlining the connected letters over and over. "This tattoo is stunning, by the way. I had no idea Arabic script was so beautiful."

"I think so, too. Especially because of what it says." He clasps one hand around mine and reverses the direction of my strokes. "But Arabic is written right to left, not left to right. Like this."

I shake my head against him, awed. "Someday, I'll know all these worldly facts you've got stored up inside your head."

His heartbeat drums steadily against my ear. "Not someday. It all starts tomorrow. How long will you be gone?"

"Three months."

His fingertips press into my side. "That's a long time."

"Yeah. I know."

"Not that I'm complaining," he says. "I'm genuinely happy for you. I'll even give you a ride to the airport. *Nat Geo*'s sending me to Malaysia tomorrow, anyway."

"Really?"

"Yeah. I'm flying to Kuala Lumpur in the evening."

We don't talk for a while. I run dreamy, sated fingers across his eight-pack, tracing the grooves between the muscles. He'll wait for me, I know. And I'll wait for him. Still, I almost ask if I can tag along to Asia. But at this point, we've waited fourteen years.

What difference will three more months make?

AFTER

By morning, we've christened four other pieces of furniture and still have fifteen to go. We've also gotten roughly two hours of sleep, and that much only at my absolute insistence. Apparently, age hasn't robbed Grayson of the ability to function on fumes, but I suppose nobody's perfect.

We breakfast in the kitchen in our underwear, trading bites of omelet. Grayson insists on lighting the lantern and putting it on the kitchen table, and I don't argue. I even consider getting a tattoo of the thing, then decide he already has enough for the both of us.

After eating, he goes through my suitcase, tossing out half the clothes I'm convinced I'll need and adding a few basic pieces he insists will save space because they can be layered. Then he asks where my outlet adapters are.

I give him a blank stare. "Um…my what?"

"Your adapters. You don't think you can just plug your American computer into a European outlet, do you?"

"No." I scoff. "Of course not. I'm not *that* dumb."

He peruses my suitcase, then turns solemn eyes on me. "You absolutely thought that, didn't you?"

I can't help it. I laugh. "Hey. I've never done this before, remember?"

His mouth snicks up at the corners. "Why do you think I'm checking your work?"

Thankfully, he's got spare *outlet adapters*. He lugs my suitcase out to his red Batmobile and transfers a couple plugs from his bag to mine. "I like to keep an extra set with me. Just in case."

"Thanks," I say. "That would've sucked."

"Anytime."

Before I know it, it's noon. Time to go. In the car, he holds my hand atop the gearshift and whips us out of the driveway at breakneck speed.

I squeal, even though I secretly love it.

I don't look back.

Halfway to Seattle, I finally ask, "What is this thing, anyway? A Lotus?"

Grayson huffs. "What? No. It's a Dodge Viper."

"Oh. Are those really different?" Mostly, I say it just to see the look on his face, which is nothing short of comical.

"Jesus Christ," he says. "I don't know if I can marry you now."

"That's fine." I smile, taunting. "I've already done the marriage thing, anyway. Wasn't all it's cracked up to be."

His eyes widen, as if he can't believe I said that, and he goes quiet for a while. Then, "Do you hate Michael? For what he did?"

I look out the window. That's a question I'll probably be trying to answer for the rest of my life. "I don't know. Do you?"

"Yeah," he says. "More for your sake than mine. But yes."

I nod. "Well, wherever he is, maybe he's with Lily. Maybe she's taking care of him and he got what he wanted. Maybe we all did, and that's all that matters, in the end."

Grayson squeezes my hand. "Maybe."

I don't really believe that, but hey. Anything's possible.

That's for damn sure.

At Sea-Tac, Grayson wheels both suitcases inside. I try to take command of my own, but he insists on being chivalrous, and I don't fight him *too* hard.

It's nice to be taken care of.

Still, my nerves buzz as we pass through the sliding doors of the terminal. I don't want to say goodbye. God, I don't want to say goodbye...ever.

But I know I have to go.

We find the line for my flight first. Grayson has already checked in electronically—something I'll probably have to figure out one of these days.

As I move to join the mile-long queue, he catches at my elbow and pulls me close, making us into an island of stillness amid the heaving crowd. When I look up, my breath snags in my lungs, as if I'm seeing him for the first time all over again.

His golden hair tumbles over one eye, gleaming in the light from the windows. He studies me while a girl squeals his name in the background.

Neither of us turn to look.

"I want to ask you something," he says.

My breath thins. "Okay?"

"Not to stay, of course. I'm not that selfish. But I was wondering if...maybe...you'd let me come with you?"

The airport falls silent, its bustle a thousand miles removed from this moment. "What, to Greece?"

"Yeah," he says.

"Right *now*?"

"Right now."

"Instead of Malaysia?"

"Yep."

A tingle sweeps through me. "But what'll happen if you don't show up to your assignment?"

"I don't know. They'll fire me, probably. Who gives a shit?"

"*I* do. I can't just let you torpedo your career for my sake."

"Why not?" A smile plays around his mouth. "It's not like I wouldn't have another one lined up. Siobhan'll welcome me with open arms."

I stare, my heartbeat unfolding inside me like a song. "You mean the two of us? Hopscotching around the world together?"

His expression turns almost shy. "That's the idea. What do you think?"

"I think... Dear god. Yes." I pull him down and kiss him, frantically, right there in the atrium. Neither of us seems to care about our audience, because his tongue goes diving into my mouth as if we're alone.

When I finally come up for air, I find Grayson's arm outstretched, his middle finger aimed at a teenage boy with elaborate camera gear who's enthusiastically taking our picture.

I force his hand down. "Oh my god, what are you doing? Is this what life is going to be like with you?"

His grin turns wolfish. "It's not too late to change your mind."

I pretend to consider.

"You know what?" He plants another kiss on me. "Never mind. It's *way* too late to change your mind. I have no idea why I just said that."

I snake one arm around his waist. "Well, in that case, then I think you owe that poor boy an apology. He's probably just a... What was it you said? A broke, hungry kid who likes to take pictures? Give him something he can use, at least."

His eyes narrow. "Like what?"

I spiderwalk my fingers up his chest. "You could let him take a picture of your tattoo. *My* tattoo. Let him be the very first one."

He looks distinctly unamused. "You want me to pull my shirt up right here? Just flash all these people?"

I smirk. "Why not?"

He heaves a sigh, but in the end, he actually does it, holding my eyes with a mock look of suffering. Somewhere behind us, a girl shrieks in delight, and the teenager frantically snaps away, and it's absolutely the most ridiculous situation I've ever participated in, but at the same time, it's also one of the most intoxicating.

At the check-in desk, Grayson plops down his credit card and books a thirty-six-hundred-dollar last-minute ticket to Athens.

I wince as he scribbles his name on the receipt and tosses the pen aside. The twenty-something desk girl stares at him with naked awe.

"Are you sure about this?" I say.

He shrugs. "I still owe you a ticket to Greece, don't I? At least you're actually letting me buy one this time. Even if it's my own."

I hearken back to that day on the sidewalk, outside my great-aunt's house. "How *were* you going to pay for my ticket, anyway? Weren't you broke back then?"

"Completely. But I had Michael's credit card. You have no idea how disappointed I was when I didn't get to see the look on his face after charging it." He chuckles, soft and sad.

I mirror his melancholy smile.

"Anyway," he says, "I can afford it now. Not that I'm rich, or anything. You do know that, right? I spent my TV money on the Viper, but... I just live in a normal house like a normal guy."

"Really?" I raise my eyebrows. "I thought all famous people were rich."

"You'd think. But at the end of the day, I'm just a photographer."

My fingers sneak into the gap between his T-shirt and jeans, brushing against warm, solid muscle. God, I can't seem to stop touching him. "It's okay. I don't mind being your sugar mama. Though you might have to find ways to continually earn it."

He grins. "Oh yeah?"

"Yeah."

"I think I can live with that," he says.

THE BEGINNING

I hold Grayson's hand while we take off.

He isn't afraid, exactly, he says. Not like Michael was. But his inner pilot knows that takeoff and landing are riskiest, and Lily's fate has left him with a shadow of doubt, if not a bona fide phobia.

He leans his head against the seat and closes his eyes while I draw loving circles on the back of his hand and watch the mist-shrouded earth fall away.

The past—all the heartache and frustration, my grief and my pain—retreat along with the foggy world below. They're not gone, of course. They'll always remain, part of a vague silver distance that once formed the solid ground beneath my feet. But now I'm free of those yesterdays. I've cut myself loose, launched into the sky. Turned my face toward today.

When the seat belt sign dings off, Grayson opens his eyes and cradles my face. We break free from the clouds. Spears of sunlight lance through the window, kindling golden flecks in the turquoise of his eyes.

I study each one. How funny. I don't think Michael had those. If so, I never noticed.

"What do you want to do tomorrow?" he says.

His smooth, aged-bourbon words conjure daydreams of dusty plazas infused with gnarled, olive-scented trees. I think of the winding, white-bright sun-soaked alleys of Athens and how I want to wander until we end up in a hole-in-the-wall restaurant somewhere, eating moussaka and drinking ouzo until Grayson decides to whisk me back to our hotel room and take all my clothes off.

But in the end, there's only one right answer. "Tomorrow? Haven't you heard? There's no such thing."

It catches him off guard, but then a brilliant smile lights up his face. He drops a kiss on the tip of my nose. "That's my girl. God, I've missed you." His voice hitches.

I grin, then turn to watch the world fade to a wash of emerald and silver, all crowned by the setting sun.

I don't let go of his hand for the entire flight. But not because I'm worried about what's coming. Or about what we've endured to get here.

It's just that right now, this is all I need.

★ ★ ★ ★ ★

ACKNOWLEDGMENTS

The process of writing *When We Had Forever* was a deeply personal one for me—this book is an amalgamation of my hopes, dreams, and experiences, and was written for anyone who's ever grappled with the question of how to wring every last drop from this wild adventure we call life. It's also my love letter to travel and loving recklessly and taking chances. The list of people who've had a hand in bringing this book to publication is nearly endless, as is my gratitude, but firstly, I'd like to thank you for reading. I hope you enjoyed Mina and Grayson's story.

My deepest thanks go to Beth Miller, my incredible agent at Writers House—I'm so relieved you saw through the murk of WWHF's first draft to the *real* story at its core. This book is exponentially better for having passed through your hands (multiple times!) and I am eternally grateful for your thoughtful edits and tireless hard work. Not to mention the fact that you scooped me out of the slush pile to begin with. I couldn't have done any of this without you, and working with you has been a dream.

To Cat Clyne, the most fabulous editor I could have hoped for—I'm still pinching myself that you saw something special in Mina and Grayson's story and chose to bring it to life. From the moment I read your edit letter, I knew WWHF had found the perfect home, because you understood aspects of this story that even I didn't. With your guidance, it's turned into something far shinier than I could have managed on my own, and I count myself lucky to work with someone so talented and inquisitive. You are the best.

To my incredible cover designers, Elita Sidiropoulou and Magen McCallum, I'm awed that you captured the vibe and heart of this story so flawlessly. I can't stop staring at it and somehow love it more each time. (How is that even possible?) To Greg Stephenson, thank you for your eagle-eyed copy edits, and I'm sorry I'm so bad at hyphenation (or lack thereof). To the whole team at Canary Street Press—I couldn't be more thrilled that this book has found a place with such a wonderful group of professionals.

To Siri Kristenson, thank you for challenging me to write a novel in the first place. I think I was always waiting for someone to give me permission, and you were that someone. To Evan James Clark, for being the very first person to read my early (and thoroughly embarrassing) writing attempts—your kindness and encouragement were instrumental in my decision to stick with it, and I appreciate it more than you know.

To my author besties: Nisha Tuli, you once called me your writing soulmate, and damn, why didn't I think of that first, because it's the perfect term. Our friendship has seen me through so many ups and downs and means the world to me (and then some). Furthermore, I'm so relieved to know I'm not the only one who thinks Adam Driver is hot. Lacie Waldon, thank you for the many Marco Polos in which you've made me laugh, think Deep Thoughts, and decide to keep on going. You told me this book would sell and you were right, and you've been an absolute lifeline through this entire process. Windy Prasert, I'm so lucky that we connected on that beta swap website all those years ago. Having you in my corner has been a privilege, even if it does mean I now have a daily planner. You deserve all the Campbell's split pea soup in the world.

To Sunyi Dean and Scott Drakeford and the entire Growlery crew, I don't know how I landed among such an overabundance of talent, but I'm oh-so-grateful that I did. Thank you for all your transparency and encouragement, not to mention the steady infusion of gym selfies and pet pics. To the Romance Writery— what an incredible group of women. It's been a pleasure creating this cozy little corner of the internet with you. Never leave me.

To Atima Kim and Brenda McQueen Neil, my beta readers extraordinaire, your assistance was invaluable in helping me dig to the heart of this story. Lyndsey Gantert, thank you for reading an early (messy) draft of this and loving it anyway. You're my favorite broken pencil of all time. To Chelsea and the team at House of J's Coffee in Arvada, thank you for keeping me sufficiently caffeinated and for allowing me to loiter on your premises long enough to write an entire book.

To my incredible family: my loving parents for believing I could do this, and my wonderful in-laws for also believing I could do this—thank you for the enthusiasm and well-timed childcare and votes of confidence. I love you all, though I do hope you skipped over the sexy bits. If not, please at least pretend you did, next time we talk.

And lastly, but not leastly (it's a word, I'm pretty sure), to my husband, Krishna. Where do I start? You are my rock. My real-life, tall-dark-and-handsome book boyfriend, my everything, my reason. You have single-handedly ruined me for all other men and I couldn't be happier about it. Thank you for putting up with the many long hours I spent refining this manuscript, and for all that you do. You're the best thing that's ever happened to me.